D1348283

CHILDREN OF WAR

MARTIN WALKER

Quercus

First published in Great Britain in 2014 by

Quercus Editions Ltd
55 Baker Street
7th Floor, South Block
London W1U 8EW

A CIP catalogue record for this book is available
from the British Library

HB ISBN 978 1 84866 401 2
TPB ISBN 978 1 84866 402 9
EBOOK ISBN 978 1 84866 403 6

10 9 8 7 6 5 4 3 2 1

Printed and bound in Great Britain by Clays Ltd, St Ives plc

Typeset by Ellipsis Digital Limited, Glasgow

For my fellow members of the ancient and honourable

Confrérie du Pâté de Périgueux

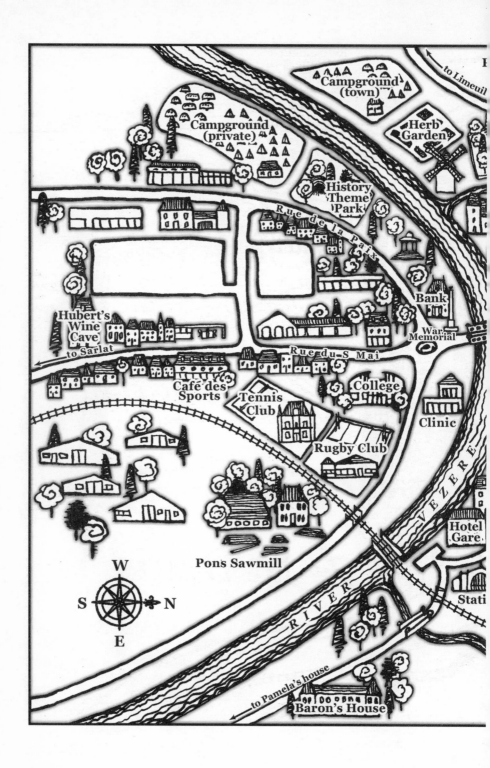

Pompiers

Retirement
Home

to St Alvère

Lespinasse
Garage

Rue de la Republique

Tourist
Office

Church

Father
Sentout

Gendarmes

The Royal

Rue de Paris

Photo
Shop

Bar

to
Périgueux
& to
Bruno's
house

Ivan's

Rue Gambetta

Mairie

Fouquet's

Rue de la Liberation

St Denis

ion

to Les Eyzies

1

Benoît Courrèges, chief of police of the small French town of St Denis and known to everyone as Bruno, had witnessed too much violent death. After twelve years in the French army and eleven as a policeman, he had seen the gruesome effects of artillery shells and machine guns and then of the hot metal of automobile crashes on the human body. And while he often hoped to forget the impact of a bullet on his own flesh, the sullen ache in his hip with the coming of each winter's damp would remind him of the shot that had sent him tumbling into the snow in the hills above Sarajevo. He'd never forget the brightness of the French *tricolore* on the sleeve of the medic who had worked on him until the helicopter came. Any sight of his country's flag now always brought back to Bruno the red of his blood against the white of the snow and the blue helmet he'd been wearing as a United Nations peacekeeper.

But Bruno had never seen anything quite as grim as the sight of the dead man now lying trussed and half-naked before him. Rain trickled down the corpse's chest and stomach, gleaming on the fresh burn marks where the stubs of male nipples had been. The body was lit by the headlamps of Bruno's own van and the large fire engine of St Denis. Flickering flames on the tyres of the burning car defied the steady rain and the white foam the firemen had used to douse the fire. Breathing through his mouth to avoid the doubled stench of charred flesh and burning rubber, Bruno checked his watch. Dawn was still an hour away.

It was not only the smell that turned his stomach. He felt sickened by a personal sense of outrage that such an evil killing had taken place on his turf, almost within sight of the town he was sworn to protect. Even though the dead man was a stranger, Bruno felt the manner of this man's death had been a kind of pollution of these woods that he knew so well. He'd never be able to bring his horse or his dog this way without thinking of it. And this atrocity had been carried out by people skilled in the blackest arts of death, professionals who were notoriously hard to bring to justice. But he'd find them.

'He's certainly dead and it's obviously murder. Did you see the wound under the chin?' asked Fabiola, a doctor whose presence was legally required to certify death. Bruno nodded. A stiletto up through the soft skin of the mouth and straight into the brain killed quickly and with very little blood. It was one of the assassin's tricks taught to troops in special forces.

'I can't even give you an approximate time of death,' she went on. Fabiola was the best doctor at the medical clinic of St Denis and a good friend. She wore no hat and rain had plastered streaks of her dark hair to her face, covering the scar on her cheek. Without make-up her face was pale in the headlights and her eyes enormous. The thought struck him how beautiful Fabiola could be.

'Normally I'd use an anal thermometer for body temperature, but he's been badly sodomized and then the fire . . .' Her voice broke off.

'The ground is dry beneath his hips,' said Bruno. 'The storm broke just after two this morning, so presumably they chained him to the tree before then.'

'You were awake for the storm?' she asked. He nodded. The lightning had not disturbed him but the quick scuttle of Balzac into his bed had jolted him awake just as the thunder came. Usually barred from his master's bed, the basset hound was still young enough to be granted a dispensation during the tempests that occasionally gave this gentle valley of the river Vézère a brief taste of an Indian monsoon. Bruno had risen, gone to the window and looked out to see if the rain was hard enough to damage the vineyards now that the harvest was due.

After a lapse into a steady drizzle, the rain was coming harder again, the tail-end of a storm front that had swept in from the Atlantic. Once Fabiola had finished her examination, Bruno tried to cover the body with a plastic sheet. It protected the charred bones of the feet and lower legs but didn't stretch as far as the man's wrists, still handcuffed around the trunk of a young chestnut tree. The poor devil would have to stay that way, arms stretched out behind his head, his legs staked apart and his back arched like some medieval torture victim, until the forensics team arrived from Périgueux with their cameras and checklists.

'Do you think he was killed before the fire burned his feet away?' Fabiola's voice sounded forced as she tried to control it.

Bruno shrugged, a gesture that turned into a shudder as he thought about it. 'That's more your expertize than mine. I don't know how you'd tell.'

'The autopsy will confirm it. After death the heart stops pumping blood.'

There was no doubt that this murder would require an autopsy. It was worse than brutal. Bruno suspected the feet had been burned deliberately before the car was set on fire. The blaze might have scorched the legs but it could hardly have devoured them. He guessed the killers had poured petrol onto his feet.

The only time Bruno had heard of that being done was in the Algerian war. It was a cruel joke of the rebels, who called the white colonists on their land the *pieds-noirs*, the black feet, after the black boots the French troops had worn when they first conquered the country in 1830. 'We'll give you black feet,' they taunted the French prisoners as they poured the petrol. Hercule had told him that; an old friend, now dead, who had served in the vicious conflict France had fought in vain to keep Algeria and its oil.

'No identification?' Fabiola asked. 'I'd say North African heritage with that hair and the olive skin.'

'Nothing on him and the registration plates were removed from the car.' Bruno had taken the VIN number from the engine block but he didn't expect an answer until much later in the day. Fabiola was staring at him, expecting him to say more. 'All we know is that Serge up at the farm was getting up for the cows and saw the explosion in the woods. He called the *pompiers* just after four. You may as well go back to bed, but I'm stuck here until the forensics team arrives.'

Bruno yawned and stretched. It had been a broken night, the phone call with the special tone waking him before midnight. Then he had dozed, expecting to be called again, until the storm had woken his dog. He'd slept again, Balzac tucked in against his shoulder, until Albert had called him to

4

report the fire in the woods. At least the storm had stopped it from spreading. Like most of the rest of southern France, the *Département* had recently issued a forest fire alert after the dry summer.

'It's too late to go back to bed and I wouldn't sleep, not thinking about this.' Fabiola gestured with her chin at the plastic-covered corpse. 'I'll go back and shower and put some coffee on. Feel free to come and have a cup once you can get away.'

'Thanks, but it will be some time. I might have to leave the horses to you this morning.'

'Poor Bruno. Nobody should have to see scenes like this. If you need something to help you sleep . . .'

He smiled his thanks but shook his head. It was thoughts about women and his confused love life that kept him awake some nights, not memories of war and corpses. Fabiola quickly kissed his cheek and then briefly took shelter with the *pompiers* in the cab of the fire engine to sign the certificate of death before heading home.

The burned-out car was on a rough gravel track about a hundred metres from a minor road, just at the entrance to the commune's old rubbish dump. It had been closed since the building of the modern *déchetterie* where all the refuse had to be sorted into different containers. The dead man lay a few metres from his charred vehicle. The car had been stopped just beyond the entrance to the dump, beside a pile of logs being seasoned before sale. Bruno raised one end of the topmost log to assess its weight; at least fifty kilos. He could lift it, but he couldn't carry it far.

Four charred logs lay on the track behind and beneath the

car. Bruno guessed the driver had been lured along this path, and then found himself unable to reverse because somebody pretty strong had been waiting to toss thick logs behind his wheels. But why had the driver stopped? Bruno walked on up the sloping path and round a sharp bend and his torch picked out some broken twigs and crushed grass. He saw tyre tracks; a second car had been parked here, blocking the way. It could have been waiting, then switched on its headlights to force the oncoming car to stop. Then an accomplice would have used the logs to immobilize it. He'd be looking for at least two men, and forensics might get something from the tracks.

The spread between the wheel markings looked too wide for a car. He went back to his vehicle for a metallic tape measure and spanned from the inside of each tyre mark to record a width of one metre thirty in his notebook. He'd have to check this against the width of various types of truck when he got back to his office.

He loosened the hood of his anorak to make room by his ear for his phone and punched in the speed-dial number for the Brigadier, the shadowy official from the Interior Ministry who had given him the phone during a previous case. It was supposed to be secure from wire taps and it rang with a special tone when someone else on the Brigadier's private network was calling. That had been the tone that had woken him before midnight. The caller had identified himself only as Rafiq and said he was coming onto Bruno's territory and might need support. He'd said he would call again, but had not done so.

'Duty officer,' came the voice in Bruno's ear. He identified himself, described the call from Rafiq and reported the death and the evidence of ambush and torture. 'It may be Rafiq.' Bruno stooped to protect his notebook from the rain and read out the VIN number. 'If that's Rafiq's car there's no sign of his phone. It could be compromised.'

'We'll check and call you back.'

He began to give his location and was interrupted.

'We know where you are. With that phone your GPS co-ordinates come up on my screen. Have any other police officers been alerted?'

'Just Commissaire Jalipeau, chief of detectives for the *Département*,' Bruno said. He had pondered calling the Gendarmes, but J-J's team had the expertise and the forensics lab. And the call from Rafiq on the special line had made him cautious. Bruno, employed by the town of St Denis, got on well with the local Gendarmes, but J-J, like many detectives of the *Police Nationale*, had little time for them, seeing them mainly as traffic cops.

'Good, keep it that way.' The duty officer closed the line.

Bruno trudged back through sodden leaves toward the fire engine. Fabiola's car had already departed but the *pompiers* were happy to stay, warm and dry in their cab and drinking coffee from a thermos. Bruno was just finishing the cup they gave him when his phone rang again.

'It's me,' came the voice of J-J. 'We're just coming into St Denis. Can you guide us to the place? I can't make this damn GPS work and I don't want to have to ask the Gendarmes.'

Bruno gave directions and told them to watch for the lights of the fire engine. He went to tell the *pompiers* that the police were on their way and they could go home soon. Would French policing be any more efficient if they were all one service, he wondered, or at least if they could overcome the traditional rivalries and learn to work together? His phone buzzed again with the special tone, and this time it was the Brigadier.

'The VIN number fits. It's Rafiq's car. Are you with the body?' Bruno confirmed that he was. 'Check the upper left arm for a tattoo.'

He went back to the corpse, lifted the plastic sheet and loosened the remains of a leather jacket and shirt from the left shoulder and saw a tattoo that brought back memories.

'Yes, there's a tattoo, looks pretty old, two digits, one and three.'

'That's him,' the Brigadier replied. 'He was a good man. I'll come down for the autopsy.'

'J-J is on his way here,' Bruno said. 'Should I tell him about Rafiq?' The 13th was a regiment of paratroop dragoons, an elite unit that was part of the French brigade of special forces. Bruno had served alongside some of them in Bosnia. The 13th specialized in discreet reconnaissance in hostile territory. They thought of themselves as the French version of Britain's SAS. Rafiq would not have been easily subdued, even by two or three men.

'I'll call J-J now and put him in the picture,' the Brigadier said. 'Expect me later today, probably early afternoon. I'll fax a letter to your Mayor to say you're being seconded to my team. And keep an eye out for Arabs. Rafiq was working undercover on jihadists.'

'Better call J-J right away,' said Bruno. 'I can see the lights of his car.' He rang off and stood in front of the fire-engine headlights where J-J could see him.

'Can we head off now?' asked Albert, calling down from the

cab. 'We'll have fresh coffee and croissants at the fire station if you want to join us.'

'As soon as J-J takes over and lets me sign off. Here he is now.' With the stench of charred flesh still in his nostrils, Bruno would not feel like eating for some time.

2

By the time Bruno left the crime scene, the sun was up and a brisk, warm breeze was sweeping away what was left of the storm clouds. At Pamela's house, tree branches were swaying and as he stepped out of his police van he heard the stable door banging in the wind. He went to secure it and saw that the stables were empty. Pamela's car was gone. She was probably out shopping. She was allowed to drive again but Fabiola hadn't given her permission to resume riding, after a bad fall that had broken her collarbone. Fabiola must have taken the horses out. Coffee, orange juice and one of Stéphane's yogurts with a jar of honey were waiting for him on Pamela's kitchen table. He drank the juice and coffee and took a shower. He shaved with the razor he kept in Pamela's bathroom for those occasions, not as frequent as he would like, when he was invited to spend the night.

Rather than offend Pamela, he gulped down the yogurt and left a note of thanks. Then he headed for the Domaine to ask Julien if the grapes had suffered in the storm. Most of Bruno's savings were invested in the town's vineyard. As he turned into the lane that led to the small château the sun was already high enough in the sky to shine directly through the windscreen into his eyes. He pulled down the visor to see knots of grape-pickers at work amid the vines that were nearest the river. He stopped the car, enjoying the calm familiarity of the scene that pushed back the memories of Rafiq's body and reminded him why he loved this land so much. Feeling refreshed if not restored, he drove and found Julien in the *chai*, checking the grapes before they went into the press.

'You're the third worried investor I've seen this morning,' Julien greeted him cheerfully. 'The Mayor was here first, then the bank manager. The grapes are fine. We always trim the higher bunches so the lower ones get protection from the leaves.'

Bruno nodded, reassured but still a little confused. He'd been reading up on wine-making and while one chapter had told him that mildew was the wine-maker's great enemy, another had waxed lyrical about *Botrytis*, the noble rot that produced such dense sweetness in the Sauternes and Monbazillacs of the region.

'No problems with mildew?' he asked, hoping it sounded as if he knew what he was talking about.

'Not this late in the season when we've almost finished picking. And this wind is drying off the grapes. This time of year it's not a bit of rain but the possibility of hail that worries me. I've seen whole vineyards flattened.'

Bruno nodded. In the storms that came around the equinox, in March and September, he'd known hailstones the size of golf balls, big enough to break roof tiles and demolish greenhouses and coming down so thickly they lay ankle-deep on the roads. He declined Julien's offer of a glass of wine but accepted a cup of freshly pressed grape juice, warm and sticky. He rinsed his hands and left for the *Mairie*. French schools had reopened after the summer and the rush of tourists had gone, but there were still British families and older Dutch and German couples enjoying the September sun as they breakfasted on Fauquet's terrace and watched the river flow beneath the old stone bridge. Yogurt and honey were a fine mixture but not what Bruno thought of as breakfast, so he stopped at Fauquet's for a coffee and croissant.

'Albert was in just now, told us about the murder,' said Fauquet, leaning over the bar with the conspiratorial air he liked to assume when pumping Bruno for information. 'Terrible sight, he said it was. Legs all burned away. Do you know who it was?'

'There'll be a statement later today from the *Police Nationale* in Périgueux,' Bruno told him. 'They're in charge now. I just went to secure the scene until they arrived.'

'Philippe was here when Albert came in. He's gone up there now, said he'd be taking photos of the police at work,' Fauquet went on, handing Bruno his espresso. 'He was asking if you'd been in.'

As he bit into his croissant and took his first sip of coffee, relishing the way the two tastes seemed made for one another, Bruno resigned himself to being pestered by Philippe Delaron. A cheerful young man, Philippe ran the town's camera shop, with a lucrative sideline in taking photos for *Sud Ouest*, the regional newspaper. A huge family of siblings and cousins gave him contacts in every walk of the town's life. Philippe often knew as much about local developments as Bruno, but tended to see them in a far more sensational light. Bruno helped Philippe when he could and told him frankly when he couldn't. They had few qualms about using each other for their own ends, which made for a reasonable if somewhat wary relationship.

'And Father Sentout wanted to know if there might be a burial,' Fauquet added. Bruno shrugged but remained silent, knowing that if he said the dead man was probably a Muslim it would be all over town and on Radio Périgord by lunchtime.

Bruno put a two-euro coin on the counter and reached for the café's copy of *Sud Ouest*. He began glancing at headlines as he chewed his croissant, a signal that he wanted no more questions. Fauquet shuffled along the bar to talk to a bunch of regular customers, doubtless hinting that he'd learned far more from Bruno than he could ever reveal. Gossip was as much his stock in trade as coffee and croissants.

The front page carried the latest depressing news about rising unemployment in France and more violence in the Middle East. The inside pages, by contrast, were filled with happy scenes of grapes being picked in the vineyards, photos of the new schoolteachers and of couples celebrating fifty years of marriage. The sports pages covered in great detail all the doings of the local rugby, tennis and hunting clubs. That was why people bought *Sud Ouest*, he thought, for the chance of seeing local news and pictures of people they knew. He closed the paper, made his farewells and left for his office.

A stack of mail awaited his attention on his desk inside the *Mairie*. He turned on his computer and leafed through the envelopes while it booted up. The ding of an incoming email drew him to the screen. The email address of the sender tugged at his memory; ZigiPara, a name he had not heard for a decade and more. Zigi was a shortened form of Tzigane, or gypsy, which was what the army called anyone of Roma origins. His real name was Jacques Sadna and he came from the Camargue, the vast wetlands at the delta of the River Rhône where gypsies had settled for centuries and raised their famous horses. Zigi had been a corporal, like Bruno, when they first served together in the Ivory Coast and each had been promoted sergeant during some covert operations on the border between Chad and Libya. Zigi was with the paratroops and Bruno with the combat engineers. He recalled hearing that Zigi had since become an officer.

'Hi Bruno, a heads-up from an old mate, even though you are a Pékin,' he read. 'I'm at Nijrab, adjudant-chef, and a muj has showed up claiming to be French from St Denis. Calls himself Sami Belloumi, says he knows you and has a dad named Momu. Seems simple-minded, scars on his back from whippings. Toubib says badly traumatized. He wants to go home but no documents. Photo attached. You know him? Let me know before this gets into official channels. Zigi.'

Bruno smiled as the old army slang came back to him. A Pékin meant a civilian. Nijrab was the French army base in the Kapisa region of Afghanistan. Bruno couldn't remember whether they were still doing combat patrols or if the mission had been changed to training the Afghan army. A muj was a mujahedin. A *toubib* was a doctor. Bruno's grin turned solemn as he read on. He knew Sami Belloumi, a young man who had left St Denis three, maybe four years earlier, supposedly to go to a special school for autistic youths run by a mosque in Toulouse. Sami was the nephew of Momu, the maths teacher at the local *collège,* and now adopted as his son. Momu was also the father of Karim, who ran the Café des Sports and was a star of the town rugby team.

Bruno clicked to open the photo and it was Sami sure enough. Bruno remembered him being as tall as Karim, but now he looked so thin he was almost skeletal, with prominent

14

cheekbones that emphasized his bulging eyes. He had a long beard and his head had been shaved. The photograph brought back memories of Sami at the tennis club, serving ace after ace, always placing the ball precisely in the corner. Bruno had been able to get back perhaps one serve in three. But Sami had no interest in anything but serving. He never returned a ball, never played a forehand or backhand. He would stay on court alone for hours with a basket full of tennis balls beside him, practising his perfect serves. It was the same with basketball. He could sink the ball from anywhere on the court, but that was all he wanted to do. He wouldn't pass the ball, wouldn't dribble or run. And like his tennis serve, he practised sinking the ball for hours.

Momu said it was something to do with the way his brain worked. Sami seemed able to repair anything electrical or mechanical, from toasters to computers. He could do mathematical puzzles, but if he'd learned to read or write, they were skills he never used. While he was polite and friendly, always shaking hands whenever he saw Bruno, the boy hardly ever spoke. Old Dr Gelletreau at the medical centre had said he was autistic and there was nothing to be done. Momu had tried to get him into a special school, but the lack of them was one of the scandals of the French education system. It was sad, Bruno thought, that Fabiola had arrived in town too late to treat him. It wasn't that the other doctors of St Denis weren't good but that Fabiola was special, a gifted healer with an intuitive way of dealing with her patients and establishing trust. Perhaps she might have been able to draw Sami out. Perhaps she could do so now once they had him back home.

He made a routine call to the passport office to see when

Sami had applied for one and to establish its number. What had Sami been doing in Afghanistan, he wondered. Zigi had called him a muj, and in the drab brown garment that was all Bruno could see on the photo Sami was the very image of a Taliban. But most Afghans in the countryside probably looked similar.

There was one obvious reason why a French citizen, a Muslim of Arab origin, would make his way to Afghanistan. Had Sami somehow been radicalized? Bruno doubted whether the boy he had known had much sense of politics or religion, and he had been brought up in Momu's secular home. Momu had little time for religion and Bruno had never known him to visit a mosque, except to enrol Sami in the special school. Perhaps Sami had become a devout Muslim and then been persuaded or dragooned to go to Afghanistan. Could he have volunteered for jihad? Zigi's account of the whipping scars made that sound unlikely. Bruno knew he was speculating with too few facts to go on. What mattered was that Sami was a son of St Denis and he wanted to come back to his family.

The passport clerk finally replied. Sami Belloumi had never applied for a passport.

'Hi Zigi,' Bruno tapped out in reply to his old comrade. 'If they made you adj-chef, the army is in more trouble than I thought. Good to hear from you and thanks for message. That photo is our Sami, French citizen and member of respected local family but last heard of at special school for autistic kids in mosque in Toulouse. Can we bring him home? Bruno.'

The Mayor looked old and tired when he returned from a meeting of the *Conseil-Général*, the governing body for the

Département, with its endless arguments over budgets in times of austerity. Usually Gérard Mangin used the stairs, bounding up them with the energy of a man half his age. This time he emerged from the lift with shoulders bowed. He spotted Bruno helping himself to coffee from the communal pot and gestured for Bruno to join him in the mayoral office. Bruno took a seat on the straight-backed and uncomfortable wooden chair the Mayor offered visitors to dissuade them from staying too long.

'You must be in worse shape than you look if you're reduced to drinking that dreadful stuff,' the Mayor said, nodding at the mug in Bruno's hand. He buzzed his intercom twice, a signal to Claire to make some proper coffee from his private store.

'I need some of that after this morning's meeting,' he went on. 'They're trying to raid the little pot of money I've been saving for the new sewers to pay for road repairs in those communes who were too idle to do proper maintenance. They're coming up with all sorts of threats to make me give way but I won't have it.'

'I'd have thought they knew you well enough by now,' Bruno said, with a slow smile. 'You always guard the commune's money as if it were your own.'

'More carefully, Bruno. I've seen mayors go to prison because they were too free and easy with town funds.'

'What are they threatening?'

'They want me to sell off the *collège* apartments, agree a three-year hiring freeze at the *Mairie* and sell off part of our town park for development.'

Bruno winced. He'd spent his spare time the previous winter in repainting and restoring one of those apartments, offered at a subsidized rent to attract teachers to work at rural schools.

Florence the new science teacher lived there with her infant twins. And the town park was sacrosanct, Bruno thought, or it ought to be.

'So what was decided?'

'Nothing, which is usually the case with committees. I said we couldn't even consider the matter of the apartments until we had a legal opinion on the status of the teachers' tenancies and they would have to pay for that. I had no objection to a hiring freeze so long as it included all the other communes, not just ours, but I made a counter-proposal that we organize a census of all public employees in all the *mairies*. They didn't like that.'

'And on the park?'

'None of their business. I simply pointed out that it belongs to the citizens of St Denis and so nothing will happen without a referendum. And I added that of course any member of the *Conseil* would be welcome to come to St Denis and campaign for a sale of the park but I wouldn't guarantee their safety if they did. Anyway, they're not having our money and that's that.'

Bruno nodded, pleased to see that the Mayor was himself again, invigorated as he refought his committee battles.

'Now tell me about this mysterious murder they were talking about on the car radio as I drove back.'

As Bruno related what he knew about Rafiq's death, the Mayor skimmed through his inbox and pulled out the faxed letter of request for Bruno to be seconded to the Interior Ministry under the Brigadier's command. He took his fountain pen from his desk drawer, scribbled an approval on the letter and handed it to Bruno. The door opened and Claire brought in two cups of espresso from the machine the council had bought to mark the Mayor's twentieth anniversary in office.

'Something else has come up, in Afghanistan of all places,' Bruno began when Claire had left. Halfway into Bruno's explanation of the reappearance of Momu's nephew, the Mayor rose, crossed to his shelves and plucked out a manila file bound in white tape. Back at his desk, he opened it and pushed across to Bruno copies of Momu's original application for his nephew to obtain French citizenship, along with a copy of the formal naturalization and of Sami's *carte d'identité*.

'I remember it well. I did most of the paperwork myself. Did we have any idea this young man was no longer at that special school in Toulouse?'

'No,' Bruno said. 'And the passport authorities have no record of his ever being issued with a passport. Heaven knows how Sami got out to Afghanistan. As soon as the school breaks for lunch I'll go and see what Momu has to say. I can't imagine he didn't know that Sami had left Toulouse.'

'You may be right, but if Sami decided to become a jihadi I'm not surprised Momu kept it quiet,' the Mayor said. 'Still, the sooner you let him know that Sami is alive and well the better.'

Bruno explained that Sami's appearance at the French army base had not yet reached official channels. So far, this was a private tip-off from an old army chum who seemed ready to keep the whole affair informal. There were regular French military flights back and forth to Afghanistan, and with luck Sami's return need never become an official matter. In Bruno's experience, armies were usually content to let sergeants resolve tricky problems in their own way with a minimum of paperwork and a maximum of discretion and dispatch.

'I presume that copy of the ID card will be sufficient for your old army friend,' the Mayor replied. 'If not, I can probably pull some strings in Paris. I seem to recall some regulation about the repatriation of distressed French citizens from danger zones. If we need to give some guarantee of paying an air fare we can find the money somewhere. Sami's one of ours, so let's do what we can to get him back. In the meantime, what's an undercover agent with an Arab name doing getting himself killed in St Denis?'

'Tortured as well as killed, as vicious as anything I ever saw,' Bruno replied. 'So he was probably being questioned before being put to death in a very professional way, a stiletto under the chin and into the brain. I only know what I told you, which is what I heard from the Brigadier. Rafiq sounds Arab, if that's his real name, and Fabiola said she thought the dead man had North African origins. It seems quite a coincidence that he gets killed just as Sami resurfaces.'

The Mayor looked thoughtful. 'Indeed it does, suspiciously so, particularly when our shadowy Brigadier is involved. It usually spells trouble when he turns up, and trouble with our traditional blend of politics, intrigue and diplomacy.'

Bruno grinned. 'You left out the sex.'

'This is France, Bruno. We take that for granted.'

3

Back in his office, Bruno scanned the documents about Sami that the Mayor had given him and emailed them to Zigi with a note saying these should suffice to establish Sami's identity. The ID card and naturalization papers each carried a thumbprint. Then he called the *collège* secretary to check the teachers' timetables. Momu was still teaching but would be free in the last period before lunch and he'd probably find him in the staffroom.

Bruno put on his cap and strode the short distance across the bridge to the school that educated the young teenagers of St Denis and the other nearby communes. It was a standard building of the 1960s, an unimaginative array of oblongs in concrete and glass around a playground and small sports field. The pupils had dubbed it 'the shoebox'. The rooms were baking in summer and none too warm in winter and the temperamental boiler was one of the Mayor's priorities for replacement in his battles over the budget.

Bruno squeezed past an unfamiliar white van that was blocking the entrance. He thought it might be some workman doing maintenance but there was no company sign on its side. He put his head round the door of the secretary's office to say hello and ask about the van. She shrugged and said she knew nothing about it. Puzzled, Bruno took a note of the number, recognizing from the figure 31 that it was a Toulouse registration.

Glancing through a side window, he saw on the passenger seat a print, an enlargement of the kind of photo taken for a passport or ID card. To his surprise he recognized the features of a much younger Sami Belloumi, the youth who was supposed to be in Afghanistan.

Bruno tried the van doors. All locked, and the windows on the rear door had been covered with paper on the inside. He looked at the width between the tyres and at their treads and pulled out his notebook to check the dimensions he'd recorded earlier. It wasn't conclusive but the width could fit. Bruno opened the engine cover, removed the distributor head and detached the cables from the battery. He told the secretary to refer the driver to him, took out his phone and called the Gendarmerie. Sergeant Jules answered and Bruno called for urgent back-up and asked him to get someone to check on the registration number of the van from Toulouse.

He climbed the stairs to the upper level where the science labs and Momu's mathematics classroom were located along with the teachers' staffroom. The final teaching period of the morning had not yet begun, and instead of the noisy anarchy of break-time, the place was quiet, disturbed only by the faint sounds of teachers' voices.

But the corridors were not empty. Ahead of him two men in jeans and leather jackets were going from one classroom to the next, bending to peer through the single pane of clear glass in each door, evidently looking for somebody. One of the two men turned at the sound of Bruno's footsteps and nudged his colleague. They exchanged glances at the sight of his police uniform.

'*Bonjour, messieurs*,' Bruno said politely. 'Can I be of assistance? You appear to be looking for someone.'

They looked like North Africans. One was tall and heavy-set with the build of a rugby player, dark skin and tightly curled hair cut short. He was clean-shaven and held his arms away from his sides as if readying for action. The shorter man had a small, neat beard and was carrying some kind of baton against his thigh. A box, the size of a thick dictionary, hung from a strap over his shoulder. They moved as if they were used to working as a team. The big man walked directly towards Bruno, his face impassive, while his partner with the beard moved to one side, ready to come in against Bruno's flank. He smiled and tried to distract Bruno by saying they were looking for a friend.

The best form of defence is attack, Bruno thought, and strode quickly toward the greater threat, holding out his hand in greeting to the taller of the two men but ready to defend himself. The big man stopped in surprise but then lunged forward with both arms as if to wrestle him. Bruno used his momentum to pivot on his left foot and sent his right boot crashing into the side of his opponent's knee and the man fell heavily to the floor. Bruno thought he'd have time to turn and deal with the smaller man. He was wrong.

A pain more piercing and intense than anything he had ever known hit Bruno on his left side and he felt himself go rigid in shock, his scream of anguish cut off as his throat seemed suddenly to jam closed. Then his limbs seemed to collapse at once and he crumpled to the floor, his nerves jangling and his heart hammering. He had no idea what had happened to him but could barely see for the stars and flashes before his eyes when the appalling pain came again, in the pit of his stomach this time, and he felt his limbs jerking of their own accord, his feet and the back of his head hammering on the floor.

The pain stopped, and again he had the sensation of his nerves firing random impulses all over his body. He seemed to have no power over his muscles and felt his bladder empty itself, wet and warm. Some form of self-control came back into his mind and he wondered if he was having an epileptic fit. A spasm from his stomach turned him onto his side in time to vomit onto the floor rather than over himself. He smelt burning and looked down to see smoke curling from a scorch mark on his uniform jacket. Had he been shot? He could see no blood. His senses were returning and he heard dragging footsteps and looked up to see the two men stumbling away down the corridor, the bigger one leaning heavily on his partner.

Doors were opening and people were looking out. He tried to shout at them to stay inside the classrooms but only a squeak came from his throat. He could hear the siren of the Gendarmerie van drawing closer. Suddenly someone was kneeling at his side, taking his pulse and calling for water and a cloth, and he recognized Florence. Then another teacher was cleaning up the pool of Bruno's vomit and Florence was bathing his face with a damp cloth. He forced himself to sit up, his nerves still quivering, and he realized he had been given two bad shocks with an electric cattle prod. The power must have been turned up very high.

He tried to say 'Gendarmes, alert,' but his throat didn't seem to work. Florence gave him a cup of water and he swallowed.

He tried to roll to his feet but she held him down and he could see he was surrounded by a ring of schoolchildren staring down at him. A voice said dismissively, 'He's drunk.'

'Get kids back in their rooms. Danger. Two men, Arabs, one beard, white van outside,' he gasped out. 'Hide Momu. They hunt him.'

The siren was continuous, just outside. Then there was shouting and the sound of engines revving hard and the siren began moving away. Bruno's mobile phone was ringing. Florence answered it.

'This is Bruno's phone. He's been hurt and can't speak. Who is speaking, please?'

A pause. Then she turned to Bruno and said, 'It's Sergeant Jules. They are chasing two men who just stole a car. They flagged it down, pulled the driver out, hit him with a rifle butt and sped off.'

Into the phone, she said, 'Two men attacked Bruno here at the *collège*. We are calling the *Urgences*. Bruno needs treatment. Nobody else is hurt.'

Other than the knowledge that he had been beaten up by experts, Bruno was starting to feel a little better. He took his phone from her hand and said, 'I'm OK, Jules. They hit me with a cattle prod. I don't know if they have other weapons but we need to talk to them about the murder last night. Is there anything I can do? I'll stay here, by their van. I immobilized it.'

Jules replied that they were in chase on the road to Belvès and other Gendarmes had been alerted. He rang off.

'What the hell happened here?' asked Rollo, the headmaster, who had just arrived. 'What's this about a murder?'

'Get the kids back in their classrooms and we need to take

Momu somewhere safe,' Bruno said. He dialled J-J's number and found him in his car.

'I was just coming to see you, Bruno. I was almost at the *Mairie* but then we heard the sirens and the Gendarmes went by like bats out of hell. The police radio net has just put out an all-points bulletin for a silver-grey Renault Laguna.'

Bruno explained briefly and J-J said he'd join him at the *collège* within minutes. Bruno closed his phone, rose gingerly to his feet, and watched the kids troop reluctantly back into their classrooms, stewarded by their teachers. Rollo, Momu and Florence remained, their eyes wide at what they had heard from Bruno's briefing of J-J.

'I have to stay here to meet J-J and search that white van,' Bruno said. 'Rollo, I need you to drive Momu home, collect his wife and take them to the *Mairie*. They'll be safe there. Florence, thank you for your care. I'm feeling better now and I'll talk to you later. Momu, I wasn't going to break it like this but Sami has surfaced in Afghanistan and he wants to come home. The two men who attacked me are looking for him and I think they came here looking for you. While they're on the loose, you're in danger and so is anyone at your house.'

A different siren was now audible and getting louder. Everybody looked around for the source of the sound except Momu, who asked, 'Sami's alive? He's coming back? Have you spoken to him?'

'That will be J-J. I have to go and talk to him. Momu, he's alive and coming home and that's all I know. Rollo, Momu, please do as I say. I don't have time to explain further.'

He limped off down the corridor toward the toilets, stripped off his trousers and fouled pants and cleaned up as best he could. His legs felt as if he'd played an exhausting game of rugby and there were burn marks on his side and his stomach where the prod had shocked him. He dashed cold water over his face and decided against looking at himself in the mirror. When Bruno got outside into the schoolyard, J-J was examining the white van. The blue light was still flashing on the roof of his car.

'It just came over the radio, the Gendarmes lost them,' said the big detective. 'They turned off down country lanes and got clear before we had the roadblocks organized.'

'That's their van, and I think it might also have been the one involved in the killing in the woods,' Bruno said, as a familiar Renault Twingo turned into the *collège*, just ahead of the red van the *pompiers* used for emergency medical services. Fabiola braked the Twingo, climbed out leaving the door open and marched up to Bruno, took his wrist to feel his pulse and looked searchingly into his eyes.

'Were you unconscious?' she asked.

'No, I was hit by two electric shocks from a cattle prod. I just collapsed. And I wet myself. Then I threw up. I feel better now, just aching.'

'I'm not surprised. Where were you shocked?'

He pointed and she dropped his wrist, opened his jacket and pulled his shirt out to look at the two places.

'Those are the same kinds of burn I saw on the anus of the dead man last night, or rather this morning,' she said. 'Count yourself lucky you didn't go through what he did. That's no ordinary cattle prod.'

She put her hands to the sides of his neck, palpating the glands. 'Follow my finger with your eyes.' She waved her finger across his vision, then up and down, then close to his nose.

'You'll live,' she said. 'When you're done with J-J, come see me at the clinic.' She turned on her heel, crossed to the *pompier* truck to tell them they would not be needed and got back into her car.

'Quite an assertive young lady,' said J-J. 'You sure you're in good enough shape to talk? You look like shit.'

'You heard her, I'll live,' Bruno replied. 'Lend me a set of evidence gloves and let's take a look inside this van.'

The driver's and passenger's doors had both been unlocked and the key was in the ignition, where they had tried in vain to start the vehicle. The blown-up photo of Sami had gone. The charging wire for a mobile phone was inserted into the hole for the cigar lighter. There were paper cups of coffee in the brackets between the two front seats and sandwich wrappers tossed onto the floor.

'Lovely,' said J-J. 'Lots of fingerprints and DNA from the cups. The intelligence boys will think it's Christmas.'

Bruno looked inside the litter basket at the entrance to the school, removed the distributor head from where he had hidden it and handed it to J-J. Then he opened the rear doors to see a mattress with two sleeping bags and a heavy-duty battery pack, which he assumed was used to recharge the cattle prod. A long wooden box was behind the two front seats, covered with a blanket. Bruno pulled the blanket aside and opened the box.

It was empty save for a lining of rubber foam, cut out in the shape of a bolt-action rifle. A second, smaller cutout suggested the shape of a telescopic sight. On the inner lid were stencilled letters and digits: FR-F2. Bruno recognized the designation for the standard sniper's weapon for the French army throughout his time of service. Two ten-round magazines were wrapped inside camouflage rags and tucked between the foam rubber and the side of the case. They were both filled with NATO standard 7.63-millimetre rounds.

Under the driver's seat was a small notebook, filled with words in Arabic, and a passport-size photo of Sami, the original of the one Bruno had first seen. There were other prints, larger, of a man who seemed unaware of the photos being taken. They might have been surveillance photos. He was snapped entering and leaving a car, at a café table and among a crowd of Muslim men praying. Bruno could not be sure but he thought it could be Rafiq, the dead man he had seen handcuffed to a tree in the woods a few hours earlier. He thumbed through to the latest blank page, turned back, and saw the words St Denis in Roman letters, Arabic writing below. He showed it to J-J, just as Rollo came out of the main school entrance, Momu close behind. Bruno called him over.

'Can you read this?' Bruno asked, showing the notebook. 'Wait.' He gave Momu a set of evidence gloves and helped him put them on before handing him the notebook.

'It's my and my wife's names, our home address and the address of the school,' said Momu.

'I wasn't joking when I said you were in danger,' Bruno said. 'Collect your wife and go to the *Mairie*. As soon as the Gendarmes get back we'll move you there while we sort out something better.'

Momu nodded. 'What about Karim and Rashida and the baby?' he asked.

'Is there anything in the notebook about them?'

Momu leafed through it and shook his head.

'Then I don't think you need worry about them. I'll go and see Karim and let him know what's happened. You and I need to talk about Sami, but in the meantime go with Rollo. I'll find you later.'

J-J was on the phone. He looked across at Bruno and mouthed, 'The Brigadier.' He listened briefly and then handed the phone to Bruno. 'He wants to speak to you.'

'I hear you've had a bit of a shock,' came the familiar voice.

'Two, in fact.'

'I'm on my way from the airport at Bergerac and I'll see you at the Gendarmerie in St Denis as soon as you've been to the medical clinic. J-J says the doc insists on checking you over. I want you with a clean bill of health. That's an order.'

Bruno handed back the phone and was about to ask J-J for a lift back to his van when he heard the sound of an ancient Citroën *deux-chevaux* being driven too fast and then Pamela's car raced around the bend. She braked hard and climbed out, looking dishevelled as if she'd left the house too quickly to look at her hair or change out of gardening clothes. She advanced upon Bruno.

'What on earth have you done to yourself this time?' she demanded, anger in her voice but concern in her eyes. 'Fabiola said you'd been attacked but didn't go into details.'

'She looked me over; she must have told you I was OK.' He briefly explained what had happened, downplaying the incident, but Florence was in earshot and decided to intervene.

'He was writhing in agony, throwing up and he couldn't stand or walk for a few minutes. I was very worried for a while.'

'It wore off,' Bruno said. 'I'm fine now.'

'I can't bear this,' Pamela snapped, her eyes blazing. She wagged a muddy finger at him. 'Each time you leave I never know what sort of trouble you might be getting into. You're a magnet for it, Bruno, and I don't think I can take much more.'

'It's alright,' said Florence, taking Pamela's arm. 'He's going to the clinic now for a proper check-up.' With her eyes, she gestured for Bruno to leave. He climbed into the passenger seat of J-J's car. After a moment J-J squeezed himself behind the wheel and asked, 'Where to? The clinic?'

'No, the *Mairie*. My van's parked there and I want to go home and clean up.' He turned to face J-J. 'Do you get this kind of reaction from your wife?'

'Yes, I think we all do,' J-J replied. 'It's one of the reasons so few cops can make their marriages last. Mine left me once because of it, but then she came back. Funny thing was, after that time when I got shot, she was fine and she never worried again. She said she'd been through the worst that could happen.'

'Sounds like a drastic sort of cure,' Bruno said.

'They're doing counselling now for spouses. Male or female, when a cop gets wed the partner is offered a course in the pressures of being married to one of us, support networks, all that. Do you want me to see if we can get Pamela into one of those?'

'I doubt it. She's British. Her idea of treatment is a nice hot cup of tea. And she does not see herself as my spouse, not even as a partner.'

'So you say, but she certainly acts like one.'

4

Having already been home to shower, change his clothes and feed his chickens, Bruno dutifully presented himself at the clinic, where Fabiola made him strip for a full physical. She spent some time examining the burn marks from the cattle prod, listened carefully to his heart, tapped his chest and checked his reflexes. Finally she drew some blood for tests.

'You're in a state of shock,' she said, 'and I don't want any jokes about cattle prods. You've had a hell of a jolt, which is a strain on the heart, and your heartbeat is still much too fast. I want you to go home and go to bed and put some extra blankets on. No food, no alcohol, no activities and take a lot of water. I'll come by later with some bouillon and I want to see you again in the morning.'

Bruno, who had great faith in Fabiola's medical skills, promised to take her advice, or at least most of it. He explained that he had to attend a meeting at the Gendarmerie but promised to go straight home afterwards.

'Did you have to tell Pamela about this?' he asked. 'She came straight to the _collège_ and gave me hell, as though it was all my fault.'

'You're her lover so she has a right to know,' Fabiola replied, looking at him levelly. 'The two of you virtually live together even if you don't want to admit it. And if Pamela was cross with you it's because she cares. Dammit, Bruno, I get cross with you when I see the kind of trouble you get into. Concussions, burns, punch-ups, near-drowning in a wine vat, asphyxiation, hypothermia in that cave. Does that old bullet wound from Sarajevo still give you trouble?'

'The hip aches a bit when the weather changes, tells me there's rain coming or winter's on the way. That's all.'

'I'd rather you didn't attend any meetings, but if it's important, just be sure you go straight home afterwards. If you pass out halfway through, don't say I didn't warn you. I'll see you later with the bouillon, probably after I exercise the horses.'

He stopped briefly at the *Mairie* to check his mail and email and saw he already had a reply from Zigi: 'Paperwork good. But if we send him out through Bagram the Americans and the Afghans will be involved. We'll try to put him onto a French military flight on our own route through Dushanbe. I'll let you know.'

Bruno knew that Bagram was the big airbase outside Kabul, run by the U.S. military. But the French had their own transport link and airfield facilities at Dushanbe, in Tajikistan, the country immediately north of Afghanistan. Bruno remembered that if the French military could possibly find a way to be independent of their American allies, they would. He was glad of it, imagining the kind of bureaucratic hurdles required to get a mysterious French civilian through American security checks.

He was just sending a quick reply when the Mayor came into his office and closed the door behind him. 'What's this I hear about your being attacked at the *collège*? Philippe Delaron called to ask me about it.'

Bruno groaned inwardly. At least Philippe had not got a photo of him writhing on the floor, throwing up and worse.

'I'm just heading to the Gendarmerie for a meeting about it with the Brigadier and J-J.' Bruno described the events of the morning. 'The only reason to target Momu would be something to do with Sami, and it looks as though he's on his way back here.'

'You mean Sami is the real target, and Momu is just the way these men think they can get to him?'

'That's right. Sami disappears from a mosque in Toulouse four years ago and turns up in Afghanistan, after doing heaven knows what. Then he arrives at the French military base, which means somebody in Afghanistan will be wondering what happened to him. His story suggests that people at a mosque in France are funnelling French Muslims to the Taliban. Presumably those people would want to stop him from talking, which could mean killing him. But first they have to find him, and Sami's last known contact is Momu here in St Denis. I assume they planned to question Momu, probably brutally.'

'So Sami coming home could put the whole of St Denis in danger?' the Mayor asked.

Bruno shrugged. 'The two tough guys they sent barely got away. I'll be making photofit sketches of them this afternoon and I believe the Brigadier has been keeping that mosque under surveillance anyway. I don't think they'd take the risk of coming back here.'

Bruno tried to sound more convinced than he felt. The Mayor did not look reassured. He shrugged and sighed in a way that seemed to express all the anger and frustration that Bruno himself felt at the invasion of their placid town by murderous forces from the incomprehensible world outside. This was a time of year when St Denis should be thinking of little but the wine harvest and the coming of the new rugby season.

The Brigadier had taken over the commandant's office in the Gendarmerie, and he and J-J were each talking on separate mobile phones when Bruno was shown in by Yveline Gerlache. Her supposedly temporary appointment as commandant of the small squad of Gendarmes in St Denis had been extended so often it looked like becoming permanent. After a rather nervous start earlier in the year, which Bruno put down to its being her first time in command, Yveline had settled in well, and she gave him a warm smile and a firm handshake when she came out to greet him.

Yveline had been a star athlete at the officer training school in Melun and almost made the French Olympic team for field hockey. She'd already won the women's final in the annual tournament of the town tennis club. Once she had learned that Bruno was training a girls' team to play rugby as well as the usual boys, she'd volunteered to help. The regular coach trips to away matches had given them time to talk and get to know one another a little better. Fabiola had arranged a dinner for Yveline to meet some of the other women in town and had asked Bruno to help her cook. He'd been delighted to do so and had made a joke of it, dressing as a waiter and serving the food and wine before leaving them to their desserts and coffees. They had gone on long after midnight, Fabiola later told him.

'Glad to see you looking alright,' said the Brigadier, closing his phone. As always, he looked as if his hair had just been cut. Like many soldiers he seemed to transfer the neatness of parade uniforms to his civilian clothes. He wore a starched white shirt with tightly knotted silk tie and an anonymous but well-cut suit of navy blue. Despite his trip by helicopter the trousers looked newly pressed. His shoes were black lace-ups and his sole idiosyncrasy was to keep a white silk handkerchief in his sleeve.

'The doc said to warn you I might pass out and I'm to go straight to bed once this meeting's over,' Bruno said.

'In that case you'd better take my chair,' said Yveline, rising to perch on the window ledge.

The Brigadier waited until they were settled and said, 'I've just been talking to Paris. They've accepted my recommendation that we keep watching the Toulouse mosque but take no further action at this time. It's more important to know what's going on than to go in bull-headed and provoke all sorts of Muslim complaints about police discrimination. I know you won't like it but that's policy. It's what we've been doing for twenty years, infiltrating the bastards and turning them rather than just arresting them. It's my belief that's why Paris hasn't been through the kind of hell they've seen in New York, London, Madrid.'

'I thought we were looking for two murder suspects,' Bruno objected. 'We also have to stop a second killing. I don't think they were carrying that sniper's rifle for fun.'

'That's not the priority,' the Brigadier replied, his voice as crisp and official as his appearance. 'The priority is to establish just how far this mosque is tied up with Afghans and jihadis and to find out who is behind it. The chief Imam is on the government's advisory board on Islamic assimilation, so if he's involved it would be very embarrassing. You probably know that glib deputy of his from the TV talk shows, Ghlamallah, the one who speaks oh-so-reasonably about a new Islam that's being reformed to integrate with European democracy. You may have seen an op-ed piece he wrote about it for *Le Monde*.'

The Brigadier made no effort to keep the sneer out of his voice, and J-J snorted from his perch on the corner of the desk. Bruno noted with interest that Yveline kept her face impassive. He suspected that like him, she didn't agree with the Brigadier's mockery. Bruno had heard Tayeb Ghlamallah speak on the radio and thought he'd made a lot of sense. There were six million Muslims in France, nearly a tenth of the population, and an even greater proportion among those under the age of twenty. Without assimilation and a more tolerant, less defensive Islam, France faced a difficult future.

Bruno, aware that he was feeling light-headed, made an effort of will to keep his voice reasonable. 'If they mean what they say, then the Imams should be eager to help us track down a couple of murderers, all the more so since Rafiq was one of their own. I presume he was a Muslim.'

'Rafiq may have been born into a Muslim family but he never went to mosque until we asked him to start doing so,' the Brigadier said. 'We inserted him into that new prison at Seysses and he managed to get himself recruited. He's been in that mosque for three months; a nice little operation until he got himself killed. But we don't know how much these thugs got out of him first.'

'Preliminary autopsy says he was still alive when they set his feet on fire,' said J-J. 'But they'd tortured him first, that cattle prod up his backside.'

'I had a taste of that cattle prod and I'd have told them anything they wanted to know,' said Bruno. 'But there's another part of this which may be connected. A young Muslim guy from St Denis has just turned up at our army base in Afghanistan, wanting to come home. He was supposed to be at the special school they have attached to that mosque in Toulouse. His name is Sami.'

'Special school? You mean he's retarded?' J-J asked.

'No, he's smarter than you or me at maths puzzles. He's just different, autistic. He hardly ever speaks.'

'What was he doing over there?' the Brigadier asked.

'I don't know, but he's coming back here as a distressed citizen in a danger zone. The Mayor looked up the regulation. Here's a copy of his file.'

'Sami Belloumi, born in Algeria, arrived in France as a child fifteen years ago and adopted by his aunt and uncle, Momu al-Bakr of St Denis. Naturalized as a French citizen the following year,' the Brigadier read aloud. He looked up and asked Yveline, 'Have you got a scanner here? Then when we've finished perhaps you could scan this thumbprint on his ID card and email a copy to my office. Let's see if that tells us any more about him.'

The Brigadier put the file on the desk before him and looked thoughtful. 'This could be just what we want to smoke out the jihadis. They think he's here, or on his way, and presumably they'll want to stop him talking. That means they'll be coming here again, and this time we'll be waiting for them.'

'But they'll know he's autistic and doesn't speak much, and anything he says isn't the kind of evidence that is likely to convince a court,' said Bruno. He hated the idea of Sami being used as live bait, let alone turning his town into a killing ground. 'Why would they take that risk?'

'Thanks to Rafiq, we know quite a lot about that mosque already,' said the Brigadier. 'We've been monitoring their phones and computers for months.'

'Did Rafiq explain what he was doing before he got killed?' asked J-J.

'Just that two men he called the action team were up to something and he'd follow, observe and report. We know their names and we can pick them up whenever we want, but right now I'd rather just watch them. It's not the toughs we want, it's the guys who are pulling the strings.'

'Did Rafiq have a family?' asked Bruno.

The Brigadier shook his head. 'Divorced, no kids. We don't use family men for undercover work.'

'There'll be friends from his regiment who'd want to know,' said Bruno.

The Brigadier shook his head. 'We'll keep this quiet. An unidentified man has been found dead by a burned-out car. Police are trying to identify him. That's all we say to the media.'

'The guys who did it left him handcuffed to a tree,' said Bruno. 'It seems to me they knew he was undercover and they're sending you a message.'

'Of course they are,' the Brigadier replied. 'But that's no reason for us to respond. If pressed, J-J can leak to a friendly journalist that it looks like a gangland killing. Not a word about mosques or anything else. I'll bring down a team to babysit Momu and his wife, and Sami when he gets here. Any idea when that will be, Bruno?'

'He should be on the next military flight from Dushanbe, but you'll probably know before I do. I assume the flights come into the Creil airbase.' It was the main airfield for France's military transports, a big base outside Paris that Bruno had used several times in his army days.

'That's right, but there might be media there. We'll arrange for this one to land at Évreux instead,' the Brigadier said. Not for the first time, Bruno was struck by the wide authority the Brigadier seemed to have in the French military as well as its police and intelligence services.

'I'll make sure it all goes smoothly at that end and I'll get them to fly him on to the Mérignac airbase outside Bordeaux so you can pick him up there. In the meantime,' the Brigadier went on, 'there's a shrink we use, deputy head of the prison psychiatric service, name of Deutz, a very smart guy with lots of diplomas.' Deutz, he explained, had noticed and then studied the way jihadis were recruiting in prisons. He had drafted profiles of the kinds of prisoner they recruited and proposed strategies to counter them.

'He probably knows more about French jihadis than anyone else, but he's also a top-notch psychologist. Or is it psychiatrist? I never know the difference. Anyway, he's got all the necessary security clearances and I'd like him to look at Sami and see how much we can learn. He could be an intelligence gold mine and this fellow Deutz is just the man to get it out of him. Here, take a look at this analysis he wrote.' The Brigadier pulled a slim, photocopied report from his briefcase and pushed it across to Bruno.

'We might have trouble persuading Momu to cooperate,' Bruno said, glancing at the report. It came with a Ministry of Justice heading above the title, *Challenges and Opportunities of Jihadists in the Penal System.*

'That's your problem, Bruno. Just tell Momu that this is the price he has to pay to get Sami back into France without trouble. If he doesn't like it we can whip Sami straight into jail as a terrorist suspect. There's a facility for psycho prisoners at Fleury-Mérogis just outside Paris, and it would be easier for Deutz to see him there. But I want Sami down here where the Toulouse jihadis know where to find him.'

'So Deutz would stay here in St Denis?'

'We'll probably put him up at the *Ecouteurs* school up the valley; cheaper that way.'

Bruno knew the place, an old château converted into a training academy for the translators who worked with French intelligence, monitoring phone and Internet traffic.

'Be nice to Deutz, Bruno, he's very well thought of. The Brits and the Americans both invited him over to talk about jihadi recruitment in prisons. He's an athletic type, alpinist, a bit of a ladies' man, I hear. You and he should get along well,' the Brigadier said with the suspicion of a wink.

'Sir,' said Bruno crisply. He had learned in the army that this monosyllabic answer sufficed for most occasions, particularly when he had no idea what to say. Once again, Yveline's face was impassive. New as she was to the Gendarmes, she must have become accustomed to the macho banter that had characterized police and military establishments throughout Bruno's career and doubtless long before. Some policewomen tried to join in, which never worked. Some made waspish comments, which made matters worse. Most ignored it and developed the kind of blank, distant stare that Yveline had mastered.

'Just to clarify, sir,' said Yveline, addressing the Brigadier. 'We have the murder of an employee of the French state on our patch. We know of two suspects, armed with a sniper's rifle and a cattle prod, who also stole a car and got away from a pursuit by my Gendarmes. We have witnesses who can identify these two suspects, who also committed an assault on the chief of police here. We know they are based at this mosque in Toulouse but we do not seek to find or arrest them. Is that right?'

'Absolutely,' said the Brigadier, raising his eyebrows and studying Yveline as if for the first time.

'And you agree with this, sir?' she asked J-J.

'The ministers of Justice and of the Interior have put the Brigadier in charge of this matter so, yes, I agree,' said J-J, looking amused. He knew the form, as did Bruno. Yveline was about to be introduced to the way that French law really worked once the intelligence agencies were involved and the crime in question carried political overtones.

'I'll need that order in writing, sir, otherwise I'd feel it my duty to tear that mosque apart to find these killers.'

She spoke with a flat, unemotional politeness that impressed Bruno. Once, he might have made the same objection, even used the same phrase. But he was older now, more experienced in some of these informal aspects of law enforcement. Above all, he saw the sense in the Brigadier's strategy. Bruno's job would be to ensure none of this damaged St Denis or its citizens, including Momu and Sami.

The Brigadier studied Yveline for a long moment and then

picked up his mobile phone, looked up a number and called it. 'Ah, my dear general,' he began when it was answered. 'Brigadier Lannes here from the minister's office. Did you receive my note about this nasty murder just outside St Denis this morning? You did? Excellent. Perhaps you would confirm to your estimable commandant in St Denis that she comes under my orders until further notice. Thank you.'

He passed the phone to Yveline, who listened briefly, said, 'Yes, sir, thank you, sir,' and handed the phone back.

'Any more questions, comments, suggestions?' the Brigadier asked.

He paused, glancing from Bruno to Yveline and back again before speaking.

'Let us not forget that when the intelligence phase of this operation is complete, then you, *Mademoiselle Commandante*, and you, Bruno, will have the agreeable duty of arresting these two murderers. We're not bringing them to justice now, but we will most certainly do so at a time that suits us.'

5

Bruno awoke the next morning feeling wonderfully refreshed but guilty when he realized how late it was. He couldn't recall the last time he had slept past nine. He fed his chickens, went for a fast run in the woods, showered and headed directly into town, still sipping from the bottle of orange juice Pamela had brought him the previous evening, along with the bouillon Fabiola had promised.

After the meeting with the Brigadier, Bruno had got home mid-afternoon. Earlier he'd identified his two attackers from a selection of surveillance shots on the Brigadier's laptop, taken at and around the mosque. The one with the cattle prod was known as the Ali the *Caïd* and the other was known only as *Zhern'ber*, the strong man. After checking his chickens, Bruno had gone straight to sleep as soon as he lay down on his bed.

He'd been woken a few hours later by Pamela's arrival. Darkness had fallen and he'd been unsure of the time and surprised to find himself drenched in sweat. Visions of Rafiq's body in the rain still churned in his head from a disturbed dream. He had a fierce headache and felt weak as a kitten. He had to take Pamela's arm to climb from his bed and stagger into the shower. By the time he returned, she had changed the sheets, laid out one of the clean rugby shirts he used instead of pyjamas, and put the hot bouillon in a mug alongside a bottle of aspirin on the bedside table.

'I didn't mean to be angry at you,' she said when he was back in bed, sipping at the bouillon. 'I was angry at me for feeling so . . .' Her hands groped at the air, looking for the right word. 'For feeling so involved.' She seemed to have trouble forming the word.

'Apart from anything else we are to one another, I'm your friend,' he said quietly, choosing his words with care. 'You'd feel just as involved if Fabiola was hurt. You weren't conscious to see it, but she reacted pretty fiercely when you fell from your horse.'

Pamela brushed his words aside. 'But it's the anything else that matters here, Bruno, don't you see? Here in your bedroom, where we've been – I don't need to spell it out. I've had that Jacques Brel song in my head all day, "La Chanson des Vieux Amants".'

Suddenly, she'd stood up and collected her bag. 'Fabiola said I wasn't to stay too long and not to upset you. I'm sorry.'

She bent and kissed him chastely on the forehead. 'Your fever's gone. Sleep well and don't worry about the horses in the morning. Unless we hear otherwise we'll expect you in the evening.'

She left him groping for the words of the song, about two lovers confronting one another in a bedroom whose walls still seemed to echo with the memories of their pleasure and their passion.

The song had stuck in his head as he sipped at his bouillon. He tried to recall that other line of the song, about how they managed to grow old without ever growing up.

He loved Pamela dearly, enjoyed being with her and could even imagine growing old with her. But she had taken the firm decision that she did not want children, and that, for Bruno, was the insuperable problem. With each year that passed, he felt more and more the need to be a father and to find the right woman to bear his children and help raise them. He sighed and sank back on the pillows, expecting a long and sleepless night of self-questioning and sadness at being childless. And then he thought of the great lottery of parenthood, never knowing how the young would turn out once they became themselves. His thoughts turned to Momu and Dillah, the grief that young Sami must have caused them and the mixture of joy and guilt and confusion they were probably feeling at the prospect of his rejoining them, and the next thing he knew it was morning and he was very late for work.

The usual mail was on his desk and atop the pile lay an envelope, addressed to the Mayor and already opened. A yellow Post-it note was attached which asked, in the Mayor's careful handwriting, for Bruno to deal with the contents. 'This comes as news to me,' the Mayor had added.

The envelope was of heavy paper, and the name and address of a Paris law firm was embossed on the flap. The address was on the Rue de la Paix, which Bruno knew to be close to the Opéra, a desirable and presumably expensive location. Bruno skimmed the opening greetings and then, increasingly fascinated, sat down in his swivel chair to read.

The lawyer, who signed himself Yacov Kaufman, was acting for the estate of a client who had recently died, a wealthy Parisian doctor named David Halévy. The will provided for a bequest to the town of St Denis in gratitude for the shelter it had given him and his sister when they were children during the war. The doctor and his sister were Jews, and the town had probably saved their lives. The bequest, however, was somewhat complicated and the lawyer proposed that the Mayor let him know a convenient day to visit the town and discuss the matter. Bruno noted that one of the partners in the law firm was also named Halévy, and then he sat back to reflect. He knew quite a lot of the town's history, but he had never heard of Jewish refugees being given sanctuary.

The Mayor, who had for several years been writing a definitive history of the town where he had been born and bred, was the real expert on local history. He would know of any refugees being taken in, if anyone did. But he'd already seen the letter, confessed ignorance and had asked Bruno to take care of the matter. Bruno called Jo, his predecessor as town policeman, and at the same fired up his computer to google David Halévy, *médecin*. Jo had been in the village school in the war years, and while there had been a lot of refugee kids, mainly those of French stock who were expelled from Alsace once the Germans took control, he didn't recall any Jews, or anyone named David.

Google provided an obituary in *Alliance*, a Jewish Internet-magazine, which revealed that David Halévy, a retired surgeon and professor of medicine and a member of the *Légion d'Honneur*, had died the previous week at the age of eighty of a heart attack at his home on the Boulevard St Germain in Paris. He had never married and had no children, and was survived by a sister, Maya, who lived in Israel. The obituary listed a number of publications, the older ones on problems of the heart and circulation and the more recent articles relating to the links between psychology and health. Which was he, Bruno wondered, a heart surgeon or a psychologist? The obituary added one interesting detail, that Professor Halévy had for many years been the honorary president of the *Eclaireurs Israé-lites*, the Jewish Boy Scouts.

Bruno called the lawyer's number in Paris, identified himself and was put through to Maître Kaufman, who instantly asked if he was speaking with the Mayor of St Denis. Bruno explained that the Mayor had asked him to make a preliminary inquiry about the bequest.

'I will need to go into this with your Mayor, but I can say that the instructions from Professor Halévy were somewhat complex,' Kaufman said in a formal, almost old-fashioned French, although his voice sounded young.

'Might I just clarify,' said Bruno. 'We are talking of Professor David Halévy and his sister Maya. That's an unusual name.'

'You know of them already?' Kaufman asked, excitement coming into his hitherto formal voice.

'Just the names, David and Maya; am I pronouncing that right?'

'Yes, it means water in Hebrew. When they were in hiding she called herself Marie. Those are the two children. The Professor hoped that his bequest could be used to fund some form of memorial to the people in St Denis who had risked their lives on his behalf. Depending on the nature of the memorial, the bequest could be significantly increased. That is why this is more complicated than a simple bequest.'

Bruno felt confused. 'Does this mean this is some kind of test? If we come up with the right kind of memorial the bequest will be more generous?'

'Precisely.'

'But Professor Halévy is dead, so who decides whether the memorial justifies a larger bequest?' Bruno asked.

'His executors, who include his younger sister. She was also given refuge in St Denis and has very fond memories of the region.'

'Could you give me some idea of the kind of money Professor Halévy had in mind?'

'I'm not at liberty to reveal the potential sum, I'm sorry. But I can say that the initial bequest, whatever memorial you plan or even if you don't produce a memorial, is fifty thousand euros.'

'*Mon Dieu*,' said Bruno, thinking that St Denis might even be able to afford the indoor sports hall that he'd been raising money for with jumble sales and collection boxes. 'He must have been a wealthy man.'

'Indeed. Now, when would it be convenient for me to call and pay my respects to your Mayor?'

'I'll ask him and get back to you by email. Just one more thing,' Bruno said. 'This all happened a long time ago and most of that wartime generation are dead. Did Professor Halévy provide any details about his time in St Denis, his hosts, where they lived, perhaps his schooling?'

'I'm afraid not. I only know that it was thought unsafe for him and his sister to go to school. They studied alone, at the farmhouse where they lived.'

'With the farmer's wife?' Bruno asked. 'Do you have her name?'

'Sorry, no. I'll look out for your email about coming down to see the Mayor.' He rang off.

Bruno sat back, pondering how to start finding out about two children living in secrecy some seventy years ago. He looked out of his window at the familiar scene below, the old stone bridge over the river Vézère, the square full of parked cars and locals gossiping by the postbox. The tables at Fauquet's café were filled with people caught in that curious morning moment when it was neither too late for coffee nor too early for an apéritif, and some of the customers had compromised by ordering both. The buildings were mostly unchanged, and he tried to imagine how it would have been seventy years ago, with no cars because there was no petrol, except for the occasional German staff car or military truck. The streets would have been patrolled by Vichy's *Milice* in their black berets and the shops would have been mostly empty because of food rationing.

He remembered Jo, reminiscing about his wartime childhood, saying the men were always unshaven because of a shortage of razor blades, and the children had their heads shaved against lice. The women would paint a thin black line up the back of their legs, an attempt to suggest the seams of the stockings that were no longer available. In his family, Jo recalled, they had washed with bran soaked in water because there was no soap. On the posters outside the *Mairie* the watchwords of the French Republic – *Liberté, Egalité, Fraternité* – had been replaced by Vichy's slogan: *Patrie, Famille, Travail,* Homeland, Family, Work.

Bruno sighed at the thought of France, of his own village, defeated, occupied and humiliated. But he knew there had been sparks and small flames of resistance, young men living rough in the woods to escape the forced labour conscription to Germany, and others gathering in the small hours to light the beacons that would guide the Royal Air Force planes that would drop guns and explosives. And there had been somebody risking arrest and torture to hide Jewish children. No wonder it had been kept secret. Bruno braced himself and turned back to his quest.

There was no synagogue in St Denis but Daniel Weiss, a local insurance broker whom Bruno knew through the tennis club, was a member of the congregation in Périgueux. He called Weiss, explained the situation and asked his advice.

'I'd start with the rabbi, but leave it to me,' Weiss said. 'Let me be sure I've got the details right – David and Maya Halévy, here in 1943 and 1944. I'll see if anybody in the community knows anything, though I can't say I ever heard of any Jewish children being sheltered here. We came long after the European war.'

For Daniel Weiss and his family, and many others who came to France from Algeria, the phrase 'the war' meant the bloody insurrection and guerrilla war that finally secured Algerian independence in 1961. The Second World War was always 'the European war'.

'If I were you I'd start by asking the Shoah Foundation in Paris; they keep a lot of records. You might also try Yad Vashem, the big research centre in Israel for Holocaust studies,' Weiss added. 'That's probably the biggest database and they're on the Internet. It would be quite something if St Denis were to join Les Justes, the Righteous among Nations; that's the list of people and places honoured for risking their lives to save Jews.'

'Indeed it would. Let me know if the rabbi comes up with anything.'

Bruno hung up and looked through his notes. He did another Google search to get an address and phone number in Paris for the Shoah Foundation and for the Jewish Boy Scouts. He then opened the website for Yad Vashem and began to explore, looking for references to France. In a section called Torchlighters, he came upon the thumbnail photo of a woman named Denise Siekierski with a French flag beside her name, and opened it. In a short filmed interview, interspersed with still photos of the young woman in wartime and then of German soldiers herding people onto railway wagons, Bruno heard her say, 'In the Scouts, we learned to serve, and at that time that meant saving Jews.'

Fascinated, he listened to her account of working with Protestant pastors to smuggle Jews out of Marseille and then to find refuge for dozens of Jewish children in the remote villages of the Auvergne. He began to look further, but caught himself. This always happened on the Internet; one thing led to another and before he knew it, hours had flown by and he did not have the time. But he had an idea. This was the kind of research project that would interest Florence, the science teacher at the local *collège* and founder of its very popular computer club. If there was anything about the Halévy children on the Internet, they could find it.

First he had to see the Mayor. 'You're the town historian,' he began. 'Do you know anything about Jewish refugees in St Denis during the war?'

The Mayor shook his head. 'I never heard of any Jews round here, and I can't understand why not. I'd have thought people would have been proud of it, after the war. It sounds odd to me; that's why I want you to look into it. Tell me about this bequest the lawyer mentioned. Is it serious, do you think?'

'Very serious. The lawyer wants to come down and talk to you directly.' Bruno explained the unusual nature of David Halévy's will and the prospect of more money if his executors approved the memorial. 'But I need to make more inquiries. We need to know something about these children, when they were here, where they stayed, who cared for them and who brought them here.'

'You might want to check the town archives in the basement,' the Mayor suggested. 'There are still files down there from the Vichy years. There might be ration cards or school enrolment lists that may have some trace of the children.'

'I'm going to be tied up seeing Momu and the Brigadier, and nobody knows those archives like you do . . .' Bruno let his voice trail away.

'Point taken.' The Mayor smiled, and Bruno was relieved to see that the old man suddenly looked rather less tired. 'Leave the archives to me. It will make a pleasant change from fighting against cuts in the roads budget.'

Bruno headed back to the *collège*. Florence had started the computer club soon after being hired as a science teacher. She began by rescuing discarded laptops from the town's *déchetterie*, then persuaded local businesses and the *Mairie* to donate their old computers and convinced *France Télécom* to provide free Internet access. Half the school was now enrolled, learning to write programs, tackle viruses and engage in video conferences with pupils in twinned schools in Scotland and Holland. The latest project was to build an online game and hope to sell it.

'I'm sure they'll love the idea of tracking down Jewish children in St Denis, but after what just happened to you, Bruno, you'll have to convince me that it won't be dangerous,' Florence said, spooning out a thick tomato soup to her twin toddlers. Living in one of the subsidized apartments for teachers in a block adjoining the school, she could quickly go home for lunch with her children before taking them back to the *maternelle* for the rest of the afternoon. She handed Bruno a bowl of soup and scattered some basil leaves on top before serving herself.

'It will be up to them, of course, to decide whether to take this project on,' she said. 'I can recommend it and you might want to come along and explain why it's important. But the whole point about this club is that the kids have to run it.'

'I'll be happy to do so. This bequest could be worth a lot of money to the town,' he said. 'This soup is great.'

'We made the herbs and tomatoes,' little Daniel told him proudly. 'We made the garden with *maman* and water it every day. That's *basilic* in your soup and I planted it.'

'I put in the lettuce,' said his twin, Dora. 'We want a garden as big as yours, Bruno, and maybe have chickens like you.'

'You already have the chickens in the school garden *maman* made,' said Bruno. He'd been impressed by the way Florence had persuaded Rollo and the education department that getting the *collège* pupils to create their own garden and raise their own chickens was the best way of teaching them environmental science. Once upon a time almost every pupil in the school had come from one of the surrounding farms and was raised knowing about animals and crops. But those days were long gone and more and more of the kids thought that food came from supermarkets. Bruno reckoned that something of traditional France had died when a sandwich ceased to mean a *baguette* stuffed with ham and cheese and became sliced bread with some dubious filling, sold in triangles of plastic wrapping.

'Would you like to share the omelette I'm making to go with Dora's salad?' Florence asked from the stove. 'They're our own eggs.'

'I'd love to, but I have to go. I should have been at the Gendarmerie ten minutes ago,' Bruno said, wiping his lips, finishing his glass of mineral water and kissing the children goodbye. 'Let me know when I should come and talk to your computer club. And thanks for that delicious soup.'

6

Bruno barely registered the calls of '*Au 'voir*' and '*À demain*' and the clatter of feet on old stone stairs as the *Mairie* closed for the day. He was rapt, eyes fixed on his computer screen, making notes as he read the material the Shoah Foundation had sent him on the *Eclaireurs Israélites de France*, the Jewish Boy Scouts, and their founder, Robert Gamzon.

Bruno had long been fascinated by the tangled myths and realities of the Resistance and the various underground movements that sometimes seemed as concerned with political rivalries as with fighting the Nazi occupation and the Vichy régime. He had read widely, talked at length to some of the survivors and thought he knew the subject quite well. But now he felt on a voyage of discovery, learning something that was at once entirely new to him and deeply moving. It revealed a whole aspect of what it meant to be French.

He learned that France had not one Scout movement, but four. There was one for the Roman Catholics, another for the Protestants, yet another for the Jews and now one for the Muslims. Nor had he known how prescient many of his countrymen had been, beyond De Gaulle and that handful of politicians who had sounded the alarm on Nazi aggression in the 1930s.

Robert Gamzon, an engineer and devoted member of the Boy Scouts, had been one of them. When the British and French governments signed the Munich pact in September 1938, surrendering Czechoslovakia to Hitler's demands, Gamzon acted. As founder and commissioner for the Jewish Scouts, Gamzon bought a farm near Saumur to establish a school for Jewish refugees from Germany. At the same time he raised money to buy houses in remote rural areas and began moving into them Jewish children from the cities. Convinced of the Nazis' intentions towards the Jews and fearing the prospect of France's defeat, he thought it an essential precaution. He moved the administrative centre of his Scout movement to Moissac, deep in south-western France, and persuaded those of his scoutmasters who were too old for military service to move to the south and set up more safe houses.

Gamzon himself went into the French army. In May 1940 he won the Croix de Guerre for blowing up the main telephone switchboard and control system in Reims while under fire. After Marshal Pétain took power amid the French collapse and sued for peace, Gamzon headed south to establish schools for the children he had moved to the countryside. There he launched another organization to help the Jewish refugees who had fled to France from elsewhere in Europe. They were now being pushed into internment camps, by the Nazis and the Vichy government in the truncated southern half of France nominally ruled by them.

Through contacts he made in Vichy, Gamzon established an intelligence network that warned him of planned arrests and round-ups. This was the origin of the *Sixième*, the clandestine wing of the Scouts, which forged documents and provided fake identities and ration papers, and found jobs in hospitals and on farms.

Meanwhile, his wife Denise was based at Moissac, which had become a sanctuary for Jewish refugees. But the noose was tightening in the summer of 1942 when the Vichy police began the *rafles*, the raids to round up Jews. In Paris on 16 July, over 13,000 Jews were rounded up in *Opération Vent Printanier*, Operation Spring Breeze, and handed over to the German authorities A third of them were children, and Bruno was sickened to read that several thousand members of the French fascist party helped the police arrest and cram them into Paris's Vélodrome d'Hiver to await the trains that led to Germany and finally to the death camp at Auschwitz.

Shortly before that *rafle*, Denise had received a phone call from her husband who said only, 'Send back the bills for 1936.' When she protested there were no such bills, he replied, 'Think.' Deducing that he meant the Jews who had arrived that year in France she sent the three men concerned into the woods. At dawn the next day the house was raided by Gendarmes. Denise then contacted an old friend, Hélène Rulland, who ran the Protestant Girl Guides. Hélène found remote villages to hide another thirty Jewish children.

Bruno began scribbling notes to himself. Almost certainly the Halévy children had been given false papers, so there would be little point in searching for traces of them by name in St Denis. The Protestant connection seemed promising, since Bergerac had been a Protestant stronghold in France's wars of religion and there were churches and pastors locally he could ask. He read of the small village of Le Chambon, in the Auvergne highlands, whose pastor André Trocmé organized sanctuary for some five thousand Jewish children in the remote woods and valleys. His cousin Daniel, the local teacher, was later shot by the Gestapo along with the village doctor, Roger le Forestier. Bruno made a note of all the names he could, planning to cross-check them against the St Denis records to see if there might be a family connection.

He sat back, feeling he was making progress, but wondering why all this was not much better known in France. It was something to be proud of, that an entire community was prepared to take such risks for the children of strangers. And it gave him a stirring tale to tell the young people in the *collège* computer club.

It was time to go. Bruno reluctantly closed his computer and called Fabiola to tell her he was on his way. She was already in the stables, saddling Victoria. By the time he arrived, Balzac at his heels, Fabiola had also saddled Hector, Bruno's own horse. He kissed Pamela in greeting. She smiled but said nothing and returned to checking over the bridles and leathers. Bruno wasn't sure whether she was embarrassed by the previous evening's exchange or was damping down her frustration at not being allowed to ride. Pamela insisted that her collarbone was completely healed from her riding accident. Her doctor disagreed.

'One more week,' Fabiola said briskly, in what Bruno thought of as her doctor's voice, the one that brooked no argument. 'Then you can start some gentle trots around the paddock.'

'But I can't think about buying a new horse unless I can give it a test ride. I keep missing absolute bargains because you won't let me back into the saddle,' Pamela complained, petting Bruno's dog and fondling the long, floppy ears. People who liked horses were invariably fond of dogs, Bruno had noticed.

As Balzac snuffled his way around Hector's legs to greet the horse whose stable he often shared, Bruno sat on the bench to put on his riding boots. He understood Pamela's frustration, unable to ride but equally unable to keep out of the stables, watching Bruno and Fabiola take out the horses while aching to join them. Without complaint, she performed the physiotherapy and exercises Fabiola had recommended to get her muscles into shape, ready to ride again. He knew she spent hours on the Internet looking at horses for sale.

While she never spoke of the horse on which she'd been injured, she kept a photo of Bess on the table by her bed. Bess had broken a leg in a rabbit hole while galloping down a slope, throwing Pamela, who had been knocked unconscious and broken a collarbone in the fall. Bruno knew that he had no choice but to put the animal out of its misery; the bones had been shattered. Although Pamela had said he'd been right, he suspected that in some corner of her heart she would never forgive him. They hadn't spoken of the incident since, but Bruno sometimes felt her resentment. Perhaps a new horse would ease matters. He hoped so.

Their relationship had never been easy for him to navigate. After an unhappy first marriage in Britain, Pamela insisted on her independence. She made it clear that she saw no permanent future with Bruno, but was content to treat him as a dear friend whom she welcomed, although less frequently, to her bed. At first, Bruno had assumed this was the result of the abstinence enforced by her injuries, but his doubts were growing. Pamela remained warm and loving, but while he could not define precisely the change he felt in her manner toward him, he felt a reticence in her embraces. One night after a lovemaking that did not seem to have pleased her, he had asked her if something was wrong. 'It's not you, Bruno, it's me, still sad about Bess, I suppose,' Pamela had replied, kissing him fondly. 'It will pass.' But it hadn't.

He rose, stamped to settle the fit of his boots, and kissed her cheek. 'You'll be riding with us any day now,' he said. She nodded and returned his embrace but her smile seemed distant. He led Hector out into the yard, climbed into the saddle and followed Fabiola up the track that led towards the ridge. When he turned in the saddle, expecting to see Pamela waving at them, she had gone inside.

That suggested he could forget the usual invitation to dine with Pamela and Fabiola, let alone spend the night. Very well, he'd dine alone; something he rather enjoyed from time to time. He had some spinach in the garden which he could pick, wash and quickly simmer. He could slice some of the ham hanging from the beam in his kitchen and chop it into *lardons*, fry it, and mix them into the spinach, and then poach two fresh eggs from his garden and serve them on top with some freshly ground black pepper. With some of that morning's baguette, lightly toasted and rubbed with garlic, and a glass of cool white wine, it would be delicious. He could almost taste it.

Then he remembered making that dish for Pamela one evening at her home, and as they finished, a disc of opera she had been playing suddenly turned into a tune he knew; the Barcarolle, from Offenbach's *Tales of Hoffman*. It was a lovely, slow but stately piece. With the last taste of wine on his lips, he had extended his hand, raised Pamela from her chair, and led her into a gentle waltz around her kitchen until the music ended. He could even remember the wine, a Tour des Verdots, with its lingering sweetness from a little Muscadelle grape added to the usual Sauvignon–Semillon blend. She had then pressed a couple of buttons on her CD player and the music had played again and then again as she drew him down to the vast sofa that filled one wall of her kitchen and they had made tender, rhythmic and almost dreamy love as the melody unfolded. He felt tears pricking at his eyes at the thought of what he and Pamela had known together, and the premonition that it might be drawing to a close.

Hector picked up speed, easily passing Fabiola, who was riding a much older horse. As his mount stretched into a fluid canter, Bruno's troubled thoughts of his future with Pamela blew away with the pleasure of the ride. He reined in as they reached the ridge, gazing down over the lush valley of the river Vézère below. Balzac was the first to join him, the young dog now grown enough to keep pace, or at least to keep Hector in sight, rather than ride in the old binoculars case slung around Bruno's neck that he had used as a puppy.

'Give her time,' said Fabiola, drawing alongside. 'As soon as Pamela gets a new horse and starts riding again she'll be fine.'

'You're probably right,' Bruno replied, wondering whether this was what he truly wanted. He had enjoyed the affair with Pamela, but lately had begun asking himself if he should continue a relationship that had no future, even if they could return to the easy affections they had enjoyed before Pamela's fall.

'No more grape-pickers in the vineyard,' he said, shading his eyes to peer down at the ordered ranks of vines that stretched behind the small château. 'The harvest must be in.'

'I've been invited to the *vendange* supper but Julien hasn't told me yet when it is,' she said. Like Bruno and half of St Denis, Fabiola was a shareholder in the town's vineyard.

'They can never fix a date because they never know in advance when they'll be picking. And the pickers will be moving on to another vineyard tonight. I imagine it will be at the weekend, Saturday or Sunday evening, when the pickers can come back to enjoy it.'

Bruno knew he would be involved in the cooking, which would mean filling and lighting the firepit the previous night. Four big *sangliers* provided by the town's hunting club were already waiting in the giant freezer of the town's retirement home. They'd go onto the spits for roasting soon after dawn. He made a mental note to check with Julien, who ran the vineyard, about the arrangements. He hoped the event wouldn't clash with Sami's return. That reminded him of something.

'How much do you know about psychology?' he asked Fabiola.

She turned to look at him in surprise. 'Why do you ask?' She picked up the reins as if eager to ride.

'It's about an autistic young man from St Denis called Sami, a nephew of Momu,' he said, and explained the background.

'I did some at medical school but it's not really my field,' she said, shrugging. 'Let's ride.'

She kicked her heels into Victoria's flanks and started off along the ridge, a trot that became a canter and then a gentle gallop, as fast as Fabiola's aging mare could handle. They stopped close to the end of the ridge, where the woods began to creep onto the high ground and the slope down to the river fell steeply away. From here, the town of St Denis nestled in the glow of the evening sun, half gold and half red as it sank through the scattered clouds to the horizon. Bruno had never known better sunsets than those he saw from this point. They made him think of the lowlands stretching to the estuary of the River Gironde and the long thin strip of the Médoc peninsula that produced the great wines of Margaux and Pauillac, of St Julien and Sainte Estèphe. He wondered whether they would someday sink beneath the waves of a rising sea, taking with them part of the soul of France.

'What are you thinking?' she asked.

'About wine,' he replied.

'As your doctor, I sometimes wonder whether I should warn you not to drink too much.'

'You aren't my doctor,' he replied. Rather than mix friendship with medicine, Bruno usually consulted an elderly doctor in the next village whose brother produced excellent wines near St Foy la Grande, just over the border from the Bordeaux *appellation*, and who accordingly counselled his patients that a glass of good Bergerac *rouge* before retiring would help almost any ailment. In more difficult cases, a glass of the same wine on waking might also be recommended. On the infrequent occasions when Bruno went to see his doctor, he more often left with a bottle of the family's Château Puy-Servain than with a prescription.

Before they turned off onto the bridle trail through the woods that would take them to Pamela's house, Bruno looked back to the east. The twilight was stealing over ridge after ridge as the land rose to the Massif Central, the high plateau of dead volcanoes that lay at the heart of France and was the source for most of its rivers. Other than the large town of Brive, there were no cities in that direction until Lyon, more than three hundred kilometres away. And Toulouse was nearly as far to the south, with only Cahors along the way. Doing the sums in his head, Bruno reckoned there were close to a hundred thousand square kilometres in those sparsely populated uplands where the Jewish children of wartime had found sanctuary. Little wonder that many of them had been able to stay hidden.

'I'm on call tonight, so I've been invited to eat pizza with the *pompiers* in the firehouse,' Fabiola said as they rubbed down the horses. As in most of rural France, the firemen also provided the medical emergency service, so the duty doctor often spent the evening in their friendly company. Bruno had an open invitation to join them, but that spinach supper, alone with Balzac and the latest Prix Goncourt winner he'd borrowed from the town library, sounded attractive. He wasn't sure how much he'd read of *L'art français de la guerre*, despite his interest in the novel's theme of France's colonial wars in Vietnam and Algeria. He wanted an early night and felt too tired to be good company.

As he knocked on the kitchen door to say goodnight to Pamela, he saw that the table had been set for two. A tureen of *potage* was already steaming on the table and he could smell roast chicken and lemon, one of her dishes he could never resist. She had changed out of her jeans and put on a blue dress she knew Bruno liked, and she was wearing make-up, which she seldom did for informal suppers at home.

Did that mean she'd like him to stay the night? Or had she dressed to look alluring so that he would feel all the more chastened, knowing what he was missing? At least with

French women he felt a kind of intuition, a shared cultural understanding that allowed him to decipher much that was unspoken. But Pamela was not French, however well she spoke the language. And sometimes he felt that all the dictionaries in the world would not suffice to help him fathom the subtleties of her meaning.

'I need to talk to you,' Pamela began, ladling some of the home-made mushroom soup into his dish. That sounded ominous, he thought, particularly after her visit to his bedside the previous evening. She spooned in some *crème fraîche* as he opened the bottle she had put on the table, a very drinkable red from the town vineyard. 'It's about Fabiola,' she added. 'I'm worried about her. You know she went up to Paris at the weekend, to see Gilles?'

Bruno shook his head as he sipped at his soup. No, he hadn't known, but he was not surprised. Gilles was a journalist he had known in Sarajevo during the Bosnian war, now working for *Paris Match*. They had renewed their friendship over recent months when Gilles had come down to St Denis on two different stories and had been attracted to Fabiola. Having seen them dining together one evening, Bruno reckoned that Fabiola seemed equally attracted to him. He approved: Gilles was a fine man, honest and kindly. Bruno's one concern was that Gilles might lure away the best doctor St Denis had known to join him in Paris.

'Did she tell you how it went?'

'She didn't have to. She came back early, obviously unhappy, but refused to talk about it. Something must have gone wrong.'

'It's her own business, Pamela,' he said.

'I know, but I was just wondering if you might ask Gilles

67

what happened, if they are still seeing each other. He's your friend, after all.'

'Men don't much ask one another about that sort of thing.' He poured a splash of red wine into the small amount of soup that remained in his bowl, swirled it around to mix it and then raised the bowl to his lips and drank. Called *chabrol*, it was a custom of the Périgord.

'Well, I'm pretty sure they hadn't slept together before and she was quite excited when she left, looking eager and happy. I think the weekend in Paris was meant to be it, you know, as though she'd made her mind up to go to bed with him. After all, she's been here a year and there's been no other boyfriend.'

'I thought they were doing fine. They seem well suited,' Bruno said, wondering how long it would be before he was allowed to taste the chicken that smelt so good. 'But if it didn't work out in Paris, I'm not sure we can do anything about it, nor even if we should. This is something between the two of them.'

'Maybe there's a misunderstanding that we could help them clear up. You could have a man-to-man talk.'

Bruno could imagine himself squirming with embarrassment as he tried to probe into his friend's love life. Bruno was about to say that he wouldn't like it if somebody asked about his affair with Pamela, but thought better of it. That could start another conversation Bruno did not want to have, so he decided to change the subject.

'I love that lemon chicken of yours and it smells wonderful. I can hardly wait, but let me tell you about this strange bequest St Denis might be getting.' He launched into an explanation of the Halévy children until Pamela rather grumpily cleared the soup plates and opened the oven to bring out the chicken.

As he spoke, into the back of his mind crept the piquant thought that it was intriguing to be dining with an attractive woman and not know whether he would be invited to sleep with her that night. He found himself making an extra effort to be charming, in the hope that Pamela would soften. There might be no future for them, but this was the present. The future could take care of itself.

7

The Mayor had decided that his own status, as a former member of the French Senate, would smooth Sami's path at the airport. It would also, Bruno thought to himself, cement the Mayor's support among the handful of Muslim voters in St Denis. His car was much more comfortable, so Bruno was happy to agree. The bench seat of his elderly Land Rover would have crammed him, the Mayor and Momu too tightly together and left no room for Sami.

The message from Zigi had been waiting in Bruno's emails: 'Your boy en route to Dushanbe with returning platoon of troops. We burned his clothes, shaved his head and beard to remove lice, showered him twice and fitted him with some old fatigues. He ate like a wolf. His ETA Évreux tomorrow 10.40 then chopper to Merignac ETA 14.30. Toubib sedated him heavily and gave him all the shots we get. You owe me big dinner, Zigi.'

Landing at Évreux meant the Brigadier had intervened to shift the port of entry, which must have annoyed the army, having to ferry the returning platoon back to Creil. It should also mean a minimum of bureaucracy at Mérignac on the military side of what was mainly a civilian airport.

'I'm sorry you didn't feel you could tell us that Sami had

disappeared from Toulouse,' the Mayor said to Momu as he took the road for the autoroute that led to Bordeaux. He and Bruno had agreed that the Mayor would lead the questioning. It would seem less of an interrogation if he spoke while driving.

'We didn't find out until we went down for one of our regular visits,' Momu replied quietly, looking straight ahead through the windscreen. Bruno leaned forward from the rear seat, not wanting to miss a word.

'When was that, exactly?'

'Four years ago, in May, about a year after Sami had gone to the school.'

'Did you hear from him again?'

'One postcard, in September that year, posted from Germany. It just said he was well and thinking of us.' Momu paused, and then spoke in a rush. 'I didn't think he could write, that somebody else had written it for him. But it was him alright, from something he said about Karim, a place they used to go to catch *goujons*. They called it the beach, a private name they had. He loved those little fish, all fried with lemon juice.'

That made Bruno smile. Each summer he'd take the kids from his tennis class down to the river with nets to catch the tiny fish, take them back by the kilo, roll them in flour and fry them up in the kitchen at the club.

'And that was all you heard until this week?'

'Yes. We thought he was dead.' Momu's voice was heavy with guilt.

'What did they tell you at the mosque?'

'At first they said he'd decided to leave with some friends, without saying where they'd gone. We were frantic. It was only when we said we'd call the police that they said he had gone with friends to study in Pakistan, to a madrassa. Even then they didn't say he had gone jihad. We suspected it, of course, but we didn't want to get him into trouble so we said nothing.'

Momu's voice broke off and he wiped a hand over his mouth before he spoke again. 'I'm sorry, that was probably a mistake.'

'The main thing is that he's alive,' said Bruno from the back.

'Will he go to jail?' Momu asked.

'He might have to go to a hospital, somewhere where he can get treatment,' said Bruno, avoiding the question. 'They're sending in a top man, a real expert, to treat him.'

'But they'll want to find out what he's been doing.'

'I think they'll want to find out more about his autism, if it's genetic or if something caused it,' said the Mayor.

'That's what we thought, that it was the shock he had as a little boy,' Momu replied. 'We thought that with time and care and his family, he'd get over it. But he never did.'

Bruno had not known the circumstances in which Sami had come to France, only that his parents had died in the civil war there in the 1990s. He was about to speak when the Mayor beat him to it.

'So what happened to the boy in Algeria?'

'You know about the war,' Momu began. It had started when the Islamists won the elections in 1991, and the army intervened with ruthless efficiency to stop them taking power. The Islamists split and the most radical of them formed the GIA, the *Groupe Islamique Armée*, and began committing atrocities.

'It was wholesale slaughter,' Momu went on. 'Thalit, Souhane, Rais, hundreds of villages where they killed everybody, raped pregnant women, cut off their heads. There wasn't much interest in France until a monastery was attacked and some of your priests were killed.'

'The monks of Tibhirine,' said Bruno. He had seen the film that was made about the event. It had won the César, France's Oscar for best film.

'My wife's brother, Nesrullah, was not a monk. He was a teacher in a poor village called El-Abadel in the Ouarsenis mountains, where he lived with his wife, his twin daughters and Sami.' Momu's voice was flat, empty of emotion, as he recounted the dreadful tale. Nesrullah's wife was pregnant. It was the thirtieth of December, 1997, the first day of Ramadan, the holy month of fasting, and the GIA had declared that anyone who was not fighting the regime was *kafir*, an infidel, deserving of death. They attacked four villages that night, to show how strong they were.

'We had asked Nesrullah to come to France with his family. Teachers were always the GIA's first target. But he would not leave. Sami was one of three people left alive in the whole village, each of them boys, each of them tied to a table to watch as their family was raped and slaughtered before their eyes, one by one. Sami was found there two days later, still tied to the table, his family's blood drying on his legs and the heads of his mother and sisters lined up on the floor before him.'

Bruno and the Mayor were silent. There was nothing to be said. Momu took a freshly ironed handkerchief from his pocket and wiped his eyes.

'We heard what had happened the following week from another teacher who had known Nesrullah. He and his family were looking after Sami in their home in Algiers. I flew out and since Karim was already on my passport, I brought Sami into France as my own son, so he was here illegally. Then you helped to get him French citizenship. I never returned to Algeria. I never will.'

Sami was huddled into a ball when they saw him, squatting on the floor, face tucked between his knees and arms over his shaven head. He was dressed in an old and oil-stained set of military dungarees that looked as if the storeman should have thrown them out years ago. Momu went to him at once, knelt to embrace him and spoke quietly into his ear. Sami was oblivious at first, as though determined to shut out anything outside his own being. Then he seemed to recognize something in Momu's voice and Bruno saw him open one eye and squint at his uncle. Then he slowly unwound. He ran his hands over Momu's arms, then his face.

'*Abu, abu*,' he murmured. Father, father. Tears rolled down his cheeks as he embraced Momu and then lowered his head to rest his brow on Momu's feet.

The Mayor, the red ribbon of the *Légion d'Honneur* in his lapel, drew the airbase adjutant to one side, showed his ornate ID card from the Senate and said he would take care of whatever paperwork might be required. Bruno asked a hovering sergeant if he knew whether Sami had eaten and if they had a bathroom nearby and a towel. Momu had brought some clothes. Bruno, ever practical, had brought a baguette filled with cheese, some apples and a bottle of water.

He helped Momu to raise the youth, who towered over them both as he stood to his full height of almost two metres. They took him to the bathroom, stripped him of his dirty clothes and got him into the shower. He was frighteningly thin. Some scars on his back were ridged and old but others were more recent, still scabbed over. His feet were like clubs, covered in hard calluses as if he had gone barefoot on rough ground for months or perhaps years. They helped him dress in the loose tracksuit that Momu had brought. His feet were too swollen for the espadrilles Momu had provided, so the sergeant brought back the army boots Sami had been wearing. When he took the baguette and wolfed the first mouthful he seemed to recognize the man who had given it to him.

He stopped eating and stared at Bruno, and took in Bruno's police uniform, looked at his face again. Through a mouthful of cheese and bread, he said something that sounded like 'Bruno?'

'It's me, Sami. Bruno from the tennis club.' He mimed tossing a tennis ball into the air and serving it. Sami's face broke into a first smile.

'There's a note here from the medical orderly who was with him on the flight,' said the orderly officer, and handed an envelope to the Mayor, and a box of pills. 'These are the sedatives he was given. Now he's all yours.' He saluted the Mayor and departed, leaving the sergeant to see them off the base.

'Is it true what they said, that he was a muj?' the sergeant asked Bruno quietly.

Bruno shook his head. 'From what I heard and those scars on his back, I think the poor bastard was some kind of slave, whether for some warlord or for the mujahedin, I don't know. But thanks for all you've done, and now we'd better get him home.'

'There are a lot of rumours about this guy, according to one of the escorts who brought him down on the chopper.

Apparently all during the flight he just rolled himself into a tight ball on the floor.'

'Rumours, rumours, that's the military for you,' Bruno said, grinning and shaking hands with the sergeant. 'At least, that's how it was in my day. Maybe you could put the word around that whatever happened back in the *bled*, he was under duress. You saw the scars and the psychological state he's in.' Bruno used the old army slang word for a war zone.

'Understood,' said the sergeant, returning the handshake. 'Don't worry about the boots. Let him keep them, I'll fix the paperwork, but I don't think I'll be able to fix the rumours.'

Bruno took the front passenger seat as they drove back, leaving Sami and Momu together on the rear seats. Sami's eyes scanned the cars and houses they passed as they navigated the Bordeaux suburbs and headed for the autoroute that led to Périgueux. Were these scenes somehow familiar to him, Bruno wondered, or had the years in Afghanistan overwhelmed the memory of the towns and landscape where Sami had grown up? So far, he had spoken only the Arabic word for father and something that sounded like Bruno.

They passed vast rows of vineyards, grape-pickers busy among the vines, and road signs for Pomerol and St Emilion. These were villages whose wines summed up for Bruno something at the very heart of France, but he doubted whether they would make any impression on Sami. There would have been no alcohol in Afghanistan, and while Momu liked his glass of wine, Bruno doubted whether Sami had ever been served it when Momu and his wife raised him.

Bruno remembered what a quiet boy Sami had been, even when he was being given a normal upbringing in St Denis. His skin was relatively pale and he'd looked like any other skinny French boy in jeans, T-shirt and trainers. He went to school and *collège* with the rest of his age group. He had never been bullied. Karim, who called him his little brother, had seen to that.

But Sami had never been accepted, never brought into the boys' rituals of sneaking cigarettes behind the toilets, raiding the apple orchards and playing impromptu soccer games beside the town campground. Bruno grinned at the memory of all the kick-abouts he had seen, and of the age-old rule that if you kicked the ball into the river, you had to get it out, whatever the temperature.

Momu and Karim had given Sami as normal a boyhood as they could, Bruno recalled. Karim would take him fishing and looking for birds' nests, and cycle with him on Saturday mornings to the kids' showings at the cinema in the next village. In the summer, Momu had taken Sami to the beaches around the big bay at Arcachon with the rest of the family and up to Paris to see the sights.

He'd been enrolled in the tennis club, and took part in Bruno's rugby training sessions, content to run up and down the pitch but never passing the ball nor making any effort to catch it when it was passed to him. But he'd enjoyed place-kicking and became good at it, putting the oval ball at different spots around the pitch and then booting it through the posts from thirty and forty metres. There had even been talk about bringing Sami onto the team for that one skill, which seemed to guarantee three points for every penalty against an opposing team and another two points for each try he converted. Place-kickers could win matches on their own, but most of them would at least take part in the rest of the match. Sami never would.

Bruno had been watchful as Sami approached puberty, wondering what the inevitable storm of hormones might do to the boy. But while Sami grew tall and the occasional words he uttered showed that his voice had broken, puberty seemed to have little effect upon him, except for enhancing his fascination for all things mechanical. He dismantled and repaired the toaster at the tennis club and fixed the mechanism of the spits they used to roast lamb and wild boar. He'd spent hours at Lespinasse's garage, at first just watching the cars being serviced and overhauled. Then Lespinasse had given him tasks to do and declared Sami to be a born mechanic. He promised that when Sami left school there would be a job for him.

Maybe he should remind Momu of that, Bruno thought, but Sami needed to heal before a full-time job could be considered. There was also the threat of the thugs from Toulouse and the Brigadier's various ploys. Karim would be vital to Sami's recovery, and perhaps meeting Karim's children would help. And maybe this psychologist, Deutz, could prove useful.

The car radio was playing quietly, tuned to the Périgord station of France Bleu with its local news. As the bulletin gave way to music, Sami leaned forward from the back seat, shrugging off Momu's arm, and gestured for Bruno to increase the volume.

'It's Mozart,' said the Mayor. 'One of the piano sonatas.'

Bruno and Momu exchanged glances. Bruno raised his eyebrows, hoping Momu would understand that he was asking if this appreciation of Mozart was new. Momu shrugged, as if to say it seemed new to him. Sami's face was rapt and his long, thin fingers were beating time on his thigh. Bruno increased the volume and Sami settled back comfortably into Momu's arm, his eyes closed, a calm smile on his face, his fingers still keeping time.

The Mayor leaned across from the wheel and popped open the glove box. Bruno pulled out a stash of CDs and picked out one of Horowitz playing Mozart. He waited until the music stopped on the radio and then inserted the disc. Momu grinned happily and nodded his head firmly at Bruno, who resolved to buy Sami some Mozart CDs.

Bruno felt his phone vibrate with the brief tremor that signalled an incoming message. He checked the screen and saw it came from the Brigadier. 'Targets in Toulouse. Security in place. Call me,' it read.

Bruno decided to wait until the journey was over to call, but he used the email system to send a brief word of gratitude to Zigi at his distant army base: 'Sami home safe. Big thanks, bigger drink.' Whatever Zigi would be drinking, he'd earned it.

'You haven't told me where I should be going,' the Mayor said as the car approached the junction where the road forked to St Denis or Les Eyzies. 'Momu's place, the Gendarmerie or what? Is security still the issue?'

Bruno asked him to pull in at the next lay-by, called the Brigadier, waited for the green light on the phone that told him the conversation was secure and began by asking if he thought it safe to return to Momu's house.

'No, that's why I wanted you to call. I want this low-key for the moment, nothing official, but I don't think your Afghan boy and his family should go back to a known address. We're watching Toulouse and I have a security team heading for St

Denis but the family could be at risk. Do you have any suggestions?'

'If there's a budget for it, we could get one of the empty tourist *gites*,' Bruno replied. 'Somewhere in a nearby commune, remote but a place we can secure.' Secure was a relative term, he thought, when the opposition had a sniper's rifle and a scope that could secure a kill at eight hundred metres.

'Funds aren't a problem. Arrange some place with decent mobile phone reception, then rendezvous with my people at the Gendarmerie at six this evening and take them out there. I want you to stay with the family full-time. Wear civilian clothes but be armed. I'll call you at seven.' He rang off.

Bruno thought about the number of rooms that would be needed. A pool and tennis court would help Sami's recuperation. If possible he'd like an internal courtyard that a sniper could not see. He called Dougal at Delightful Dordogne, an agency for villa rentals, telling him this was confidential police business. He needed a place to safeguard an important witness and he wanted it from tonight.

8

Dougal's suggestion of Le Pavillon Placide in the neighbouring commune of St Chamassy was perfect. It was not a single house but a complex of old farm buildings built on three sides of a square with a stone wall and arched gateway protecting the fourth side. A terrace with tables and benches and a large herb garden filled the closed courtyard. Bruno took a room in the main house where Sami and his family would stay and assigned an attached house to the security team. A separate barn at the rear, probably used to dry tobacco in the old days, served as a garage and shielded one side of the swimming pool. The pool house shielded another side, with a lean-to and a horse trough outside. It must have been a stable and hay was still stored in one of the stalls. This gave Bruno an idea. He could patrol the perimeter more quickly and perhaps arouse less suspicion on horseback.

They stopped first at Bruno's home, where he changed into civilian clothes, packed a small suitcase and his hunting guns and loaded Balzac and his gear into his Land Rover. The Mayor took Momu and Sami to the Pavillon at St Chamassy, where Dougal met them with the keys. Bruno drove his Land Rover to the *Mairie*, took his police pistol from the safe and called Fabiola to check that she'd be free to exercise the horses with him. He picked up Momu's wife, explained the situation and helped her pack. They spent over a hundred euros at the supermarket buying food and another thirty on Mozart discs. Dougal had told him there was a sound system at Le Pavillon. Bruno took a roundabout way to get there, using quiet roads where he'd see if he was being followed.

The Mayor, whose own hunting dog had been the mother of Bruno's old hound, Gigi, was a better shot than Bruno. They shared out the weapons discreetly in the garage. The Mayor took Bruno's old military Lebel rifle and began to clean and oil it even though Bruno, who took care of his weapons, had done so the previous weekend.

'I have to go and pick up the Brigadier's security guys so I'll leave you on guard,' Bruno told him.

'I'm trying to think of the last time a Senator of France was armed on active duty,' the Mayor said, a twinkle in his eye. He was evidently enjoying himself. 'Should I give Momu the other shotgun?'

'I'd tell him where it is, but let's keep the guns out of sight for the moment. I don't want to worry Sami or Dillah.'

After her joyful reunion with Sami, Momu's wife Dillah was already clattering pans in the kitchen, Sami and Momu were sitting and watching her cook when Bruno left for the Gendarmerie. The two waiting security men introduced themselves as Gaston and Robert. They usually worked together, they told him, and they had the full kit in the four-by-four; weapons, infrared scanners, high-beam lights, Kevlar vests and an extra walkie-talkie for Bruno. He explained that he would be bringing his horse to Le Pavillon later, along with a doctor to check Sami's condition. At St Chamassy he showed them around, introduced them to the Mayor, Momu and the family, and gave them the large-scale map of the locality he kept in his Land Rover. Then the Mayor drove Bruno to Pamela's place, where he found Pamela and Fabiola waiting and the horses already saddled.

This evening, there were no arguments about Pamela being allowed to ride. He explained Sami's return and the security arrangements and suggested he and Fabiola ride to Le Pavillon, barely three kilometres away as the crow flies, on bridle trails and forest rides they knew well. Bruno strapped Fabiola's medical bag to the pommel of her saddle, kissed Pamela and they set off.

'What can you tell me about this young man?' Fabiola asked as they walked the horses through the paddock to the lane. 'All I know is that you said he's been in Afghanistan and he's somewhere on the autistic spectrum.'

'He looks half-starved, and he's been whipped, both in the past and recently. He was heavily sedated when they flew him here. He curled up into a ball and refused to respond until he saw Momu. But then he recognized me and he seems devoted to Momu and Dillah. And I learned today that he likes Mozart.'

Bruno went on to describe what he recalled of Sami's boyhood in St Denis, and the trauma of his family's slaughter in the Algerian civil war. 'We have no idea what happened to him at the mosque in Toulouse, nor how he got to Afghanistan. I think he must have gone barefoot a lot. His hands are thin and his fingers delicate but his feet look like sides of beef. From his hands, I don't think he was a fighter. Weapons and combat tend to roughen them up.'

'And you want me to look at him,' she replied, her voice

disapproving. 'I trust you aren't asking for an instant diagnosis.'

'I'm hoping you can check him over for general health, see if there are any immediate problems,' he replied. 'I'm not asking you to take him on permanently or treat him.'

'Is this connected with that dreadful scene in the woods, the man who was killed?'

'It looks that way,' he said. 'I think the guys who killed him are the ones who attacked me in the *collège*. They were looking for Momu as a route to Sami and I presume they want to kill him, too.'

'Thoughtful of you not to explain all this to Pamela. She worries about you quite enough as it is,' Fabiola said, raising an eyebrow. 'Let's canter or we'll never get there.'

From Le Pavillon came smells of cooking and a watchful greeting from Gaston. They rode around to the lean-to stables, where they heard the sounds of splashing coming from the pool and squeaks of excitement from Balzac. At the sight of Fabiola, Sami huddled close to Momu, turned his face away and sank down into the pool until only his head was visible. Fabiola, nodded, smiled and told Bruno she'd wait in the kitchen with Dillah until Sami was dressed and felt able to face a female.

'I'll leave you to unsaddle the horses and brush them down,' she said, unstrapping her medical bag and marching off.

As soon as she left, Sami clambered out of the pool, unconcerned by his nakedness, and scooped Balzac into his arms, careless of the scratches the dog's paws were raking on his chest as Balzac clambered up to lick his face.

'I'll get him some swimming shorts tomorrow and some more clothes,' Bruno told Momu, who was smiling at Sami's obvious pleasure.

'Maybe you should get him a dog, too,' Momu said, as Sami began running around the rim of the pool and letting Balzac chase him. Momu called Sami to come and get dressed and Bruno went to take care of the horses, wondering why Sami had not responded to them as he had to Balzac. Maybe it was a matter of size. His phone vibrated and as he opened the call he saw the green light. He checked his watch; he'd forgotten to call the Brigadier.

'I heard from the security men that you're all settled in. Who's the doctor?' the Brigadier began. Bruno explained that Fabiola was from the St Denis clinic and was checking Sami for any urgent medical problems. He asked if there was any news from Toulouse.

'All quiet. The good news is that we got the number of that phone they were charging. We knew where they'd been in the woods and at the *collège* and then the route they took, so we triangulated it from there. They made a lot of calls while driving, several of them to numbers we didn't know about. Make sure your guests don't start using their own phones; the Toulouse gang may turn the phone trick against us and establish your location. I'll call again tomorrow.'

When he entered the kitchen, Bruno saw that Fabiola had recruited Dillah, who was one of her regular patients, to help make Sami comfortable with her presence. Dillah stood with her arm around Sami as Fabiola examined him, stethoscope around her neck. Balzac sat at Sami's feet, staring up at him patiently. Sami began to stroke the dog with his bare feet until

Fabiola asked him to sit still. Bruno left them to it and went outside to discuss with Gaston and Robert how they would share out the hours on watch.

'Just like being back in the army,' said Gaston, and Bruno asked which unit. Gaston had been in the paras and Robert in the *chasseurs*, but they had then served together when they transferred into the 13th Paratroop Dragoons, Rafiq's old unit. That made sense, Bruno thought; the Brigadier would automatically recruit his security men from the special forces.

'Did you know a guy named Rafiq?' he asked.

The two men nodded grimly. 'We heard he got the chop,' said Gaston, the shorter and stockier of the two. 'The word was he died hard, nasty stuff.'

'He was killed by the same bastards we're guarding against here,' said Bruno.

'Understood,' said Robert, and gave his FAMAS assault weapon an affectionate tap. 'If they come back, we know what to do. We'd better set a watch list for tonight.' By the time Momu called him in to supper they had agreed a schedule.

'We live on frozen pizza and there's a microwave in our house,' said Gaston. 'We'll eat later, one at a time. We already had a snack at that bar by the Gendarmerie before we met you.'

'You don't know Dillah,' Bruno replied. 'You can be sure there'll be food for you. I think it's chicken cous-cous. She said it was always Sami's favourite.'

Places had been set for everyone at the big kitchen table, but Fabiola said she'd better ride back while there was still light. Sami clutched at her arm as she turned away and stroked her hand. She smiled at him, receiving a wide grin in return.

'*Demain?*' Sami said, in a questioning tone, asking if Fabiola would be back tomorrow.

'*Demain*,' Fabiola replied, gently patting Sami's cheek. Bruno escorted her outside and asked for her verdict. Sami was malnourished, she reported. He also had hypertension, very high blood pressure and some gastric and bronchial infections that she'd identify when she had the results of the blood and other samples she'd taken. He would need major dental work, a broken bone in his left arm would probably need to be reset, and she thought a specialist had better look at the whipping scars on his back. Some of them weren't healing.

'He's in poor shape, but in no immediate danger as far as I can see. As for the problems I can't see, I'll get the blood-test results in a day or so and I'll let you know what they find. Physically, he needs rest, a good diet and some antibiotics. I've started him on a course that should clear up the infections in his scars. Dillah has the tablets. He seems calm enough, so I've stopped the sedatives. Psychologically, he's in a bad way.'

'Is it straightforward autism?' Bruno asked.

'There's no such thing, and a lot of us are no longer convinced it's a useful term,' she replied. Autism used to be seen as morbid self-absorption, she explained, then it was said to be the result of bad parenting, and more recently that it was genetic. Some specialists thought it came from mercury poisoning or some other new toxin in the environment. All modern medicine could truthfully say was that autism was a catch-all word used for people who did not react convention-ally to current social norms. They could be mute, hyperactive, extraordinarily gifted in some ways and almost psychopathic in others.

'What happened to him as a child in Algeria was likely to trigger some kind of extreme reaction. Post-traumatic stress in children often presents itself as elective mutism, they just decide not to speak,' she went on. 'But whatever condition Sami had when he was growing up here has been hugely complicated by the new traumas he went through in Afghanistan. On the bright side, he's obviously capable of strong affection. He shows it for Dillah and Momu, and for your dog. That may be a good sign, but from the way he reacted to me he might have something we see in orphanages, a reactive detachment disorder. Kids starved of contact and affection when young will often grab desperately to any adult in sight.'

'Do you think prison psychologists will be able to help him?'

She said nothing but looked at him solemnly for a long moment and then at the rifle slung over his shoulder and sighed. She turned away to mount her horse, and said, 'I don't think I'm qualified to judge.'

'Will you be back to see him tomorrow?' Bruno asked. 'You told him you would.'

'I'd like to, but I'm not sure your prison psychologists would want another doctor getting involved,' she said. As she settled in the saddle she added, 'If I'm needed, of course I'll come. In any event I'll call you when I get the test results.'

At table, Sami used a spoon to devour his food and kept his left hand curled around his plate as if to protect it. Dillah was watching Sami, and she put her hand on his arm and told him gently, 'It's alright, Sami, there is plenty of food. We won't be hungry.'

Sami smiled at her but continued to bolt his food. He seemed unconcerned at the sight of Bruno's rifle leaning against his chair. He was evidently accustomed to the sight of armed men, even when they kept their weapons to hand as they ate. That was probably commonplace in Afghanistan, Bruno thought, but perhaps not if Sami had been kept as a slave.

'This cous-cous is great, Dillah, and thank you for helping with Fabiola,' Bruno said. 'I was worried he might not want to be examined by a woman.'

'So was I,' she replied, smiling. 'But when he came in with your dog, Balzac went straight to Fabiola and she picked him up like an old friend. Sami seemed to think that made her his friend, too. And I told him Fabiola was my doctor, and Momu's, and that she had delivered Karim's baby. Anyway, I asked her to take on Sami as a regular patient and Momu signed the form. We're still his guardians.'

'But he's over eighteen,' Bruno said. 'Guardianship lapses once he becomes an adult.'

'Yes, but when we were trying to get Sami into a special school he had to be declared incapable of running his own affairs. We had to go before the *Juge des Tutelles*, and Momu and I were appointed *tuteurs*,' Dillah said. Bruno nodded; he knew that the court of guardianship usually appointed family members to manage the affairs of someone judged incapable. 'That means the guardianship is extended until the medical diagnosis changes.'

Momu cleared his throat, the sound of a man intent on changing the subject. 'How long will we have to stay here, Bruno?'

'I don't know. As long as the situation lasts that puts you and Sami at risk.'

'When can I go back to teaching?'

'It's the same answer, Momu. They know where you teach and where to find you. If you aren't at the *collège*, that means less danger for the schoolchildren and your colleagues. This is not an address they know, and if they find you, you're guarded. And that reminds me, I have to ask for your mobile phones. We don't want them tracking you through them.'

'Can Karim and his family come to visit us here?'

'Yes, of course. I'll go to see Karim and make the arrangements, pick them up myself and bring them here.'

'Presumably they know who you are,' said Dillah. 'These men could be tracking you as easily as us.'

'I have a special phone. It's as secure as we can make them.'

'I'm worried about Karim and the babies,' she said. 'Shouldn't they be here with us? There's plenty of room.'

'That's up to you and Karim, if he feels he can afford to close the café and forgo the income,' Bruno said. 'I don't think it's wise for him to commute back and forth to work from here. We simply don't know if these thugs are aware of Karim. His name wasn't in their notebook we found. And if he disappears along with his family, they might alert somebody. We don't know if they have any sympathizers around here . . .' Bruno saw Momu's face darken.

'At the mosque, they know about Karim,' Momu said. 'When they agreed to take Sami into their special school, they wanted to know everything, names, relatives, how much I make, did I own my house, did I have a mortgage or a loan to buy my car? That was how they worked out how much we should pay.'

Bruno had not been aware that Momu had been paying the mosque. 'How much did you pay them?'

'Rather more than I could afford,' he said. 'And they were

furious when I stopped paying when Sami disappeared. They said their religious court had ruled against me and I still owed money. I told them I'd see them only in a French court and they climbed down. I understand now why they were so nervous at the idea. It would have meant questions about where Sami had gone.'

'I'd better take some food out to those two nice young men,' said Dillah. 'I can't stand the idea of them living on frozen pizza, not here in the Périgord.'

9

The next morning Bruno drove into St Cyprien to buy more clothes for Sami, dog biscuits and a pay-as-you-go phone. If he wasn't allowed to use his own mobile, he still needed to communicate with people. And he wanted to continue his search for any trace of the Halévy children. He picked up some croissants and then drove back by a roundabout route to call at Karim's Café des Sports. He parked around the corner by the rugby stadium and looked at the cars parked outside the café. They all carried the number 24 on the licence plate, which meant they were local. Even so, he knocked on the back door and Rashida opened it, an infant crawling at her feet and her new baby in her arms.

'Karim called the Mayor to find out where they are but he won't tell us,' she said when he'd slipped inside and closed the door. Automatically, she began making coffee.

'I'll take you there tonight if you like, after the café closes, but you must only go when I take you. It could be dangerous,' Bruno explained. 'Don't say anything about this to Karim unless you're alone.'

'Should I bring some food, maybe some clothes?'

'That's all taken care of. Dillah is feeding us. And you might want to bring your swimsuits. There's a pool.'

She grinned. 'Karim thought you'd have them all in some police barracks or on an army base. It sounds more luxurious than that. But how long is this going to last?'

'I wish I knew,' he said, and was about to take his leave when Karim came in from the door that led to the café, his height and bulk instantly filling the room. As soon as he saw Bruno his eyes blazed.

'What the hell is going on, Bruno? Where are my mum and dad?'

'That's why I'm here,' he replied calmly, and thanked Rashida as she handed him a cup of coffee. 'They're still in danger, along with Sami, but I'm hoping to arrange for you to see them this evening.'

Karim took the baby from his wife's arms and said, 'I came in for some more sugar. We're almost out. Could you see to the bar, please? And I was making two double espressos for Julien and Manuel. They'll also want some of their usual lottery cards.'

As Rashida left, saying that little Pierre had yet to be fed, Karim sat heavily at the kitchen table, scooped up his toddler with his free hand and tried clumsily to seat the little boy in his high chair. Bruno put down his coffee and took the baby and Karim settled his son and began to feed him some yogurt. Bruno bent down to sniff the baby's head, a scent that always enchanted him.

'Who are these bastards?' Karim asked, keeping his voice mild to avoid upsetting his son.

'Jihadis, Salafists, the same kind of zealots who wiped out Sami's family in Algeria, and now they're here in France,' Bruno replied. 'They want to kill Sami because he's the living proof that they've been funnelling French Muslims from the mosque to fight in Afghanistan. If they have to kill your parents or your children to get to Sami, they'll do it.'

'You saw them at the *collège*, you know who they are. Why haven't you arrested them?'

'If we do that, the people who are behind this will send somebody else. It makes more sense to watch them, monitor their phone calls and their movements and build up a picture of the whole organization, not just these two thugs. They're just pawns.'

'You make it sound like my parents are pawns, too,' Karim said, but Bruno felt there was no malice in his words, simply a sense of frustration that there was so little he could do for his family.

'We don't see them as pawns,' Bruno said, knowing his words were pompous but they needed to be said. 'We're doing all we can to protect them, renting a discreet location, installing round-the-clock security guards.'

Karim nodded. 'What about Rashida and the kids?'

'We found a notebook in their van. It had your dad's name and address but not yours. Still, Momu says he listed the entire family when Sami went to the mosque, so they may know about you. If you want to join your parents, we can do that.'

'I can't afford to leave the café.'

'Rashida and the kids could go, but it might be risky for you to stay on alone. These people are armed and ruthless.'

'*Putain*, why not round up the whole mosque? Close the bastards down.'

'Because this is France. We have laws. I have to go, Karim. We can discuss all these issues later. I'll pick you up this evening after you close the café. Go to the tennis club and I'll take you out the back way, just in case someone is trying to follow you.'

Bruno kissed the baby, handed it back to Karim and strolled up the quiet side street that led to the empty rugby stadium. He used his key to enter the clubhouse and used the office phone to make the calls he had planned. He started with the Mayor, then Florence to learn if the computer club had approved his appeal for their help in the search for any records of the Halévy children. They'd already begun, he was told. Finally he called Pamela.

'Fabiola came back last night and we ate here. She told me all about it, made it sound very cloak-and-dagger,' she said. He could almost hear the smile in her voice. 'I suppose you'll have to arrest me now I know the secret of where you've taken them.'

'They should be safe there.'

'Did Fabiola say anything about that problem with Gilles? And have you called him?'

'No, she said nothing, and no, this isn't something I could ask him about on the phone.'

'What's this number you're dialling from?' she asked. 'I don't recognize it.'

'I'm not using my usual phone for security reasons.'

'Take care of yourself. Should I call this number if I need you?'

'No, there's another number, a disposable phone I bought.' He gave the number. 'So long as you're not calling to tell me to interrogate Gilles about Fabiola.'

She laughed, a sound he loved to hear, and it made him hope things were better between them again.

His calls to the Jewish Scouts and to the Shoah Foundation brought no new details, but gave him the names of some of Halévy's friends in Paris to whom he might have confided something. He got voicemails, secretaries, but finally Halévy's sometime partner in a medical practice came on the line, happy to talk about his old friend.

'You'll never guess what he told me once,' Bruno heard. 'He said that he was never healthier than in the war. He never ate too much, no sugar, only water and milk to drink, and everything fresh from the garden and the farm.'

'So he lived on a farm? Not in a town.'

'He was briefly in a town, in an attic belonging to an old lady who brought them bread and hot milk for breakfast. But mostly he was on a farm, with a couple, and he always called the man Monsieur. He called the wife Tante Sylvie. Apparently they were very devout Christians, and the man wore a porcelain mask. David spoke of it when that musical was popular, the one about the phantom living under the Paris Opera. He said the Monsieur had been like that, a *gueule cassée*.'

Bruno almost jumped from his chair. This was a vital clue. A *gueule cassée*, literally 'broken face', was one of the many who had suffered severe facial injuries from the Great War, usually a victim of artillery fire. Some were so disfigured that they were given ceramic masks, along with a small pension, which meant there should be an official record somewhere of all those in the region with these facial mutilations. Where might the records be kept? He called the Préfecture in Périgueux and was put through to the archives, only to be told the relevant records had been lost or perhaps destroyed. He tried the military archives at Les Invalides in Paris, and was transferred to the archives of the *anciens combattants* in Caen.

He reached a woman who tried to be helpful when he explained his search. The archives were filed by name, and he had no name, and only a rough idea of the region. But there were more than a hundred thousand *gueules cassées*, he was told. Did they all have porcelain masks? No, only about a third of them. Would it be possible to track down those fitted with such masks in the Dordogne? That's not how the archives are organized, he was told. And there was no centre for fitting the masks in the *département* of the Dordogne.

Bruno then called Jo, his predecessor as the town policeman, and asked him for any memories of a *gueule cassée* in the region during the Occupation. Jo could recall two: one, named Barrachon, had lived in St Denis and worked in an insurance office; the other had been an *Inspecteur de Tabac* in Ste Alvère. Bruno took their names, but neither one was a farmer. Jo promised to ask around.

Bruno knew someone in the town with the name of Barrachon, who would probably be a relative. He called the house and an elderly woman answered. It was her son that Bruno knew, also an insurance agent. He explained his search and asked if an ancestor had been a *gueule cassée* and found he was on the right track. The woman's grandfather had been fitted with a mask in Limoges, and had been secretary of the local branch of the *Anciens Combattants*. She still had his papers up in the attic. Would Bruno like to come and look through them?

Two dusty hours later, Bruno had a long list of names of the local *mutilés de guerre*, organized by the nature of their wounds. It sobered him. He knew from the town war memorial that almost two hundred sons of St Denis had fallen in the Great War, around one in eight of the commune's male population in 1914. And there were two hundred and seventy names of the *mutilés*. There were the blind, those who had lost one or both legs, those missing one or both arms, as well as the victims of poison gas.

Bruno had known intellectually of the appalling toll of that war, and as a veteran soldier he could guess that for each one who died in action, two or three would be wounded. He understood from his own experience how that simple word 'wounded' could not begin to describe the pain and frustrations of hospital and operations, the endless tedium and discomforts of convalescence.

His own recovery had been complete. Yet now he felt weighed down by the presence of hundreds of thousands of men whose lives had been permanently transformed and diminished by wounds and disfigurements that lasted for the rest of their days. Blinded, legless, deafened, barely able to breathe for the gas that had scoured their lungs, the costs of war endured for whole lifetimes, condemning the victims and their wives and families to but a fraction of the lives they had expected. And it was not only Frenchmen, but Germans, Russians, British, Austrians, Americans, Turks, Italians, a polyglot host of smashed bodies and broken minds that spread around the globe. What a gross and terrible madness that war had been.

On the list in his hands were fourteen *gueules cassées*. Five of them were listed as receiving pensions for being one hundred per cent disabled, so he presumed they would not be able to continue working their farms. Of the remainder, five were farmers. Three of them were in the commune of St Denis, one was in St Chamassy and one in Audrix.

Bruno noted the names and addresses, and went to the *Mairie* to find exactly where the farmers from St Denis had lived and the names of the current owners of the farms. The *cadastre*, the vast map of the commune on which every lot of land was marked, was cross-referenced to the taxation records. Two of the names he crossed off his list, since the men had died before 1942. He called the other *mairies* and found that the *gueule cassée* in St Chamassy had died in 1941. That left him two names. The farmer in St Denis had land adjoining the road to Les Eyzies, which did not seem sufficiently remote a secret shelter.

So he drove to the tiny *mairie* of Audrix and asked the Mayor if he could consult the *cadastre*. He found that the farm had been abandoned and had paid no taxes since 1944. The farmer's name was Michel Desbordes and his wife was Sylvie. The Mayor rang the oldest inhabitant of the village and asked if he remembered the couple. He did, so Bruno and the Mayor walked through the small square flanked by the medieval inn on whose terrace Bruno had often dined to the modest house where the old man lived with his daughter, a widow and retired in her turn.

'I'll be eighty-four next month, but there's nothing wrong with my memory,' said the old man, pouring a glass of his home-made *vin de noix* that he insisted his guests taste. It was indeed good, although a little sweeter than Bruno's own version. 'Monsieur Desbordes, our local bogey man. We were all frightened of him, all the children. My grandma would say she'd get him to come round if we were naughty. We hardly ever saw him and his wife was usually the one who went to market. They had a little cart and a donkey.'

The Desbordes had no children and had kept to themselves, since they had been the only Protestants in the commune, the old man recalled. Theirs had been a small farm of no more than ten hectares, raising goats, chickens, rabbits and a couple of scrawny cows. The land had been too poor for tobacco, so the Desbordes had been little more than self-sufficient. But he had some kind of pension as a *mutilé*, enough to keep himself and his wife in salt and soap and an occasional pair of shoes.

'Are you sure there were no children, perhaps relatives who came to stay?' Bruno asked.

The old man shook his head; not that he had ever seen. He remembered one thing. There had been a time when Desbordes had fallen and broken his mask. For weeks he had worn a cloth that his wife had sewn to cover his face until he went to Limoges for a new mask. But yes, there had been relatives, a man who wore a white collar like a priest, but he was accompanied by a woman whom he had introduced as his wife.

'It was the first I knew that Protestants let their priests marry,' the old man said. 'But I never saw any children and I never saw Desbordes or his wife after the liberation.'

Bruno drove out to the farm, at first along a single-lane tarmac road. But then at a junction it became a dirt track and after another junction it was no more than an overgrown space between two tangled hedgerows. Bruno stopped his Land Rover, climbed out and pushed his way through the jungle of vegetation. Nobody had been this way in years. The going eased as the track led through a small patch of woodland that had grown dense and dark through lack of management. As he emerged from the trees, he saw that he was in a small bowl of gently sloping land, perhaps two hundred metres wide and a little longer where the land fell away to a small stream lined with overgrown willows and the remains of a wooden fence.

The farmhouse lay to his left. It had been built just below the crest of a ridge, to be sheltered from the winds, which could be fierce up here on the plateau. Its front faced the rising sun and at the rear and southern side there was a terrace. Like the walls, it was made of local stone and was still in good repair; only a scattering of weeds had found purchase in the cracks. The roof was almost gone, just a few rafters and a handful of tiles remained. The wooden door was cracked but still firm and locked.

Bruno cleared some of the bracken that had grown around the walls and clambered through a gap that had once been a window. He found himself in what could have been the kitchen, with a stone sink and a broken-off chimney pipe hanging above the spot where a stove would have stood. A small hallway, with the remains of a ladder going into the attic, led to two empty rooms, most of their ceilings gone and open to the skies. Presumably Desbordes and his wife had one and the Halévy children used the other.

He went out to the terrace. A large stone barn, in better repair than the house, stood across a cobbled yard. At one side of the yard he found an ancient well in the yard and the rusted remains of a pump. A small pile of stones overgrown with wildflowers had presumably been the outhouse. Beyond it a low, single-storey building set into the slope of the hill could have been a pigsty or perhaps a donkey's stable. It was too small for a horse. The place felt like a refuge, quiet and protected from the outside world, and the only sound audible was birdsong. It was a spot where people of quiet tastes could be content and where children of war like Halévy and his sister could find peace.

He climbed to the top of the ridge and knew at once where he was, at the southern end of one of the stretches of woodland that contained a long firebreak that he sometimes rode. He could get here on horseback. It must once have been a pleasant farm, and with a tractor to clear the approach lane and a lot of work would make a charming holiday home. Fix up the barn, turn it into a dormitory and it would make a fine camp for children.

Bruno paused as the idea struck him. It would make a good centre for Boy Scouts and Girl Guides. Halévy had been a Scout. Maybe that would be the right project for Halévy's estate, turning the house where he and his sister had been sheltered into a memorial to them both that was also useful for a new generation. He used his mobile phone to take some photos. He'd ask some of the builders in St Denis to take a look and give a rough idea of what it might cost to restore the place.

Bruno looked at the sun and checked his watch. He had meant to get back to Momu at Le Pavillon with croissants in time for a late breakfast, but he'd been gone for half the day. He plucked out his disposable phone but there was no signal. They must be wondering what had become of him. And the Brigadier, who had told Bruno to stay with Sami and the family, would probably be furious. Nonetheless, Bruno reflected as he ploughed his way back along the overgrown lane to his vehicle, his time had been well spent. When he got back to Audrix he had a signal and his first call was to the Mayor, to tell him that the Halévy mystery was solved and they now needed to find out what they could of the Desbordes family. And with his croissants growing stale beside him, Bruno headed back to Le Pavillon.

10

The thought crossed Bruno's mind that he should offer to cook for the group assembled at Le Pavillon. But he knew that Dillah, expecting the arrival of her son, daughter-in-law and grandchildren and with her long-lost adopted son returned, would be outraged if anyone tried to replace her in the kitchen. Trying to think what Sami might like and also what he might need, Bruno went briefly by his own garden to fill a basket with apples, pears and blackcurrants. From the look of him, Sami had eaten little of anything in Afghanistan, let alone the fruit and vegetables that would do him good. Finally, remembering one of Sami's favourite treats from his days at the tennis club, Bruno stopped at the supermarket and bought a large carton of vanilla ice cream.

'All quiet in Toulouse,' Gaston told him when Bruno drove into the courtyard where he could park out of sight. 'Nobody's stirring, they tell us. But the boss is on his way. Apparently there's been a development.'

Bruno found Sami, barefoot and dressed in loose tracksuit trousers and a vest, dozing by the pool, Balzac snoozing on his chest. One of Sami's hands was shading his eyes, the other lay on Balzac's back. Bruno stripped off to his shorts, dived into the pool and began swimming short lengths, crawl one way, backstroke the other. The splashes woke Balzac and jerked Sami to sit upright. He saw Bruno's basket lying close to hand and picked out a pear.

'Have you swum yet?' Bruno asked, pausing at his turn. Sami shook his head and then stripped and rolled into the pool. He floated on his back, arms outstretched and eyes closed as Bruno continued his lengths, wondering what news the Brigadier would bring and whether his idea of turning the Desbordes farm into a Scout camp would unlock more money from the Halévy bequest. How long would the Brigadier want to take, monitoring the phones and emails at the mosque and building intelligence before judging it was time to move in, arrest Rafiq's killers and let Momu and his family resume a normal life?

'Car coming,' called Gaston. Bruno climbed out of the pool, quickly towelled down and put on some fresh shorts and sandals from the sports bag in the back of his Land Rover. He strapped on his handgun and joined Gaston at the archway. Robert had the high ground in the *pigeonnier* tower with a view in all directions.

'It's the doc's car,' he called down, and Bruno recognized Fabiola's old Twingo as it rounded the bend. Far off in the distance and barely louder than the buzzing of a bee he could hear the beat of a helicopter.

'I got the lab to expedite the blood tests. They'd never seen anything like it,' Fabiola explained. 'He's had hepatitis, amoebic dysentery and jaundice which is still not cleared up, and he's still got anaemia, hookworms, trichuriasis and they're still checking for tuberculosis. It's amazing what a human body can put up with. I've brought him enough antibiotics to cure a regiment, but you have to make sure he takes them, Bruno. How has he been today?'

'He slept in and had a big breakfast, eggs and yogurt and that flat bread Dillah makes,' said Gaston. 'He spent the rest of the morning stroking your horse. Then he sat by the pool with Momu and your dog. He's got a thing about animals; they like him, the way he touches them.'

'Touch seems very important to him as a way to communicate,' Fabiola said. 'He doesn't seem to trust speech much, as if he hasn't had much practice in speaking. Anyway, since I'm here, let's go and see how he is.'

Sami must have heard her voice and came loping round the corner, Balzac in his arms, still dripping water from the pool and his face beaming a wide smile at the sight of Fabiola.

'Fab'ola,' he said, in a voice that creaked like a rusty door. He stroked her forearm as if he were petting a dog.

Fabiola's hair was piled up atop her head and she wore no make-up. The old mountaineering scar on her cheek stood out plainly and Sami drew close to look at it. He touched it gently with the back of his hand as if to feel its texture. Fabiola smiled and then turned him to examine the scars on his back. He was still wet from the pool.

'Brigadier will be here in twenty minutes,' Gaston interrupted, his head cocked as he listened to the voice in his earpiece. 'The chopper put him down by the big quarry. He wanted to be sure we were all here.'

'Why not land here?' Fabiola asked.

'It would draw attention,' said Bruno. 'Not many holiday rentals come with helicopter service.'

Fabiola took Sami's hand to lead him indoors and asked

Bruno to bring her medical bag. Once in the kitchen and beginning her examination, with Dillah again standing beside Sami, Fabiola said she had something important to tell them.

'These worms Sami has are highly infectious. You need to wash your hands very thoroughly after you touch him, every time. And wash him with this special soap first thing in the morning, whenever he goes to the bathroom, before meals and when he goes to bed.' She put a large white plastic bottle on the kitchen table and then turned to Bruno.

'Dogs are very vulnerable and they are also carriers to humans, so I'm giving Balzac a de-worming course.'

'What about horses?' Bruno asked. 'Sami spends a lot of time stroking Hector.'

'I don't know. I'll check and get back to you. And make sure those two security men are brought into the picture, because all this applies to them. Dillah, every time Sami uses the bathroom, please wash everything with bleach – shower, hand-basin and toilet bowl. Here, I've brought you a big pack of rubber gloves. Use them once only.'

Dillah's eyes widened in alarm but she nodded firmly.

'One more thing,' Fabiola went on. 'No babies and no lactating mothers may visit until I say so. I'll do more tests in a few days. The antibiotics and other treatments should have killed the worms and eggs by then. But babies are very vulnerable and breast milk from an infected mother can be lethal.'

She turned to Bruno, who was thinking that there would now be no visit by Rashida and her children. 'You might want to remind them of the legal situation on quarantine,' she added as she climbed into her car. She drove off.

Bruno nodded as he waved farewell, recalling one of his

lectures at the police academy and a section of the legal code that he had not studied for years. But he remembered the extraordinary powers that French doctors could assume to impose strict quarantine to prevent public health risks. Briefly, he explained that Fabiola could have them all kept here behind barbed wire and watched by armed sentries, if she thought it necessary.

As he finished, Bruno heard Gaston's voice warning of an approaching car. It must be the Brigadier. Bruno told the rest to stay inside for the moment and went out to greet him. To his surprise, the Brigadier was being driven in the private car of the Mayor of St Denis and the Mayor gave him a cheery wave as he parked. Two new security men climbed out from the rear seats, nodding amiably at Gaston and Robert.

'All in order, Bruno?' the Brigadier asked, shaking his hand.

'Yes, sir. The doctor has just been scaring the pants off us with awful warnings about some intestinal worms that Sami picked up when he was overseas. It looks like we'll all be bathing in bleach from now on.'

'Do whatever she says,' said the Mayor, coming forward to shake Bruno's hand. 'If we get any kind of infection like that we can say goodbye to next year's tourist season.'

'In that case, gentlemen, you'd both better wash your hands after shaking mine. It's a pleasure to see you, *Monsieur le Maire*, but a bit of a surprise.'

'I'll explain,' said the Brigadier. 'The situation has changed rather dramatically since we last spoke. You remember that small château in the vineyards we used for the summit during that Basque business? We've found a similar place, only rather more remote, for your boy and his family. The buildings are being secured by the army as we speak and facilities are being installed, beds and so on. Deutz will be there tomorrow and he wants the family kept together, so you'll all be moving there. I want you to stay there with them, Bruno, and be sure you're armed. And we may be getting somewhat crowded. It looks as though we'll have to convene a tribunal on his mental competence.'

Bruno frowned. That was usually only needed if there was a trial in prospect. 'Are charges being brought?'

'Not yet, and not by us, but I suspect we'll be getting an extradition request from Washington. There's been quite a dramatic development. Remember we were checking Sami's thumbprints? Those prints are all over some of the unexploded IEDs they found in Afghanistan. It looks like your boy is the expert the Americans call the Engineer.'

Bruno's jaw dropped. He recalled reading articles in the French press about this legendary bomb-maker, his innovative designs and the meticulous craftsmanship of his work, never a centimetre of wire wasted nor a junction that wasn't doubly soldered. A caption to a photo in *Paris Match* of one of the bombs that had been defused said it looked as professionally made as the interior of a mobile phone or a computer.

'Even if this wretched young man is not the Engineer himself, at the very least he worked with him. So your Sami may be responsible for dozens of deaths. Under a whole shelfload of anti-terrorism agreements we had no choice but to inform our allies that we've got him,' the Brigadier said. 'I wish to heaven that he'd never left Afghanistan.'

Bruno kept his face expressionless as he absorbed the news and the visceral shock of horror that it brought. Bruno had seen men he knew maimed and killed by roadside bombs and cleverly rigged artillery shells that could be timed to spew shrapnel into a passing column. *Mon Dieu*, if Sami had been guilty of that . . .

He took a deep breath and tried to fit the image of Sami as a star bomb-maker, putting together the intricate timing mechanisms of bombs and booby-traps, with the pathetic figure huddled in a ball as they had first seen him at the airbase. Bruno recalled Sami smiling beatifically as Balzac lay in his arms. It didn't add up. But the image fitted only too well when he recalled a much younger Sami fixing the appliances at the tennis and rugby clubs and helping Lespinasse repair the ignition in a car so old they had to make their own spare parts. Could that Sami be the Engineer, Bruno asked himself? Recalling the careful artistry of Sami's repairs in St Denis, it seemed all too possible.

Then the wider implications began to occur to him, of extradition hearings, court appearances and outraged American politicians demanding that the French hand him over so that the Engineer could be brought to justice.

But if Sami was formally declared to be mentally unfit to stand trial, or had been acting under duress, what then? Like most policemen, Bruno suspected that pleas of insanity were open to wide abuse. Most people, he believed, knew the difference between right and wrong. But in the case of Sami, whom he had known as a strange and troubled boy, and whose unspeakable childhood trauma he had learned from Momu, Bruno felt in his bones that the conventional legal rules of guilt and responsibility and medical evidence could hardly apply. Momu had phrased it best: Sami was put together differently. He was not like other people.

And how would the French state react? After its own terror attacks in Paris, France had been one of the strongest voices for international conventions against terrorism and the extradition of suspected terrorists to stand trial. Could Sami, could the massed ranks of the French psychiatric profession, stand against the overwhelming demand of realpolitik that Sami be surrendered?

French soldiers had been killed in roadside bombings in Afghanistan. French public opinion would be unlikely to stand up for Sami after that. The best that could happen was that Sami would be tried in France and condemned to a psychiatric prison hospital for the rest of his life. Something else occurred to him. Bruno already knew why the men from the Toulouse mosque wanted to find Sami and to silence him. Now he understood just how desperate they must be to kill him before he might talk.

'I see you understand the implications of this,' the Brigadier said. 'As we speak, letters are going out to the legal attaché of the United States embassy in Paris, along with the proper representatives of our British, German, Dutch and Canadian and Australian friends, all of whom have lost men to these damned IEDs. I have no doubt we'll be getting formal applications for extradition. The British and Germans can simply send us European arrest warrants and he'd be handed over to them almost automatically.'

'Well, it would be automatic unless we charge him first under French law,' the Mayor said. 'That would take precedence and it means we'll be in charge of the procedure and set up medical tribunals to assess competence and so on. I've been talking to the Minister of the Interior and he's been talking to the Elysée and this is the way we're going to handle it.'

'Yes, sir,' said Bruno said. 'At what point does all this become public? I ask because I think there will be considerable media interest.'

'It becomes public when formal charges are laid or if it leaks, and it had better not be leaked from here in St Denis,' the Brigadier said, menace into his voice.

'It won't just be the media, Bruno,' the Mayor said. 'I can think of quite a lot of our home-grown politicians who will want to make use of this. A young Algerian immigrant, now a naturalized French citizen, a bomb-making terrorist whose work has killed French soldiers . . . You know as well as I do what the anti-immigrant politicians will do with that. Then there'll be Muslim hotheads trying to turn Sami into some jihadist martyr.'

'That's why we're going to move all this into the château, where we can secure the grounds and close the roads if we have to,' the Brigadier said. 'And if all this rebounds badly on St Denis, you two gentlemen have only yourselves to blame for arranging to bring Sami home.'

'Yes, sir,' Bruno repeated. 'There might be one legal way to keep this area buttoned up. The doctor reminded me of her powers under the public health regulations. If necessary, we can get this whole area declared to be under quarantine and sealed off.'

'Good thinking, but let's not get ahead of ourselves, Bruno. That might be useful to bear in mind for the future, but we're not going to persuade our medical tribunal to convene in the middle of a plague zone, or whatever you plan to call it. The immediate priority is for you to take a full set of Sami's finger-prints and DNA samples, just so we can be absolutely clear who we are dealing with.'

'Any news from Toulouse about those two guys who killed Rafiq?' Bruno asked.

'They're still holed up in the mosque, as far as we know,' the Brigadier replied. 'Don't worry, Bruno, we'll get them when we're ready. But in the meantime perhaps the Mayor had better explain to Sami's family that this is likely to become an inter-national incident.'

'In that case, sir, we're likely to be holed up in the château for some time. If your extra security guards are available you won't need me. Might I take this last night off and join you at the château tomorrow? If you need an extra vehicle, the keys to my Land Rover are in the ignition. I'll take my horse.'

The Brigadier nodded and turned away. The Mayor caught Bruno's arm and asked, 'Are you riding all the way home?'

'No, just to Pamela's place; I know Fabiola's on duty tonight so I have to exercise the horses. Our human affairs come and go, but we still have to take care of the animals.'

'You and I need to talk about the Halévy bequest and the Desbordes farm,' the Mayor said. 'This Paris lawyer is coming down tomorrow, so he'll be here in time for lunch. He was very pleased that you'd tracked the place down. I've spoken to the Brigadier and he's prepared to spare you for the day.'

'You know my thinking about turning the Desbordes farm into some sort of country camp for the Scouts,' Bruno said. 'You can prepare something on that for the lawyer without me.

But that's in another commune. Do you know of any Desbordes link to St Denis itself?'

The members of Florence's computer club were helping the staff of the *Mairie*, the Mayor explained, hunting down the names of the Desbordes' cousins, in-laws, along with local scoutmasters and Protestant pastors.

'My money's on Florence's kids,' Bruno said. 'They'll be faster and won't try to charge overtime. But how do you think the Halévy family will react to this business of Sami as an Islamic militant? It can hardly make them feel better about St Denis.'

'I think we'd better warn the lawyer,' the Mayor replied. 'St Denis is a community that believes in the virtues of our *République*, a town that gave refuge to Jewish children and also tries to deal honourably with its Muslims, whatever the consequences. There's nothing else we can say.'

'And it happens to be true,' added Bruno.

11

Bruno felt a touch of nervousness as he led his horse down the bridle path that led through the woods to the paddock behind Pamela's house. He told himself that he was being ridiculous; they were old friends as well as lovers. And yet the word lovers seemed to Bruno to overstate the relationship, at least in the way that Pamela had defined it. She had once suggested, in a way that she had evidently assumed he would find agreeable and even flattering, that they were affectionate friends who on occasion shared their pleasures in bed. Bruno's immediate instinct had been to take offence, but he knew better than to surrender to instant reactions in dealing with the opposite sex.

Women, in Bruno's experience, usually thought before they spoke, while men seldom did. Women were more fluent in the language of feelings, emotions and relationships, and gave much more thought to them. Men lived and thought in two or at most three dimensions, while women were at home in a dozen or more. Bruno believed he could usually tell when a man was lying, but women were much harder to read, far more familiar with the many shades and nuances of truth.

So while he had taken Pamela's words at face value, he had understood her to be saying something more subtle: that there were some clear limits to their relationship, and that the intimacies they shared in her bedroom did not auto-matically transfer to the rest of her life. She had also made it clear that she had no intention of living with him or any man on a permanent basis, far less of setting up a joint home and starting a family. She would let him know when he was welcome in her bed, and he should understand that to take her body or her loyalty for granted would be unforgivable.

This had been more than acceptable to him in the past, but two elements had changed. Since Pamela's injury, she seemed less at ease with her life, less patient with him and with others. Perhaps that would change when she got back on horseback, as Fabiola kept reassuring him. Bruno was not so sure. Her mother's death had left Pamela financially independent and in future she would no longer need to rent out her *gîtes*, nor to do all the cleaning and gardening herself. She was already planning a holiday in Venice with an old school friend and was musing about a trip to the sun this winter, perhaps a safari in Africa. Pamela seemed to Bruno like a woman preparing to make some major changes in her life.

The other change had been in his own circumstances. The final breach with Isabelle had affected Bruno more power-fully than he had expected. He had always known their affair was doomed, however gloriously it had begun in that golden summer when they had fallen so tumultuously in love. Once she had made the decision to move to Paris to pursue what was becoming a brilliant police career, he knew there was no place in her baggage for a country policeman, even if he could have given up his home and garden, his horse and dog and his love of the Périgord to follow in her wake.

At first the blow of parting had been cushioned by the righteous anger he felt at learning that she had aborted their child without even telling him she was pregnant. But while the anger faded, the sense of loss remained, somehow deepened now that Isabelle had moved from Paris to The Hague for her new job with Eurojust, the European Union's judicial arm. She was no longer even in the same country.

Before he could start to feel sorry for himself, Bruno saw the trees thinning and the familiar broad and grassy ridge began to appear. Soon he'd be able to canter and then to gallop, the wind of his passage sweeping away these gloomy, self-absorbed reflections. What simple creatures we are, he thought, that we feel so much better and more alive through the simple sensation of speed. A horse might gallop at a fraction of the speed of a car or train, but the ride felt infinitely faster and more thrilling.

He found Pamela in her garden wielding secateurs and wearing an enormous straw hat. Tendrils of her reddish-bronze hair were loose around her neck and she smelt pleasantly of herbs and feminine warmth when he ducked beneath the rim of the hat to kiss her.

'I hope you can stay to dinner,' she said. 'I'm deluged with tomatoes, green peppers and courgettes but I'm not sure how best to serve them. With pasta, do you think?'

He shook his head. 'I'll make soup. Do you have any of Stéphane's *aillou*?' Bruno loved the mixture of *crème fraîche* and *fromage blanc*, to which Stéphane added garlic and chives, smeared atop vegetables that had been grilled with the merest hint of walnut oil. 'And if you have any of that *farine de blé* flour and some yeast, I'll make some bread. And we have the pâté we canned last winter. Open one of those and it makes a perfect supper.'

'I just picked some pears, so that's dinner arranged. We're on our own this evening since Fabiola is on duty. I'll finish in the garden and you take care of Hector and then make the bread and we can have a swim together before supper.' Bruno noticed a sparkle in Pamela's eyes that suggested that a swim was not all she had in mind.

'Do we have the pool to ourselves?' he asked, knowing that two of her *gîtes* were currently being rented by British families.

'Yes, they've gone to Sarlat for dinner and a concert. They won't be back until late.'

Taking off her hat, she came up to him and raised her lips to be kissed. She locked her hands behind his neck to hold him in place and kissed him very thoroughly indeed. Thinking that this woman always had the capacity to surprise him, and that this was not how he had been expecting the evening to begin, he responded with enthusiasm until she released him, murmuring, 'I'll go and pick the courgettes and you'd better take care of your horse.'

Once Hector was rubbed down and settled, Bruno washed his hands, took down the half-kilo bag of whole wheat flour and turned on the oven. He mixed the flour with a generous tablespoon of salt and put it into the oven to warm. Then he added a spoonful of brown sugar and a packet of dried yeast to about half a litre of hot water and put it to one side to work up its froth. He buttered a big baking tin and went off to take a quick shower.

By the time he returned in his swimming trunks, there were a good three centimetres of froth on the yeast liquid, but he stirred it well anyway. Then he brought out the warm flour, put it into a mixing bowl and little by little he began adding the yeast liquid as he stirred and mixed the dough. Once it had become a smooth ball he scattered some more flour on a wooden board and began the final pounding of the dough with his hands. He stretched it and folded it back over itself and formed it into a rough cylindrical shape that would fit the baking tin. Once in the tin, the dough was pressed down to leave no air pockets. He scattered more flour over the top, covered the dish with a cloth of moist muslin and left it by the oven to rise.

Bruno's summer soup was quickly made. He chopped two green peppers, peeled and sliced a cucumber and put them all into the blender with two cloves of garlic, two glasses of white wine and half a glass of olive oil. He poured boiling water over four tomatoes to loosen their skins, peeled them and squeezed out the pips and added the tomato flesh to the blender. Once liquidized, it went into a large tureen with some ice cubes and he put it into the fridge.

When he reached the pool, Pamela was wearing a filmy dressing gown of white linen that seemed to float around her. She laid a large soft rug on the grass and tossed onto it a couple of cushions from the chairs by the pool. She turned to look at him, poised to dive in.

'I'm surprised at you, Bruno, wearing trunks. Why on earth should you think you'll need them?' Pamela slid off the gown, the only garment she wore, and dived neatly into the water.

Wearing a towel around his waist, Bruno lifted the baked loaf out of its tin and tapped its underside to be sure it was properly done. He opened his nostrils to enjoy the heady scent of fresh bread. He left it on a wire rack to cool and began loading the tray with pâté and cheese, plates and glasses. He served his summer soup, now well chilled, in tall glasses, and opened a bottle of a new discovery, Château Briand, a charming Bergerac Sec white wine made by the daughter of the wine merchant Hubert de Montignac, whose *cave* was one of the treasures of St Denis. With the tray loaded, he carried it out to the small table at the side of the pool, poured out a glass and took it to Pamela. She was lying face-down on the rug, her chin propped in her hands, smiling lazily as she watched him approach.

'I love it when you cook for me,' she said. 'And in the nicest possible way you've given me quite an appetite. I can smell the bread from here and it's always best when it's warm.' She had draped the dressing gown around herself in a way that revealed almost as much as it concealed.

Bruno took her a glass of the white wine and kissed her shoulder, where the gown had slipped away. In the pool house, he plugged in the electric hotplate, washed and sliced the courgettes she had picked. He used his finger to coat them thinly with the walnut oil. By the time he returned from the kitchen with a bottle of mineral water and the bread they had started to sizzle and he turned them.

Pamela had taken the cushions from the sun chairs and piled them into a heap so they could lounge back as they enjoyed their picnic. She pulled the fresh loaf apart, plunged her nose close to catch the scent, then dipped a crust into the bowl of *aillou* and washed it down with a mouthful of the chilled soup.

'It feels wonderfully decadent to feed so many appetites at

once; eating a picnic with my fingers, a glass of fine wine and making love in the open air,' she said, and patted the cushions for Bruno to lie down beside her. 'It reminds me of all the fantasies I had when I decided to move to France.'

'I'm glad I could help you bring them to life,' he said, smiling as he lay down.

'A good thing you happened to be around,' she replied, and kissed his chest. 'For some reason I was feeling amazingly romantic this afternoon. If the postman had turned up, I might have leaped on him.'

'I know your postman,' he said. 'He's on the verge of retirement and he's only got three teeth.'

'That goes to show just how sexy I felt. But then Prince Charming arrived, just in the nick of time.'

He put down before her the plate of lightly charred courgettes and Pamela proceeded to feed him, putting a small dab of *aillou* on each slice and then holding it to his lips before taking one in her turn. She handed him his wine glass and said, 'Now I've got your complete attention I want to talk about Fabiola.'

Bruno spluttered and some of his soup went down the wrong way. When he had recovered, he raised his eyebrows and prepared to listen, knowing there was no escape.

'She finally told me what happened when she went to Paris. She likes Gilles a lot, really a lot, and went up to see him quite determined to take him to bed. But at the last moment she couldn't. He was very sweet and patient, she said, and they cuddled and slept together. But there was no consummation.'

'How very sad for them both,' said Bruno, trying to damp down the mental image her words evoked. 'Did she say why?'

'She just said that she had to work out something from her past. I asked if she meant she was still in love with someone else, but she shrugged in that way of hers and changed the subject. I always got the impression of a doomed love affair hanging over her, perhaps a married man who refused to leave his family.'

That could be it, thought Bruno. But Fabiola never talked about her private life, nor much about her past.

'It could be something else,' he said, thinking aloud. 'You know how much time Fabiola spends at that shelter for abused wives in Bergerac. Maybe she'd been badly treated or beaten up herself.'

Pamela shrugged. 'Who knows? When I first got to know her I even wondered if she was gay. Anyway, you know Fabiola; she's a very private woman. I asked if she had tried seeing somebody for counselling, or a good psychologist, but you know what doctors are like when it comes to treating themselves. She said she'd tried talking with her gynaecology professor, whom she admired, but it hadn't done much good. Apparently she came from the Périgord and planned to return when she retired. That was one reason Fabiola came here.'

Bruno shook his head, feeling concerned for his friend but without enough knowledge to do anything. But this could not be allowed to rest there. Bruno knew his own nature; if there was a problem, he'd always try to resolve it. Fabiola had once told him he always assumed there was a solution to any problem, but as a doctor she knew that some cases were hopeless. Perhaps she'd been talking of herself? He'd have to think of a way to help. But he must start by finding out what had gone wrong. Whatever the ordeal, people could often recover. He knew that from his time in the Bosnian war.

'You're miles away,' Pamela said, breaking into his thoughts. 'What are you thinking?'

'Sorry.' He reached out to put his hand on hers. 'I was wondering how we might persuade Fabiola to try again to find someone who might help her.'

'No, you weren't,' she said gently. 'You had that soft look on your face that you get when you're remembering something.'

He smiled at her, thinking how well this woman knew him. 'You're right. I was recalling some women we knew in Bosnia who had been forced into being sex slaves for Serb troops. But some of them seemed pretty resilient, as if they were determined to recover. Knowing Fabiola, whatever happened to her I'd have thought she'd be the same.'

Pamela shook her head. 'The problem is that we don't really know what happened to her. At least she's started to talk to me about it. And she's not running away from Gilles. Fabiola still wants to make that relationship work, and I think we should do whatever we can to help. After all, Gilles is your friend. You brought him down here and introduced them. So in a way, you're responsible. And we both love Fabiola so we have to help her.'

'I agree,' Bruno said. 'If she lets us.'

12

Since it was one of Bruno's varied duties to manage the traffic problems of St Denis, the Rue de la Libération was one of the few aspects of his job that caused him misery. Sometimes he thought it should never have been built. It led from the roundabout in the central square along a narrow street that finally opened out into the main road to Les Eyzies. It was listed as a two-lane road, but there wasn't really enough room for a truck and a car to pass. The pavements were too cramped for safety, barely wide enough for one person, let alone two. On one side were tall, narrow houses built in the nineteenth century and shoehorned into the narrow space between the road and a steep hill that blocked any light from the rear windows. On the other side of the street slightly newer buildings were squeezed into the equally tight space between the road and the twelve-metre vertical drop down to the quayside and the river.

The result was a town planner's nightmare. Without demolishing the houses on one side or the other, there was no way to widen the narrow road. St Denis could not afford to demolish the houses, which would mean paying compensation to the owners. And yet the Rue de la Libération, once a healthy commercial thoroughfare with shops and restaurants at street level, was slowly dying as pedestrians shunned the narrow pavements and busy traffic. Shopfronts were empty or boarded up. The dry cleaner had gone, and so had the estate agent, once he realized there was too little room for the few passers-by to study the photos of houses for sale in his windows.

It was into one of these vacant shopfronts that Bruno and the Mayor now entered after taking their early coffee and croissants at Fauquet's café. The two men began to climb the narrow stairs that led to small rental apartments on the upper floors. Cheaply modernized a generation ago, the apartments contained one small bedroom, a living room with a kitchen corner and a tiny shower room with a toilet. They were now used for unemployed families or single parents whose rents were subsidized.

Bruno led the way to the empty attic on the top floor which had neither shower room nor kitchen, and forced open the reluctant door. The bulb did not work when he flicked the switch and the skylight was too small and grimy to help. He turned on his torch and shone the beam around the dirty floor to pick out two broken chairs and a rusted pot-belly stove. A dusty wooden box held ancient crockery, most of it cracked.

'I'm pretty sure this must be the place,' said the Mayor, breathing heavily after the steep stairs. Tax records had shown that Madame Poldereau, the widowed mother of Sylvie Desbordes, lived here until her death in 1944. Once Bruno had supplied the name of Desbordes for the owner of the farm, the Mayor himself had tracked down a wedding certificate for the Desbordes, with Madame Poldereau listed as witness and mother of the bride.

'We don't know why she didn't move into the farm with her

daughter; there'll be a story behind that, maybe she didn't get on with her son-in-law,' the Mayor said.

'Halévy's partner told me the children had stayed in a small town for a while before moving to the farm,' Bruno said. 'And he specified St Denis.'

'She was one of the few Protestants in town, so if you're right about the Protestant connection this is where they probably stayed. But I don't know how we could prove it.'

'What did they do for water?' Bruno asked, curious.

Even the apartments below had no kitchens in those days and no bathrooms, the Mayor explained. There had been a standpipe in that tiny yard at the back and a communal latrine. At night they would use chamber pots and take them down to empty every day.

Bruno went out to the hallway, unscrewed the light bulb on the landing and used it to replace the broken one in the attic, but the extra light revealed little more. He pushed open the door that led to the second room but it seemed empty except for dust and mouse droppings. On the walls were remnants of old wallpaper, a floral pattern of faded roses against a grey background. Some strips of it hung down like ribbons. Maybe a good forensic crew could pick up some finger-prints, Bruno thought, but he had none of Halévy's prints for comparison.

He played the torch around the room at waist height and below, wondering if there might be some childish scrawls, but saw nothing until by the door frame he stopped and bent down to peer more closely. Lifting one of the hanging strips of wall-paper he brought the torch closer and a childhood memory came back of his cousins' house in Bergerac, a small mob of kids being lined up against the door frame while a grown-up stood there with a ruler and pencil.

'What's that?' the Mayor asked, coming across the room to join him.

'Not sure, but I think this could be where they stayed.' Bruno pointed to the two short parallel lines drawn on the paper. One was about twenty centimetres higher than the other. 'Remember when you were a kid and you tried to measure your height against the wall?'

Under the glare of Bruno's torch, some faded letters could almost be made out. Beside the higher line the wallpaper had been torn, but something remained that might have been the letter D and beside the lower was written Mar and perhaps an i.

'Marie,' said the Mayor, squinting through his spectacles. 'It's the wrong place.'

'The lawyer told me she used the name Marie. It was close to her real name, Maya,' said Bruno. 'I think this must be the place.'

He tried to visualize the scene; two Parisian children and an old woman, a stranger who probably spoke patois rather than the classic French the children could understand. All three of them cooped up here together for however long it took to arrange their move to the Desbordes farm. The children must have been frightened, hardly understanding what was happening to them or who was this stranger trying to help them and give them shelter. In Paris, they would have known kitchens, bathrooms, tucked into bed each night by a loving mother. Bruno shook his head at the thought of the Halévy children, who must have felt like fragile leaves tossed here and there by the great storm of war. The old grandmother, trying to divert them while keeping them hidden away indoors, had thought of measuring them and comparing their heights.

'We have the place, both places,' Bruno said. 'What we need now is a plan to turn this into something the Halévy executors will support.'

'This reminds me a bit of the Anne Frank house in Amsterdam,' the Mayor replied. 'Obviously we can preserve these rooms, bring in some furniture from the period, try to make it look as it was when the children were here.'

'That makes sense,' Bruno agreed. 'But I'm not sure we'll persuade many tourists to climb those narrow stairs just to see some attic rooms. Could we turn the whole house into a museum, maybe about St Denis during the war, something to explain who the children were and why they were in hiding?'

'If we can get funding from the bequest to do that, we could probably raise some more money elsewhere. The Ministry of Education would be the place to start,' said the Mayor. 'We could mount an exhibition on the Resistance here in the Périgord.'

'Why not think of something more ambitious that could take in the other houses in this row?'

'You mean a real town museum, the history of St Denis as well as the wartime and the children?' said the Mayor, a note of excitement in his voice as he pondered the potential of such a project.

'If we plan this carefully, we might be able to use this idea to solve the problem of this street,' Bruno said. 'I've always thought we'd have to demolish these houses one day and widen the road, but there's another solution. What if we removed the ground-floor shops – they're all empty anyway – and put in stone pillars to support the upper floors? Then we could use the ground floor for a much wider pavement, a kind of covered pedestrian precinct.'

'There are six houses in this row. That would be a big museum.' The Mayor was looking worried. 'Can we justify that?'

'Let's get an architect to draw up some ideas and then run it past the local businessmen and see what they think. A museum like that would need a café and a gift shop. Maybe they could think of other commercial possibilities. At least it gives us a real project to propose to the Halévy trustees.'

'We could call it the Halévy Museum,' said the Mayor. 'They'd like that.'

'We'd need to emphasize that we want to use it as an educational centre. When I was researching the Halévy history I certainly learned about things I'd never known before,' said Bruno. He explained that there could be one room on the history of the Jewish Scouts and their work in protecting children and another exhibit on their role in the Resistance with the fighting unit they formed. There could be another room on the role of the Protestant pastors, he suggested, and there would still be space for the town's own museum of St Denis. There could even be a small cinema to show educational videos.

The Mayor nodded, but then he frowned. 'But what do we do with the social housing people? We've got nearly twenty families in these houses. We'd need to find alternative accommodation and there's no money for that.'

'You're right, but let's lay out the problem to the trustees and say here is our idea for a really ambitious project but we'd like their thoughts on how we tackle the various challenges it throws up,' said Bruno. 'I get the impression that the trustees want to do something serious and impressive, so we need to propose something that can catch their imagination. And it would do a lot of good for St Denis.'

'But where do we rehouse those families?' the Mayor persisted.

'You've been complaining for years about the waste of that old cooperage off the Rue Gambetta,' Bruno said. It was a fine stone building, with a big courtyard and that long workshop where they assembled the barrels. It had stood empty for years, since long before Bruno's arrival. Properly converted, he suggested, it could house twenty families, and in much better conditions than these cramped apartments.

'Get an architect to come up with some sketches and we can call it *Résidences Halévy*. It's a historic building so there'll be restoration grants we can apply for. Let's think big. We can always scale it down later if we have to.'

'Every time you suggest something, Bruno, it raises the costs even higher. You know how tough things are with the budgets these days.'

Bruno knew there were times when it was best to give the Mayor the last word, and this was one of them. Then at the landing, the Mayor stopped and turned to face him.

'A lot of this is going to depend on the amount of money available under Halévy's will,' he said. 'We couldn't hope to do this from our own resources. So you're going to have to make sure we make a very persuasive presentation to those trustees.'

Bruno was not despondent. He'd been thinking about the presentation and wondering whether some glossily professional drawings by an architect might be too predictable. The key to this whole project was the children in the attic and building a fitting memorial to them and the people who sheltered them. That was why he would focus on the educational aspect of the museum, and why he was determined to involve the young people of St Denis.

Thanks to Florence, the town's *collège* students knew computers, and they could come up with some plans for the museum and maybe also for the farm. Why not get Florence and the students to make part of the presentation, rather than leave it in the hands of the Mayor and some local architect more accustomed to designing house restorations and super-markets?

As he headed for the airport to collect the lawyer from Paris, Bruno knew his Mayor's wily political brain would be at work, balancing votes and budgets. The Mayor would see the advantage of using the schoolchildren of today's St Denis to pay homage to the children of the war years. And doubtless he was also thinking about his own legacy as Mayor. From the Palace of Versailles to President Mitterrand's giant new Arc at the end of the Champs Elysées in Paris, French kings and presidents had sought to build great monuments that would carry their names down the centuries. A project like this, properly handled, could do the same for the Mayor of St Denis.

13

Two people descended from the small turboprop aircraft that landed at Périgueux airport from Paris. Bruno had expected the first, a slim young man wearing an elegant dark suit, white shirt and sober tie. He carried one of the bulky briefcases that lawyers used. The second, an attractive young woman in a classically cut suit in burgundy with glossy dark hair spilling artfully from the loose bun atop her head, surprised him. She strode confidently forward to embrace him, announcing in almost perfect Parisian French, 'Bruno, I've heard so much about you from Isabelle. She said to give you her love.'

Bruno had little choice but to kiss her cheeks in return and welcome her to the Périgord. He then turned to shake the lawyer's hand and introduce Maître Kaufman to the woman. She was perhaps in her mid-thirties. Her face seemed slightly familiar, although he was sure he'd never met her. Perhaps she'd been in one of the photos Isabelle had shown him on her phone of her life in Paris.

'Yacov and I met on the plane,' she said, waving vaguely at the lawyer. 'I'm Nancy Sutton, from the American Embassy. I think the Brigadier may have told you to expect me.'

That was how she knew Isabelle, Bruno realized, trying to gather his wits. He presumed she would have some kind of security liaison role at the Embassy. Women in that world would be rare enough to know one another. He wondered just how much Isabelle had told the American.

'As one of the legal attachés, Mademoiselle Sutton is well known in judicial circles in Paris,' Kaufman said. 'I understand she has an appointment in Périgueux with the *Procureur de la République*.'

The *Procureur* was the chief legal officer for the *Département*. That suggested to Bruno that she was probably intending to file, or at least to discuss an extradition warrant for Sami. If the American was an Embassy lawyer, then she probably knew Isabelle through her new job with Eurojust. It had meant an important promotion for Isabelle, while neatly extracting her from the staff of the disgraced Minister of the Interior. Untouched by the scandal that had erupted around the Minister, the high-flying career which was Isabelle's top priority had been preserved. There had been a time when Bruno had hoped he would be Isabelle's priority, but now he knew better.

'There was supposed to be a cab waiting for me,' Nancy said, as one of the airport staff unloaded one small and one large suitcase from the hold of the plane. Kaufman took the smaller case.

'Since there's no taxi here, perhaps we can give you a lift, Mademoiselle,' said Bruno, taking the larger case and leading the way to the Mayor's car. He'd parked as close as he could get to the runway, his blue flashing light perched on the car's roof. The Mayor had said that neither Bruno's police van nor his elderly Land Rover would be suitable to collect the Parisian lawyer.

'Call me Nancy,' she said, and took the front passenger seat, although Kaufman was already holding one of the rear doors open for her. Bruno grunted at the weight of her suitcase as he loaded it into the back of the Mayor's Citroën.

'Perhaps you could take my case on to my hotel in St Denis,' she called. Bruno and Kaufman exchanged glances; this was a woman who knew how to get her own way. 'I'm booked into Le Manoir and I'm picking up a rental car in Périgueux.'

'So you know Isabelle from The Hague?' Bruno said, making conversation as he drove into town. He could not identify her scent, but it was pleasant, slightly stimulating and discreet in the way that Frenchwomen prefer, knowing that a hint of fragrance was far more enticing than the crude impact of an overpowering perfume.

'I saw her there recently, but we really got to know each other in Paris,' she replied. 'Isabelle said she'd told you about our group of women in this business who meet informally for dinner together every month. And I visited her in hospital when she was wounded. That's when she told me about you.'

Bruno was confused. Isabelle had been talking of a band of women in the security service. Was Nancy Sutton a lawyer or a spook? Or perhaps both? And what exactly had Isabelle told Nancy about her former lover deep in the French countryside?

'And what brings you to our Périgord?' he asked.

'You know perfectly well what brings me,' she replied, keeping her eyes on the road but somehow signalling to Bruno that she did not want to speak openly with Yacov Kaufman in the rear seat. 'That engineering matter.' She turned in her seat to address the lawyer. 'I know from our conversation on the plane that you're here about a bequest. But why is a policeman meeting you?'

'The bequest relates to someone in our commune, so Maître Kaufman has an appointment at the *Mairie*,' Bruno said smoothly. 'The Mayor asked me to meet him as a courtesy. This is the Mayor's own car. He'd have come himself but he has a meeting of the regional council.'

'I gather your Mayor is quite well connected in Paris,' Nancy said. 'Didn't he once work for Chirac?'

She was well informed, Bruno thought, or she had done some efficient research. Maybe Isabelle had told her; it was the sort of detail that Isabelle had always made a point of knowing. 'Yes, when Chirac was Mayor of Paris, before he was elected President,' he said, slowing the car and steering it between imposing iron gates into a gravel courtyard. He stopped at the base of the steps that led into a large stone building flanked by tall pillars, 'Our Mayor's political background has certainly helped us in St Denis. And here you are, Mademoiselle Sutton, at the office of the *Procureur*.'

He was about to climb out of his seat to open her door, but Kaufman had slipped out from the back seat and beaten him to it.

'Thank you, Bruno,' she said, leaning across the seat to peck him on the cheek. 'I'll hope to see you for a longer chat in St Denis later today.' She swivelled her legs with practised grace to leave the car, shook Kaufman's hand as she thanked him, and strode up the steps as if leading a delegation.

'An interesting woman,' said Kaufman, taking her seat in the front of the car. 'A lawyer, a temporary diplomat, and career FBI.'

'How do you know that?' Bruno asked, steering back into the tree-lined avenue, the Cours de Turenne.

'We do a lot of work for the Israeli Embassy,' Kaufman replied. 'They speak of her with respect. What's this engineering business that brings her here? It doesn't sound like her usual work.'

'That's all I know,' said Bruno, thinking he had said quite enough. 'Business-related, I imagine. What's her usual work?'

'I told you, she's FBI, high-level liaison on law enforcement and security issues with the French government, Interior Ministry, Justice and DST.'

The *Direction de Surveillance du Territoire* was more counter-espionage than law enforcement, Bruno reflected. No wonder she knew Isabelle and the Brigadier.

'Not your field of the law, then?' he asked Kaufman, his tone light.

'Not really. I hear you have some good news for me on the Halévy matter.'

'That's what the Mayor wants to discuss with you. We've found the house in St Denis where the two children first stayed, and the farm where they spent most of their time.'

'Yes, Maya will be pleased. I think the prospect of seeing those places again might tempt her over here.'

'And she lives in Israel?'

'She moved there with David after the war, but he came back to Paris for his medical studies and remained here to make his career. She stayed in Tel Aviv and built up her business.'

Once she left university, Kaufman explained, Maya Halévy had taken a job in the Ministry of Education, researching the textbooks that the infant state of Israel wanted to have translated into Hebrew for use in schools. As a native French-speaker, she had looked first at French books, but the Ministry had decided to use American ones. Believing this was a mistake, she resigned, married an army officer and went into business for herself, translating and publishing French textbooks on mathematics, and then German books on the sciences and electronics for the Israeli military. She then went into partnership with an English publisher of scientific journals, launched her own electronic versions, and by the time her husband had retired as a General she had become wealthy enough to invest in the first Israeli start-up companies. Now widowed, she had become one of the country's leading venture capitalists, still active in business despite her age.

'She's also my grandmother,' Kaufman concluded. 'So I also want to see these places in St Denis. My mother would never have been born without them.'

'That means David must have been your great-uncle,' Bruno said as he turned off from the old *Route Nationale* for the road that led to St Denis. 'And I gather he never married.'

'No, but he was very kind to me and my mother when she came here from Israel. She met my father when they were both working on a kibbutz. They fell in love, got married, and she came back with him to France and I grew up here. So David became my honorary grandfather.'

'What kind of law do you specialize in?' Bruno asked.

'Patents. I'm just doing this business of the bequest for the family.'

'It's a strange bequest. I never heard of anything like it. I didn't even know you could do something like that under French inheritance law.'

'You can't, but the money in question is not David's, at least not under French law. His own property has to go to the family but the bequest money would come from a family trust. Since David used his savings to back my grandmother when she was starting out, she always gave him a lot of say in what the trust does. It's complicated, but one of the trust's purposes is education and another is Franco-Israeli friendship, so that was why the bequest was set up the way it was. It was Grandmother's idea as much as David's. She always reckoned it was no good to just give money, you had to prompt people to do something on their own in return.'

'That's why you've challenged us in St Denis to come up with a plan?'

'Exactly; it means you get to feel ownership in the whole project.'

'One thing still baffles me about all this,' Bruno said. 'Why did nothing about the Halévy children and St Denis emerge until now? You'd have thought people would have been proud of it, after the war, but nobody seems to have heard of these children being sheltered. And why did David and Maya never refer to it before, never come to visit the town or make inquiries about the family that looked after them?'

'I don't know,' Kaufman replied. 'I've asked myself the same question and I asked Grandmother, but she just changed the subject. Until David died, I'd never heard of St Denis and never knew how they survived the war. They just said that thanks to the Boy Scouts, they were able to hide in the countryside. One thing David always insisted was that all the children in the family had to join the *Eclaireurs*.'

'Are you still involved with them?'

'Yes, I'm a scoutmaster.' There was a note of pride in Kaufman's voice.

'You mean you wear khaki shorts and take kids on camping trips?' Bruno asked, grinning.

'It did me a lot of good when I was a boy and I still enjoy it. We did a week walking in the Ardennes this summer, and last year it was the Alps. Next year we're going to Israel and do some hiking with Israeli Scouts, which I did when I was thirteen. It stood me in good stead when I did my military service.'

'You mean in Israel?' Military service had been phased out in France by the time Kaufman would have been old enough.

'Yes, it's a family tradition. David and Grandmother would never have spoken to me again if I'd ducked it. I was in the navy on patrol boats but they taught me sailing and navigation, a bit of scuba diving, Frankly, I rather enjoyed it.'

'Are you still in the reserves?'

'Two weeks a year for another eight years, and they can call me back any time in an emergency.'

Bruno pulled up in the car park in front of the *Mairie* and checked his watch. They had made good time, in spite of the detour to drop off Nancy. Kaufman had twenty minutes before his appointment with the Mayor. He offered their visitor a coffee in Fauquet's café but he declined, saying he'd seen his hotel down the street. It was the Hôtel St Denis, a comfortable but considerably more modest place than the Manoir where Nancy was staying. Kaufman said he'd walk there, check in, unpack and be back at the *Mairie* on time. Bruno knew that Kaufman intended to stay overnight; it suggested his inquiries would be thorough.

Bruno nodded, gave him his small suitcase, and then darted into his office in the *Mairie* to start a computer search for information on Maya Halévy and her venture capital business. Google gave him an article on Israeli entrepreneurs on *Les Echos*, another in *Capital* on Israeli start-up companies and yet another in *L'Expansion* on Israeli companies that were listed on the American Nasdaq market. He jotted down the market capitalizations for the companies listed in her name, totted up the sum and whistled. Her U.S.-listed companies alone were valued at close to eighty million dollars, but he could find nothing on Google.fr about the family trust. There was no time to try to fight his way through the English version of the search engine, but he was able to brief the Mayor and return his car keys before Kaufman trotted up the old stone steps for his appointment.

The Mayor did the talking, first over coffee in his office and then upstairs in the attic room where the children had briefly stayed and he pointed proudly to the two lines that had marked the children's height. Kaufman took endless photos on his mobile phone. Bruno had his Land Rover ready for the trip out to the ruined farmhouse, but first the Mayor had arranged lunch at Ivan's bistro. He'd invited Florence to join them to talk about her computer club and the way the schoolchildren of St Denis would become an integral part of the Halévy project.

At the Mayor's suggestion, they all chose Ivan's menu of the day. A tureen of vegetable soup appeared, plus a half-litre of his house red and another of house white. As always in the dying days of summer, the soup mainly consisted of tomatoes, based on a stock from duck bones. Whether or not Ivan had been told that Kaufman might not eat pork, the next course was a fish terrine, avoiding the usual *charcuterie*. By the time they reached the *blanquette de lapin*, Kaufman was finishing his second glass of wine and talking enthusiastically with Florence about the benefits of getting the children to help repair the computers she salvaged from the local garbage centre. Bruno and the Mayor exchanged satisfied glances; it was going well.

'Let me tell you something that impresses me here,' said Kaufman, sitting back as Ivan removed his empty plate and replaced it with his latest dessert, peaches marinated overnight in white wine with a little fresh thyme.

'The food,' said Florence, laughing. Kaufman grinned back, evidently taken with her.

'Not just that. I'd been expecting a slick power-point presentation from some local marketing firm, architect's sketches, a budget with grandiose forecasts about future sponsorship income. I thought I'd be meeting a hastily convened committee with a bank manager and a local rabbi.'

'Maybe I should have thought of that,' said the Mayor, with a slightly embarrassed shrug.

'I don't think so,' Kaufman replied. 'I think I get a better sense of St Denis from meeting the Mayor, the village policeman and the teacher than I would from some high-powered committee whipped together by professional fund-raisers. And given what you've found already about David and Maya, you're doing fine on your own.'

After coffee, and Kaufman's stunned expression as Ivan gave the Mayor some change from a fifty-euro note for the four lunches, Florence went back to the *collège* and the three men set out in Bruno's Land Rover for the Desbordes farm. It was a slightly cooler day, with some high cirrus clouds and occasional flurries of wind that suggested rain to come in the night. Bruno looked across to the west but saw no sign of a storm. With a dubious look at the lawyer's elegant moccasins, he lent Kaufman a pair of rubber boots and went on ahead with a machete to clear the worst of the undergrowth on the track to the farm.

Kaufman said nothing as he explored the dilapidated building and the barn. He tried the rusted pump, poked around what had been the outhouse and took out his phone to take more photos. They climbed to the top of the slope above the farm and looked down at the land stretching down to the stream at the bottom of the valley.

'David once said something about swimming here,' he said. 'Could we go down and take a look?'

At a spot where two brooks tumbling from each hillside fell into the larger stream, the banks had been eroded to form a welcoming pool. Fringed on the far side by reeds, the near bank was dominated by a large, flat-topped boulder that felt warm to the hand. It sloped down to the pool. Bruno broke off a weedy sapling and from the boulder's edge he poked it down to test the depth of the water.

'Over a metre,' he reported. 'This must be the place David remembered.' He turned and saw Kaufman sitting on the rock, taking off his rubber boots and trousers, obviously intent on taking a dip.

'I've got a towel in my sports bag, in the back of the Rover,' Bruno said.

'I'm too old for this lark. I'll get the towel,' said the Mayor, and began trudging back up the slope.

Like two schoolboys just released from school, Kaufman and Bruno stripped to the buff and slid whooping into the water, striking out for the far side to get over the shock of the water's initial chill. After a moment, it felt cool and refreshing, with a silken smoothness on the skin that only river water gives.

'If ever I become famous enough to have an entry in *Qui est Qui?* I'll list as my main recreation swimming in rivers,' said Kaufman as his head emerged from the water. 'There's nothing like it.'

Dragonflies were humming along the edge of the reeds and butterflies fluttered over the long grass on the hill that led up the farm. A kingfisher darted between the trees downstream in a fleeting blaze of colour. As Bruno felt for the river bed with his feet, he was conscious of something exploring his toes with the gentlest of nibbles. There would be crayfish here; the water was pure and there was no sign that humans had come to this spot in years.

'Next time I come, I'll bring a bottle of wine and a girl,' said Kaufman. He began to breaststroke slowly down toward the trees where the stream narrowed again.

Bruno headed upriver to where the stream fell over a boulder in a shallow waterfall, barely half a metre in height, but enough for him to duck beneath its flow and feel the water showering onto his head and shoulders. There was no bottom beneath his feet and he dived down to encounter another boulder, eroded over the years by the tumbling water to a smooth flatness. Bruno turned onto his back and let the current drift him downstream, closed his eyes and told himself this was a perfect pool. If this didn't convince Kaufman of the merits of St Denis's proposal for the bequest, nothing would.

He heard the sound of voices and rolled over to see the

Mayor sitting at the pool's edge, his shoes off and his trousers rolled up and feet dabbling in the water. Kaufman was beside him, still naked, and using Bruno's towel on his thick dark hair.

'You really think we could restore this house and the barn for less than a hundred thousand?' Kaufman asked.

'The barn roof is sound and all the walls are in good shape,' the Mayor replied. 'You'd need a new roof on the house, doors and windows, a big septic tank. We'd need to clean out that well and test the water flow and depth. The biggest unknown is going to be the cost of running electricity out here, but you wouldn't need to pay those brigands at *Electricité de France*. We've got our own works department, our own heavy equipment. We could do it for cost or maybe you could rig a solar power system. Then it's a just matter of installing bunk beds in the barn and a basic kitchen, and there you are, Camp David. Or maybe Camp Maya for the Girl Guides.'

'Camp David,' Kaufman repeated, rolling the words, evidently enjoying the sound of it. 'And all this land we can see from here is part of the farm. We could pitch twenty, thirty tents on that flat land down toward the stream.'

Bruno was uncomfortably aware that Kaufman and his family trust would not need St Denis if all they wanted to do was to turn this old farm into a camp and hostel for Boy Scouts. They could buy and restore the place themselves and let the *Eclaireurs Israélites* run the place in David's memory. It would be a pleasant tribute to the old boy but it wouldn't do anything for St Denis. He held his tongue; the Mayor knew what he was doing. Kaufman tossed him the towel as Bruno climbed out of the water.

'It seems a pity to leave this place,' Kaufman said as they headed up the slope towards the Land Rover.

'You could come back tomorrow,' Bruno said, hoping to get a sense of Kaufman's plans for the following day.

Kaufman nodded amiably but said nothing until they climbed into the car, and said, 'And now perhaps you'll let me buy you two gentlemen a drink before I settle down with my laptop and catch up with the work I should have been doing in Paris.'

14

Bruno couldn't help but be impressed by the speed with which the French state had organized almost overnight a secure centre for the medical tribunal, Sami and his family and the security guards. As he reported in to the château, removal vans, newly emptied, were pulling away and one armed sentry at the gatehouse watched him while another checked his ID against a list. In the courtyard, a sergeant from the catering corps was ticking off cases of plates, glasses and cutlery. Bruno was steered to another sergeant, who checked his ID again, ticked his name on a list, and told him he'd been assigned a bed in one of the side buildings that had been designated as the dormitory for the guards. He'd find a locker at the foot of his bed, with a key in the lock, and he'd be responsible if it was lost.

A harassed-looking captain wearing badges for the army medical service led him to a grand reception room with a painted ceiling that featured plump cupids against a background of light blue. The room had been hurriedly fitted out as an office with trestle tables and folding chairs. A middle-aged woman in civilian clothes was ignoring two ringing phones and hovering nervously over a signals technician who was trying to link the room's several computers to a large printer.

She gave Bruno's police uniform a dismissive glance when he asked for the Brigadier and was told to wait. She pointed vaguely at a row of chairs where a tall and fit-looking man of about Bruno's age was already sitting. He was concentrating on his mobile phone, thumbs poised as if about to send a text. He was wearing a suit of grey corduroy, an open-necked white shirt and desert boots and his head was shaven. Bruno took an adjoining chair and introduced himself.

'Deutz,' said the man with a quick smile. He had a craggy face, hard blue eyes and a bone-crushing handshake in which he did not seem to put any effort. 'Are you the cop from St Denis who knows this young man Sami Belloumi?'

'That's me,' Bruno replied. 'I know you're a psychologist with the prison service and an expert on Muslims, but that's about all.'

'I think they called me in because they can,' Deutz said, with an engaging grin. 'I work for the state, so I couldn't say no. But it sounds a fascinating case. I dropped everything to get here as soon as I could.' He paused. 'I shouldn't have said that about him being a case. He's a human being, like the rest of us. I'll need to talk to you and other people who knew him growing up.'

Bruno felt reassured. 'Do you have much experience with autism?'

'Enough to know the word doesn't tell us very much. It's a whole spectrum of issues that affect people, can even enhance some things. How about you?'

'Almost nothing. I just know Sami, at least I used to, even though I knew nothing of what he'd gone through before he came to France.' Bruno explained briefly Sami's ordeal when his village had been attacked back in Algeria. Deutz's eyes widened and he whistled softly, shaking his head.

'I liked him,' Bruno went on. 'There didn't seem to be anything unpleasant about the boy even though we couldn't really communicate much. He never spoke a lot. I've no idea what happened to him since he left France.'

'That childhood trauma is probably the key to it all, I think, intensified by what happened to him in Afghanistan and perhaps the overall context of the Islamic shock.'

'How do you mean?'

'I don't think we've understood yet what a series of shocks and traumas the Islamic world has been going through,' Deutz began, and embarked on what Bruno quickly suspected was a well-honed lecture. Across Africa, the Middle East and Asia different communities and traditions of Islam were going through their version of the Renaissance, rethinking their traditional attitudes to the world around them, and at the same time through their equivalent of the Christian Reformation, rethinking and arguing about the nature of their religion. 'Simultaneously they were going through the Enlightenment and the industrial revolution, and now they're being hit with the information revolution and probably the feminist revolution as well,' he went on.

'Remember it took Western civilization six centuries to digest all that, and we went through civil wars, religious wars, class wars, genocides and revolutions in the process. Arabs and Muslims are reeling with culture shock, psychological trauma and wars, all at the same time. And we haven't done much to help those who live in the West to feel settled here or comfortable with our own culture.'

Bruno nodded, interested and impressed by Deutz's way of voicing some complex ideas. It made a kind of sense. But even while Bruno shared the instinctive French respect for intellectuals he didn't see how it helped understand someone like Sami.

'Let me see if I can get us past this dragon lady and in to see the Brigadier.' Bruno pulled out his special mobile phone and texted him: 'Waiting outside your office with Deutz, Bruno.'

Bruno turned back to Deutz. 'The Brigadier gave me your report on jihadi recruitment in prisons,' he said. 'I had no idea it was so widespread, nor so well-organized.'

'Nor did I when I started that survey. Did you know . . .' Deutz was saying when a pair of double doors opened and the Brigadier beckoned them into the large room beyond. This ceiling had even more cupids circling a naked woman who was lounging on a bed of flowers. Heavy curtains of red brocade hung at the long windows that looked onto parkland. Other than the Brigadier's laptop, the only element in the room older than the eighteenth century was a spindly modern table lamp atop the ornate desk.

'Welcome and thanks for joining us,' the Brigadier said briskly. 'Bruno, I'd like you to take Doctor Deutz to meet Sami in the family rooms. They have to get acquainted and he'll probably respond better if you're there. The army caterers have promised to have some kind of meal for us all at eight, which gives you a couple of hours. The other two tribunal members should get here tomorrow. I've got a car meeting their train at Périgueux. Everything has been speeded up by the American pressure.'

'I met Mademoiselle Sutton from the Embassy this morning

when she landed at Périgueux. She said she had appointments with the *Procureur* and with you.'

'I saw her this afternoon. She's a tough professional and it's her job to get Sami into American hands. She went through West Point before taking a law degree and joining the FBI, so she's military-trained. She's also well-connected. One of her uncles is a Congressman. Her father retired as a general and now sits on the President's intelligence advisory board. Bear all that in mind and try to stay out of her way.'

'Has Sami been charged with anything yet?' Bruno asked.

'Not so far. There's still no evidence linking him directly to any of the French deaths in Afghanistan. The *Procureur* has a couple of holding charges ready which we can file at will, but once he's formally in custody we'll have to get him a lawyer and we may have trouble persuading his family to stay here with him. And because Momu is still his guardian the legal situation is confused.'

'I've met this American diplomat; she's no fool,' Deutz said, speaking with an easy self-confidence. 'I'm sure she'll understand the top priority is to pick Sami's brains of every bit of intelligence he has.'

The Brigadier nodded. 'She knows that and I think she might be open to a deal under which the Americans get to sit in on the debriefing sessions. That's the outcome I want, and of course we'd then share the intelligence with our other NATO partners in the usual way.'

'Meanwhile we let our political masters decide who eventually puts him on trial and locks him away,' said Deutz.

Bruno noted the sarcasm in Deutz's voice when he used the phrase 'our political masters'. He was more troubled by the assumption that Sami's memories and knowledge could be peeled open as if he were a tin can. He doubted that the jumble of thoughts and fears inside Sami's head would be so easily extracted. Nor was he sure how much Sami really knew of the personalities and politics, communications systems and finances of the Taliban and al-Qaeda, which were presumably what the intelligence experts wanted. Bruno suspected he'd been kept alive and used for his tricks with bombs and electronics, rather than invited into the governing circles of the jihadis.

'You know Sami,' the Brigadier said to Bruno. 'The security boys at Le Pavillon reported that you have a good relationship with him and his family, so I want you to work alongside Deutz to keep Sami and his family happy while Deutz picks his brains.'

Deutz shook his head. 'We might want somebody else involved. Two people and we tend to fall into the hard cop, soft cop pattern. Since he's a Muslim, it might be easier if a third person were another man.'

'I'm not sure,' said Bruno. 'He responds well to women, including our local doctor who examined him. And I don't know if this is important but he loves animals. He's formed an attachment to my dog and also to my horse.'

'What about this American woman?' the Brigadier asked. 'Her first degree at Yale was in psychology, before she went on to study law. How might she fit in as a third person for your sessions?'

Bruno thought before replying, 'She can be somewhat intimidating.'

'I know, but that's not a problem, I can work with that. It

might even help me,' said Deutz, with an easy self-confidence. Bruno wondered how long that would last once he confronted the formidable Nancy Sutton.

'Where did you meet her?' he asked.

'Usual diplomatic circuit before I went over to talk to their FBI people. She helped set it up.'

'All friends together,' said the Brigadier, drily. 'Let's keep it that way.' He marched for the door to dismiss them.

'Just one thing,' said Deutz. 'Whether or not this American woman sits in, this process is going to take time. Normally this kind of assessment would take weeks, but I imagine we're on a tighter schedule. How long will I have with him?'

'As much time as we can persuade our American colleague to give you,' the Brigadier replied. 'I don't know how long we have before the news leaks and the media starts clustering round this place. So I think we are all going to be extremely courteous and helpful with Mademoiselle Sutton.'

Sami had been unconcerned at the change from Le Pavillon to the château, Momo told Bruno with relief. He'd been excited to explore the medieval tower and its battlements and he gazed in wonder at the eighteenth-century additions to the château which contained the bedrooms. Now in a large wood-panelled room with french windows that opened onto a terrace and walled garden, he sat on the floor at his aunt's feet. He was calmly stroking Balzac, who was curled up sleepily on his lap. Balzac was the first to respond to Bruno's arrival, leaping to the door as soon as his master appeared. Sami beamed as he rose, saying Bruno's name in a sing-song voice as he stroked his arm. Bruno patted Sami's shoulder, noting that the dark hollows had gone from beneath his eyes. Sami looked behind Bruno as if searching for another familiar face and asked, 'Fabiola?'

'Not today, Sami,' said Bruno, smiling at the young man before going to greet Momu and Dillah. He introduced Deutz as the medical specialist, feeling a twinge of deceit as he did so. Nonetheless, he put his arm around Deutz's shoulders as he introduced him to Sami, to show that he regarded the psychologist as a friend.

Deutz could not have been more charming. He was deferential to Momu, courteous to Dillah, and friendly to Sami. He steered them all back to their places and sat cross-legged on the floor beside Sami, who had resumed his place at Dillah's knee. Bruno sat beside Momu on the sofa and put Balzac down on the floor, giving him a gentle push to return to Sami.

Bruno had not known what to expect of Deutz's technique. Deutz was accustomed to dealing with prisoners, presumably in confined and guarded locations. Deutz's own personality seemed assertive and Bruno had wondered if this meant he'd present himself to Sami as an authority figure. But it was soon clear that Deutz's priority was to establish a friendly, non-threatening relationship. He smiled constantly and took turns with Sami in stroking Balzac.

On a low table beside Sami, Bruno noticed the parts of a dismantled radio. Momu murmured that it hadn't worked for years. He'd brought it from home in the hope that Sami could repair it. So far he seemed only to have taken it apart.

'Sami,' Bruno said, pointing to the radio. 'What's that?'

'Broken,' he replied and turned to look at it. 'Sami fix.' He simply put the pieces back together, pressed a button and the tinny strains of a baroque minuet from *France Musique* blared out.

'Mozart,' Sami announced. He turned the volume down and his fingers began softly tapping a beat on Balzac's back.

Deutz brought out a drawing pad and crayons and asked Sami to draw his family. Sami stared at him in silence, tears welling in his eyes. Then he took the crayons and began. Bruno had expected him to produce images of Momu and Dillah but instead he drew one large circle and two smaller ones beside it. He began adding dots that might have been eyes, lines for mouths and then took a red crayon and began slashing crude red lines beneath the faces. With a jolt, Bruno realised Sami had drawn the severed heads of his mother and sisters.

Deutz squeezed Sami's arm in reassurance and began sketching figures, asking Sami what the shapes looked like to him. One that looked like a man Sami said was Momu. A second card he thought was a rugby ball and the third was a car. Another reminded him of Dillah and the next of Balzac. Another shape was a slim figure in trousers with long hair.

'Fabiola,' said Sami, delightedly.

'Who is she?' Deutz asked.

'Lady doctor,' said Sami proudly. 'My friend.'

Deutz nodded in apparent agreement and then drew more images. Sami identified one as a croissant, another as a fish and a third as a cloud, until came a card that might have been a cabbage or a perhaps a pumpkin. Sami's face fell. He squeezed his eyes shut and turned away.

'Bomb,' he said. And then he quickly glanced back at Bruno, a flicker of something intelligent and watchful in his eyes, as if Sami were watching to see what reaction he'd got.

'Bad card,' said Deutz. 'Bad card.' When he had Sami's attention, he tore the offending card in half and gave the two pieces
to Sami, who tore them in half again, and then again until
the remaining pieces were too small to tear again.

'Bomb gone,' he said. 'No more bomb.' This time Bruno
saw Sami's eyes dart at Deutz, who seemed not to notice as
he put the cards away. Thinking this was a rather different
Sami, Bruno wondered if he was watching the kind of survival
mechanism that had kept Sami alive in Afghanistan, trying to
learn what won approval.

Deutz put the pad and crayons away and brought out a
pocket set of checkers and asked Sami if he knew this game.
Sami nodded, looking pleased, and briskly set out the white
pieces. Bruno recalled how Sami had been able to beat all
comers in St Denis at chess, including Momu, who had until
then been the town champion. Deutz set out the blacks and
signalled Sami to go first. Sami trounced him in a dozen
moves. They switched colours so that Deutz went first and
this time it took him a few more moves, since Deutz had
manoeuvred his last pieces into a guarded corner and kept
moving them back and forth. Sami quickly devised a strategy
to break up the corner and grinned cheerfully as he cleared
the board.

They were on their fifth game when Bruno rose to answer
a discreet knock on the door. The Brigadier signalled him
to come into the corridor, where Bruno saw Nancy Sutton
standing to the side of the door. She had changed into a baggy
sweatshirt and cargo pants. Her hair was loose and her face
washed clean of make-up. It made her look younger and rather
more vulnerable than the fashionably packaged woman who

had stepped off the plane at Périgueux that morning. She gave Bruno a hesitant smile and they shook hands.

'I'd like Mademoiselle Sutton to sit in,' said the Brigadier. 'Will you make the introductions?'

'Please, call me Nancy,' she said, and then went on, 'That business with the bomb sketch was interesting.' When she saw Bruno's questioning look, she said, 'We were watching the video feed.'

'Maybe you should ask Deutz.' Of course the rooms would have been wired. 'He's trying to establish a rapport with Sami. A new face might disturb that.'

'I'll take responsibility,' said the Brigadier, and opened the door to steer Nancy inside. Bruno followed quickly and took Nancy's arm to signal to Sami that they were friends. Deutz remained on the floor, looking irritated. He raised his eyebrows at Bruno, who shrugged, as if to say this was none of his doing. Bruno made the introductions, ending with Balzac, who approached her wagging his tail and then clambered onto her lap as she sat beside Sami on the floor. Balzac had always liked women.

'This is the dog Isabelle gave you,' said Nancy, as if to establish that she knew Bruno well. 'He's wonderful. How big will he grow?'

'Thirty kilos or so.'

Nancy's eyes missed nothing: the radio on the small table, the game of checkers, the crayons and sketches.

'I have some cards, too, different cards and all pictures,' she said, pulling a plastic envelope from her shoulder bag. 'Can we play, Sami? Tell me if you know any of these people.'

The photos were a mixture of police mugshots, stills from

surveillance cameras and snapshots taken on the street, paparazzi-style. She showed them to Sami one at a time.

He shrugged at the first two, photos of bearded men with sunburned faces except for their foreheads, where their turbans had been removed for the police cameras.

'Emir,' he said, at the third photo, one of the world's most famous faces, Osama bin Laden himself.

'Did you meet him?' she asked with a friendly smile.

'Saw him,' said Sami, his eyes darting to Nancy in the same watchful way. 'Never spoke.'

He took the remaining stack of photos from her and began sorting them into piles, speaking names as he laid some of the cards down. He tossed discarded cards carelessly to one side. 'Don't know,' he said of them, shrugging. 'Never seen him.'

Once he had finished, he pointed to the smallest pile, of eight photos. 'Friends,' he said, and rattled through a list of names: 'Ali, Mustaf', Ibrahim, Yassu, Fati, Hamid, Dullah, Adja.'

Bruno had never heard Sami speak so many words at once. Bruno wondered if he'd guessed that the American was a woman he needed to impress. Thinking of Fabiola, Bruno wondered if Sami simply responded better to women. Nobody was taking notes, but Bruno knew the microphones would pick up Sami's words and the video cameras would allow them to match each of the names to faces.

His second pile was larger, perhaps twenty photos. 'I know them,' he said, and pulled out four. 'Bad men,' he said of the first three, and repeated their names, this time using surnames: Bahdad, Yemani, Azaid. The fourth one was a face Bruno recognized, the shorter of the two men who had attacked him.

'This one is Ali, in Toulouse mosque,' Sami said of this fourth photo. 'He hit me with electric stick.'

From her chair Dillah gave a small sob. Bruno thought electric stick was not a bad way to describe the cattle prod.

'In Peshawar, Yemani and Azaid beat me, tied me up,' Sami went on, and then turned to the pile he'd called friends. 'Ibrahim and Ali made him stop and gave me food when I fix things. Hamid played basketball and Adja gave me sweet figs. Adja from Chechnya, Fati from Bosnia, they showed me photos of their homes.'

The room was utterly silent. Even Balzac seemed frozen in place. Bruno had never heard him speak so many words at once. For the first time he began to think that they might be able to access the gold mine of intelligence in Sami's head. A glimmer of hope began to grow. If Sami was able to go on providing useful information, the Americans might settle for that rather than cause a political storm by demanding his extradition.

'Very good, Sami,' Nancy said, and beamed at him. Bruno thought her warmth seemed genuine, as though she was not simply professionally pleased at Sami's revelations but also enjoyed his company.

'That was a good game and you did very well. Maybe we can play that game some more.' She patted the back of Sami's hand, now resting on Balzac's back. 'Is Balzac your friend, too?'

Sami looked startled by the question, and then to Bruno's surprise delivered the clearest sentence he'd ever heard Sami speak. 'Balzac is Bruno's dog, and Bruno is my old friend from before.'

Nancy nodded, and turned to Bruno. 'Does Balzac run well?'

'Well enough to come jogging with me.'

'Can we jog with him this evening, maybe around the grounds here? They seem big enough.' She turned to Sami. 'Do you jog, Sami? Do you want to run with us before dinner? And maybe a dip in the swimming pool?'

'I like the pool,' said Sami, brightening.

'Could be a good idea,' said Deutz, grudgingly, looking at his watch, as if trying to resume control of the session. 'We have an hour or so but I want to run some other basic tests this evening, a Bender-Gestalt for a basic neuro-psychological screen and at some point a Wechsler intelligence test for his cognitve skills.'

'Are his linguistic skills up to it?' Nancy asked.

'I'll just use coding, picture arrangement, pattern completion and see where that takes us. As for this idea of a run, he needs a break. Perhaps we'd better clear it with the Brigadier. I don't know if the grounds are secure.'

The Brigadier had no objection, so long as Sami was not obviously recognizable. With his shaven head and minus his beard, he looked nothing like the photo of him that had been left in the white van.

Sami looked a little bemused but happy to join in when he realized that Balzac would be coming. Once Sami was kitted out in an army tracksuit, they gathered in the courtyard and Nancy led off. Deutz sprinted around Bruno to catch her. After a moment she slowed, dropping back to join Bruno, who was running alongside Sami and Balzac, leaving Deutz running alone ahead of the group. Bruno smiled to himself, thinking that the dynamics between her and Deutz would be interesting.

She had taken over his session, changed the agenda, secured an important result and made Deutz accept it; a formidable woman, this American. Bruno could understand how she and Isabelle had become friends.

15

Karim's voice on the phone sounded frantic and in the background he could hear Rashida shrieking something that sounded like her son's name, Pierre.

'They used a kid to lure me away and they've taken Pierre,' Karim shouted. 'Bruno, you've got to get down here.'

'On my way, Karim, but who's got him? Who is they?'

'Those jihadists. Rashida told them about Le Pavillon. Just get here.' He rang off.

Still in his jogging gear, Bruno ran to his Land Rover, hardly noticing that Nancy was half a step behind him. He punched in the speed-dial for the Gendarmerie and told Sergeant Jules to get to the Café des Sports and inform Yveline that they had a kidnapping on their hands.

'Wait,' Nancy shouted as he unlocked the vehicle door. 'You aren't armed and you'll need back-up.'

Bruno stopped and looked at her, about to say his hunting rifle and shotgun were still in the locked cabinet in the back of the Land Rover. But she was right, they needed back-up.

'Call the Brigadier and I'll get weapons and be back here as soon as I can,' she said, and raced off.

Bruno briefed the Brigadier, who calmly said he'd have one of his security teams meet Bruno at Karim's café. The other team, Gaston and Robert, were still at Le Pavillon, packing up, and he'd warn them. He took Bruno's directions to the café and added he'd call the hostage specialists in Paris and find where the nearest ones would be. Nancy was running back towards him, a heavy sports bag swinging from one arm. She climbed into the passenger seat and he accelerated away.

'Two handguns and one of your assault weapons, three magazines,' she said. 'I told the guardhouse it was an emergency, Brigadier's orders.'

'Karim is Momu's son, married to Rashida. They have a baby and a toddler called Pierre. He's the one that's been taken, he said by jihadists.'

'Jesus, they'll try to trade the kid for Sami. But they must know we won't let that happen.'

'Apparently Rashida told them about Le Pavillon, the place where we kept Sami and Momu before we moved here. The Brigadier is warning the security team that's still there.'

'How do you want to play this?'

Bruno was thinking as he hurled the vehicle down the lane, honking before each bend.

'We go to Karim's first and find out what happened, how many they are, what vehicles and weapons they have, and then we take a back road to Le Pavillon and try to catch them between us and the security team. I know them, they're good.'

'Makes sense.' Nancy was checking the handguns, taking out magazines and testing the springs. She pulled from the sports bag a FAMAS, the French army automatic rifle, pointed the muzzle at the floor and began to strip it. She evidently knew what she was doing.

'Should you be doing this?' he asked.

'They're my enemies, too. Besides, it's an emergency.'

Sergeant Jules's personal car was parked askew in front of the café. That meant the Gendarmerie van was out on patrol somewhere. He and Karim came to the door as Bruno honked his horn and pulled in, noting that the café's plate-glass window was broken. As he turned off the engine Bruno heard Rashida having hysterics in a back room.

'The big café window was broken by a couple of kids,' Karim announced. 'I ran after them and caught one and we've got him here but the other boy, a black kid, ran away. They're strangers, not from here, both *beurs*.' Karim used the slang term for North Africans.

'When I was catching him, two guys came in with guns, submachine guns not pistols, grabbed Pierre from Rashida's arms and demanded to know where Sami was.'

'Was she hurt?' Bruno asked.

'She was pushed to the ground and they put a gun to her head when they asked about Sami. One of the customers, Valéry, tried to stop them but they hit him with a gun butt. I think they broke his jaw. We've called the doctor. They took Pierre and ran back to their car, a black Toyota four-by-four. They had a driver waiting.'

Valéry was one of Karim's teammates on the town's rugby squad, an aggressive wing forward, just the type to take on armed men, thought Bruno.

'What direction did they take when they left?'

'South, toward Le Buisson.'

'You saw just the two guns?'

'Yes, short ones, all metal with curved magazines.' Karim glanced curiously at Nancy, still in her tracksuit, handgun at her side, watching the road while Bruno asked his questions.

'Did they speak French or Arabic?'

'Both. One of them used French to tell the customers to sit still after he belted Valéry, but he had an accent. The one who knocked Rashida down and grabbed Pierre called her bad names in Arabic and then he asked about Sami.'

'They were in black leather jackets and jeans, little woollen skullcaps,' chimed in Gervaise, one of the customers who worked at the farmers' co-op just up the road. 'The driver of their Toyota had a map open on the steering wheel in front of him. I got the number plate and here's one of the little bastards.'

Sergeant Jules was holding a brown-skinned boy of twelve or so firmly by one arm. The boy was just short of puberty, wearing dirty jeans and sweatshirt and a faded denim jacket that was several sizes too big for him. On his feet were a pair of new and expensive trainers and on his face an expression that was both surly and defiant.

'He hasn't said a word,' Karim said. 'The other kid was about the same age, a bit bigger and ran a lot faster.'

At the sight of Bruno the boy curled his lip. Bruno ignored him, shook Karim's hand and asked after Rashida.

'You can hear her, she's in a bad way. Monique is with her. She was buying lottery tickets when it all happened.'

Bruno eyed the boy. 'What's your name?' he asked.

'*Va te faire foutre, flic.*'

Despite the situation, Bruno almost laughed at the strangeness of the obscenity coming from such young and apparently innocent lips. Sergeant Jules shook the boy a little, evidently restraining himself.

'I know all the Arab families round here and this kid's a stranger,' said Karim. 'There was nothing in his pockets except for a few ten-euro notes and this phone.' He pointed to it on the counter. It looked cheap, like a disposable, and was wrapped in a plastic bag.

'I saw it in his pocket so I borrowed Rashida's washing-up gloves to take it from him. I thought about fingerprints.'

'Good for you,' said Bruno, slipping on a pair of evidence gloves and then opening the phone's list of recent calls. There was only one incoming call listed, from a mobile that began with 06. They might be able to trace that. The address book contained only a single number and it began with 0534, which meant Toulouse. *Merde*, thought Bruno; this was starting to get complicated.

The big blue Gendarmerie van pulled up on the forecourt and Yveline, in civilian clothes, stepped down and stood looking at the broken windows before going to the rear of the van and opening the door. Bruno went out to join her and saw, inside the van, Françoise on the bench clutching a second youngster firmly to her side. She was determined not to let him go but knew the rules on the treatment of minors too well to put handcuffs on him. They would probably have slipped off his young wrists, thought Bruno. There was a strong smell of petrol. This boy was black, wore spectacles and also had new trainers.

'Caught him at Momu's house, trying to make a lighter work,' said Yveline. 'There was a plastic can of petrol against the back door. If he'd got it alight, he'd have been the first victim.'

'Good work,' said Bruno. 'How did you find him?'

'Just a hunch,' she said. 'I thought if they'd gone for Karim they might also be going to Momu, so I went along the river-bank to the back door while Françoise drove up to the front. The kid was crying because he couldn't make it light.'

'Get any names from the boy?' Bruno asked.

'He says he won't say a word until he sees a lawyer, must be a hardened criminal,' she replied, her tone mocking. 'I called the social department but it will be an hour or so before they get here from Bergerac. We have to wait inside. Can't take the little dears to the Gendarmerie.'

'Don't let the two kids talk to each other,' said Bruno, and used his mobile phone to photograph each boy. 'One should stay inside, the other in the van. Was yours carrying anything in his pocket?'

'Forty euros, a Toulouse bus pass and those glasses are prescription,' Françoise replied. 'There's an ID number on them so we'll be able to trace him through the optician.'

'Attempted arson is serious stuff, even for a minor,' Bruno said, loud enough for the boy to hear him. He opened his phone and called the Brigadier to pass on the news. As he put the phone away, he saw a military jeep draw up with an army driver and two men in camouflage uniforms. One carried a sniper's rifle and the other a Heckler & Koch assault weapon. This would be the Brigadier's security team. He went across to shake hands and brief them.

'You know about the kid, Pierre, not yet two, can barely walk?' he asked.

'The Brigadier briefed us and said you'd tell us the rest,' said the sniper. 'I'm Marcel and this is Raymond. The driver is Jacquot. I'll need to talk to Gaston and Robert. Who's the woman?'

Bruno explained and then left Yveline in charge at the café as he and Nancy climbed back into the Land Rover. He took the side street past the rugby stadium to get onto the road to Audrix and take the back way to St Chamassy. He handed Nancy his phone and asked her to call the Brigadier. The line was busy so Bruno left a message about the black Toyota and its licence plate. Then he asked Nancy to look up Gaston on the address book.

'This is like Isabelle's phone,' she said. 'One of the special ones.' She handed it back to him when she heard it start to ring at the other end.

'It's Bruno,' he said. 'Have you heard from the Brigadier?'

'Yes, and we're ready,' Gaston replied. 'I'm in the pigeon tower on lookout, Robert is in the courtyard. No sign of them yet.'

'They don't know the area, they'll be looking. They're in a black Toyota four-by-four.'

'They may have another car.'

'I know. I'm coming in from the north-east in my Land Rover, from a village called Audrix. I've got a good rifle and a partner with a FAMAS and two of your friends, Raymond and Marcel. They're in a jeep. From the direction the Toyota took, you should expect the bad guys to arrive from the west, through the village of St Chamassy.'

'Got it. I'll call if we see them and you call me when you're in position.'

As Bruno turned off through Audrix, the Brigadier called him back. A white Peugeot 206 had been seen leaving the

Toulouse mosque that morning with two boys in the back seat. The driver was identified as one of the mosque's security team and an alert had been placed on the car's number plate. Bruno scribbled down the registration.

'The driver must be getting worried about the boys,' Bruno told him. 'Probably he'll have chosen somewhere central to pick them up. There can't be many places in town. I have photos of the two kids, you might be able to identify them from the surveillance cameras at the mosque. We'll email them now.'

'Who's we?' the Brigadier snapped.

'Our American ally,' said Bruno, closing the phone. Nancy grinned at him as she sent the two photos.

Bruno took his rifle from the locked box in his Land Rover and left the vehicle at the last bend in the single-track road before Le Pavillon came into view, perhaps five hundred metres away. He approached the jeep and then called Gaston to tell him, and heard there was still no sign of the black Toyota.

'Le Pavillon isn't easy for strangers to find,' Bruno said. 'We are now on foot. Marcel and Raymond will set an ambush from the treeline, as close as we can get to you. They'll be to your east. I know the country so I'll be on open ground to your south, trying to get them in a crossfire.'

'Got it. I'll call you and them when I see the Toyota. Make sure your phone's on vibrate.'

Bruno heard an echo of Gaston's voice from the small radio clipped to Marcel's collar. The security men had their own communications link.

'Are you OK with the plan?' he asked Marcel.

Marcel nodded. 'The Brigadier said rules of engagement are

open, just save the kid and leave at least one wounded prisoner to interrogate. We'd better let them out of their vehicle first. We don't want to leave one of them inside with the boy.'

'The driver stayed inside at the café, so maybe they'll leave him with the car.'

'If so, I'll take him out first, then immobilize the vehicle.'

'What if they have run-flat tyres?'

'This is a twelve point seven calibre,' he said, patting his heavy rifle. 'It'll blow the wheel hubs off.'

A crackle from Marcel's radio told them the Toyota was in sight, advancing slowly from the west.

'Showtime,' said Marcel, and trotted along the treeline, Raymond following.

'So I come with you?' Nancy asked.

'I'd prefer you to stay in the Land Rover. We might need to give chase and it's the best cross-country vehicle. If you have time when you're chasing, pick me up.'

She nodded and he took the PAMAS handgun she held out him, made sure the safety was on and stuck it into the belly pocket of his tracksuit. Rifle in hand he headed, crouching, onto the plateau. He picked up some dirt from the ground as he trotted, spat onto it and rubbed it into his cheeks and brow. He kept moving north towards Le Pavillon and west toward the Toyota. It was still out of sight, visible only to Gaston in the pigeon tower.

The plateau's ground was uneven. There were folds and small hillocks and he headed toward the furthest north of these and ducked behind it. He was perhaps two hundred metres from Le Pavillon when his phone vibrated. It was Gaston to say he had Bruno in view. The Toyota was heading at crawling pace over the rough ground toward Le Pavillon and was no more than a hundred yards to Bruno's ten o'clock. Gaston added that Marcel had the Toyota in his sights.

'Keep this line open.' Bruno said, and peered carefully around the side of the hillock.

'It's stopped,' Gaston said.

'I see it,' Bruno said. Apparently confident that it had not been spotted, the Toyota began moving again slowly. There was a driver and one man in the front, another man in the rear, who suddenly opened his door and stood, feet still inside the car, his right arm wrapped around the bars of the luggage rack, his gun pointing at Le Pavillon.

Suddenly everything happened at once. The Toyota revved its engine and surged forward, stopping just to one side of the arch that formed the entry. The passenger door opened and a man jumped out. Looking bulky, as though wearing a rucksack under his jacket, he sprayed bullets from his assault gun at Le Pavillon as he ran. The sniper rifle crashed and the windows of the Toyota shattered The man leaning out of the Toyota began firing at the pigeon tower and Bruno sighted carefully and fired once, then a second time, and saw him slump.

The sniper fired again and the Toyota sagged, a front wheel collapsing. Gaston was firing from the pigeon tower and Bruno switched his aim to the bulky man who was running toward the courtyard. He fired twice without success and then the man jerked and spun at Bruno's third shot. But he limped on and ducked inside the arch, careless of the gunfire.

The gate seemed to disintegrate as a large explosion took

place and Le Pavillon disappeared in an eruption of flame and black smoke.

A suicide bomber, Bruno realized, cursing. He should have thought of that. He began running toward the Toyota, shouting into his phone for Gaston as he ran. There was no reply. He pulled the handgun from his belly pocket as he reached the Toyota, partly sheltered from the blast by the stone wall around the building but with loose stones strewn across its roof and hood.

Carefully, he peered under the car, the gap narrowed because the sniper had destroyed one of the front wheels. The man he had shot was slumped on the earth beside the Toyota, not moving and no weapon in his hands. The driver had been blown off his seat by the heavy sniper's bullet and his body was crumpled in the foot well of the passenger side. There was not much left of his head and the whole interior of the Toyota seemed to have been sprayed with blood. He could hear Pierre screaming from inside the vehicle.

Bruno opened the rear door, scooped out Pierre from where he lay on the floor behind the front seats. Quickly he examined his limbs and Pierre stopped his shrieking and began sucking in great gulps of air that turned into sobs. None of the blood on the child seemed to be his own. Bruno held him tight against his chest, trying to murmur words of comfort, and suddenly Nancy was there with the Land Rover. He handed the child to her and told her to take the boy back to the jeep and then come back.

He checked the man sprawled half in, half out of the Toyota. He'd been hit twice in the shoulder but was still alive. His gun was on the ground out of reach, a large stone on top of the breech. It was too heavy for Bruno to move, so he thought the wounded man would be unlikely to free it.

Bruno tried Gaston again but still got no reply. The smoke was clearing and the pigeon tower's roof and the window where Gaston had been on watch had both gone. He crept into the courtyard and saw complete devastation. The front wall and roof of Le Pavillon had disappeared and the courtyard was a mass of stones and roof tiles. What was left of the house was burning fiercely. A crater close to where the main door had been was all that remained of the suicide bomber.

Bruno half-ran, half-jumped across to the pigeon tower, picking his way between the loose stones that covered the steps. He clambered up to where Gaston had been. Gaston was slumped below the window, unconscious, with blood on his face and his limbs slack. But he had a pulse. Bruno slung him over his shoulder and carried him down to the courtyard, staggering under the weight and the obstacle course beneath his feet, and out to the Toyota. Nancy was coming back in the Land Rover, followed by the jeep with the driver and the other two security men aboard.

They loaded Gaston into the back seat of the Land Rover and the wounded terrorist into the rear.

'The kid can go on your lap in the front seat,' Nancy told Bruno. 'Let's go.'

'Just one moment,' he said, and turned to Marcel. 'We'll take them to the medical centre in St Denis. Can you stay here, see if there's any trace of Robert and report in to the Brigadier? And ask him to tell the *pompiers* to hold off until we can clear away the Toyota and the weapons.'

Marcel nodded dully, his eyes on Gaston in the back seat.

'If only I'd thought, I could have stopped that bloody Toyota long before it got close enough . . .'

'Then we'd have lost the kid,' Nancy said. 'Pull yourself together, man, we've got to get your guy to a doctor.'

Pierre shocked and silent in his arms, Bruno jumped in beside her as she let in the clutch and bounced away over the rough ground to the track. A thick plume of dark smoke was rising and drifting slowly to the east, visible for miles. Bruno called Yveline to see if she could spare any Gendarmes to keep curious locals from driving up to see the source of the explosion and the smoke. Then he called Karim to say Pierre was safe.

He was trying to call the medical centre to warn them he was bringing two gunshot wounds when Nancy said, 'Don't.'

Bruno glanced at her in surprise.

'Brigadier's orders. We're taking them to the château. The French army have a better-equipped medical team there, with more experience of gunshot wounds. And it's secure.'

Bruno closed his phone with a sigh. 'He can't keep an explosion like that secret. If only I'd thought . . .'

'Don't blame yourself,' said Nancy. 'I didn't think of a suicide bomber either. And the little boy is fine.'

Bruno looked down at the child now sleeping in his arms. As soon as they'd delivered the wounded men to the medical team at the château he would drive Pierre home to his parents. Perhaps he'd better try to clean him up first.

As Nancy turned into the lane that led to the château, Bruno's phone rang. It was Yveline. The white Peugeot had been spotted at the Intermarché car park. The driver was under arrest and had been taken to the Gendarmerie. In the car was a receipt from a filling station just outside Cahors for a full tank of petrol and an extra five litres plus a plastic can. He'd paid cash but the car's *carte grise* showed it was registered to the welfare department of the Toulouse mosque.

16

The story broke the next day, in a wire report from Agence France-Presse in Kabul. Quoting NATO sources, it said simply that in a dramatic coup for French intelligence, the expert terrorist bomb-maker known as the Engineer had been found by French troops in Afghanistan in the course of a special operation and was now in French custody.

This was followed within minutes by Associated Press, date-lined Washington, which said that U.S. officials were liaising with the French authorities over his fate. Reuters from London, in a story titled 'The most wanted man in the world', then reported that the Engineer had been secretly smuggled out of Afghanistan in a French military plane and was now being held in an unknown location in France.

Within minutes, United Press International was quoting senators and congressmen in Washington demanding that the Engineer be delivered to American custody. One senator called him 'a mass murderer of American boys'. Then Deutsche Presse-Agentur filed a story from Berlin that a European arrest warrant would be sent to the French government, asserting that the Engineer had been responsible for the deaths of at least four German soldiers, and requiring him to stand trial in Germany.

Soon the official spokesmen and politicians were all over the TV screens, and the press secretary of the European Union's commissioner for external relations launched a new angle. In response to a question from a reporter from Holland's *De Telegraaf*, he agreed that it would be against European law for any suspect to be handed over to American jurisdiction if there were any prospect of the death penalty.

The newspaper's headline was: 'Europe to Washington: Thou Shalt Not Kill'. Asked to comment, the official spokesman for the U.S. Justice Department retorted, 'In that case, we'll settle for life in Guantanamo.'

Bruno followed the gathering media storm closely. A regional paper, *Le Républicain Lorrain*, close to the German frontier, gave the next new lead. They ran it as an exclusive on their website edition, not waiting for the next day's newspaper. They quoted a returning French soldier that an Afghan in French uniform had been huddled, drugged and weeping, aboard his plane from Dushanbe. The soldier complained that he had lost part of his leave since their flight had unexpectedly landed at Évreux for unspecified security reasons. There had then been a special flight to Bordeaux for the Afghan.

Bruno decided not to answer several calls from Philippe Delaron, the local correspondent for *Sud Ouest*. Philippe was no fool. He knew that something unusual was under way at the château. Furniture and food had been delivered, military helicopters were coming and going and soldiers were guarding the gates. He also knew that Bruno had been viciously attacked at the *collège* in St Denis and would probably soon learn that the Muslim teacher, Momu, had taken a sudden leave of absence and disappeared, along with his Muslim wife. And Gendarmes had turned Philippe away when he'd tried take a picture of the ruins of Le Pavillon and get more details of the mysterious propane gas explosion which had supposedly caused it.

'I don't think we have long, sir, before the media knows that the Engineer is here and that he has something to do with Momu,' Bruno said.

Bruno and Nancy were in the Brigadier's office, sipping some of their host's Bowmore malt whisky. They were looking in something close to disbelief over the transcripts of that day's session with Sami. He had identified over sixty photographs, remembered precisely where and when he had seen them and how often.

When Nancy brought out a map and asked him how he had got from the Toulouse mosque to Afghanistan without a passport, Sami had recounted his journey step by step, starting with a long car ride to Germany, a charter flight full of Turkish families going back to Ankara and another charter flight to Abu Dhabi. Finally a rusty merchant ship, flying Liberian colours, had taken him and his companions to the Pakistani port of Karachi. He remembered addresses, names of the couriers who had met his Toulouse group and handed them on to the next stage. He was proving to be an extraordinary source, and he took obvious pride in pleasing Nancy in being able to answer her questions.

'I'd like to check these reports about his skills at electronics,' Nancy said. 'Can we learn how he turns cellphones into detonators? We can get it on video, send it to your guys in Paris and mine in Washington. I'd like to know if he was building these IEDs from scratch or just assembling them to order.'

Bruno made a note. Florence's computer club had a box full of broken electronics awaiting repair. One of the Brigadier's staff was drawing up a chronology of Sami's Afghan sojourn. His memory was uncanny. He remembered names, dates, times and places and cheerfully recounted them all. He rattled off radio frequencies and mobile phone numbers for remotely controlled bombs, and remembered the addresses on the packaging in which they had arrived. He recalled email addresses and credit card numbers he had heard being used. He seemed to have forgotten nothing he had seen or heard.

'We knew this media fuss would happen,' replied the Brigadier calmly. 'That's why we are here in the château, sealed off and guarded. The media may speculate but all inquiries must be made to the Interior Ministry in Paris.'

'The White House press corps won't swallow that,' Nancy retorted.

The Brigadier looked at her patiently. 'Is not our work here of considerable importance?'

'You know it is,' she replied. 'This is the best intelligence out of Afghanistan I've ever seen. We've got teams back at Fort Meade correlating Sami's names and dates to all the SIGINT in the databases. We're getting voice prints, cellphone numbers, emails, connecting all manner of dots. It's a gold mine.'

'So our priority is to continue our work and not permit the media to distract us. Anybody who matters in Washington and Paris knows the value of what we are gleaning here. In the meantime our press officials will give full but empty answers to the media hordes; that is what they are paid to do.'

'Washington doesn't quite work like that.'

'In that case, my dear Nancy, you have my profound sympathies. Paris, thank heavens, does work like that.'

*

Bruno knew that St Denis worked in a different way altogether, but even he was startled by the text message he received later that day from Gilles at *Paris Match*. He went straight to the Brigadier to warn him that the storm was about to break over their heads.

'*Fabiola told me full story about Sami, Pavillon, chateau,*' Gilles had texted. '*She insists Sami innocent victim and unfit to stand trial. On my way to St Denis. Will you call me or do I run the story?*'

'I assume he's going to run the story anyway whether you call him or not,' said the Brigadier, once Nancy had been summoned to join them.

'Probably,' said Bruno. 'I can try asking him to hold off, but Fabiola would just go to Philippe Delaron at *Sud Ouest*. And remember, Sami is officially her patient. I'm surprised she hasn't turned up already, demanding to see him.'

'Maybe there's a way we can make this work for us,' Nancy interjected. 'We tell the truth. Sami is autistic, long since declared legally unfit to take care of himself. These jihadis viciously used this poor, pathetic boy, even whipped him to build bombs. Let's spin this against the bastards.'

Bruno felt instantly that Nancy was right. The strategic objective was not simply to penetrate al-Qaeda, and not even to break open the network of European jihadis that funnelled young Muslims to the Taliban. These were simply tactical goals that did not address the fundamental issue of politics, religion and public opinion. The crucial task was to force a separation between the jihadists and the millions of peaceful Muslims all across Europe, by exposing their ruthless and cynical treatment of someone like Sami.

'It's a question of how we build the narrative. If we spin this right, we can make Sami into a hero,' Nancy went on.

'If we are going to build this story around Sami, it might help to offer some media access,' Bruno said. 'I'm thinking of photos of Sami playing with Balzac, some photos of the whipping scars on his back. Maybe *Paris Match* is the best vehicle for it.'

'If we offer them an exclusive, we can keep some control of the story,' the Brigadier said, thoughtfully.

The other two members of the medical tribunal arrived later that day. Under French tradition, a medical tribunal that seeks to establish the mental competence of someone charged with a serious crime consists of a psychologist, a psychoanalyst and a practising psychiatrist. Pascal Deutz, deputy head of the prison psychiatric service, fulfilled the last of the three roles. The psychologist was Bernard Weill, an eminent professor from Paris who had also taught in London and Chicago. In his sixties, Weill had a fringe of bushy white hair above his ears and the back of his neck, but his scalp was bald and suntanned. Bruno was surprised that someone whose life was spent probing the unconscious minds of unhappy people could look so cheerful. Weill's dark eyes twinkled and his round face broke into frequent smiles. Bruno liked him at once.

The psychoanalyst was Professor Amira Chadoub, a plump and motherly-looking woman in her early fifties. She came from a family of Moroccan immigrants and had been raised as a Muslim. There was no sign of her Moroccan heritage in her clothing; she was wearing a blue linen dress, high-heeled shoes, a pearl necklace with matching earrings, and her grey hair was pulled back into a neat bun. Usually such a tribunal was assisted by a secretary from the Justice Ministry, a role that in this case had been assigned for security reasons to the Brigadier.

Once his two colleagues had unpacked, Deutz introduced them to the Brigadier, who made brief welcoming remarks and offered them coffee or drinks. Nancy had made herself scarce. Bruno was described vaguely as the local policeman who had known Sami since he was a boy and was invited to join them. The Brigadier evidently wanted to set some ground rules.

There were two essential issues, he began. The first was whether Sami was able to distinguish right from wrong and be responsible for his actions. The second, equally important, was whether he was fit to stand trial, to be aware of the nature of judicial proceedings against him and able to be responsible for his own defence.

'If we judge the answer to either of those questions to be No, then he will not stand trial and will remain under medical supervision. Am I right?' asked Professor Weill. The Brigadier nodded.

'Just one thing,' Deutz said. 'I've heard that the signs of whipping on this man's body are being taken to mean he was under duress. That might not be right; self-flagellation is common among some Islamic sects.'

'How much time do we have to spend with this young man before we decide?' Chadoub asked, ignoring Deutz's remark.

'I'd like to say as much time as you need,' the Brigadier replied. 'In practical terms we are under some time pressure. Bruno, when we have finished our coffee perhaps you could find Sami and bring him to the main salon.'

Bruno set off to find Sami in the family rooms. He found Dillah, reading a magazine, who told him that Momu and Sami had decided to explore the château. He'd probably find them in the tower, she said. He climbed up the endless stone stairs but eventually found them by the austere battlements that ran from the tower the full length of the main building.

The view from this height was spectacular. He could see across the outer wall and down into the valley with a clear view of one of the long, slow bends of the river. Just beyond the stretch of water, glinting in the sunshine, were the pale grey cliffs of limestone that defined the region and had sheltered its human inhabitants for tens of thousands of years. When Bruno had first arrived in St Denis a decade earlier, he'd been told that humans had lived there for forty thousand years. Now the archaeologists said it was at least eighty thousand years, and some thought it was far longer, citing the flint tools found at Tayac near Les Eyzies that dated back over two hundred thousand years.

A map of the local area was spread out on the stone in the gap between the battlements before the two figures. Momu was pointing to the rounded hills that enfolded St Denis as Bruno approached. Sami had Balzac clutched to his chest as his eyes followed Momu's pointing finger until Balzac's puny bark alerted him to Bruno's arrival. Sami put Balzac down and let him scamper to his master.

Sami grinned as he pointed out familiar places to Bruno and then located them on the map. Momu had been showing him the scale printed on the corner of the map and Sami was using the length of his finger to work out how far away each place was from where he stood. At one point, as Sami leaned over the battlement, Momu gently pulled him back to safety, warning him of the dangers of the drop.

Sami was still wearing the army tracksuit in which he had been jogging that morning. He looked happy and very young. Just a few days of good food and medical care had done him good. The contrast was striking with the image of the fanatical and calculating professional bomb-maker presented in the media.

'The tribunal is here, and they want to get started,' Bruno told Momu, who sighed and began to fold the map. Looking disappointed that the map game was over, Sami shrugged and followed them down the stairs to the salon.

'I think we only need Sami for this meeting,' Deutz said firmly when Bruno showed Sami and Momu into the large room, well lit by four tall windows that opened onto the park.

'Monsieur Mohammed Belloumi is Sami's adoptive father and has been appointed his guardian by the courts,' Bruno said. 'There are no legal grounds to exclude him.'

'This is a medical examination, not a legal proceeding,' Deutz replied, turning to the Brigadier for confirmation.

'I have no objection to the father staying,' interjected Weill, and Amira agreed. Bruno drew up a chair for Momu and then left the room, pausing to give Sami's shoulder a comforting squeeze as he passed. Nancy was hovering at the corner of the corridor and asked him to describe the other two members of the tribunal.

'It's smart to have a Muslim on the tribunal, even if she's no longer religious,' she said when he'd described them. 'Washington had a query about the other boys who went jihad from the Toulouse mosque with Sami. Do we know who they were, what happened to them?'

'Momu is in with Sami. Let's ask Dillah.' Bruno led the way to the family rooms, but they were empty. Finally they found her in the grounds, sitting on a wooden bench that faced the château, some knitting on her lap that looked as if it would become a baby's jacket. But her hands were still and her eyes blank, almost as if she were dozing. She jerked upright when Bruno called her name and then explained why he needed her help.

'I've been thinking about those other poor boys,' she said, and Bruno scribbled down the names she gave him. 'Momu and I tried to get their parents to come with us when we complained to the mosque. But the first one, Kader, had a French mother, a convert to Islam. They're always the worst. She said she was proud her son had gone jihad. The others were frightened of making a fuss. I think their immigration status was in trouble, or maybe it was asylum. Their son had already been in trouble with the police, so they put him in the madrassa.'

'Tell me about this school attached to the mosque,' said Nancy. 'Was it specially for autistic boys?'

They had first heard of it from the social welfare office in Sarlat, Dillah explained, when they were told there were no schools in the *Département* suitable for Sami. They had said this mosque school looked after troubled boys of various kinds with specialist teachers and doctors for boys like Sami. The Imam was a respected figure and his deputy who ran the school was often on TV, speaking what she and Momu thought was sense about the need for a European Islam, adapted to a modern democracy.

'You mean Ghlamallah,' Bruno said. Dillah nodded. 'Was it Ghlamallah you saw at the mosque?'

'Ghlamallah came in to tell us the boys had gone. He insisted they'd planned it themselves and there was nothing the mosque could do. He was sorry and he refunded us the fees for that term.' Her mouth tightened. 'He seemed to think it was the money we cared about.'

Nancy said they needed to see Olivier, the one going through the videotapes to make a chronology of Sami's journeys, to give him the names of the other boys from the mosque. Nancy also wanted to see the file on Ghlamallah.

There was a fat file on him, but none of it damaging. Even with Rafiq's reports, all they had were suspicions. The precise organization of the mosque was far from clear. The elderly and deeply devout Imam was nominally in charge, and he was highly visible, sitting on the board of France's national Muslim council, a delegate to the global ecumenical council and to the European inter-faith assembly.

'He seems to be a figurehead,' Olivier said. 'Everybody's favourite Muslim, but apart from chairing the weekly board meeting it doesn't look as though he actually runs the place.'

'So Ghlamallah is the one in charge?' Nancy asked.

Olivier shrugged. 'He's more like the public spokesman, spends a lot of time giving speeches and writing his books and articles. His phone calls and emails seem pretty innocent. We're running a clean-up program on some of the audiotapes on calls that we think were using a vocal modifier to disguise the speakers' identities. Maybe that will tell us more.'

'In his emails, does he send a lot of photos?' Nancy asked.

'Funny you should ask, but it's like he keeps a photo diary of everything he does, photos of audiences at his meetings, of him being interviewed, events he attends. He sends hundreds of them.'

'Have you run them through a pixel scanner?' she asked.

'What's that?' Bruno asked.

The National Security Agency at Fort Meade in the U.S. had found microscopic messages embedded in individual pixels in a photograph that could contain hundreds of thousands of them. The NSA had developed an automatic scanning system to look for such odd pixels, blow them back up to normal size and then run the message through the decryption programs.

Olivier shrugged. 'Not that I've heard. We don't do the analysis ourselves.'

'Maybe it would be a good idea to check,' said Nancy. 'On an operation like this, where we're working closely together, I'm sure the NSA would be glad to help.'

Olivier raised his eyebrows. 'I'm sure they would,' he said, in a voice loaded with sarcasm. 'I'll put it to the Brigadier.'

'Don't bother, I'll do it myself,' she said. 'But who else seems to be running the mosque?'

Olivier went through the list. There was the *kayim*, or caretaker, who seemed to do most of the administration; a *khalib*, who led Friday prayers, and a *nazir*, the treasurer. He controlled the money, at least that part of it that could be traced through the banking networks. Then there were various departments: the madrassa or school; the social service that ran charities and welfare; the sports association and medical centre; the

186

publishing company; the job training office and the women's organization.

'It's huge,' Olivier said. 'Twenty thousand worshippers, so many they spill over into the streets, and about two hundred people seem to be employed full-time. The annual budget is around twenty million euros, at least that bit of it we can see.'

'So which section are those guys in that attacked me at the *collège*?' Bruno asked.

'We call it the security section. They call themselves the monitors, the guys who keep order at Friday prayers,' Olivier explained. 'The man Rafiq was interested in before he was killed is the *Niqab*, the captain, second-in-command. We know this man was in the paras, invalided out after two years when he had a training accident when his chute didn't open properly. He's a bit of a mystery, French-born with an Algerian background but no next-of-kin ever listed, never seems to send emails, never makes phone calls, never leaves the mosque. The smaller of the two guys who attacked you is his chief aide, Ali, known as the *Caïd*.'

Olivier paused, looking at his computer screen. 'Well, look who's turned up.'

He hit a couple of keys and what had been a small window on one corner of the screen expanded and Bruno saw it was a live feed from France 24, and a familiar face was being interviewed: Ghlamallah.

'Whoever this so-called Engineer might be, there can be no question of handing him over to the Americans,' Ghlamallah was saying. 'We know from Guantanamo and the Abu Ghraib prison scandal how the Americans treat their prisoners, even when they don't fry them in the electric chair or inject them with lethal chemicals. Many French people, not just Muslims, have severe doubts about the American operations in Afghanistan, the countless deaths of innocent civilians in drone attacks. If this Engineer is in French hands, he must be dealt with under French law.'

'But France has also been part of the NATO effort in Afghanistan, in support of the elected government and against the Taliban,' the interviewer objected.

'Some of us question that policy, which seems neither to have produced stability nor a decent government in Afghanistan and certainly has not defeated the Taliban,' Ghlamallah said, sounding very reasonable. 'We think it's time to put down the guns and start negotiating.'

'Glib son-of-a-bitch, isn't he?' said Nancy, her arms folded as she watched the screen. 'Just made for prime time.'

Ghlamallah was wearing Western dress, a dark suit with open-necked white shirt. His short beard was carefully trimmed and his teeth, which he displayed often as he smiled when making his points, had that too-perfect white symmetry that suggested expensive dentistry. His dark hair was trimmed short and neatly parted. Bruno saw Nancy's point; the man was a highly skilled TV performer.

'The sooner we get that pixel-scanning operation running, the happier I'll be,' she said, and turned to Bruno. 'So how is Monsieur prime-time there going to spin it when *Paris Match* breaks the news that the Engineer came from his mosque?'

'I imagine he'll say exactly what he said to Momu and Dillah,' Bruno replied. 'He'll say the three young men left of their own accord, choosing the path of jihad in the service, perhaps mistaken, of what they saw as their victimized Islamic brethren. Nobody could be more sorry than him about Sami's eventual fate, but the fault lies with the Americans and tragically mistaken policies by successive French governments. Was it his fault if there were too few special schools in France for autistic children, particularly if they were Muslim? The mosque did their best to help, but they were not running a prison camp. The students were given considerable freedom and they chose jihad.'

'Not bad,' said Nancy, nodding her head in approval as she glanced at him. 'Needs a little polish, but if he sticks to his guns he could just get away with that. Maybe you have a future in politics.'

Her tone was light and joking, but suddenly Bruno was aware that Nancy's eyes were still on him, as if reappraising what she saw. He felt a sudden spark flash between the two of them that went beyond the professional relationship they had established. But with the stir of attraction he felt for her came an automatic caution. It was partly a sense that duty came first, but he knew it came also from his uncertainty at navigating delicate terrain. Almost automatically he responded as a policeman.

'That's why I want those bastards who killed Rafiq and hit me with that cattle prod,' he said, and saw the spark fade from Nancy's eyes. 'If we have them facing murder charges we can go in and turn that mosque upside down.'

'Not with twenty thousand devout worshippers standing solidly as a human chain to protect their mosque, you can't,' Olivier interrupted.

'Are you telling me that mosques are off limits?' Nancy asked, dragging her gaze from Bruno.

'Usually yes, with a mosque this big and this well connected,' Olivier replied. 'But there is one way in. They run a small orphanage that operates as a kind of extortion racket. A gang of kids go into a shop, start breaking and stealing stuff, and of course they're too young to be arrested. Then the *Caïd* comes along to apologize and explains how underfunded the mosque is in trying to deal with those poor fatherless boys. The shop-keepers get the message and fork out to the welfare fund and the kids move on to the next store. That's the lever we'll use when the time comes.'

17

The sun was still warm in mid-afternoon and Bruno was in his garden wearing a polo shirt and shorts when he heard a car lumbering up the lane. Gilles had called to say he was on his way. Balzac darted off down the drive to investigate the new arrival. Bruno had been weeding his vegetable patch and filling a wicker basket with tomatoes that he would turn into a compote for freezing. Some olive oil, garlic, chopped onion and balsamic vinegar and he'd have more than enough to keep him through the winter. And there'd still be plenty of tomatoes left over for the *tarte* he planned to make for dinner.

He stood, stretching his back, put the basket by the kitchen door and went in to take some beers from the fridge and glasses from the freezer. Gilles had taught him that trick, and Bruno was looking forward to seeing him, although not to fulfilling Pamela's request to probe him about the stalled affair with Fabiola. Once the Brigadier had told him to leave the château for the rest of the day and concentrate on Gilles, Bruno had called Pamela and Fabiola and invited them to supper.

'You've lost weight. You're even thinner than you were in Sarajevo,' Bruno laughed, welcoming his friend with a hug. He shook the hand of the photographer who accompanied Gilles, an unshaven young man in jeans who looked too frail for the big camera case he carried. He was introduced as Freddy, and his eyes darted inquisitively around Bruno's property, the restored old cottage, the line of truffle oaks, the chicken coop and *potager*.

'I don't think Freddy is quite used to the countryside. More of an urban guy,' said Gilles, fondling Balzac's long ears, which always made the puppy roll onto his back to have his tummy scratched. 'He's going to leave us to talk, and if you can show him the château on the map he'll take some exterior shots if that's OK.'

'We might be able to do better than that,' said Bruno, handing each of them a cold beer. 'We can arrange for you to have an exclusive: photos of Sami and his family, the scars on his back and as much of an interview as you're likely to get from an autistic young man who's been through hell.'

'You're kidding.' Gilles looked amazed.

'No, we thought it was time to tell Sami's full story, including the way he was let down by one of France's biggest mosques, run by two of France's most respected Imams. But you and I need to talk anyway and the full photo shoot can't be till tomorrow, so let Freddy go and take his exterior shots and maybe he'd like to join us for dinner.'

Freddy declined, blushing, saying he had a date with one of the girls who had checked him into their hotel. Quick work, thought Bruno, but his absence would make the dinner conversation easier. Gilles's rental car map didn't show the château, so Bruno lent Freddy his local map and marked his own house, the hotel and the château.

'Fabiola will be joining us for dinner, along with Pamela,' Bruno said when Freddy had gone. 'I hope that's OK.'

'No problem on my side. Does she know I'm coming?'

'Yes, and she sounded pleased. I know things didn't work out too well when she came to Paris and if you don't want to talk about it, that's fine. But you can expect Pamela to quiz you, so be prepared.'

Gilles grinned. 'I know you too well, Bruno. You're making out Pamela to be the tough cop so I'll spill the beans to you. Don't worry, I was going to tell you all about it, because I want your advice. Fabiola is the woman I want in my life. I'm head over heels in love with her and I just want to make it work. Do you know what happened between us?'

'Not really, just that she was coming to see you in Paris for a weekend, apparently determined to spend most of it in bed. That was Pamela's interpretation.'

'And mine. And we did, except that we just talked, and held each other and slept. Somehow when it came to it, she couldn't make love, not properly.'

'Did she say why?'

'She wouldn't talk about it. I thought after we'd slept together, just holding each other, she'd be used to me and it would be fine in the morning. But it wasn't. It was like she was furious with herself, which was why she dressed and stomped out from my apartment, saying it wasn't me. It was all her problem. That was it. We've talked a lot on the phone since then, but she just refuses to go into it or even to talk to a woman psychologist. I asked some medical contacts and some female colleagues for recommendations, but Fabiola said she'd been let down by women like that before.'

Bruno did not know what to say. He'd have recommended

patience, platonic embraces and some female counselling for Fabiola but Gilles had already tried that.

'Pamela and I are on your side,' he said. 'We think you make a great couple. Pamela says Fabiola's in love with you, buys every copy of *Paris Match*, follows you on Twitter, has your name on Google alert so everything you write online goes straight into her inbox. Apparently it's the modern way of romance.'

Gilles looked pleased. 'You forget the other part of modern love,' he said. 'The gym; that's why I've lost weight. I'm trying to get into better shape so I don't feel like a fat slob if I ever do get her into bed properly. This is the first beer I've had in ages.'

He took a long sip, put down his glass, and said, 'In fact, I went to one of these women psychologists who'd been recommended by a colleague at *Paris Match*. She said all the usual things, be patient, give her time. But she also asked whether Fabiola had ever been able to resolve what had happened to her. She called it closure. I hate these psychobabble words but I know what she means.'

Bruno nodded. 'It's an interesting thought, but since Fabiola refuses to talk about it in any way, we have no idea what happened. Pamela thought it might have been a love affair that went sour, perhaps with a married man who abandoned her.'

'I was hoping that maybe Pamela, being so close to her, could find out more and then we could decide what to do next.' Gilles broke off and finished his beer in a couple of swallows.

'I'm sure she will. Now, I've got to make some dinner for us. It's going to be very simple: *tarte aux tomates*, roast pigeons with *petits pois* and then pears in red wine.'

'So much for my diet. But it sounds wonderful. I stopped off at the *cave* and picked up a couple of those bottles of Château Haut Garrigue you recommended. It's called Terroir Feely now and the wines have got funny new names. They call the white sauvignon Sincérité and the red is Résonance, but Hubert assured me it was the same wine. And he made me try some of the Château Briand dry white his daughter makes, so I got a bottle of that, too. Let me contribute those to the dinner, and I'll watch you cook while you tell me more about Sami.'

Bruno plucked four juicy pears from the tree as he led the way into the kitchen. To save time, he'd already bought some pre-made puff pastry. He scattered some flour and then rolled it out on his big wooden block into a rough circle, and put it on a plate inside the fridge to cool. He turned on his gas oven and set the heat at level six, picked out some of the best-looking tomatoes and put them on his scales. When they topped one and a half kilos he began slicing them thinly. Earlier, he'd mixed the juice of two lemons into a half-litre pot of Stéphane's thickest cream, since he objected to paying the price of the mascarpone he should have used. He now mixed the thickened cream with about half as much aged Cantal cheese. He'd picked a bunch of fresh basil leaves from his garden, but never used a knife to chop them, always ripped them with his hands. He'd never understood the chemistry but metal turned the basil black. He added the basil, salt and pepper, and left it to rest while he carefully cleaned the pigeons.

Cooking familiar dishes came almost automatically to him, so Bruno began talking about Sami as Gilles sat on the high stool by the kitchen counter, took notes and sipped at his beer. As Bruno mixed an egg, some soft butter and two chopped shallots into the ground pork that would be the stuffing, he described Sami's life in St Denis and why Momu had turned to the mosque in Toulouse. Meanwhile he added some nutmeg, salt and pepper, mixed the stuffing together and inserted it into the pigeons. Pamela always maintained the stuffing was the best part whenever she ate roast fowl. Then he reached for the big ham that hung from the beam in the kitchen, and carved off four slices, as thin as he could make them. He carved an extra slice, a little thicker, for the expectant Balzac, who wolfed it down and sat back, looking especially appealing as he hoped for more.

'Whether people at the mosque helped him go to Afghanistan, we don't know yet for certain,' Bruno said. 'But they were responsible for Sami and they let him down. The schools inspector who gave them a rating of "acceptable" has some explaining to do. Maybe that's another angle for your story.'

Bruno began mixing spices and sugar into half a litre of Bergerac red wine as he described Sami's voyage to Pakistan, and then his brutal treatment at the Peshawar madrassa. He grated lemon zest and ginger into the wine, added a splash of cognac, poured it all back into the wine bottle and replaced the cork. In his head he calculated the timings; thirty minutes for the first cooking of the *tarte aux tomates* and then another forty minutes when he'd turned down the heat to mark two on the gas stove. The pigeons would need about forty minutes at mark six. Pamela and Fabiola were due in about thirty minutes. Allowing for time for drinks and chat, he could make it all work, but he'd cheat a little by using a tin of *petits pois* rather than abandon his guests to make them.

He spread the thickened cream and Cantal mixture over the pastry. Then he layered the sliced tomatoes, each one fitting over the next in a long spiral that ended in the centre of the pastry. He filled the final hole with some more slices, sprinkled walnut oil and ground some fresh pepper over it all and put it in the oven, setting his timer.

'Given Sami's limitations, he's been enormously helpful,' Bruno told Gilles as he washed his hands. 'He's identified people from photographs, at the Toulouse mosque, in Germany and in Abu Dhabi, in Pakistan and in Afghanistan. He remembers every place and date and the names of the terrorists who starved him and whipped him to make him work. The intelligence guys are very happy.'

'Should you be telling me this?'

'I'm authorized to say he's being very helpful and cooperative. And if the Taliban know Sami, they know he's got an extraordinary memory. That's why they want to kill him'

'Has he told you yet how he escaped?' Gilles asked.

'Not yet, but we know that he learned about the French troops from a radio he repaired in a village south of Herat. When it was being tested he heard a news bulletin that said the French were at the Nijrab base in Kapisa, and that's when he began to think he might escape and get home. Then he says he just slipped out of the village, walked all night, hitched a couple of rides but walked most of the way. One of the soldiers here who served out there says people like Sami are seen as holy fools, said to be touched by Allah.'

'It sounds a better way than we think of them. When can I see him?'

'Tomorrow morning. Will that work for your deadline?'

Gilles nodded. 'That's great. This autism problem, how well does he express himself?'

'His speech improves every day, and he looks better, putting on a bit of weight. He seems very glad to be home but expect very short and simple sentences. I don't think it will be your usual kind of interview.'

'Can I quote you by name?'

'Anything about his life in St Denis before he went to the mosque, certainly. Anything after that, just call me a French official involved in Sami's debriefing. You can also meet the American colleague who's been sitting in on the debriefings, but you'll have to check with them about sourcing. And it might help if you took along a CD of Mozart. He loves Mozart, don't ask me why.'

'What about this mysterious gas explosion they were talking about on the car radio? There were reports of gunfire.'

'I've been tied up with Sami,' Bruno said, shrugging as he loaded plates, cutlery and wine glasses onto a tray. He took them out to the table in the garden, Balzac following hopefully at his heels. Gilles brought his notebook and a bottle of the Bergerac white.

'What's going to happen to Sami?' he asked. 'Do you know?'

'Nobody knows. It may depend on the way you write this story,' Bruno replied, opening the bottle. 'You've got the exclusive, you'll set the tone. Right now the world knows Sami as the Engineer, the ruthless bomb-maker with dozens of dead to his name. You now know it's a lot more complex than that, but you have to make your own judgement. This may be the most important story you ever write.'

Gilles was silent, looking away over Bruno's land and over the woods and ridges into the far distance.

'Jesus, this is a time when I wish I'd never given up cigarettes,' he said, and fell silent. Bruno poured him a glass of wine but Gilles left it untouched.

'You probably know that journalism isn't doing too well, but you don't know that they're offering redundancy payments at *Paris Match*. If too few of us take the money and leave, some will be laid off. We don't know how many, ten per cent, twenty, maybe more. Advertising is down with the financial crisis, sales aren't great. That means, I suppose, that I need this story. It could save my job. God knows there aren't many alternative jobs in journalism these days.'

'Well, at the worst you'll go out on one of the world's great scoops,' Bruno said, hearing the familiar sound of an underpowered car labouring its way up the steep lane to his house.

Fabiola's battered Renault Twingo lurched round the final bend and into Bruno's driveway. Balzac galloped to meet it with his ears flapping almost as if he hoped they would turn into wings and let him take to the air. And once the door on the driver's side opened, the dog seemed to soar onto the driver's lap, and Bruno heard his friend chuckle as they watched Balzac smother Fabiola with affection. He was glad to hear it. So focused had Bruno been on Sami's story and Gilles's reaction, he'd forgotten that for Gilles the deeper meaning of this evening was his new meeting with Fabiola. Gilles's fingers were plucking nervously at his shirt collar as if trying to adjust the tie he wasn't wearing.

Fabiola walked briskly from the car, a warm smile on her face. She thrust Balzac into Bruno's arms as she strode straight past him to take Gilles in a strong embrace, her arms locked around his back, her face tucked against his chest.

'I miss the beard,' she said, a catch in her voice. 'And you're getting too slim. I like you a bit more cuddly.'

Balzac still in one arm, Bruno leaned forward to kiss Pamela, but she took his face in her hands and kissed him soundly on the lips. 'I find all this affection rather catching,' she said, and kissed him again.

At last, all four of them were sitting in the evening sun with glasses of wine in hand, Balzac scampering from one to the other and squeaking in pleasure. Bruno pointed to the sweaters he'd put out in case the evening turned cool, raised his glass to his friends and rose to head for the kitchen, where his timer had just pinged. 'I must see to the food.'

Bruno took a very dry *cabécou* of goat cheese from his pantry and crumbled it in his hands. He turned down the gas, laid a slice of ham over each of the pigeons and slipped the roasting dish onto the bottom shelf of his oven. Having scattered the crumbled goat cheese over the top of the tomatoes and then tasted the spiced wine for the pears, he decided to add a touch more cognac and ginger before heading back to the table on the terrace, where his friends were talking about Sami.

'. . . even if he stays out of prison, Sami is still likely to go into a psychiatric hospital, not because it will do him any good but because that's the least the politicians and public opinion will accept.' Fabiola shook her head in frustration. 'He's Sami, he's not this monster we call the Engineer.'

'The point is that Sami is two people,' said Gilles. 'He's both Sami, this autistic kid who can't really be blamed for what he was forced to do, but he's also the instrument of mass murder.

Even if we drop this emotive name he's still a bomb-maker. But from what you've been saying, Bruno, Sami is also a third person, an extraordinarily valuable source of intelligence.'

'Are you saying that compensates for the bombs he made?' asked Pamela.

Gilles shrugged. 'Probably not, but it must go into the balance.'

Bruno headed for the kitchen, with a quick detour to the herb garden to pluck some more leaves of basil and one of his lettuces. He washed and rinsed it for the salad he'd serve after the pigeons, took the *tarte* from the oven and shredded some fresh basil on top. Finally he turned up the heat on the pigeons and took the first course out to his friends, where Pamela was lighting the candles and Gilles was opening the bottle of Sincérité.

'I was just telling Gilles that if he wants Sami to open up you ought to be there,' Fabiola said to Bruno as he joined them. 'Maybe you should take Balzac. He loves that little dog.'

'He's fond of you as well,' Bruno told her, slicing the *tarte*. Pamela handed him the plates, each in turn. 'At some point the tribunal will need to talk to you as his doctor. Maybe we should both introduce Gilles so Sami knows he's a friend.'

Bruno described the two new members of the tribunal. Fabiola perked up at the name of Amira Chadoub, saying she had read one of the woman's books on psychological issues for immigrants and had been impressed by it.

'I'll have the photographer with me as well,' Gilles said.

Bruno nodded. 'I'll pick you all up at the medical centre at ten in the morning. But now let's enjoy our dinner.'

'Pastry, cheese and tomatoes, it looks like a French version of pizza, and I smell goat cheese under all this basil.' said Pamela, picking it up like a slice of pizza to eat with her hands and taking a healthy bite. 'Mmm, good.'

'Seemed like a good way to use up some of my vast crop of tomatoes,' said Bruno, and then added thoughtfully, 'Maybe next time I should add some onions, perhaps a little ham.'

'Don't,' said Pamela firmly. 'Learn to leave something well alone. This is perfect just as it is.'

'I agree,' said Fabiola cheerfully, as if she didn't have a care in the world. 'And you can start cutting me another slice, Bruno. You can make this dish to get rid of your tomato crop with me whenever you want.'

18

Bruno had ensured that the names of Fabiola, Gilles and his photographer had been put on the approved list to get through the security checks at the château. Even so, they had to show their ID cards and Freddy's camera case was thoroughly searched along with Fabiola's medical bag. They rolled their eyes when Bruno showed them the sports bag containing broken laptops and junked mobile phones that he'd picked up from Florence. Balzac was well enough known that the guards relaxed their stern expressions and grinned at the sight of him. One bent down to pat and fondle his ears. With a chill, Bruno remembered that one of the special tricks of the Engineer had been to hide bombs inside the roadside corpses of stray dogs.

Nancy and the Brigadier came down the steps together to greet them. Despite the warm September day the Brigadier wore one of his usual dark suits and a forced smile, as though not happy to welcome the press but determined to make an effort. Nancy was in the casual pants and sweatshirt that she usually wore around Sami. Perhaps she suspected that more formal dress might change his response to her. Her eyes met Bruno's and he felt that frisson again, but she gave him a quick smile and then braced herself as Balzac greeted the American woman as an old friend, jumping happily into her arms as she bent to stroke him. Fabiola observed this with interest and then gave Bruno a quizzical look.

Introductions were made and the Brigadier handed Gilles a press statement that would be released once the new issue of *Paris Match* was published. His eyes skimmed over it and then he passed it to Bruno. It was a bland summary of the facts. There was something mind-numbing about official prose that could turn a profound human drama into lifeless bureaucratic verbiage, thought Bruno, but perhaps that was the point.

'How long do we have with Sami?' Gilles asked. Freddy already had one camera in hand and another slung around his neck.

'About an hour,' the Brigadier replied. 'We don't want to take too much time from the tribunal. He's in the garden with his parents, if you'd care to follow me.'

'Here, take the dog,' said Nancy, handing Balzac to Gilles. 'Now Sami will know you're a friend.'

'Doubly so,' said Fabiola, slipping her hand under Gilles's arm as they went through a stone archway. It led into a walled garden with a stretch of lawn, fruit trees espaliered against the stone, a long wooden bench and some chairs around a large table of sun-bleached wood laden with coffee and bottles of mineral water. Momu and Dillah looked up at their approach and Sami bounded toward the new arrivals, beaming and calling out, 'Fabiola.'

Balzac squirmed from Gilles's arms, made the perilous leap to the ground and sprang up to meet Sami's outstretched arms and start lapping at his neck. Bruno heard the mechanical clicking as Freddy fired off photo after photo. Nancy and the Brigadier were moving quickly toward the flight of stone steps that led up to the balcony, where Bruno saw Deutz standing, his arms crossed, glaring at them all. Nancy reached him first and put a hand on his arm and the Brigadier tried to steer him back inside the building, but Deutz shook them off and Bruno heard angry voices.

'Who in hell are all these people?' he heard Deutz bark, before the Brigadier's voice cut him off. By now others had noticed the confrontation and Bruno heard Fabiola's sharp intake of breath, as if bracing herself for something. Sami, intent on Balzac, was oblivious to it all, but Bruno moved at once to block Freddy's camera, which was now turning toward the balcony scene.

'That's not what you're here to photograph,' he said, keeping his voice low and friendly but taking a firm grip on Freddy's arm. 'The deal is you photograph Sami and his family. The American woman and the Brigadier are off limits or I'll confiscate your camera gear.'

Gilles, putting his small tape recorder on the table while trying to talk to Sami, seemed not to have noticed this by-play, but Fabiola looked stunned. She stood a moment with her hand to her face, watching as the scene on the balcony went quiet and the Brigadier led Deutz back inside.

'Are you alright?' Bruno asked quietly.

'Fine,' she said harshly, turning away to open her medical bag. She took out a stethoscope and asked Dillah if Sami had been taking the pills she'd given him. Briskly, she donned some surgical gloves, took his pulse, blood pressure and a small sample of blood. Then she asked him to slip off the tracksuit top and used her stethoscope on his chest and back, the occasion for Freddy to photograph the scars on Sami's back. When Freddy nodded that he was done, Fabiola patted Sami's shoulder, helped him dress again and sat down again close to Gilles.

Sami seemed more settled and more open to conversation than when Bruno had last seen him. He responded to Gilles's questions with whole phrases, even a few complete sentences, rather than in the monosyllables he had used when he first returned. Perhaps the questions, about the whippings and how he had managed his escape and his motives for leaving Toulouse, had become familiar.

Some of the answers Bruno had not heard before. Sami said he had been woken at night in the Toulouse mosque by his friends, Hamid and Khaled, and taken by car to a bus station. He gave the registration number of the bus and the towns it passed on the way to Germany. Gilles asked if he knew where he was going. Sami said no, but he was happy to be with his friends and he'd been excited to hear that he would be going on a plane.

What happened to his friends? He had not seen Hamid since Pakistan. Khaled had died after being wounded in Helmand, when an ambush had been prepared using one of Sami's roadside bombs but the British troops had some kind of radio beam that exploded the bomb before their convoy reached it. Sami said he'd been starved until he devised something that could neutralize the anti-bomb device. He took Gilles's notepad and made a quick but careful sketch of an electrical circuit to show what he had developed. Then he drew another sketch to show how he used a mobile phone to detonate a bomb.

No, he had not lived in a cave, Sami said. He only slept in a cave a few times, when crossing from Pakistan. Usually they stayed in villages, never more than a few days at a time. Once he went to Kabul, and he described the mobile phone shop where he'd stayed while adapting mobile phones to become detonators and going through catalogues of electrical goods, marking the ones he would need. Sami gave the shop's address, the manager's name and the catalogue numbers of the items he'd ordered. Gilles whistled softly as he began to realize just how much intelligence Sami's extraordinary memory could provide.

'Don't use that,' Bruno said. 'It's operational intelligence.'

Gilles nodded and asked, 'What do you want to do now, Sami?'

'Play with Balzac and Fabiola, swim with Bruno and run with Nancy,' Sami said, and opened his arms as if to embrace them all. 'Live with Momu and Dillah and Karim, fix things and hear Mozart.'

'Tell me about Mozart,' said Gilles. 'Where did you first hear his music?'

'In Pakistan, always Mozart on the playlists. Mozart like maths, only liquid. You know what's coming, until you get surprised.' He laughed happily. 'And always messages on playlists.'

'Messages?' Bruno asked, suddenly alert.

'On playlists they send by Internet, iTunes, Spotify, it doesn't matter,' Sami replied innocently. 'Just run acoustics programme, see the thick bar, copy it, slow it down, decompress and there's the message. All encrypted, very secure.'

Bruno nodded reassuringly and realized Gilles was looking at him fixedly. He must have picked up on the revelation that the jihadists were using playlists to hide their communications.

Bruno shook his head at Gilles. This could be too important to be shared with the readers of *Paris Match*.

'Can you fix this?' Bruno asked, handing Sami a dead laptop from the sports bag he'd brought. It was a cheap Taiwan-made model that looked very like the one Bruno had bought on special offer at the supermarket for four hundred euros.

Sami opened it and found it dead when he tried to turn it on. He rummaged in Bruno's bag until he found a connecting cord that fitted and looked around for a power point. His eyes scanned the garden and saw a small stone outbuilding, its door open and what looked like a lawnmower inside. Sami trotted to it, looked inside and came out with an extension cord wrapped around a wheel. He plugged the power cable into the back of the computer and waited briefly. Then he turned it over and neatly removed the battery and the power plug and pressed the On button for a count of perhaps thirty seconds. He replaced the battery, switched it on again and was rewarded with a momentary flare of tiny green and orange lights above the keyboard before they faded and died.

'It's OK, only needs new battery,' he said casually, and looked hopefully at Bruno. 'You have more? And tools?'

The rules for Gilles's interview with Nancy were no photos, and he had to agree to refer to her simply as an American diplomat. Freddy was told to put his cameras back in his bag. Fabiola had left quickly after Sami had gone back with Momu for another session with the tribunal. Bruno had passed on to the Brigadier Sami's sketches and his revelation about the Mozart playlists. Nancy was delayed by relaying the information to Washington. Gilles kept checking his watch.

Nancy finally emerged, having changed into a blue linen skirt and a plain white shirt, sleeves rolled up to her elbows, flat-heeled leather boots. Bruno thought he detected a touch of eye make-up and she was wearing a soft red lipstick and silver stud earrings. Again he had the sense of having seen that face somewhere before, but still could not place it. As she sat, Bruno was aware of a subtle hint of perfume. No longer needing to look comfortably rumpled for Sami, she seemed more at ease in this relatively formal dress. She gave a polite smile with the aplomb of a woman who had handled or chaired many such meetings.

No one asked Bruno to leave, so he listened to Gilles's questions, and was interested to note the careful courtesy with which Nancy treated them, although she answered either briefly or with diplomatic caution. Her remarks disappointed Bruno. So far she'd given the verbal equivalent of the Brigadier's press release, and Bruno wondered what Gilles could do with it.

'You seem very comfortable with Sami,' Gilles said suddenly. 'Have you come to like him?'

'I think anyone would sympathize with what he's been through and it must have taken guts and initiative to escape from the terrorists,' she said, with a smile that added something human and convincing to the words.

'So you believe his story?'

'We'll have to see what the medical tribunal says, but so far everything he says checks out and he is being very helpful.' Again, her body language and facial expression added emphasis. Bruno was aware that she was deliberately setting out to charm Gilles, even while a transcript of her words would read blandly on a page. He decided to intervene.

'I'm not sure our American friend has yet been briefed on the traumatic events of Sami's childhood,' Bruno said. 'It wasn't part of the initial diagnosis, but we heard it from his adoptive father. And it helps explain his problems today.'

Briefly, he outlined Sami's experience in the Algerian civil war, watching the rape and slaughter of his family while tied to a table for two days and two nights as he stared at their severed heads while their blood dried on his legs.

Nancy's eyes went wide in horror and she brought her hand to her mouth. For a moment Bruno thought she was going to be sick.

'That's incredible, except that I believe it,' she said, her voice hoarse, as if her throat was dry. 'I'd better make sure Washington knows; it's important context for everything else about Sami.' She shook her head and stared at Bruno. 'Kind of hard to see him as a ruthless terrorist after learning that. How old was he?'

'About five, I believe. You might want to ask Momu about it.'

'Was that on the record?' Gilles asked. 'Hard to see him as a terrorist once you know that?'

Nancy looked at him in silence, considering, and then shrugged. 'Why not? It's what I think. I can't imagine how anyone wouldn't be shattered by it. And with that memory of his . . .' Her voice trailed off.

'Do you think Sami should be sent back to the United States to face justice?'

'We and French officials are still trying to establish exactly what happened to him in Afghanistan, before we start considering judicial issues.' She rose. 'OK, I think we're done here.

You have a deadline and I guess you'll want to see Momu as well, to get some details about this terrible incident in Sami's childhood.'

She shook Gilles's hand, nodded to Bruno and said, 'We need to talk.' She led the way out of the walled garden in silence and into the park where they usually went for their jogs. Bruno restrained his curiosity and waited for her to begin.

'I gather you've seen Deutz's report on jihadists in prison,' she began once they were in the fringe of the trees. 'What did you think?'

'Impressive but unsettling,' he said. Parts of the report had sickened him. 'Heaven knows what a human rights lawyer would do with it.'

Deutz had used a wing at the top-security prison where the cells had been wired for sound and video. In the first phase, he had simply monitored the recruiting techniques deployed on the new arrivals. But then he had started using standard prison management tools, inserting stool pigeons and then hardened trusties sent in to challenge the jihadists' power. One of them ended dead in the showers, hanging from a pipe. It was listed as a suicide, with a note that the video had not been functioning that day. Deutz tried using tame Imams, but the prisoners simply refused to talk to them. His best results had come from inserting homosexual prisoners into the wing and using the resulting photographs to blackmail the jihadists into cooperating with threats to send still photos of the resulting encounters to their families. Once that first moment of cooperation was on film, Deutz could threaten to expose the man to his fellow jihadists as an informer.

'It's not something we'd get away with in Guantanamo,'

Nancy said drily. 'Not after those photos came out from Abu Ghraib.'

'I didn't think we could get away with it in France,' Bruno replied. 'And I'm not sure what Deutz means when he talks of success. Getting them to inform on one another is one thing, but they're still jihadists and they'll hate us all the more.'

'That's what I think. I'm sick of us being seen as the bad guys.'

'Is this what you wanted to talk to me about?' he asked.

'In a way, but there's also Deutz's claim that the scars might not have been punishment. He could be right. Maybe Sami was not whipped into obedience.'

'Sometimes I wonder about that,' Bruno replied. 'There are occasional flashes in Sami's eyes, I don't know whether it's intelligence, or if he's slyly observing us to see how we react to him. Maybe it's a survival mechanism he developed in Afghanistan, watching to see what he has to do to win approval. I think Sami knows his bombs killed people, you remember how he reacted to that card he thought looked like a bomb.'

Nancy swept her hand through her hair impatiently. 'You mean he did what he had to do to stay alive?'

'Yes, but he's still an autistic kid. I don't know what goes in in his head. That's what Deutz and the tribunal are for.'

'Deutz sees himself playing devil's advocate, I guess. But it's not just that, it's the methods he describes using in that paper. They worry the hell out of me. Do you think they might backfire on us if that paper of his leaks? We could pay for it down the road when details start to come out.'

'I thought you Americans were his big supporters.'

'Some are, those who want quick results and big headlines. There's a growing number of us who think this could be a much longer kind of war and we need to be a lot more subtle in the way we wage it. What about you?'

He shrugged. What would a high-flying diplomat want with the views of a village policeman? 'There's always a problem with balancing short-term results and long-term concerns. Break a man today and his sons make you pay for it later.'

'Not many politicians look that far ahead,' she said.

'I've noticed.' They had reached the edge of the parkland, where the scattered trees began to thicken into the woods that climbed all the way up the slope. Oaks, chestnut and walnut trees mainly, good country for wild boar. He led the way to the side, away from the wild woodland.

'Thanks for steering Deutz away when Gilles turned up,' he said.

'The Brigadier took care of it, but I don't think it was Gilles that set Deutz off. It was Fabiola. He kept asking who brought her here.'

'Professional rivalry?'

She shrugged and they walked on in a silence for a while. Bruno broke it by asking her whether she'd ever worked in the Arab world.

'A few liaison visits to Saudi and Jordan, one tour in Iraq, that's all. I don't speak it. Why do you ask?'

'You seemed surprised about what happened to Sami in the Algerian civil war.'

'It's like when you read about the Taliban shooting girls who're learning to read and burning their schools. Unless it's one girl you can see and identify with it doesn't stick, unlike those wretched photos of prisoners in Abu Ghraib that went all round the world. They defined us.'

'And you're worried that Deutz could define us all over again?'

'Yes, and then wondering if we really know what we're doing. There's a line of poetry about ignorant armies that clash by night. That seems to sum us up.'

Bruno glanced at her, surprised by her frankness as much as her views. He'd assumed she'd follow the Washington conventional wisdom. But he understood her snatch of poetry. He'd been in armies like that, like the mess in Bosnia when he'd been attached to the United Nations peacekeepers with an ill-defined mission and no coherent chain of command. But he'd also been in good units with good leaders, clear goals.

'Isabelle told me you were in that secret war in Chad, fighting the Libyans.'

Startled that she knew of it, and wondering how much else Isabelle had told her, Bruno glanced at her. She was watching him with polite interest rather than with an inquisitor's gleam in her eye. With some distant memory of stern lectures on security before the Chad operation, he tried to brush the topic aside. 'Nothing very secret about it, mainly a training mission. We were teaching the Chad troops to use modern weapons while they taught us how to move in the desert.'

Nancy shrugged and nodded, then looked at her watch, and said, 'Sorry, just checking when I can reach somebody in Washington.'

Bruno tried to remember the time difference, six or seven hours. It would still be four in the morning at the CIA or White

House or wherever she was planning to call. 'I presume they're pressing you to deliver Sami,' he said.

'I think we're getting more out of him here. It's a matter of persuading people of that despite the politicians and the talk-shows.'

'So you're on our side,' he joked, wondering if she'd smile. He was also wondering why she'd brought up Isabelle's name. Nancy did not strike him as the sort of woman who did anything by chance.

'Just temporarily on your side,' she said, and her smile looked genuine enough, coming with a twinkle in her eyes and a rather impish look that suited her. For a moment it gave him a sense of what she must have looked like when she was a teenager. 'So don't count on it lasting.' She took his arm companionably and they strolled in silence for a few paces.

'I hear you met Deutz before?' he said.

'Yes, when he went over to Quantico, where our psychological people are based. They didn't like him. Apparently he was rather too confident of his French charm succeeding with the women. One of them nearly brought a sexual harassment case, so then it took a lot of phone calls to get him into Guantanamo.'

'I thought our government didn't approve of Guantanamo.'

'It doesn't, officially, but at this level we can all be flexible. Did you read all of that report Deutz wrote?'

'Yes, there was nothing about Guantanamo in there.'

'No, but it was clear that he knew our smooth-talking Imam, Ghlamallah.'

'I must have missed that.'

'First rule of academic papers: always read the footnotes and the acknowledgements,' she replied. 'Ghlamallah is thanked for his cooperation and insight. Reading between the lines, it sounded as though he saw Ghlamallah as one of his tame Imams. You know Ghlamallah was in Saudi Arabia, working with them on their de-tox programme?'

'No, and I don't know what you mean by de-tox.'

'De-toxification, using Islam to persuade jihadists of the error of their ways.'

'Does it work?'

'In some cases, but it's slow,' she said. 'The fact is, we're groping in this world, so we'll try anything.'

'I don't think we're groping with Sami. I mean, he's doing his best to help.'

'That's why it's so frustrating to sit around this place while the tribunal gives him Rorschach tests or whatever they do. I've got a whole lot more mugshots sent over that I can't wait to try on him. As it is, I'm going stir-crazy here.'

She stopped, let go of his arm and turned to face him. 'You know this area. Where should we go for dinner? Your favourite place, my treat, or at least, Uncle Sam's treat.' Her face had that impish look again.

'Well, there is one thing I was hoping to do this evening, if the Brigadier lets me out,' said Bruno, smiling. 'It might make it easier if I'm taking you. But it will be very noisy, very French, a lot of people, many of them good friends, and a lot of wine. It's the *vendange* supper at the local vineyard, to celebrate the end of the harvest. And I should warn you that Gilles will probably be there, if he finishes writing in time. Have you ever eaten fresh-roasted wild boar?'

19

The smell of roasting meat grew stronger as Bruno and Nancy walked down the long avenue, already lined with parked cars, that led to the Domaine. Bruno had little choice but to leave his Land Rover by the entrance gate, a long stroll from the winery where the *vendange* party was being held. It gave him time to explain to Nancy how the vineyard had been saved from financial trouble by the Mayor's plan to raise cash by selling shares to the citizens of St Denis. Since shareholders, who included Bruno, were given discount prices, they then from self-interest and loyalty became the best customers.

'The party's late this year, so the grapes will already have been pressed,' he explained. 'They had to rush the picking because of the weather. So you won't be able to taste the fresh grape juice.'

'And is the wine you make here good?' she asked, turning her head to look at him as they talked, and sounding genuinely interested.

She was looking splendid, with that easy style that comes from deep self-confidence. Nancy was wearing a red roll-neck sweater, a leather jacket and jeans tucked into knee-high brown boots. Her dark hair fell in natural curls, flattering her rather square jaw with its slightly prominent chin. Except for her generous lips and eyes that were lively with intelligence, Bruno would have thought it a face too strong for beauty. But there was something special about her, perhaps the proud way she carried her head or the way she took part so easily in the male world of politics and security. Whatever it was, he knew he'd remember this woman.

'Tell me when you've tasted it,' he answered her. 'It will be last year's wine and I think Julien usually does better with his whites, but it's all very drinkable. It may not compare with the fine wines you drink on the diplomatic circuit in Paris.'

'Some of the embassies, you'd be surprised,' she said, grinning. 'And if you knew what we used to drink in college, you'd be appalled.'

'Do you know Bergerac wines?' He raised his voice over the growing sounds of revelry as they approached the winery.

'You bet,' she said. 'Isabelle made a point of serving them at her place. That was the first time I had foie gras with Monbazillac. And there was another, a red that she said was one of your favourites, named after some baron who was always drawing his glove to challenge people to duels.'

'Château de Tiregand,' Bruno said, smiling, and privately touched to think of Isabelle shopping around the wine *caves* of Paris to find wines to which he'd introduced her.

They rounded the corner to see the golden stone of the inner courtyard turned into a rosy pink by the glow from the giant firepit on which the boars were roasting. When the twilight gave way to the dark of night, Bruno knew the whole scene would turn a rich red as the ashes smouldered. He felt the strange sensation stealing over him of time slipping, of the modern France of high-speed trains and computers giving way to a scene that was almost medieval or perhaps even older. The setting of stone and fire and meat roasting over an open fire could have taken place in this valley in days when men carried swords and wore chain mail and kept guard against English raiders, or millennia ago when they wore furs and painted prehistoric beasts on the walls of caves.

'Wow, we could be back with the knights of the round table,' said Nancy, squeezing his arm. 'This is great. You ought to sell tickets.'

He shook his head. 'This is just for us locals. It's all done by volunteers. For this to work, people need to know each other.'

'Then I'm honoured,' she replied. 'Thank you for inviting me.' She paused. 'I just realized, there's no music.'

'Not now, when people are greeting and talking and tasting the wine. But there'll be dancing later, after the food.'

The courtyard was half-filled by four long rows of tables, lit by ranks of hurricane lamps and candles in glass jars. Places were set for thirty or forty people at each one and one large crowd was milling around a makeshift bar where big jugs were being filled from barrels of wine. A second crowd was standing back from the heat at the great fire as men with wet towels round their hands wrestled to lift one of the long metal spits. The weight of the wild boar bowed it slightly as they carried it to another set of tables where two men in white aprons were already carving the first of the roasted boar.

'Where the hell have you been, Bruno?' called Stéphane jovially, waving one of the big carving knives.

Raoul clapped him on the shoulder, put a wet towel in his hand and barely giving him time to introduce Nancy to Stéphane, led the way to the third boar. Bruno helped lift the beast from the blasting heat to carry it, still dripping fat, to the carving tables. He apologized to his friends, saying duty had called him away. He was sorry to have missed the usual ritual of building the fire, stuffing the boar with thyme and sage, sewing up the belly and then sliding the beast onto the roasting spit. Usually it was Bruno who concocted the bucket of marinade, herbs, wine and honey. They applied it with long brushes made of thick branches of rosemary tied around a pole. It always reminded Bruno of a witch's broom.

'I was going to save you a wee dram, but they finished off the bottle,' said Dougal, coming to give Bruno a welcoming hug. Dougal had launched St Denis's new tradition of baptizing the beasts with a splash of whisky just before they were placed atop the fire. The men who had built the fire and dressed the boar then finished the bottle.

Dougal took Bruno's arm and turned him aside. 'When can we get the insurance inspectors into Le Pavillon?'

'Up to the Gendarmes,' Bruno said. 'Trust me, it will be taken care of.'

Julien approached, bringing two large water glasses filled with wine. Bruno took them and turned to find Nancy and saw her standing with Fabiola and being introduced to Pamela, Florence and Annette, a young magistrate based in Sarlat. He was pleased to see that Yveline, the Gendarme officer, had joined them. Her unpopular predecessor, Capitaine Duroc, had seldom bothered to attend any of the civic festivities that meant so much in the life of St Denis. Bruno excused himself from his friends and went to join the women and hand Nancy her glass.

'I'm celebrating,' said Pamela, kissing him enthusiastically.

'My brace is finally off and Fabiola says I can start riding again tomorrow. When do you get a day off to come and see the new horse I'm hoping to buy?'

Nancy seized the cue and began an animated discussion about horses, but Bruno noted that as soon as Pamela spoke, Nancy withdrew a fraction, observing Pamela in the way cops were trained to do. Watchful more than curious, there was a cool detachment in Nancy's gaze. Bruno thought Isabelle might have told her of Pamela as the Mad Englishwoman, that old nickname for her that the people of St Denis had first coined before they came to know her.

Nancy and Isabelle must have been closer than he'd assumed, Bruno thought as he felt a friendly hand grip his arm to draw him to one side. Hubert de Montignac, whose local wine shop regularly made the Hachette list as one of the best *caves* in France, handed him a glass of red.

'It's the new one Julien and I started making last year, leaving the juice in the vat with the skins,' Hubert said. Bruno had hoped the wine would benefit from Hubert's expertise. 'We kept it six months in a barrel. What do you think?'

His eyes still on the unspoken interplay between the women, Bruno sniffed; the smell of fruit was stronger than usual but there was a deeper note in the scent, a hint of maturity. He sipped, and opened his eyes in surprise. It was markedly better than the reds Julien had made in the past.

'That's a good wine,' Bruno said. 'It can't just be the barrel. There's more Merlot in this.'

'Half and half Merlot and Cabernet Sauvignon, plus about five per cent Cabernet Franc; it's what we plan to make this year.'

It had been a good harvest, Hubert went on. Having invested most of his savings in the town vineyard, Bruno was delighted to hear that St Denis was now producing a wine of which he could be proud. Bruno led Hubert back to the women, who were still talking enthusiastically about horses, and Hubert began pouring another bottle of his new red for them to try. Bruno excused himself to make a brief tour of the crowd, shaking hands and kissing cheeks and ducking questions about the explosion at Le Pavillon. He was looking for the Mayor. Finally he found him coming out of the door to the Domaine's big kitchen, carrying a big pot filled with roast potatoes.

'More pots to bring, Bruno,' the Mayor called, and Bruno helped him take out the rest and then pulled him to one side.

'Things are about to get busy,' Bruno said quietly. 'The news about Sami being here will break tonight and we'll be flooded with media tomorrow.'

'Not just media,' the Mayor said. 'We're likely to get political demos, *Front National*, anti-war types, Islamic groups. I had a word with the Prefect about bringing in extra Gendarmes and putting the CRS on standby.'

The *Compagnies Républicaines de Sécurité* were the much-feared riot police, with helmets, shields and body armour that made them look like bodyguards for some alien species. Bruno understood the need for them but winced at the thought of their patrolling the streets of St Denis.

'Ah, there you are,' the Mayor said when a figure slipped from the light of the kitchen. As she paused to blink into the darkness where the two men stood, Bruno saw the silhouette of a woman in a well-cut dress, wearing flat-heeled shoes, her grey hair flowing. He recognized the half-French, half-American historian who had become close to the Mayor after his wife died.

'Jacqueline,' Bruno said, embracing her with real affection and catching a hint of Chanel. 'I thought you'd be back teaching in Paris.'

'I am,' she said, hugging him. 'I came down for the weekend, for this. There's a rumour going round that you have a new woman in tow, an American like me. You must introduce us.'

'Gladly, but she's hardly in tow, just a colleague. In fact, she's talking horses with Pamela and Fabiola. She's at the Embassy, a legal attaché.'

'So I don't need to ask what brings her here,' Jacqueline replied, frowning. 'I might have known you'd be involved with this poor devil they're calling the Engineer. I presume your old friend the Brigadier has stashed him here.'

Bruno glanced at the Mayor, who shrugged and then shook his head, as if to say he'd told Jacqueline nothing. Bruno knew her to be a formidable woman, as perceptive as she was curious and with a fierce intelligence. Jacqueline was even more passionate about politics than his Mayor, and Bruno always felt he should have read every word in *Le Monde* for a week before joining them for dinner.

'He hasn't been stashed anywhere,' Bruno said, mildly. 'His name is Sami and this is his home and he's as French as I am, thanks to the Mayor, who signed his naturalization papers.'

'Hmm, you could pay for that,' Jacqueline said thoughtfully, glancing at the Mayor, 'unless you lead the fight to stop his extradition.' The sound of a handbell rang out over the chatter and Julien climbed onto a chair, still tolling his bell until it was quiet enough for him to say a brief word of welcome and invite them all to take their seats for dinner.

Bruno found himself surrounded by women – Jacqueline and Florence, Yveline and Nancy, Pamela and Fabiola, who kept an empty chair beside her in case Gilles was able to join them. A generous slice of game pâté, with cornichons and cherry tomatoes, lay on each plate as a starter. A large dish, filled with thick slices of roast boar, dominated the table. It was flanked by a large bowl of salad and another of roast potatoes. Magnums of red and white wine stood beside jugs filled with a thick sauce of *cèpe* mushrooms.

Bruno looked around the tables and pondered the menu with an almost professional eye, honed from many a rugby and tennis club dinner. The benches and tables and crockery had been borrowed from the clubs, he recognized. Hubert had probably provided the wine glasses; the clubs usually made do with water glasses and even recycled mustard and jam jars. Had Bruno been involved, he'd have tried to provide a soup as a starter, probably with the *cèpes*, since the woods would be full of them after the rain. Still, for a first effort at a *vendange* for this many people Julien had organized this well, he thought, as he poured wine and the Mayor began slicing a big round *tourte* of bread.

And the white wine he had drunk had been more than decent, with some Semillon added to Julien's usual Sauvignon Blanc grapes. The red wine being served was not up to the standard of the barrel-aged wine Hubert had poured, but it went well with the pâté and was sturdy enough for the boar.

'Do you have this dinner every year?' Nancy asked. She had been chatting with Annette about rally-driving, Annette's passion. Bruno had a hair-raising memory of driving with the young magistrate headlong along a wooded track, convinced she was about to crash them head-first into a tree at every bend.

'No, this is the first *vendange* since it became a town business,' he told her. 'Everyone here you see is a shareholder, getting a return on our investment. Some of them took part in picking the grapes, and I'd have joined them if this other business hadn't come up.'

'You mean Sami,' said Yveline. 'Fabiola told us all about it. And who is this guy Deutz?'

'He's with the medical tribunal trying to decide whether Sami is fit to stand trial,' Nancy said, before Bruno could frame his answer. He'd been looking for Fabiola but her chair was empty. She must have slipped away.

'Why do you ask?' Nancy went on.

'He's a lot more than that,' Annette interrupted. 'Fabiola froze when Yveline mentioned his name, like there's something personal there.'

'No doubt about it,' said Florence. 'There's something not right about this, Bruno. What do you know about him?'

Before he could speak Nancy said, 'Deutz freaked earlier today when Fabiola showed up.'

Pamela caught Bruno's eye and seemed about to speak when a cheerful shout of greeting interrupted them and Gilles appeared to slap Bruno on the shoulder, Fabiola looking happy with his arm around her. That was where she'd gone, Bruno realized. Gilles must have texted her that he was arriving. Gilles nodded amiably to Nancy and then darted around the table to kiss Florence and then Pamela.

'I need a word,' he said, coming back to Bruno and almost hauling him to his feet and then tugging him away from the courtyard. Bruno saw that Fabiola's eyes followed Gilles fondly before she turned back to her friends. He wondered if that conversation would continue now that Fabiola had joined them.

'My story is running on our wire and my tweet has gone viral,' Gilles said and held up his phone. Messages were racing past on the screen. 'That's my Twitter account, people responding and tweeting it on. They're coming in too fast to see, I've never seen anything like this.'

'Do I congratulate you?' Bruno asked. He knew little of Twitter and thought life was too short to spend more time than he had to looking at a phone or computer screen.

'This is not about me, it's the story. I'm late because I had to stop the car three times on the way here, doing phone interviews for France-Inter, the BBC and Agence France-Presse. We've got requests from al-Jazeera and CNN. Everybody wants some of this.'

Bruno glanced back to the long tables in the courtyard where Nancy was climbing from her seat. She began walking toward them, her phone to her ear.

'Not just you,' Bruno replied to Gilles, but then something happened that rocked him.

Nancy was advancing toward him in that graceful, assertive way she had, still listening to her phone but with her eyes fixed intently on his. Out of the blue he felt a jolt of sexual energy pass between them that was so powerful he felt suddenly out of breath. He saw her eyes widen and her mouth open and she stopped dead in her tracks, her shoulders back and her breasts thrusting forward. She was still staring at him and Bruno was suddenly certain that she felt this same intense rush of attraction.

He felt like leaping to take her in his arms, but something kept him rooted to the spot. He found cautionary thoughts erupting in his mind. One of them seemed to say Pamela and another said Isabelle, a third said Nancy was an American official and a fourth said half the town was present here and yet another said there was no future in this intense surge of passion.

Nancy swallowed, seemed to collect herself, dropped her eyes and half turned to concentrate on her phone call. Gilles's phone was ringing again and then Bruno's mobile began to vibrate. He felt drained, his mouth dry. Whatever this erotic rush had been he felt it passing. He took a deep breath, checked the screen and saw it was Philippe Delaron. Reluctantly, he answered.

'The Mayor told me you said it was OK for me to run the story,' Philippe began. 'We were right behind *Paris Match*, but can you give me a quote?'

Bruno fought to pull himself together and duty and habit kicked in. He pondered briefly and then said, 'You can quote me saying we're all glad to see Sami home and reunited with his family, but he's been through a terrible ordeal. He has very serious medical and psychological problems that are being addressed by some of France's best experts. Meanwhile he's doing his best to help French and American officials to understand the trauma he went through.'

'Has he been charged yet? Is he spilling the beans about the Taliban?'

'That's all I want to say for now, Philippe. But you were at school with him, so that should let you fill a page or two. Good luck.'

Bruno closed his phone, aware of Nancy standing close to his side, almost close enough to touch. She was listening to her phone and answering briefly in English. She looked at him curiously, her mouth still slightly open and her lips glistening. He forced himself to tear his eyes from her. He felt rather than saw her nod at him before walking away out of earshot.

Bruno closed his eyes and tried to think of what actions he'd neglected, what duties remained for him to do. He felt suddenly very hungry. He looked across at Pamela, expecting to see her still locked in conversation with the other women, but she was watching him, something like wariness in her eyes. He told himself to smile and went back to his table, where his plate of roast boar and mushroom sauce awaited along with a refilled wine glass.

Annette, Yveline, Florence, Jacqueline and Fabiola were huddled over Annette's mobile phone, reading with apparent approval the story Gilles had filed on the *Paris Match* website. Annette held the phone out to Pamela and she took it, almost reluctantly, and scrolled it down as Bruno began to eat.

'Have you seen this already?' Pamela asked him, briefly raising her eyes from the tiny screen. She was looking at him closely and he felt flushed. Bruno shook his head, washed down his first mouthful with a sip of red wine and made himself smile at her.

'No, but I trust Gilles and I want to eat while this is still warm,' he said.

'Better eat while you have the chance,' she replied and

gestured at the other tables. The sound of conversation was fading and Bruno looked around to see knots of his friends and neighbours clustering around mobile phones. An image from some long-ago newsreel came into his mind, of people in vintage clothing huddled around old-fashioned radio sets as they listened to news of war being declared.

Mauricette from the Hôtel St Denis and the manager of the Royal Hotel were leaving the courtyard, phones pressed to their ears. Mauricette changed course toward him.

'You could have told me this was coming, Bruno,' she said briskly. 'We were going to take time off but *France Deux* TV has just booked the whole hotel. I've let the staff go and now we'll have to work all night to get the rooms ready.'

So it begins, Bruno thought, turning back to his plate as Mauricette stalked off to her car. Music began to play from loudspeakers Julien had rigged on the table where Stéphane had carved the boars. He recognized the tune, 'Mon Amant de Saint-Jean', and the singer. It was the original version by Lucienne Delyle, recorded sometime during the war before she had been eclipsed by the rising star of Edith Piaf. Bruno would always associate Delyle with 'J'attendrai', the song of the Frenchwomen of 1940, waiting through the long years of war for their men to come home from the PoW camps. A memory of Delyle's face on an old record cover suddenly came into his head and he looked across the table at Nancy, struck by the resemblance that had eluded him.

Fabiola had put her phone away and the women were ignoring the music and talking with quiet animation among themselves. Bruno caught the Mayor's eye, raised his glass and they nodded to one another, each thinking of the intense global attention that was about to focus on St Denis.

His plate empty and the courtyard starting to fill with dancers, he joined the women to ask Pamela to dance. Bruno had never quite mastered the swing, the dance that most French people seem to absorb effortlessly in their youth, and Pamela had never learned it. So they fell into their usual dance, not quite a foxtrot and not quite a waltz, but they circled the floor contentedly, enjoying the music and the pleasure of being in each other's arms.

'What were you all discussing so animatedly?' he asked. 'Was it about Sami?'

'No,' she said, glancing behind her to see if anyone could overhear and then speaking softly, close to his ear. 'This is not for other ears. Nancy started asking Fabiola about Deutz. Then Annette and Jacqueline joined in. And you know Jacqueline, how direct she is. She asked Fabiola straight out if they'd had a relationship that ended badly.'

'What did Fabiola say?'

'She said she wants only to think about Gilles this evening,' Pamela replied. 'But I don't think this is going to stop there.'

20

Beyond his love for the town and the life he had built in St Denis, there was another reason why Bruno knew he could never leave. He suspected he would be a terrible policeman in any other setting. Colleagues like J-J, the chief detective for the *Département*, liked to say that Bruno embodied a unique store of local knowledge, familiar with every family and house in his commune. Bruno sometimes suspected that was all he had, apart from basic common sense, a lot of good advice from his Mayor and a largely law-abiding and amiable population. And nothing could be more important for a policeman than knowing the territory he covered and the people he protected and served.

Bruno stood in awe of the cops in great cities like Paris or Marseille, who dealt almost invariably with strangers. For Bruno, it was the reverse. Strangers were the rarity; mostly he dealt with people he'd known for years, youngsters whom he'd watched growing up. He'd danced with their mothers at their weddings, played rugby with their fathers, helped arrange the funerals of their grandparents and taught most of them how to pass a rugby ball and to volley at tennis.

Bruno's instinctive reaction whenever a problem arose was to ask himself whom he knew, a relative or neighbour or colleague, who could help him get to the heart of the matter. His idea of policing was based on knowing people, their backgrounds and concerns, sometimes their secrets. And so, squashing the twinge of guilt he felt at investigating a friend, on the morning after the *vendange* he rang the pathology lab in Bergerac, where one of the doctors had been at medical school with Fabiola. The two doctors were friendly without being close friends, ready to do favours for one another, but Bruno knew they seldom met.

Bruno already knew Fabiola's medical background, and a few moments on the Internet had been enough to find the professional biography of Pascal Deutz on the website of the prison service. Deutz had been a lecturer on the teaching staff at Marseille when Fabiola had been a student. It was no more than a suspicion, but Fabiola's reaction to Deutz had triggered one of Bruno's hunches.

'Hi, I'm looking for your advice about our mutual friend Fabiola,' Bruno began when the Bergerac doctor answered. He had prepared a plausible excuse, saying that her friends planned to throw her a surprise party next month but worried that it might be too close to the anniversary of the day of her climbing accident. They remembered Fabiola being really depressed around that time every year. Did her fellow medical student happen to remember when it was?

'Sure, it was a big thing at medical school,' came the innocent reply. 'It was *Toussaints*, five years ago. I remember because I'd been away for a family event at my grandfather's grave and when I got back everyone was talking about it. I don't remember the details, but a piton broke or a belay failed. I remember reading about it.'

232

'Reading?' Bruno asked. 'You mean it made the newspapers?' On a pad he scribbled 31 October, *Toussaints*, All Saints' Day, when old-fashioned French families still gathered at the family graves to commemorate the dead.

'No, it was the report the mountaineering club had to make about the accident. It's routine in the event of somebody having to go to hospital. I'm pretty sure it was a piton that failed. But as the senior guy and by far the most experienced climber, Deutz came in for a lot of criticism. He was really broken up about it because he and Fabiola had been very close all year until then. He told us at the club he blamed himself. I guess that was why he later transferred out of the school, but he's doing very well now, I hear.'

'Deputy head of the prison psychiatric service,' said Bruno.

'Not for long. I hear rumours of a professorship at Paris-Diderot.'

'Well, we'll be careful to avoid the last days of October.'

'Sure thing, give Fabiola my best. Let me know what date you pick, it could be fun to come and surprise her.'

Bruno went back to Deutz's official biography and saw he'd transferred from the medical school staff five years earlier to join the prison service. Now he had a date. He then called the medical school, was put through to the security office and asked how he might get hold of a copy of the report of the mountaineering club into an accident on the relevant date. He was given the name of the current club president, but then heard that the club secretary, another security guard, had just walked in. Within ten minutes a copy of the report had been faxed to him.

It was just one page of single-space typing, written by the

club secretary of the day after interviewing Deutz and the two other students on the climb. There had been no interview with Mademoiselle Fabiola Stern, still in hospital after suffering concussion and a broken jaw and cheekbone. She had not been wearing a helmet, in defiance of club rules. Deutz accepted responsibility for that and for placing the piton that had failed and for allowing too long a belay on the rope. That meant that Mlle Stern had fallen much further than she should. Deutz had been praised by the other climbers for bringing the unconscious Mlle Stern down the mountain and to hospital. Deutz's licence to lead climbs was suspended for a year, and he would need to retake the qualifying tests. Copies of the report had gone to the medical school director and to the Mountaineering Club de France.

Bruno sat back, pondering. That was enough to account for a certain chill in relations between Fabiola and Deutz, but it was a far cry from the kind of sexual trauma that seemed to be at the source of Fabiola's problem. Obviously he'd been barking up the wrong tree, adding two and two and getting five or even seven. So much for his hunch; he'd have to think again.

But what had the Bergerac doctor meant when he said that Fabiola and Deutz had been very close? Bruno recalled Fabiola once telling him that when she was at medical school she'd had an affair with a man she called 'a cute mountain climber'. The phrase had stuck in his head because it was an unusual way to describe a grown man. And he could hardly think of any word less fitted to Deutz, a rangy, muscular type with an assertive manner, always trying to dominate any encounter. But who could fathom the strange accidents of human chemistry that brought two people together?

There was a phrase Bruno recalled from one of those sayings of the day that *Sud Ouest* sometimes printed alongside its horoscopes and crossword puzzles. It had come from La Rochefoucauld, a name he vaguely knew as some distinguished French writer of the past, but it had stuck with him: *Love, as it exists in the world of today, is nothing but the contact of two skins and two fantasies.*

Instinctively, Bruno had disagreed, too much the romantic to accept such cold cynicism. But he understood how new lovers could construct fantasies of each other. Maybe a young woman, enjoying the thrills of mountaineering, could have seen a younger Deutz as 'cute'. Or maybe Fabiola had plucked from the air a word to downgrade the importance of a relationship that had affected her more than she wished to reveal. Maybe she thought of Gilles as cute. But what mere male ever knew how women really thought of their lovers?

He turned to the next item on his list of things to do, which was to track down the gynaecology professor Fabiola had talked to about her problem. He called the security team at the medical school again. Professor Rosalie Waldeck, now retired, had taught gynaecology and obstetrics. He took a note of the address in Villefranche du Périgord, a small town south of Bergerac, and her phone number.

His phone rang, a Paris number. It was Yacov Kaufman.

'I was just reading the news on my phone,' he said. 'Drama in St Denis.'

'You're telling me. What can I do for you?'

'It's Maya, my great aunt. She's flying into Paris from Israel today and I have to meet her at the airport and bring her straight down to St Denis. But I can't get a hotel, the media seems to have booked every room around. Can you help?'

'If all else fails, you can both stay at my place, but let me call a friend who has some empty *gîtes*. It will be cheaper than a hotel. How long will you stay and when will you arrive?'

'I'm at the airport now,' Yacov replied. 'Her flight lands in a few minutes and I have David's car here to bring her down. I wanted her to spend the night in Paris and rest a little but she insists on coming straight down to you. I imagine we'll be with you late this afternoon and we'll be there three or four days, maybe a week. She wants to see the region again and she wants to use my grandfather's old car.'

'I'll call you back.'

Bruno tried hotels he knew in Les Eyzies, Lalinde and Trémolat but there was not a room to be had. He called Pamela, who was delighted to rent her *gîtes* now that the English families had left. Bruno booked both, one for Yacov and one for Maya; he presumed a woman so wealthy would want her own bathroom. Pamela offered to feed them, if required. The media would probably have booked all the restaurants.

'I'll come with your new tenants later this afternoon,' he said. 'And I'm sorry all this has come up but it was lovely dancing with you last night.'

'It was quite an evening,' she said coolly, and he could hear none of the usual affection in her voice before she hung up.

Bruno paused, wondering whether she had observed that strange and powerful moment he had shared with Nancy at the *vendange*, before looking again at his phone to call Florence; her students would be a key part of the effort to persuade Maya that St Denis would make good use of the bequest.

He was about to inform the Mayor before driving to the château to ask the medical team about Gaston's condition when the Mayor came into Bruno's office. He closed the door behind him and said, 'Karim told me about getting his boy back. Did that have to do with this so-called gas explosion that the Gendarmes have sealed off?'

'Officially, since you approved my secondment to the Brigadier's staff, I can't say,' Bruno replied. 'Between you and me, it was a suicide bomber who thought Sami and his family were still in Le Pavillon.'

'Philippe Delaron has interviewed Karim about Pierre's rescue. He's good at putting two and two together.'

'I can't talk to him about it until this is over,' Bruno said.

'It's not just Philippe. We've got half the Paris press corps heading for St Denis. Ask the Brigadier to call me when he has a moment.'

'I'm heading for the château now. I'll ask the Brigadier if he can release a statement, or at least nominate a press spokesman. Meanwhile, the Halévy woman is arriving here later today, staying at Pamela's.'

'We'll make sure everything's ready.' At the door, the Mayor turned. 'And however you got Karim's boy back, well done.'

On Bruno's car radio, the news bulletin on Périgord Bleu identified the local château where 'the French terrorist known as the Engineer' was being held. But it then summarized Gilles's report about Sami's autism. That day's edition of *Sud Ouest* carried photos that Philippe had unearthed of Sami as a schoolboy. Another story was headlined: 'Was this the terrorist recruitment centre?' with a photo of the Toulouse mosque and another of the telegenic Imam, Ghlamallah.

'We're winning,' said the Brigadier, almost smugly, when Bruno was admitted to his office. A large TV screen had now been installed. 'These days, the media is where battles are won and lost. Look at this.'

The Brigadier worked his computer keyboard and the TV screen lit up and began playing extracts from American news programmes. One of the clips showed a man Bruno recognized, the White House spokesman, saying something about 'extraordinary cooperation from our French allies'. The CNN clip carried a headline on the bottom of the screen: 'Engineer – or victim?'

'The Mayor of St Denis asked me to tell you he'd appreciate a call, or a press statement about the explosion at St Chamassy,' Bruno said. 'He thought appointing a press spokesman might help, with all the media gathering.'

'There's one coming down from the ministry, should be here soon. I'll call your Mayor. Anything else?'

'I asked the field hospital about Gaston. They said he'd been moved to the military hospital in Bordeaux but wouldn't say anything about his condition.'

'He's badly burned, still concussed but they think they can save his eyesight. We've identified the terrorist from the mosque. He took one bullet in the shoulder joint and another in the bone. He'll lose an arm, but he can talk.'

'What happens to Sami now? Will it be life in a prison hospital?'

'We'll see. Now that the world knows he's been cooperating

with us he'll have to be somewhere secure,' the Brigadier said. 'Those Mozart playlists may be the biggest breakthrough into the jihadist communications we've ever had.'

Bruno nodded sadly. Jihadists had long memories; Sami's life and the lives of his family would be in danger for years to come. They could never resume their normal lives in St Denis. Bruno had heard of the American witness protection system for useful informers who were given a new identity in a strange town, but a French-speaking Arab family suddenly arriving anywhere on earth with an autistic young man would soon be identified.

'Some good news for you,' the Brigadier went on. 'Those photos of the two little ruffians you emailed – Olivier identified them. They're from the orphanage at the mosque. And that impressive young woman at your Gendarmerie got a very good statement from the driver of the Renault that brought them which implicates the whole of the mosque security. I gather she threatened to charge him with luring the two boys away from the orphanage for his own purposes and then asked him if he knew what happens to paedophiles in prison. She thinks his statement justifies a full-scale search warrant but she suggests instead that we get an order from the family affairs court to intervene on behalf of the kids in the orphanage. As she says, not even the most pro-Muslim politician would want to be seen blocking that. She's a smart girl, should go far. By the way, she was asking where she could find you.'

'Did she say what it was about?'

'No, but she was asking how long she'd have to keep Le

Pavillon sealed off and she's obviously curious about what happened. You can brief her but make sure she knows it's officially secret. And tell her I'm arranging for a detachment of Gendarmes from Périgueux to help her out. They'll arrive this afternoon.'

Bruno went out to the balcony to contact Yveline about the extra Gendarmes.

'Thanks, I can use them, but that wasn't why I wanted to see you. Are you free to meet? I'm at the roadblock between Audrix and Le Pavillon.'

'On my way.'

Bruno had no desire to see the place again, nor to relive those panicked moments when he'd realized that the suicide bomber had rendered all his plans futile. It was Bruno's own failure that had left Robert dead and Gaston so badly hurt he might lose his sight. They were men he knew and liked and he'd failed them. But as he drew up at the roadblock, all he could see was the ruined roof of the building and the jagged stone silhouette of the remains of the pigeon tower.

'Thanks for coming,' Yveline said, steering him out of earshot of the other Gendarme. 'How much can you tell me of what happened?'

He explained briefly, adding that she'd face the Brigadier if it went any further.

'I'd worked out something like that from the bullet holes and cartridge cases we found. But that wasn't what I wanted to talk about. You remember the *vendange*, when Jacqueline asked Fabiola about a relationship with Deutz?'

'Yes, and I since found out that he was leading the climb

when Fabiola fell and got that scar. Apparently they'd been pretty close before that.'

'I checked the records. There was a rape complaint filed against Deutz by another student, but it didn't go anywhere. It seems the medical school hushed it up. The woman was transferred to another school and then Deutz went into the prison service with glowing recommendations from the faculty at Marseille.'

'Rape?' Bruno felt a chill creep up his spine. That kind of trauma could explain Fabiola's inability to respond to Gilles. It made a hideous kind of sense and he felt a slow anger begin to build. 'Have you talked to this student?'

'I'm tracking her down in the time I can squeeze away from roadblock duty. And Annette is trying to reach the magistrate in the rape complaint that was dropped. She reminded me that there's no statute of limitations on rape, so if this case builds, she's determined to pursue it.'

Bruno nodded. Annette was a dedicated magistrate; once she got her teeth into something she never let go. He pulled out his notebook and gave Yveline the name and number of the gynaecology professor Fabiola had been to see.

'Have you talked to Nancy?' he went on. 'Apparently there was some trouble about sexual harassment when Deutz visited the FBI.'

'Seems like we've got a pattern here,' Yveline said. 'This man is a predator. But what would it mean for the tribunal if Deutz is formally accused? That's the Brigadier's priority. Would he intervene to shield Deutz?'

'I don't know,' said Bruno. 'A rape charge is very hard to stop.'

'It was stopped before, when the student withdrew her accusation.'

Bruno nodded. 'Is Fabiola prepared to file a formal charge against Deutz?'

'Annette and I talked to her today. She's wavering.'

21

Bruno liked cars without obsessing over them. He never bought car magazines nor followed Grand Prix races and had never lusted after sleek and superfast sports cars. He was deeply fond of his ancient Land Rover, as much for its history as its sturdy practicality. It had been a bequest from Hercule, his old hunting partner and the man who had taught Bruno about truffles.

But this car was different. When Bruno saw it taking up three spaces in front of the *Mairie* looking as big as an ocean liner, majestic in deep black, he stopped, stunned. Slowly he realized that his eyes were as wide as a schoolboy's and that a broad grin had appeared on his face. Scattered couples, interrupting their afternoon walks to stare and marvel, were reacting the same way. Bruno walked to the front of the car to admire the statue of the goddess and the famous radiator below it, looking rather like one of the better-preserved Greek temples. He'd never been this close to a Rolls-Royce before, and this was one of the traditional ones with stately lines.

The driver's door opened, a vast slab of metal, and Yacov stepped out, waving and opening one of the even larger rear doors to gesture Bruno inside. Most cars rocked a little when somebody climbed in or out, but this massive vehicle didn't budge. It probably ignored potholes in the same way.

'My grandmother, Maya Halévy,' Yacov said, as Bruno climbed in. The rear of the car was so wide that Bruno had to stretch forward to shake the hand of the elegant old lady with blue-tinted white hair and enormous spectacles who was smiling brightly at him from the corner of the rear seat. It could have taken six or seven people of her size.

The door closed behind him with the sound of a very discreet bank vault, reminding him that he should have spent much more time preparing for this encounter. Many of his plans and dreams for St Denis rested with this woman, whose net worth could have bought every house in his town and still left her more than rich. He should have spent more time on the presentation that was to win her support, but for better or worse that was now in the hands of schoolkids. At least he knew that he could count on Florence. And even as he chided himself for thinking of Maya Halévy in such mercenary terms, he looked at her with great curiosity. This woman had not only gone through an extraordinary childhood, hunted and hidden, but she was the first woman entrepreneur he'd ever met, and probably the richest.

He'd barely begun to say, '*Enchanté, madame*,' when he was interrupted by her surprisingly deep voice, speaking an old-fashioned French and saying as she took his hand that she had already recognized the bridge and the church of St Denis.

'Nearly seventy years ago,' she went on, still holding his hand. 'I shall need your help, young man, to protect me from my grandson, who seems to think I'm a fragile old thing who needs to be tucked into chairs with rugs and cups of thin tea in delicate porcelain cups. What I really want is a stiff drink, and Yacov removed the decanters, which were one of the treats I was looking forward to about using my brother's car. This car was the apple of his eye, perfectly maintained and waxed and polished and always in its original condition. He even refused to install a newer radio. Above all, he knew my tastes and always made sure the decanters were full when I came to visit him in Paris.'

She gestured at the rear of the front seat, where gleaming cabinetry slid down at the touch of a button to form a tray, and revealed two crystal glasses. But the space for the decanters was empty.

'Isn't that a sad sight?' she asked, with a grin that despite her age he could only describe as cheeky.

Bruno liked her at once and said, 'Are you a scotch drinker, madame? And please call me Bruno.'

'Yes, and if you want to join me you can call me Maya. I see a bar behind the *Mairie*.'

'You could certainly get a glass of decent whisky, but if you'd care to follow me to the place where you're going to stay, I'd be glad to offer you a Lagavulin.'

'A Land Rover *and* a Lagavulin drinker, and I gather you're the local policeman who found the old farm where we stayed. I don't think we had policemen like you in my day.' She pressed a button on the armrest and the window purred silkily open.

'Yacov,' she called through the window. 'Give the policeman the keys. He's going to drive me and you can have the pleasure of following behind and driving his Land Rover.'

'I'd be terrified of damaging your car, I've never driven anything this size except armoured cars,' Bruno protested, although privately he was yearning for the chance. 'And the army never worried about scratches on them.'

'Don't be silly; with a car like this, everybody else gets out of your way.'

After a brief explanation of the controls from Yacov, Bruno climbed into the front seat and set off, conscious of an extraordinary amount of power in the engine, even though he couldn't hear it. The bonnet seemed to stretch away endlessly ahead, and oncoming trucks and cars pulled into the side of the road to make way, most of them stopping to watch the vehicle's progress.

Fortunately, there was no other traffic on the single-track road that led to Pamela's house, but the gates at the entrance to her lane worried him even though they were wide enough for his Land Rover and for a horsebox. He climbed out of the car to assess the gap. He would have a couple of centimetres on each side. He reversed a little to ensure he was pointing straight at the gap and crept forward, almost brushing the near side post, and then he was through. Feeling proud of himself, he pressed the accelerator and felt the great beast surge forward like a sports car. Pulling into Pamela's courtyard, he sounded the horn and was startled by a sonorous blare that might have been an elephant's mating call.

Once Pamela had been introduced, the luggage unloaded and the *gîtes* inspected and approved, Maya was installed in Pamela's sitting room with a large scotch. She bent her nose into the glass to sniff as if it were a vintage wine, took a tiny sip and let it evaporate in her mouth before taking a deep breath. Her eyes closed in pleasure as the warmth spread down her throat and then she took a deeper drink, sat back in the leather armchair and opened her eyes to peer inquisitively around her.

Although they usually spent most of their time in the kitchen, Bruno was very fond of Pamela's long sitting room with the giant fireplace whose lines lifted the eye to the balustraded gallery and all the way up to the roof beams. Lit by two french windows that opened onto the garden, its walls were lined with books and the floor of terracotta tiles was covered in old rugs, their reds and golds still bright despite their age.

'That's a fine Qashqai and a charming little Varamin,' Maya said, looking at the rugs with an expert eye. 'Have they been in your family for a long time?'

'My grandfather spent some time in Persia during the war,' Pamela said. 'He made quite a study of their rugs and brought several back with him.'

'Me too, I love them. He chose well. That large one with the touches of green is a Bakhtiari, very hard to find in that size. This is a charming room and it's much more agreeable to be here than in some country hotel. Your *gîtes* are lovely.'

'Thank you, I'm glad you like it. My grandfather used to tell me that the thing that surprised him most about Hitler was that he loved Persian rugs and kept an Ardabil carpet in his office in Berlin. Every time we were in London Grandpa would take me to see that enormous Ardabil in the Victoria and Albert Museum and tell me its history.'

'I know the one,' Maya burst out, sitting forward excitedly. 'Do you know about the inscription?'

'Except for thy haven, there is no refuge for me in this world.,' Pamela recited. 'Other than here, there is no place for my head.'

'The work of a servant of the court, Maqsud of Kashan,' Maya chimed in. 'I'm so glad you know it. When I first saw it there they had the carpet hanging on a wall, but now it's lying flat as it should.'

The two women looked at one another with satisfaction. A bond had been established, Bruno thought. Yacov gave him a friendly wink.

'I assume you're tired after your journey, so if you'd like to relax before dinner we can leave your visit to the attic and to the farm for tomorrow,' Bruno said.

'I took Granny to the farm as soon as we arrived, before we called you,' Yacov said. 'She brought rubber boots specially because I'd told her what to expect. And don't worry, we didn't get the Rolls scratched.'

Interesting, thought Bruno, that she wanted to see the place without an escort from St Denis trying to sell her the town's plan. Perhaps he should warn the Mayor to let her make her own way up to the attic where she'd been hidden.

'It brought back a lot of memories, some of them very pleasant,' Maya said. 'Do we have time before dinner to go and see the attic in town? I really want to be sure it's the right place.'

'There's just one thing I need to point out which should convince you, and you might not find it yourselves,' Bruno said. 'But, yes, we can go now.'

'Dinner will be ready in about an hour or an hour and a half,' said Pamela. 'It's smoked salmon and then *blanquette de veau* so don't worry about getting back at any precise time.'

Maya nodded, finished her scotch and rose easily to her feet.

She was evidently very fit, thought Bruno. He'd wondered if they'd have to carry her up to the attic.

'I'm looking forward to seeing these proposals of yours in the morning,' she said. 'And at some point I'd also like to see Mouleydier, or what's left of the place. That's probably my most powerful memory.'

Mouleydier was a small town on the way to Bergerac, nestled below the long, low rise above the river that nurtured the vineyards of Pécharmant, the noblest of the Bergerac wines. Bruno knew the area well, but was surprised that it had stayed in Maya's mind. Was she talking of the battle that had taken place there? The town had been destroyed by Nazi troops, which presumably explained why she had used the phrase, 'what's left of the place'. Might this explain why she had never shown any interest in coming back to this region until her brother's death?

'I'll take us all down memory lane over dinner,' Maya said, seeing Bruno's quizzical look. 'In return, you must tell me all about this tragic young man they call the Engineer. The car radio was full of stories about him on the way down. But right now, I want to see that wretched little attic of St Denis where I was so unhappy.'

'At least it kept you alive, Granny,' said Yacov quietly. 'No doubt you were unhappy, but you survived, you and David.'

'We survived and then went through three more wars in Israel, and then putting on a gas mask all over again in the first Iraq war when Saddam Hussein was firing Scud missiles at Israel,' she said. 'And then I was in Haifa when the rockets fell there. I must be one of the most bombarded women alive.'

As he led the way out to the car, Bruno thought that Maya

must have known a lot more of war than he had, despite his spending over a decade in the French army. But that was the way of modern war, with civilians in the front lines. Yacov drove them back to St Denis in silence and Bruno led the way up the stairs of the old house to the attic. He had borrowed a light bulb from Pamela and installed it in the attic as Maya followed him up the stairs, much nimbler than he'd expected she would be. The Mayor had arranged for someone to clear away the rubbish and the place had been swept out and the tiny windows cleaned.

It still looked dreadful. Maya stood at the threshold, shaking her head, not recognizing the place at all. Then Bruno led her into the rear room and showed her the markings on the wall with her name below David's. At last she nodded her head, looked around again, peered out of the window and said, 'I remember that view.'

Yacov was examining the chest full of broken crockery and Maya picked out a large cup with a red line round the rim. 'I remember this, too,' she said.

Bruno left the two of them alone and went back down the stairs, checking the message that he'd heard coming into his phone. It was a voicemail from the Brigadier, asking him to call back.

'There's trouble in Toulouse,' the Brigadier said when he answered. 'Some right-wing militants marched on the mosque and began throwing paint and chanting slogans. People came out of the mosque and there were some rough scenes for an hour or so, some tear gas and water cannon. The police seem to have got control but there's another demonstration called for tomorrow afternoon. And they're torching cars again in Paris.'

'Is all quiet at the château?' Bruno asked.

'Yes, but half the TV crews in France seem to be camped on the road outside, except for those who raced down to Toulouse. I may go down there. Nancy was asking for you. She seems pleased with her TV interviews and says she thinks the mood might be shifting in Washington. Apparently they had a woman in the TV show, a mother whose son was killed by one of Sami's bombs. She said Sami sounded like he was just as much a victim as her own boy.'

'She's right,' said Bruno, thinking that the wisdom of ordinary people never ceased to surprise him.

'I'm pretty sure Sami won't be heading to Guantanamo after all this. And what are you up to?'

'I'm with the old Jewish lady I told you about, the one who was sheltered in St Denis as a child. We're about to have dinner.'

'*Bon appétit.* I'll call you if I need you. If I go to Toulouse tomorrow, I'll want you back here at the château. Deutz has been making a nuisance of himself, furious that your doctor was allowed in to see Sami. I thought I'd let you know.'

'It looks like there may have been a bit of personal history between the two of them,' Bruno said. 'I'm still trying to get to the bottom of it.'

'Understood, keep me informed.' He rang off.

22

Bruno hesitated before asking Maya the questions that intrigued him. What had become of the two children and their guardians, one of them a *gueule cassée*, at the end of their time at the farm, and how had they resumed their lives? And why had they never returned to St Denis, never returned to the brief sanctuary that had saved them, until after David's death?

He had wanted to ask her when Maya came out of the attic on Yacov's arm, but her face was pale and strained. She shook her head as if to forestall any conversation and then wiped away the tears on her cheeks. In the car, she took a small tube of some cream from her bag and wiped away the smudged eye make-up. She looked much older, and when they returned to Pamela's house she asked for another scotch and this time downed it in a single gulp and then took a refill. Pamela led her to the bathroom and the two women had remained there for some minutes while Yacov and Bruno talked and opened the wine.

The questions continued to nag at him over dinner, at the back of his mind even as he told Maya and Yacov what he knew about Sami as a boy, about Momu and Dillah, and of his sadness at Sami's likely fate. Maya looked herself again, her make-up refreshed, making polite compliments to Pamela about the food. She took a sliver of cheese and just enough of the *tarte au citron* to be polite. When the plates had been cleared away, she said, 'Let's stay on around the table. I always prefer talking that way and you ought to know what happened to us. But bear in mind, these are the memories of a little girl of eight, backed up by what David remembered, but he was just eleven when we left the farm.'

The attic had been the worst time, she said. She and her brother had been whisked away from Paris in the summer of 1942, just after the massive round-up of 13,000 Jews and their detention in the Vélodrome d'Hiver, the indoor cycling stadium just down the Left Bank from the Eiffel Tower. Neither she nor David knew why her parents were not arrested at the time, perhaps because her father was a doctor. Through the Jewish Boy Scouts, they had been assigned to a group of eight children who were taken first to a campsite near Blois in the Loire valley. Once there, they had photos taken and after a few days were issued with new papers that identified them as Protestant Scouts and Girl Guides to get them through the controls at Vierzon, the border crossing between Nazi-occupied France and that part still nominally ruled by the Vichy government.

They had then gone by train to Brive, and then a bus took them to a Protestant campsite. They stayed there in tents for the summer while Robert Gamzon tried to find somewhere more permanent, but the first of the round-ups of Jews in the so-called free zone of Vichy began that August. They were still at the campsite in November when German troops invaded the Vichy zone to occupy France's Mediterranean coast after the Allies had landed in Morocco and Algeria. Somehow Gamzon persuaded several Protestant pastors to find various places of refuge for the children.

'So it was November, cold and dark, on the morning when David and I left the campsite,' Maya recalled. 'A big blonde woman, very pretty, told us to call her Tante Simone. David later found out that it was Simone Mairesse, one of the people who organized homes for hundreds of Jewish children around the village of Chambon-sur-Lignon. But apparently there had been a panic after some raids and we had to be taken elsewhere.'

Maya said she remembered a train journey, and watching through the window as their train stopped and another train full of German troops went by. David later tried to track down their route but he was never sure. Then they walked along country lanes for a long time and then waited in some woods outside a small town until it was dark. Tante Simone had some stale bread for them to eat. Then she took them over a bridge into a town with very few lights. It was St Denis. She led the children to a house and up some stairs to an attic, where an old woman was waiting.

'She spoke hardly any French and I thought she was a witch. I was very scared,' Maya said. 'She was bent over as if she had a hunchback and she smelled, but she gave us some soup and tried to be kind to us. Tante Simone said we were not allowed to go out of the attic until market day, when there would be a cart to take us to a farm. It was a donkey cart, the first I ever saw. And then Tante Simone left, telling us we had to leave before dark on market day and go back to the place in the woods where we had waited together. A man with a white mask on his face who would come about midday.'

'He was a *gueule cassée*, from the First War,' Bruno prompted. 'That was how I tracked down the farm of Michel and Sylvie Desbordes. The old woman in the attic was her mother, all of them Protestants.'

'Michel and Sylvie, that sounds right. She told us to call her Tante Sylvie and we were to say we were her cousin's children if anybody ever came. But I don't remember anyone ever visiting except for the old woman from the attic once or twice. Monsieur hardly ever spoke, and when he did his voice was just grunts. His wife was very kind. I think she'd always wanted children.'

The children stayed there through the winter and all through the year of 1943 and the first half of 1944, knowing nothing of the world outside the farm. Sylvie taught them their sums, read to them from the Bible and sometimes brought back battered copies of Dumas, Victor Hugo and Jules Verne. But they only had candles to read by because they couldn't always afford the oil for the lamp, even when there was lamp oil to be had. There was no gas, no electricity and all their water came from the well. At least the wood stove kept the kitchen warm. On Sundays, the children were left alone as the Desbordes took the donkey cart to the Protestant chapel in St Denis.

They lived on the eggs and milk the farm produced, made bread from chestnuts and in the vegetable garden they grew verveine and camomile to make tea. Occasionally there would be a *poule au pot* when one of the chickens grew too old to lay. The Desbordes sold eggs and chickens in the market, vegetables in summer, and in the winter Michel knew a place where he could find truffles and would sell them, when he could find a buyer. Few people had the money except for occasional visitors looking to supply the black market, but dealing with them was a risk the Desbordes thought it wiser not to take. Ironically, as a result foie gras from the ducks was a regular part of the diet on the farm. With so few buyers the Desbordes made it for themselves.

'Apart from the foie gras, it sounds like living in the Middle Ages,' said Yacov, shaking his head.

'I suppose it was. In winter, we all slept in the same big bed for warmth, me and Madame Desbordes at one end, David and Monsieur at the other. We had to work, too,' Maya said.

Every day the children were in the woods, getting kindling for the stove, or looking for mushrooms for Tante Sylvie to sell. In the summer they took their turns with the scythe, getting the hay for the donkey. Maya had to watch the chickens when they were out in the yard and she and David both helped Sylvie in the garden. Maya was taught to sew and knit, because their clothes were falling apart. And although there was no sugar, she recalled a kind of jam from berries.

'Looking back, it was probably a very healthy way to grow up, and we loved Dou-Dou, the little dog. It was he who taught us how to swim, a sort of dog paddle that we copied from him. It was a lovely place to be, in spring and summer . . .' Her voice trailed away.

'You had no news of your family, nothing from the woman who brought you to St Denis, Tante Simone?' Pamela asked.

'Not a word. We had no radio, never saw a newspaper nor even a postman.'

The *facteur* would leave any letters at the *Mairie* and Monsieur would look in on his way to market. He had a small pension for his wounds and once a month something would come in the post and he could go to the post office and get the money. And he got ration books, Maya said, because she remembered him applying for two tobacco rations for him and Tante Sylvie so he could sell them in the market to buy needles and thread. There was no wool, except from unravelling old sweaters.

'Then came the Sunday, June the eleventh, I'll never forget it because they came back from chapel and said the war was going to be over because the British and Americans had landed in Normandy and we could go home to Paris. They would take us to the big Protestant church in Bergerac where someone could get in contact with Tante Simone. There was such excitement!'

She laughed at the memory and helped herself to more wine. 'We were sure we'd soon be in Paris, back with Maman and Papa. But of course we had to wait until after market day because there were eggs and chickens to sell. Then we had to wait another day because his ration books hadn't arrived at the *Mairie* and he thought he might need something for a bribe if we ran into the *Milice*.'

Bruno winced a little at what the black-clad Vichy police had done to sully the name of his profession. The term was still used. Anytime there was a claim of police brutality in the papers somebody would be sure to say, 'They were as bad as the *Milice*.'

So they had set off in the donkey cart in the moonlight, David and Maya in the back with Dou-Dou, the Desbordes up front with two fat chickens, their beaks and legs tied together, under Tante Sylvie's ample skirts in case an extra bribe was needed. Just before dawn they crossed the river Vézère at

Limeuil and took the old road to Trémolat, planning to cross the Dordogne at Lalinde.

But there were armed men, Frenchmen, in the streets of Lalinde and the bridge was blocked by a barrier of heavy stones, as tall as a man. The bell was tolling and a priest told the Desbordes they were expecting German troops to come by the main road from Bergerac and they should turn back. But with his *gueule cassée* the *Résistants* let their cart through the chicane in the barrier on the bridge. Once over the river, Desbordes took the dirt track up the hill that went through the woods to Couze and Mouleydier and got to Bergerac that way.

Bruno now knew what was coming. The SS Panzer Division Das Reich, which had been based further south near Toulouse, was battling its way north through Resistance ambushes to join the German defences against the Allied landings in Normandy. An SS Panzer division was twice the size of the usual Wehrmacht armoured divisions. It had been equipped with new Panther tanks and 20-millimetre flak cannon designed for use against aircraft but which could chew up a house in a few rounds. The orders from London had been blunt: slow the Panzers at all costs. The longer the Das Reich division took to reach Normandy the greater the chance that the invasion could succeed. Bridges had been blown, towns destroyed, Resistance prisoners gunned down in ditches as the ill-armed civilians tried to slow the armoured columns. And two children and two simple peasants who knew little of the war save that Allied troops had landed were heading innocently into a battle zone.

'I see you have some idea what happened to us at Mouleydier, Bruno,' Maya broke off. He tried to recall the details he'd read in the history books.

'You got there in time for the first battle, when the Resistance held the bridge for a whole day,' Bruno said. 'I know the Soleil group was there and some of the Cérisier company. There's an old man still alive in St Denis who took part.'

'I suppose you could say we took part in it, too. At least, we were casualties. I had no idea what was happening, but we were coming along the road from Varennes and I remember watching the little planes in the sky. I didn't know they were spotting for artillery. Just as we got to the crossroads where you'd turn right to cross the Mouleydier bridge, mortar bombs erupted all around us. David pulled me off the back of the cart and into the ditch. I was furious with him because it got me all dirty and I wanted to look nice for Maman.'

The donkey had been killed, and both of the Desbordes were wounded, him seriously in the leg and the stomach, Tante Sylvie in the arm but still able to walk. Some *Résistants* took them to a makeshift dressing station in a house on what was supposed to be the safe side of the river. Dou-Dou the dog had disappeared. Maya remembered being put into the cellar with David and some other children, where they would be sheltered from the mortars.

The *Résistants* had machine guns, rifles, plenty of grenades and some bazookas that had been dropped from British aircraft by parachute. They fought off two probing attacks on the bridge and then the battle erupted in the river just behind the house where the children were sheltering. The Germans had brought up a barge to take the *Résistants* in the flank, but the barge was sunk by a bazooka. The battle ended when the Royal Air Force launched a long-planned bombing raid on the powder-works, an ammunitions factory just outside Bergerac. Fearing that the *Résistants* had called in air support, the Germans withdrew.

'Monsieur Desbordes died two days later and we were left with Madame Desbordes, whose wounded arm and shoulder had been treated by a doctor with the Resistance,' Maya went on. 'She kept asking what had happened to her chickens and to the money her husband had in his pockets. My little brown paper parcel with my change of clothes had disappeared, like a lot of things. I remember the man with the *tabac* sitting on his threshold and crying because the *Résistants* had cleaned out his stock.'

Many of the people in the town had fled. A schoolteacher came and found Maya and David and they were taken to the church with the rest of the children, where at least they had food and water. David went with some of the other boys to hunt for souvenirs of the fighting and came back with some empty cartridge cases. Tante Sylvie told the teacher they had come from St Denis and were going to stay with cousins in Bergerac. Maya and David knew enough to say nothing.

The next day Monsieur Desbordes was buried in a short ceremony, the one civilian who died as a result of the battle of the fifteenth of June. When Tante Sylvie said he was a Protestant, the priest had not wanted to bury him in the church cemetery. The schoolteacher said Desbordes was obviously a veteran of the First War, a *gueule cassée*, so the priest relented. The *Résistants* took their own dead with them, to give the bodies to their families. Most of them had come from the area around Belvès, the priest explained.

'Tante Sylvie fell ill with fever. I think her wound was

infected,' Maya said, her voice very flat. 'She became delirious, shouting at the priest, anybody she could find, demanding someone take us all back to St Denis. I was terrified she was going to start shouting that we were Jews from Paris but she didn't.'

She stopped, sipped some water and then drank off her glass of wine. Bruno, scanning Pamela's bookshelves for a volume he knew was there, was counting the days in his head. He knew there had been a second battle of Mouleydier, the town's day of tragedy. Had Maya gone through that, as well?

'And then the war came again,' said Maya. 'It was the twenty-first. We were still living in the church, but all the other children had gone. They had people to look after them. We just had the madwoman, which is what Tante Sylvie had become. I was terrified of her but David kept trying to take care of her, persuade her to go back to the dressing station. Finally he succeeded, but it was deserted and we couldn't find a doctor. We raided vegetable gardens for food, I remember eating a lot of strawberries and raw courgettes.

'This time the Germans came with tanks, at least David said they were tanks but now I think perhaps they were those armoured cars you see in newsreels with wheels at the front and tracks behind. It began with a lot of shooting and then a Frenchman with a loudspeaker called on the *Résistants* to surrender. They answered him with gunfire and then the Germans came in firing cannon and the *Résistants* were defending. Suddenly the firing stopped. The Germans seemed to withdraw and people came out from their cellars. Tante Sylvie left the church and was walking up the main street. I was going to follow but David held me back, and that was when the bombardment started. Mortars, artillery, heavy guns, I don't know exactly. But within an hour Mouleydier was in ruins.'

Bruno rose and went across to the bookshelves and took down a book he had lent to Pamela. He leafed through to the page he wanted and read aloud:

'Of two hundred houses, a hundred and sixty-four were destroyed in the barrage and the fires. Twenty-two people were killed, three civilians including a nine-year-old boy, and nineteen *Résistants*, most of them shot after being captured.'

'I knew the boy,' said Maya. 'He was called Jean.'

'Jean Bouysset,' said Bruno, reading from the book. 'Then the armoured column went on to Pressignac and burned that, too.'

'You cannot imagine how Mouleydier looked, burning, smoke everywhere, houses collapsed, streets full of rubble,' said Maya.

There was no water, of course, and most of the wells had been blocked with rubble and charred beams from the houses. The schoolteacher was dead but the priest fed them. The Germans retreated into Bergerac and the *Résistants* took over the countryside and took David and Maya to a school where they stayed with some other children until the Germans left Bergerac in August. One of the schoolmistresses took them to the Protestant church there in a *gazogène*, one of the cars that had been modified to drive on charcoal gas that was kept in a large bag attached to the roof. The Protestant pastor somehow got in touch with Tante Simone. They stayed with a Protestant family until Simone could come and take them back to Chambon where she lived.

'In September, after the liberation of Paris, we learned that our parents were no longer in the city. They had been taken to Germany,' Maya said, her voice empty of emotion as though she had said this so many times before that she had no more tears to shed. 'We didn't learn until after the war that they had died in the camps. So we were orphans, living in a Jewish orphanage set up in a school near Chambon, and stayed there for three years until 1948 when we went to Israel.'

There was silence around the table until Maya said, 'There you have it, my story of two children of war, adrift in a battle and knowing that if people learned we were Jews we'd be dead. Now perhaps you understand why we never came back. There was nothing we wanted to return to, no Desbordes, no Dou-Dou, not even the donkey. But I feel there are debts to be paid, to the Scouts and the Protestants and to the people here, and just like David I want to pay them. And now I want to go to bed.'

23

Florence and her pupils had done the town proud, Bruno thought, as he followed Maya, Yacov and the Mayor into the classroom. There was a blown-up photograph of the terrace that housed Maya's attic as it now looked, and beside it an accomplished sketch on a large sheet of white paper showing how they could appear after the proposed transformation. The sketch was based loosely on Bruno's idea of turning the ground floor of the buildings into a kind of arcade. He'd been assuming some simple pillars, but the sketch showed a series of stone arches that led into a covered space, large enough for thirty or forty people to gather, that housed the entrance to the museum and the museum shop. Another shop had been sketched in and listed as an art gallery. Above the museum entrance a sign had been inked in, reading *Musée Halévy de St Denis*.

The interior plan showed a handsome new staircase and a lift, leading to two exhibitions on the first floor, one on the history of the Resistance in Périgord and the other on life in St Denis under the Occupation. On the next floor was a small cinema and a large room for the role of the Protestant Church and the Scout movement in saving Jewish children. The attic was marked simply as The Refuge and a note said it would be decorated as closely as Maya could remember to how it had been. The other attics in the terrace were to be turned into offices and an exhibition space for life in the Périgord under the Occupation.

Yves Peyreblanque, one of the older boys and the son of an ambulance driver, came forward and handed Maya a small bunch of flowers, and then Eglantine, the star of the girls' rugby team that Bruno trained, made a small speech of welcome. The two of them led Maya round the sketches, asking if she had any questions.

'What about the people who live in these houses now?' she asked.

Another youth, Maurice Cordet, whose father was a tree surgeon, led her to another easel that held another blown-up photo of the disused cooperage. A sketch showed how it could be restored and turned into housing. Above the entrance was a plaque that read *Résidences Halévy*. The final display showed a photo of the Desbordes farm as it was now, and a sketch showing how it could be, with a neat array of tents on the flat land by the stream.

Florence stood back, letting her pupils make the explanations and then leading Maya to the final display. Two large tables had been covered with a cloth, and behind them on the wall leaned a large cork board that was covered in old photographs and newspapers. One of them carried a photograph of Marshal Pétain with Hitler. Another blared out the words *Paris Libéré*. There was one exhibit that seemed to be missing, the space covered with a white cloth. Perhaps they had not had time to install it. Florence and the kids had done extremely well to get this project looking as good as it did.

The tables carried objects from the period of the Occupation, ration books and faded blue packets of cigarettes marked *Vente Restreinte*, sales restricted to troops. Bruno saw a Wehrmacht and a French helmet, well-worn *sabot* clogs carved from wood and a dress dyed in blue. The original markings from the flour sacks from which it had been made were still visible. There were armbands with the Cross of Lorraine and others marked FFI, for the *Forces Françaises de l'Intérieur*, and a handwritten receipt for food and wine, signed in the name of the FFI by a Capitaine Bousquéret.

'We went round all our grandparents asking what they might have in their attics, everyday items that came from the period,' said Yves, the youth who had given Maya the flowers. 'My great-grandfather was given that receipt and now we're trying to track down the captain's family to see if they have any mementos of him. We just wanted to give you an idea of the kind of things we'd like to see displayed, and we're glad we did it. We all learned a lot.'

He stood back to let Maya look at the various items and another of the pupils pressed a button on a small music box and the strains of 'J'attendrai' began to fill the room. She smiled faintly and her fingers traced the outlines of a piece of cloth in the shape of a star, in faded yellow.

'Strictly speaking, that's not from here, but from one of the members of our family who lived in Perpignan,' said a slender youth whom Bruno recognized from his rugby classes. He was Daniel Weiss's son Samuel, a fast sprinter who played a good game on the wing.

'This is much, much more than I expected,' Maya said, haltingly, speaking to the pupils. 'You've all done very well and

I want to thank you for all your hard work and your very creative ideas.'

'There's one final item we found, or rather that the Mayor found in the basement of the *Mairie*,' said Eglantine, and steered Maya to the wall display where she removed the white cloth.

'It's a copy of the marriage register that records the wedding of Michel and Sylvie Desbordes in 1917. And now you'll need this,' the girl said, handing Maya a magnifying glass. 'We only just tracked it down so we didn't have time to enlarge it. It's from the newspaper *Liberté du Sud Ouest* from May 1917.'

The headline read 'Soldiers marry before returning to the front', and there was a small photograph of three young men in army uniform with their brides, each of the women carrying a bouquet.

'The couple on the left are Michel and Sylvie.'

'It's before he was wounded,' Maya said, peering through the glass at the face in the photograph. 'I never really knew what he looked like before. And that's her, Tante Sylvie, looking so young.'

She turned to look at her grandson and beckoned him across to look at the couple who had taken her in and then died in the attempt to get her and her brother home and reunited with their family. Maya's eyes were glistening with tears as she took Yacov's hand and gave him the magnifying glass to peer in turn at the wedding photo of the long-dead Desbordes.

'Without those people I wouldn't be here today and nor would you.' Her head was shaking slowly as if in disbelief that so many echoes and memories of her youth could have survived and been brought back for her to remember.

'You young people have done an amazing job,' Yacov said, turning to face Yves and Eglantine, Samuel and the others. 'Believe me, you have rocked me today.'

Bruno waited for the 'But . . .' Yacov was a lawyer, trained to take no decision in the heat of the moment but only after sober and prolonged reflection. Bruno expected him to say that any further decision about the memorial would have to wait for discussions with the Mayor, a meeting of the family trustees, detailed cost estimates and so on. Yet Yacov remained silent, looking expectantly at his aunt almost as if urging her to voice support for the St Denis plans.

The Mayor chose that moment to cough discreetly and step forward.

'On behalf of the town, I'd like to add my own few words of appreciation for the hard work of our youngsters and their dedicated teacher, Madame Florence Pantowsky,' he said. 'I'd also like to pay tribute to the creative imagination of our chief of police here, who has been at the heart of this project from the start. It's a very impressive generation of young citizens we have here and it gives me great confidence for the future of St Denis. I think the traditions of humanity and decency that Monsieur and Madame Desbordes displayed are being very much upheld by these children of our town today. And these youngsters tell me, Madame, that irrespective of the eventual decision of the Halévy Foundation, they will go ahead and pursue this project of a museum, on their own if need be. And now perhaps we'd better let them return to their studies.'

The Mayor gave Maya his arm and led the way down the corridor of the *collège* to the playground and out to the forecourt where his car and the Halévy Rolls-Royce were parked, dwarfing Bruno's little police van.

And there, waiting for them with his camera at the ready, was Philippe Delaron, whom Bruno had been trying to avoid. Philippe had taken to his role as newsman with great energy and panache, and while Bruno sometimes found him to be a pain in the neck he rather admired Philippe's enthusiasm.

'What on earth brings you here?' Bruno asked.

'Who do you think took those photos and blew them up?' Philippe retorted, dodging around Bruno to snap a shot of Maya, the Mayor and the Rolls-Royce. 'I made Florence tell me what it was all about in return for doing the work.'

'Madame Halévy,' he called out before Bruno could stop him. 'Are you going to support the schoolkids' plans for the museum?'

'Certainly,' she replied, turning as she was about to step into the car. 'I can't think when I've been more impressed by a project. You have some wonderful young people in this town and they deserve everybody's full support.'

Bruno wondered if it was because he was her passenger that Yveline drove so carefully, observing the speed limits of seventy as they approached a town or junction and fifty once they were inside any urban area, even a village. She kept at ninety even on long straight roads, but handled the bends well, accelerating out of them. She glanced at her rear mirror religiously and read the road ahead. It was as though she were going through the Gendarme road test. But she was relaxed as she drove, chatting easily, and he concluded that this was simply another feature of a remarkably composed and well-organized young woman. Like so much else about her, he found it quietly impressive.

'Did you explain to this professor why we're coming to see her?' he asked.

'Not in so many words, but I said we were investigating some cases of sexual harassment, one of them involving Fabiola, and we knew Fabiola had told her about it and asked her advice. And if she asks, the *Procureur*'s office has opened a dossier into a suspected crime. Annette faxed me a copy along with a formal request to assist her inquiry.'

Bruno nodded, still not sure why Yveline had asked him to join her on the inquiry, rather than taking along one of her Gendarmes.

'We're doing this by the book,' she said after a moment. 'That's why you've been invited along. Annette thought it would be a good idea since you're Fabiola's local policeman. Nancy said it was the way they ran inquiries into sexual offences at the FBI, always a man and a woman.'

Bruno hadn't known that, but it made sense, precluding the suspect claiming he was being targeted by female cops after a woman's complaint against him.

'And Fabiola said she'd rather you were involved,' Yveline added. 'I thought I'd like to run the questioning, but if I rub the witness the wrong way, you're experienced. You'll know when to step in and change the mood.'

'You won't rub her the wrong way,' Bruno said, although he knew it was easily done. He'd seen cooperative witnesses turn hostile often enough through clumsy questioning. 'Sergeant Jules would have done, he's got that grandfatherly touch.'

'Yes, but I need someone I can count on back running the Gendarmerie, and that means Jules.'

'Have you told him that?'

'No, but I gave him top marks on his annual performance rating, a bit against my better judgement. He's sometimes too inclined to live and let live.'

She could say that about him, Bruno thought. Knowing when to turn a blind eye was part of being a country policeman; part of being a policeman anywhere.

'And whatever I might think, the other women wanted you on this inquiry and on reflection I agree with them, so here you are,' she said, glancing briefly at him before returning her attention to the road ahead. 'Do you mind? I think you ought to be flattered.'

'It's not a question of being flattered. If I have one big concern it's that I don't want Fabiola screwing herself up to take this step and then we find the evidence is too thin and the memories too vague to make a case stick against Deutz. And given his connections, it's going to have to be foolproof.'

'I know that. And you'll make sure it is foolproof. The case already looks pretty good to me – a contemporaneous witness, a retired professor.'

'What about that complaint against Deutz that went nowhere?' he asked. 'I thought Annette was contacting the magistrate who'd been involved.'

'She did and the magistrate, another woman, was furious when the student dropped the charges. She thought the medical school had applied pressure and she was right. I found the student, Monique Jouard; she's now a paediatrician in Cherbourg. One of her professors took Monique aside to say if

she dropped the charges they'd give her a good recommendation to another school. If she went ahead, she could forget
about a career in medicine. Now they've lost that hold over her,
Monique was only too happy to relaunch her accusation and
the original magistrate is taking the case. I think that's what
finally persuaded Fabiola. There's a copy of her statement in
my briefcase on the back seat,' she said. 'It's the file marked
Fabiola. Take a look.'

Not many Gendarme officers would invite another Gendarme,
let alone a municipal policeman, to poke around inside her
briefcase. It was a gratifying sign of trust. Bruno reached over
and thumbed through the briefcase to find it. There were two
typed pages with Fabiola's signature on each one.

She and Deutz had become lovers during the autumn term
at the medical school, very happily at first, he read. But Fabiola
had become aware that he was seeing other women and had
decided to break off the relationship even before the mountaineering accident. When he had visited her during her recovery,
she had told him their affair was over and he'd laughed it off.
When the medical school reopened in the new year he had
tried to resume their relations but she had repeatedly refused.
On 4 February, he had come to her lodgings, somewhat drunk,
demanding sex. When she refused and asked him to leave, he
had punched her in the stomach, thrown her onto the bed,
pulled down her pants and raped her. As he left she recalled
him saying, 'You don't say no to me.'

Despite the cold, almost forensic prose, the image was clear
in Bruno's mind. He couldn't imagine Fabiola's feelings as she
lay there, humiliated and violated. But he could almost see

the arrogance on Deutz's face as he spoke the words. Grimly, Bruno looked forward to arresting him.

Yveline slowed the van outside a small villa with a large and well-tended garden on the outskirts of Villefranche and then drove on and parked in a side street around the corner. Bruno approved. The professor would already be nervous about their visit without the added pressure of a Gendarme van outside her house where the neighbours could see it and gossip.

Although plainly nervous at their arrival, the woman who answered the door looked like the kindly and comforting sort of woman who'd play the role of a midwife on TV. She was plump with round and rosy cheeks, no make-up and her white hair cut short. Automatically, Bruno noted the flat-heeled leather lace-ups on her feet, a floral-pattern dress and cardigan, no jewelry except for a pearl necklace. She asked them to call her Rosalie, offered coffee, and almost at once brought in a tray that she must have prepared earlier. Yveline led the questioning and to keep matters formal addressed her as Professor Waldeck.

Yes, Professor Waldeck remembered Fabiola very well, one of her favourite students and a doctor with a natural touch and a bedside manner that inspired trust. And yes, she remembered Fabiola coming to ask her advice after what the professor called 'a painful and humiliating experience' at the hands of another member of the teaching staff. She was going out of her way to sound pedantic, like a stage professor, Bruno thought.

'I have thought over this matter carefully before you arrived, and I'm not proud of my failure to do more to help Fabiola at the time,' she said, lifting a notebook from a side table and putting on her reading glasses. 'I made these notes before your arrival because I wanted to be clear in my mind what I should say.'

First, she began, she believed that Fabiola had been forced into having sex against her will. That was rape. But matters were complicated, since before her accident Fabiola and the young professor had been engaged in an affair for several months. When Fabiola had tried to end it, the young man refused to accept her decision. When she insisted, he had forced himself upon her.

Second, the young man was a member of the teaching staff. Since his promising career could be ended by Fabiola's accusation, he could be expected to fight her charges against him. The other members of the teaching staff who would be sitting in judgement upon him were almost entirely male. Many of them saw him as one of the most gifted young men they had known, with a future likely to bring renown to the school. They tended to discount claims of rape between lovers, she said, thinking that once the woman had already been to bed with the man, what difference would another such bout make?

Bruno winced inwardly, remembering times he had heard sly jokes at the rugby club: 'a slice off a cut cake is never missed'. He knew Professor Waldeck was being realistic about the attitudes of most men of his generation. It was a view that Bruno had grown up sharing. Only in recent years had his experience in Bosnia and the reality of life as a country policeman driven him to change his mind. It was not that the men he knew were brutes, but once married many of them seemed careless whether the woman was willing or not. The sexual codes were evolving only slowly in Bruno's part of rural

France. Bruno had seen the eyes and hurt of women who had been forced repeatedly into sex against their will, and never wanted to see it again. That this had happened to Fabiola was intolerable.

Third, Professor Waldeck went on, Fabiola had no evidence. The incident had taken place some days earlier. She had repeatedly bathed since then and had made no complaint at the time. It would be harder to take her word for it now, with no witnesses. It would be a matter of the young man's words against hers.

'Who is this individual you call the young man?' Yveline asked coolly.

Waldeck paused a long moment. 'Pascal Deutz,' she said.

'Are you aware of any other similar incidents involving Monsieur Deutz?'

There was a long pause before Waldeck replied, 'Yes, I am. Two in fact. One was with another student, the year before Fabiola came to me, in very similar circumstances. The two of them had been on a climbing holiday together and the young woman had left early and wanted to end the affair. Deutz had returned later and had his way with her again, saying it was one for the road. Again, she came to me, and I'm afraid I gave her the same advice. I very much regret it now. Had I taken the matter up then, Fabiola might have been spared the same fate.'

'And the second incident?' Yveline pressed.

'After the end of his relationship with Fabiola he turned his attentions to another medical student, very forcefully, but without obtaining his goal. The young woman resisted, her clothes were torn, his face was scratched and her screams attracted a neighbour. Deutz left in a hurry. The woman went straight to the school authorities, not to me. The matter was hushed up and the authorities arranged for the young woman to be transferred to another medical school. Deutz left shortly afterwards. I have made a note of the names of the two women involved. I'm afraid I don't have the address of the first one, Iphigène Vaugaudry, but I believe she is now practising in Nancy. The second is Monique Jouard, graduated from the medical school in Rennes and now lives in Cherbourg.'

She handed across a sheet of paper with the two names and Bruno helped her draft a statement and sign it. The coffee that Professor Waldeck had offered them remained on the table, untouched.

As they took their leave, Waldeck remained in her chair, her head down, her hands clenched together so tightly in her lap that Bruno could see the skin white around her knuckles.

'I wanted to say that I grew up in another time,' she said quietly. 'Things were different then. And at the medical school, it was a man's world.' Her pedantic manner had disappeared.

'Women deserve to live in it peaceably, Madame,' said Yveline.

'I feel very ashamed of myself. I know what Fabiola went through.'

Yveline was grimly silent. Bruno, thinking of the way he might have made the same flawed judgement at the time, tried to offer her some comfort.

'You've done the right thing, Madame,' he said. 'If we can get statements from these other two women, I think Deutz will at last have to answer for his crimes.'

Yveline gave him a cold look, shook her head and turned to

leave the room. At the door, she stopped, looked at Waldeck and said, 'I just hope I can do a better job for any young women in my care than you did with yours. Don't get up. We'll let ourselves out.'

24

'Put the siren on and go as fast as you can to the château,' said Bruno, closing his phone. 'That was the Brigadier. There's trouble.'

Yveline complied and then, raising her voice above the electronic howl from the roof, asked, 'Trouble at the château? Does Sergeant Jules know?'

Bruno explained, briefly. It was hard shouting over the siren. There had been another riot at the mosque, the Brigadier had said. Hundreds of young Muslims had gathered to protect the sprawling complex against a planned demonstration by some anti-immigrant groups. The head of the city's social services was trying to deliver a warrant for an inquiry into the condition of the children in the orphanage, but the city police had been unable to force their way through. The Imam had been on the phone to the Elysée, saying he would calm the youths around the mosque but demanding that he be allowed to come to the château to speak to Sami and Momu. Somebody powerful on the President's staff had told the Brigadier to take the Imam there by helicopter as soon as possible.

'That story on the radio probably won't make things any easier,' said Yveline.

Almost as soon as they had started the journey back to St

Denis, she had turned on the radio to catch the local news bulletin. The second item had been announced as 'Millions from Israel for St Denis', quoting Philippe Delaron's story on the *Sud Ouest* website. Philippe had had his tape recorder running when he shouted his question to Maya as she left the presentation at the *collège*.

'Two Jewish children, hidden and saved from the Nazi death camps by St Denis, are giving millions to the town to build new housing and a museum of the Resistance,' the announcer had read. 'Better known this week as the home town of the famous terrorist bomb-maker of Afghanistan known as the Engineer, St Denis is now to receive millions from multi-millionairess Maya Halévy, who left France after the war for Israel, where she made her fortune as a venture capitalist.'

As soon as he'd heard it, Bruno felt with foreboding that he could already imagine posters proclaiming, 'St Denis saves Jews, abandons Muslims.'

And now the Imam was coming to the château, and probably carloads of Muslims were planning to follow him, while listening to the radio news about the Halévy bequest. No wonder the Brigadier was worried. Bruno looked at the road. They were on the long, straight stretch that went past the hilltop *bastide* of Belvès and there was little other traffic. He asked Yveline to turn off the siren so he could use the phone and called Sergeant Jules, to learn that the region's Gendarmes had been placed on alert and reinforcements were coming from Bordeaux. Then he called Nancy to find out what was happening at the château.

'All quiet on the outside, somewhat tense on the inside. I'll fill you in when you get here. When should we expect you?'

Yveline dropped him at the *Mairie* car park so that he could take his van. Bruno drove direct to the château, where the military were on alert. He was stopped and checked twice on the approach road. When he reached the gate for the security clearance he heard the steadily paced shots that meant somebody was using the shooting range. He hadn't known one had been established. After a thorough search of his van and a check of his papers Bruno was allowed to park inside the outer walls. He asked the sergeant of the guard where he might find the American woman, to be told she was the one on the shooting range. Bruno was directed to the outer ward, and the sergeant shouted after him, 'Pay attention to the red flags. You know what they mean?'

Bruno knew, and followed the sound of the gunshots until he reached a part of the grounds just inside the outer walls, but with a further wall before one entered the château grounds. A long, thick row of sandbags had been erected against the outer wall, about three metres high and almost as thick. There were red flags at each corner and three paper targets, each one metre square, pinned at about chest height.

'Rangemaster,' Bruno called between shots. 'Permission to enter range.'

'Permission granted, range cold,' came Nancy's voice. 'Is that you, Bruno?'

'It's me.' He rounded the corner and saw Nancy removing her ear protectors and as her hair swung free and he felt her eyes on him Bruno once again knew the rush of sexual attraction. And what was going on in Nancy's mind? She knew he was on his way to the château, so she must have expected he'd arrive to find her shooting. Was she trying to impress him or was this just the way Americans were supposed to be with guns?

Two handguns lay on the table before her, about thirty metres from the targets and the sandbags. As he came close, he saw one gun was a Glock, a standard weapon in American law enforcement. The other was a familiar PAMAS G1, the universal 9mm weapon for the French army and Gendarmes. He glanced at the target. Her shots were well grouped, all within the inner rings.

'You're good,' he said. 'Do all FBI agents shoot like you?' Each gun had its magazine removed, in accordance with usual Rangemaster rules. He approved.

'It helps to have a daddy who loved guns. The day I was born he bought me a lifetime membership of the National Rifle Association.'

'Which do you prefer, our PAMAS or your Glock?'

'Strictly speaking the Glock is Austrian, but it's the weapon the FBI prefers us to carry. Our lawyers like the triple safety system. This one's a Glock 22, chambered for the ten-millimetre round. In stopping power, they're much the same. Want to try it?'

Bruno couldn't resist. He checked the action and ensured the chamber was clear and then squinted down the barrel. It was clean. He examined the magazine and saw there were still seven rounds. That would do. He pulled a paper tissue from his trouser pocket and twisted off two strands and put them into his ears. He looked for the safety, dry-fired to test the trigger pull and then prepared to load the magazine.

'Range going hot,' he shouted.

'Range hot,' she called back. 'Firing approved.'

He moved sideways to go for one of the fresh targets. Never too proud of his shooting, he used the standard two-handed grip, holding the weapon high and then lowering it slowly to the target. He fired one shot to assess the recoil, aimed again and fired a double-tap and then another. Then he looked at the target.

His first shot had missed altogether, which didn't surprise him. The next four were all on target, two shots in the outer ring and two in the inner. It was significantly worse than Nancy's performance.

'Not bad for a new weapon,' she said. 'Try it with the one you know.'

Why am I doing this? Bruno asked himself. He was not fond of handguns and tried not to carry one on duty unless he felt a special need to do so. He conscientiously did his annual refresher course at the police range in Périgueux and scored decently, if not as well as he had in the army. Was he so childish that he wanted to show off, or did not dare refuse the challenge from a woman he found attractive? Probably, he thought, having few illusions about himself. Now concentrate, he told himself sternly. There is nothing more dangerous than a man with a gun whose mind is elsewhere.

The feel and weight of the PAMAS were familiar and there were eight rounds in the mag. The gun came up cleanly to the target as he breathed out and fired the first double-tap. He stepped to one side and fired another. He stepped aside again and went down to one knee and fired one more. Six rounds and that was it. He was done. He cleared the chamber and ejected the magazines from both guns.

'Range cold,' he shouted.

'Range cold,' she echoed. 'That looked fun and good to watch. Let's see what the target thinks.'

All six rounds were in the inner ring and he had two bulls, one of them just barely inside the black circle.

'Best shot of the day,' she said, and he felt ridiculously pleased. 'I want you on my side. Let me clear the magazines and we'll talk.'

'Range hot,' she shouted when her ear protectors were in place.

'Range hot,' he echoed from behind her, and watched as she quickly emptied each gun. Three shots, two inners, one bull, probably from the familiar Glock.

'Honours even, I'd say.' She looked at him boldly, eyebrows raised in challenge, and again he sensed that she was feeling the same attraction that he did. Maybe it was just the effect of gunfire and shooting with someone from the opposite sex. 'Except I just had more practice and you'd never fired a Glock before.'

'This is like the kids' tennis games, when I have to pick one winner for the over-sixes and another for the fives and under,' he said, smiling to take any sting from the remark. 'So you win the girls' trophy and in the absence of any competition I get the prize for the boys.'

'Your prize is you get to clean the PAMAS and I'll clean my Glock.' She pushed the pull-through and oil along the table, tossed him a clean rag and watched him strip the weapon. It had once been second nature to him; he could have done it blindfold. Showing off, he kept his eyes on her as he dismantled the gun.

'And now let me tell you what's going on here,' she said, and made a point of keeping her eyes on him as she stripped her Glock, as if to teach him two could play at that game.

'The tribunal is not getting along. That's not what Deutz says but the other two are quietly furious with him. I got this from Amira. He took each of them to one side and suggested to Professor Weill that Amira's judgement might be in question because of her Muslim background. Then separately he went to Amira and said the same thing to her about Weill being influenced by his Jewishness. He didn't seem to know the two of them were old friends. So now they both think he's a manipulative son of a bitch who wants to take control of the tribunal so it turns out his way.'

'And what is his way?' Bruno asked, squinting down the barrel after using the pull-through. 'I mean, what's Deutz's agenda in all this? What's he trying to achieve?'

'Who knows? My guess is that he wants Sami under his control in the prison system, in a hospital where he can study him at length and write the book that will make him rich and famous. *The Engineer and Me*, or *How I turned the dreaded Engineer into a compliant little vegetable*. Sorry, I'm just letting off steam. But what have you guys got on the bastard? Did Fabiola's old prof come up with the goods?'

Bruno started, surprised and impressed that Nancy knew of the trip to Villefranche; she had evidently been brought into the information network among the women. 'We got a good statement from her, confirming everything,' he replied as he put the gun back together and cleaned off the excess oil with a rag. He popped the spring from the magazine to clean that, too. 'As we speak, Yveline will be tracking down another possible witness, or rather victim. Did you know the

Brigadier is heading this way by helicopter with the Imam in tow?'

'Yes, the email was copied to all of us. I expect he'll be here sometime in the next fifteen minutes. Deutz is probably rehearsing some carefully chosen verses from the Koran as we speak,' she said drily. She put the newly cleaned Glock back together, slipped it into a fast-draw holster above the curve of her left hip and began to load a spare magazine. 'If you haven't got your own weapon here you'd better hang on to that one. It's signed out to me so take care of it. And I'd feel better if you filled at least two magazines. Just to be on the safe side. I saved the best news till last. The Brigadier didn't pass this on but I got a call from your old flame.'

'Isabelle?'

'Who else? And she made a point of telling me to be sure to tell you. It came through to her on the Brigadier's intel net, which I'm not cleared for and I suppose neither are you. It's not just the Imam who's left the mosque. The bad guys seem to have slipped out during the tear gas and the riots yesterday; the *Niqab*, the *Caïd* and the one they call the strong man. They're the ones that flattened you with the cattle prod. The Brigadier's watchers lost track of them but I suspect they might be heading this way. That's why I thought I'd get in some shooting practice.'

25

His képi held firmly on his head, Bruno stood by the windsock with the duty lieutenant watching the helicopter descend. The grit and leaves stirred up by the rotor blades made him close his eyes until the engine coughed to a halt. He saluted as the Brigadier, the white-bearded Imam in his robes and a third figure in an elegant suit and neatly buttoned collarless shirt descended in turn. The two Imams looked curiously around them at the outer walls and the imposing château before them. The Imam touched his hand to his heart and bowed his head slightly as he was introduced to Bruno and the lieutenant. Bruno recognized the third figure, Ghlamallah, from his TV appearances as the man came forward to shake hands, marking the contrast between his modern style and the courtly greeting from the Imam.

The Brigadier dismissed the lieutenant and led the two Imams to his office, gesturing to Bruno to follow. There was a tray of fresh tea, coffee and fruit juice on his desk; he must have radioed ahead, Bruno thought. The Imams took tea, Bruno and the Brigadier had coffee and the Brigadier served. Once they were all seated, the Brigadier introduced Bruno as 'the local policeman who's known Sami since he was a boy and is probably the only official Sami really trusts'.

'From what we can gather, Sami doesn't much trust you or your mosque,' the Brigadier went on briskly, staring directly at the old Imam. 'That's unfortunate but it brings us to one point I am instructed to make before we take you to see the young man. There is considerable concern in official quarters about jihadist influence in your mosque. It is very worrying that some of the young men in your care have gone jihad in Afghanistan but it's outrageous that someone as troubled as Sami should have been under so little supervision that he went with them. And now we hear more troubling news about the children in your orphanage. There will, of course, have to be an official inquiry by the regional child service authorities, and a review of the education licence for your mosque's school.'

'I welcome those inquiries, and promise you my full coopera-tion.' The older Imam spoke in a voice much stronger than Bruno had expected, from the man's frail frame. His French was precise, the accent Parisian, despite his birth in Tunis and the long years he had spent studying in Cairo's al-Azhar university.

'Thank you,' said the Brigadier, looking agreeably surprised. 'This will also mean some very thorough inquiries into your security team at the mosque. Three of them at least will be facing very serious criminal charges. A fourth is already in custody, having been found in dubious circumstances with two of the children from your orphanage, apparently attempting to burn down the house of Sami's adopted parents. Happily, he was prevented, and is now giving us full cooperation. The children are now in care.'

'I am distressed to hear of this, but relieved that the crime was prevented,' the Imam replied. 'Let me be frank, sir. I am grateful that all this has come to a head. For some time, my young colleague and I have been worried that parts of our mosque were drifting out of our control. The school, the orphanage, above all the security team . . . We had already discussed seeking the help of the authorities, but you will understand the constraints that prevented us from doing so.'

'No, I do not understand,' said the Brigadier, coldly. 'You are the Imam. You are the religious and legal authority of the mosque. Whatever happens under its auspices is your responsibility.'

'Perhaps I might help explain.' Ghlamallah spoke for the first time. 'You must know that the house of Islam is sadly divided, that traditional authority is being challenged by militants, the ones you call jihadists. Our mosque was originally founded in a modest way by our own faithful in Toulouse but was then built to the glory of Allah with considerable financial help from our Saudi brethren.'

'Thirty million euros, as I recall,' said the Brigadier. 'Almost as much as they're putting into the new *Grande Mosquée* in Marseille. And the Saudi Ambassador chairs your board of trustees. He can't be pleased at what's happening in your mosque. They didn't install you to run a recruiting station for al-Qaeda.'

Ghlamallah winced as if he'd been hit. 'There are Saudis and Saudis,' he said, and then glanced at the older Imam. 'We get funds from the Saudi monarch and then there are other donations from Saudi individuals who do not share the views of the monarchy and give their money to others, for other purposes.'

'You mean the people who have been funding al-Qaeda?'

'Not just al-Qaeda, but the extreme Salafists in Algeria, Mali, Somalia,' Ghlamallah replied. 'They are the worst of the *Ahl-as-Sunnah*, the ones who reject following any of the four traditional schools of Islam, which is why they condemn even the Wahhabis of Saudi Arabia. They are to us what your extreme Puritans or your Inquisition were in your wars of religion. They have their own funds, their own followers, and we fear they have taken over much of our mosque because we did not recognize them soon enough for what they were.'

Bruno wondered how much of this was true. The fine points of Islamic doctrine were lost on him. He could understand that the Imams felt squeezed between the conservative Saudis who held the purse strings and the increasingly radicalized young members of their congregation, but could they really have allowed the other departments of the mosque, the school, the orphanage and the security service, to be run by jihadists as separate entities?

'You two are the Imams. It's your mosque. Take back control.' The Brigadier's face was impassive but there was a tone of mockery in his voice. 'It's four years since Sami was taken off to Afghanistan. So if four years have passed since the jihadists took over the school, you've had long enough to work out what to do.'

'We have a management committee for the mosque and its various services, and it pains me to admit that it has been some time since we could count on having a majority,' said Ghlamallah. 'Ever since the Iraq war the Salafists have been winning support among the youth. It has become increasingly difficult for me to function. They've already tried to get me dismissed as a modernist, one who is prepared to abandon the traditional ways of Mohammed, peace be upon him.'

'So you're hoping we can help you get your mosque back before your Saudi benefactors notice you've lost it?'

'Yes, but you need us to help you prevent the mosque from becoming a Salafist stronghold in France, and one capable of delivering twenty thousand well-disciplined votes. Your politicians offer a great deal of protection in return for a voting block like that. I think you understand what I mean. Without our support and our invitation, I'm not sure your politicians would take the risk of sending in the police to our precincts to impose French law.'

Watching this exchange Bruno understood that this visit, supposedly to see Sami, was in fact a bargaining session with the French state. And Ghlamallah was sufficiently astute to realize that the French state, its permanent government of institutions and Prefects and *procureurs* and officials like the Brigadier, was something different from its politicians.

The old Imam, a faint smile on his face and his fingers stroking his white beard, gazed benignly on the two of them as if the conversation had nothing to do with him but they had his blessing anyway.

'Are you prepared to invite us in to enforce the order to investigate the children's services and your security team?' the Brigadier asked.

The two Imams confirmed that they were.

'Then I think we understand one another, so let us go and see young Sami and his parents.'

The Brigadier led them up the stairs and outside to the

long balcony by the battlements where Bruno remembered finding Sami and Momu playing games with maps when he'd gone to tell them the tribunal was ready. Some tables and chairs had been put out and Momu and Dillah were sipping tea and watching Sami play with Balzac when the Imams arrived. The other tables were empty except for the one closest to the parapet, where Nancy sat alone over a notebook, pen in hand and a cup of coffee beside her. She looked up briefly, gave a courteous smile and returned to her writing.

Bruno noted that Ghlamallah walked a pace behind the old Imam, as if sheltering in his shadow. Perhaps it was simply respect. Momu put down his cup and watched their approach coldly. Sami ignored them until he saw Bruno and scampered across, calling his name.

'This has become his favourite place,' the Brigadier said. 'When they saw how it relaxed him the tribunal started having sessions out here as well. In this fine weather, it's more pleasant to be outside.'

Patting Sami's back as the young man hugged him and Balzac pawed at his leg, Bruno's eyes scanned the surroundings for danger points. The main bulk of the tower protected most of the balcony from being overlooked by anyone on the far hillside, the only logical place for a sniper. The place seemed safe enough. And at each end of the balcony Bruno saw the cameras, fresh cement showing how recently they had been installed. As elsewhere in the château, every word and action was being recorded.

The old Imam walked slowly to Momu and Dillah, stopped and took Ghlamallah's arm for support as he went slowly and painfully down on one knee. He touched his other hand to his heart and bowed his head.

'I have come to apologize to you for our failure to do right by your son,' he said. 'You had a right to expect better of us. I cannot ask your forgiveness, only your understanding that I was too naïve to see that our mosque was being taken over by wicked people.'

Momu sat unmoving, refusing to respond, his face set like flint. It was Dillah who broke the silence.

'You should be ashamed,' she burst out, almost spitting at Ghlamallah. 'You, in particular, who thought all we cared about was the money we had paid, thought we could be fobbed off with a refund of one term's fees. We entrusted you with our poor boy and you did worse than nothing for him. You betrayed us, your mosque betrayed us and you only come to say sorry when the whole world knows what you did. So take yourselves and your apology away with you. I stamp my foot on it.'

Momu reached across and gripped her hand. Nobody else moved. Even Sami, still crouched at Bruno's knee where he had recovered Balzac, sat immobile, his eyes wide.

'I hoped I might say a prayer . . .' the Imam began.

'Save your prayers,' Dillah retorted. 'Save them for the grief of the mothers of those other poor boys you took in who were sent off to fight in a far-off land, to die for nothing. And do not even think of using the world martyr to me. We have had too many martyrs from you old fools who claim to speak for religion. And it's never you who die, it's the innocent children whose minds you poison.'

The Imam tried to lurch to his feet but Ghlamallah had to

help him. When he stood at last, he bowed solemnly to Dillah, turned and bowed to Sami and said, 'I am sorry we failed you.'

Sami stared at him blankly until the Imam then said something in Arabic and Sami edged back away from the old man, his face crumpling as if the language itself disturbed him.

'That's enough,' roared Momu, rising from his chair, his voice booming in a way he'd learned in mastering unruly schoolrooms. 'Haven't you tormented this poor boy enough? Leave him in peace.'

Momu stood defiantly, hands on his hips, chin thrust out, and Dillah darted from her chair to go to Sami and comfort him. Nancy rose from her own table to join her.

The Imam looked helpless and confused, like an old man no longer knowing where he was or how to find his way home. Ghlamallah led him gently back to the door where the Brigadier was waiting.

'That poor woman, I know she's not his real mother but my heart goes out to her,' Ghlamallah said piously.

'A pity your heart took four years to notice her grief,' said Bruno.

The Brigadier ignored him and said, 'Now, gentlemen, we'd better draft your statement requesting the police to intervene to protect your mosque against a Salafist and terrorist takeover. And we'll have to stress your concern for the children in the orphanage and your shock at the evidence of murders and terrorist recruitment taking place under your noses. And since you're so accustomed to being on TV, Ghlamallah, perhaps you'd draft a statement you can deliver to the cameras.'

The Imam coughed, tugged at Ghlamallah's sleeve and

murmured something in his ear. Ghlamallah nodded and turned to the Brigadier.

'I am reminded to convey to you the unfortunate news that the *Niqab*, the *Caïd* and Mustaf, the one known as *Zhern'ber*, the strong man, seem to have left the mosque precincts sometime between yesterday noon and when we left this morning. We have no idea where they have gone or what they are doing, but the Imam insists you should know.'

The Brigadier nodded and addressed the Imam directly. 'We knew that already, but I'm glad you confirmed it without being asked. It helps build a little trust.'

'The Imam would also like to know . . .' Ghlamallah went on, but the Brigadier cut in.

'The Imam is old enough to speak for himself,' he snapped. He looked at the old man. 'Well, what is it?'

'That other woman there, the Western woman, who is she? She's not a member of the tribunal, at least of those listed in the newspaper.'

'She's one of the officials who have been helping to debrief Sami and support the family as the tribunal does its work,' the Brigadier replied crisply. 'You've seen the château, the security arrangements we've been forced to put in place because of your so-called security services. Perhaps you can think what the French people are paying, in soldiers' lives as well as money, to deal with this crisis you created through your negligent handling of this young man.'

He turned to Bruno. 'Perhaps you would see these two gentlemen to the waiting room outside my office and find some pens and paper so that they can start drafting some-thing suitable. I'll rejoin you there shortly, after the tribunal reconvenes. I think the tribunal will be calling on you shortly to tell them what you know of Sami. And then perhaps you'd check on this Halévy woman whose bequest is suddenly all over the radio. The last thing we want is another security situation involving her.'

26

Bruno's experience before the tribunal was short and mostly straightforward. He described what he knew of Sami's boyhood, his amazing skills at serving tennis aces and sinking baskets and his gift for repairing anything mechanical. Professor Chadoub, who asked him to call her Amira, wanted to know how Sami had got on with other children of his own age, girls as well as boys. He answered as best he could and recommended they speak to Momu's son, Karim, who had played a sterling role as big brother. Professor Weill asked if he'd ever seen Sami perform any violent act and had smiled, his eyes twinkling, when Bruno replied, 'Only against a tennis ball.'

'There's just one more aspect of this that intrigues me, as a music-lover as much as anything else. Sami seems to have an extraordinary response to Mozart. Do you know anything about that?'

'I noticed it first in the car on the way back from picking Sami up at the airport,' Bruno said, thinking there was no reason to let the tribunal know of the playlists being used to conceal messages. 'Mozart was on the car radio and it seemed to calm him. I bought some CDs for him and he listens to them all the time. He said something about it being predictable, like maths, until it suddenly wasn't. It struck me as a perceptive way to describe Mozart's music.'

'What did you buy for him?'

'What I found in the supermarket, *Eine kleine Nachtmusik*, the *Jeunehomme* piano concerto and *The Magic Flute*. Later I took him some of my own discs, the horn concerto, Symphony Number Forty and *Figaro*. He likes them all, sometimes tries to sing along. I'd be fascinated to hear what he'd come up with if he ever learned to play the piano.'

'Indeed, so would I. And now a last, rather personal question, I'm afraid: do you like him?'

'Yes, I do, at least the Sami I knew as a boy and the Sami I have seen since his return,' Bruno said without even thinking about it. 'I find it very hard to equate that Sami with what we hear of his work in Afghanistan.'

'You're an experienced policeman,' Chadoub suddenly intervened. 'Do you think he's responsible for his actions?'

'I'm not sure he thinks as we do of the difference between right and wrong but I suspect he knows what he did in Afghanistan was deeply wrong. That's why he got out. I think he made bombs because it was the way he found to stay alive. He sometimes seems watchful of others, as if observing what actions of his meet approval. Does that make him responsible? I don't know. But I'm pretty sure he can't understand a judicial proceeding, far less be responsible for his own legal defence.'

It was Deutz who asked the key question, about changes in Sami's behaviour since his return. Bruno described seeing Sami at the airport, huddled speechless in foetal position, and his nervousness around new people. He mentioned Sami's apparent distress at being addressed in Arabic.

Even as Bruno answered, it felt odd to see Deutz in this context, thoughtful and professional. He was adept at zeroing in on the key point and played his role perfectly, neither steering Bruno nor letting him evade the question. It was impressive, but for some time now Bruno had seen Deutz in a wholly different light: as a vain man of great ambition and without self-restraint. Deutz was a rapist who had no right to sit in any kind of judgement on others, Bruno believed, let alone on a hapless youth like Sami. And he was sure that Nancy was right about the dangerous consequences of Deutz's techniques to turn prisoners into informers. Even as he tried to explain his thoughts to the tribunal there was a corner of his mind that was looking coldly at Deutz and vowing to bring him to justice.

'As a boy, Sami didn't seem afraid or distressed,' Bruno replied. 'He gave me the impression of being a contented child, always eager to help if he could fix something. He just didn't interact much with others, very seldom spoke. I still see that Sami now, when he's with people he knows or those he loves, or with animals. But since he left home he's obviously known pain and terror, and they've marked him. He's clearly glad to be back in familiar surroundings with his family.'

'We've heard from Sami's adoptive father about his dreadful experience in the Algerian civil war when his family was slaughtered. He knew pain and terror then, but you say his later childhood showed no sign of that,' Deutz suggested.

'I don't know whether his childhood in Algeria before the massacre was normal, whether he spoke and interacted like other children. Momu or Dillah might know. At the time, not having learned from Momu about the massacre, I assumed

Sami had been born that way. Now I suspect his autism, or whatever name we use to describe his problem, came as a result of his ordeal, but I'm not a doctor and not qualified to judge.'

That was all the tribunal wanted from him. As he left the balcony Nancy was waiting for him at the bottom of the stairs.

'Nice job, particularly on the Mozart. It really helps to humanize Sami,' she said. 'I was worried about the wind messing up the audio when they hold these sessions outdoors, but the video feed was fine. Now they have the feed direct in Washington, they hardly need me.'

Bruno's eyes widened in surprise. 'You mean that what I just said has already been heard in Washington? Including that part when I said I liked him?'

'And Harvard, and New York, Raleigh, Houston and Minneapolis. We've lined up some of the best psychologists in the States to monitor these hearings and give us their own reports. I don't think the West Coast is awake yet but I know there's someone from Seattle on the monitoring team. And others in the Justice Department, who'll make their own report on Sami's likely legal status.'

'I had no idea . . . all this set in train for little Sami.'

'He's going to be the most famous case of autism on the planet, and probably the most studied. The newspapers back home are suddenly full of medical experts and psychologists explaining what it is and how little we understand it. The TV footage has really helped changed the mood. He's Sami now, not the Engineer.'

'Probably because it's shorter for the newspaper headlines,' Bruno said.

'Wait till the next little drama hits: a tribunal member being arrested for rape,' she went on, a triumphant glint in her eye. 'I had a call from Annette. She's spoken to one of the other medical students who got the Deutz treatment. That's two cases as well as Fabiola. The guy is toast.'

She used the French term *pain grillé*, and Bruno shook his head, not understanding the expression.

'It means he's done, he's finished, his goose is cooked.'

Bruno grinned. He loved to hear these English idioms translated directly into French, reminding him how wonderfully inventive and quirky languages could be. And 'his goose is cooked' was one any good Périgourdin would relish.

'Then the essential question is likely to be about the timing,' Bruno suggested. 'The *Procureur* has to sign off on it first, and I imagine he'll need to talk to Paris. They won't want an arrest to overshadow the tribunal process, so they'll probably wait until the tribunal report is complete.'

'They're supposed to end the hearings today and produce their report tomorrow. The Brigadier expects it will be unanimous, but who knows. One thing worries me: who'd respect a tribunal verdict once Deutz has been disgraced?'

Bruno nodded; he hadn't thought of that. Either way would be a mess. He was glad it wasn't his decision.

'I just hope the trial isn't too much of an ordeal for Fabiola,' he said.

'A lot less of an ordeal than she'd face in the States, with a clever defence lawyer asking her about her every sexual experience. That's our adversarial system. The defence usually tries to turn the woman into a slut in front of the jury by alleging the wicked woman led the poor helpless guy along. There are times I prefer justice your French way.'

Bruno remembered something he'd read, he thought in one of Montaigne's essays, that one of the most convincing reasons to believe in a supreme being was that it held out the prospect that a perfect justice could exist, however impossible it might be for flawed humans to achieve it. He was just trying to recall the exact quote when he heard footsteps on the stairs and the Brigadier arrived, leading the two Imams and smiling broadly, a triumphant gleam in his eye.

'They have agreed to tell the tribunal what they know of Sami's time at the mosque,' the Brigadier explained, and led them up the last set of stairs to the balcony, the older Imam on Ghlamallah's arm.

'That's good,' Nancy said when they were out of earshot. 'It means we'll get Ghlamallah's voice on tape. We've got some special equipment that washes out all the voice-modifiers you can buy. There's a lot of queries about some of the voices on the phone taps and it would be useful to have something on him.'

'Whatever happened to those pixels in the photos on his smartphone?' Bruno asked, remembering Nancy had said the NSA had software that could scan them for hidden messages.

'They were clean,' she said, shrugging. 'But I'm not surprised. The jihadis have known we had that capacity for some time. But they don't know we're now reading their Mozart playlists.' She checked her watch. 'This is an unscheduled hearing. All the others are done. I was hoping it would be all wrapped up tonight and we'd have the final report tomorrow. The Brigadier said he'll stay up all night writing it.'

'And then you go back to Paris?' Bruno asked, trying to keep his voice level. He knew he'd remember her and those sudden moments when he had felt the jolt of attraction pass between them. Suddenly his mouth was dry again.

'Probably straight to Washington, a lot of meetings as we draft the three options.' She was looking into his eyes as if searching for something.

'Three options? You know already?' They were at least a metre apart but he felt she was much closer than that. There was a strange disconnect between the words they were exchanging and another quite different and deeper communication that seemed to be taking place.

'It's the way things are done in Washington.' Nancy's voice sounded faint. She closed her eyes, half-turned and took a deep breath. Whatever sudden charge had begun to flow again between them seemed to fade. Bruno supposed he ought to be grateful. She was leaving within a day or so and he'd never see her again.

'Some president, I think it was Nixon, wanted every decision that came up to him to be on one sheet of paper with no more than three options.' Now her voice was normal again, crisp and efficient, with a slight tone of mockery, as if she knew there was more to life than the politics of Sami.

'So for Sami the options have been pretty clear from the start,' she said, still looking away from him up the staircase. 'One, we demand extradition and trial in the United States. Two, we demand a trial and punishment but leave the jurisdiction to France. Three, we accept a tribunal verdict that he's not fit to stand trial and treat him as a cooperative witness who stays in protective and medical custody. The Brigadier and I have talked about it, we agree, and we're going to do all we can to get the most sensible decision, option three.'

'It sounds as though whoever drafted those options knew that one and two were hardly possible, politically. They wanted option three all along.'

'Exactly.' She turned back to face him, but without that intensity that had so stirred him a moment earlier. 'That's how bureaucracies work, how our political masters want us to work, reshaping the complexities of the world into three clear choices.'

She laughed, a warm sound, almost a chuckle that seemed to embrace him in a complicity of two professionals trying to make sense of a crazed world. 'So here we are, two servants of our separate states, conspiring to bring about the only rational outcome while standing on the landing of a stone staircase in a medieval castle and wondering about a bunch of jihadi nuts on the loose and trying to kill us and everyone in here.'

Bruno said nothing, wanting to extend this moment, to remember her as she looked now. The time stretched and she looked away again.

'We can't stay here. What are you planning on doing now?' she asked.

He closed his eyes and took a breath. It was over. He straightened his back and brought himself back to his duty. 'I'm off to track down a little old Jewish lady, Kaufman's grandma. The Brigadier is worried that she might be at risk, now the news of her bequest has gone public.'

'Oh, Arab terrorism, Jewish money, I think I get it,' she said. 'And that car certainly stands out a mile. Have you seen the *Sud Ouest* website?'

She whipped out her smartphone and called up Delaron's news story with the image of Maya waving cheerfully as she stepped into her Rolls. A second photo below showed Bruno, the Mayor and Maya coming out from the *collège*.

Bruno hadn't seen it and he was startled. The job of protecting Maya had suddenly grown urgent. And personal too: if the men who'd attacked him saw his photo, he reflected, they might think they were getting two targets rather than one.

'What are you going to do?' she asked, but he was already calling Kaufman. Nancy turned away with a natural courtesy, pretending to be checking emails, giving him space. Bruno explained briefly, listened, agreed to meet and rang off.

'They're in Bergerac, sightseeing with the Rolls-Royce. I'll drive there now to meet them and let them use my Land Rover. I'll bring the Rolls back and put it in a friend's barn.'

'I should come, too. There has to be a woman in the back to replace Maya. Besides, I've always wanted to be driven in a Roller.'

Bruno shook his head. 'We're not playing bait. We just have to get that damn magnet of a car off the street.'

'We'll be bait whether we like it or not. We're armed and we know what we're doing. We'll tell the Brigadier and he'll arrange back-up. We have a chopper and squad of troops on call. How long is the drive?'

'From Bergerac back here, thirty, forty minutes, maybe less.'

'I'll go see the Brigadier. You organize the weapons and flak vests. I've got my Glock but I want an M-16 or something like it. If we're ambushed, some grenades would be useful, maybe some smoke.'

Bruno stared at her in disbelief but she was already heading up the stairs. 'Wait,' he said. 'Look, this is Périgord, civilian country. We don't go round gunned up like that.'

'Bruno, you're not a fool. You know how these jihadists will be armed. And how else are we sure to bring them out? They aren't going to try hitting this place, it's a fortress. We've got the sniper zones covered. They'll be desperate to hit something, anything, and they won't be able to resist an Israeli million-airess in an utterly recognizable car.'

Bruno could think of nothing he could say that wouldn't sound ridiculous, but had to say something.

'You're a diplomat,' he ventured.

'I'm a law enforcement officer and these people are terrorist criminals and enemies of my country,' she snapped. 'Let's go.'

'Lead on,' he conceded, 'but we'll both go to see the Brigadier. We can't do this without authorization and only he can fix the support.'

The more he thought of it, the more inevitable the idea seemed. Maya would be at risk. Her car would be unmistakable. He had to get to Bergerac and arrange an alternative car for her. It was reasonable to take precautions, which should include helicopter reinforcements on stand-by. He found himself rehearsing the arguments he'd present to the Brigadier.

But there was no need. The Brigadier seized on the plan even before Nancy had finished explaining. 'A damn sight better idea than twiddling our thumbs here and waiting for them to come to us,' he said, and began organizing the troops for the helicopter, the communications and an ambulance.

27

The map was spread open on the hood of Bruno's Land Rover. Nancy and the Brigadier stood to his left and the young paratroop lieutenant and his three-man team to his right. Bruno said, 'We have to think like them, to know only what they know.'

Bruno explained that the jihadists knew from the media that Sami was in the château and probably out of their reach so long as he remained there. Short of artillery, the château should be deemed safe. They also knew that Bruno was based in St Denis and that Maya Halévy with her very identifiable car had been with him there that morning. They knew she was extremely rich, so they would assume she would be staying at the most luxurious hotel in the region. Without question, that meant the Vieux Logis in Trémolat. They would be wrong, she was staying at Pamela's but the jihadis weren't to know that. They would focus on the Rolls-Royce and Trémolat.

The lieutenant cleared his throat. 'My men have been listening to the local radio. They've got a reporter following this woman and her car around like she's a film star and sending in regular bulletins. She was in Mouleydier early this afternoon, apparently she was there in the war when it was destroyed. Now she's in Bergerac. She went to the Protestant temple, another place she remembered.'

'Should we call the radio station and tell them to stop?' the lieutenant went on. 'They don't know it but they're putting her life in danger.'

'No,' said Bruno firmly. 'We can use this. I know the reporter.'

He took out his phone and called Philippe Delaron.

'Philippe, it's Bruno. You owe me a lot of favours already, but here's a big one. You're in Bergerac with Maya now. You know where she's heading? No? She's having dinner at the Vieux Logis. Yes, I'm told she's staying there, hardly a surprise. It's the best place around. Anyway, if you want an interview, Trémolat is the place to be. You should be able to get a word with her on the doorstep.'

He closed his phone. 'Let's work on the assumption that they're listening to the radio. They'll have at least one car, maybe two or even three. They have one good sniper rifle and I don't know what else. Do we have any intel on their available weapons?' he asked the Brigadier.

'According to Rafiq, in the mosque they had small arms, grenades, explosives, a couple of Minimi machine guns with 200-round belts and some RPGs. That was all. We have no idea what they took with them when they left the mosque, but we'd better assume they brought all the weapons they could.'

Bruno pursed his lips. Rocket-propelled grenades were as good as light artillery at close quarters. And a Minimi could spew out a full belt in just over ten seconds, laying down a terrifying amount of fire.

'Let's not forget what we know about them,' he said. 'The *Niqab* was in the paras, until invalided out after a jumping accident. He's trained in French fighting technique, just like us. The tactics and solutions he'll go for are those we'd probably choose ourselves. And I was told the *Caïd* was a *sous-off*, again trained, but I don't know in whose army.' He turned to the Brigadier. 'Can you get me that info, and phone through anything you have on the strong man, and whether any of them went through a sniper course?'

He looked at the lieutenant and his three men, all that could be fitted into the light Fennec chopper. 'We've all been trained the same way, so if I say anything that seems unlikely to you, speak out.'

'In their shoes, I'd worry about being able to stop a car that big unless they set up a pretty powerful barricade,' he went on. 'They might try with the RPG but I think the most rational military probability is that they'll look for a sniping point by the Vieux Logis or an ambush point on the road from Bergerac. Probably both, one sniper in place and two for the ambush.'

Bruno's mind went back to the scene in the woods where Rafiq had been murdered.

'One guy, I think his name's Mustaf, is as strong as a horse, and he used logs to block another car at a previous ambush.' He pointed at the map. 'The main road from Bergerac to Trémolat goes through Mouleydier and Lalinde. The obvious route is to cross the river at Lalinde then turn off left, where the road is signposted to Trémolat and joins the D31 road to cross the river into Trémolat at this bridge. It's by the place where the river widens out to make the water-ski lagoon.'

Bruno moved his finger to the bridge. 'I wouldn't mount an ambush after the Trémolat bridge, too many houses, too much chance of being seen. I'd rather try it either here, where the D31 makes this dog-leg curve, or here, at the sharp left turn just before the bridge. Either one makes sense, but if they disable the Rolls and block the bridge, then they can't get to the Vieux Logis to pick up the sniper, if they've left him there. They could leave their car on the far side of the bridge or they might just abandon him. Any comments?'

The lieutenant spoke first, to ask where the helicopter should wait to fly in support if those were the two likely ambush points. It would have to be behind some high ground to muffle sound that might alert the jihadis. He pointed to the two likely spots, one behind the village of Cales and the other by the campsite of La Pénitie.

His sergeant objected that the first one was too close to the car's route, which wouldn't matter, but the contour lines didn't look helpful, which would.

'La Pénitie it is,' said Bruno. 'You're a bit more than three clicks from the ambush sites, say one minute flying time, a bit more to gain altitude and pick up speed. You can be hitting them from the rear in less than ninety seconds after we call you in, or after you hear gunfire.'

'Is this Rolls car armoured?' the sergeant asked.

'No, but it's so heavy it might as well be. Why?'

'I was thinking of the window glass,' the sergeant said. 'If these guys want to stick together rather than separate, and that's how they train us, then I'd use the sniper to take out the driver at one of these two turns where the car has to slow, probably the sharper of the two turns. Once the driver's hit, it will be easy to stop the car and kill the woman, or grab her as a hostage. It gives them options.'

Bruno nodded. 'I'm glad you're with us. That's the best thought yet. What's your name?'

'Duclaud, Sir, Gilbert Duclaud, *Sergent-chef*. Do we know

if any of these guys were trained as snipers? And whether they only have that FN-F2 sniper's rifle you spoke about, or might they have the big bastard, the Hécate, the one that fires the 12.7 round? In the right hands, that's a killer at over a kilometre.'

'Not as far as we know. And since they haven't used it on us here, when they might have been able to reach a target, we'll have to assume not.' Bruno smiled at him; *sergent-chef* had been his own rank. 'Right, we're running out of time,' Bruno went on. 'The sooner you guys are in place, the better. We'll test the radio link when we're on the road and if that fails we have the mobile phones.' He turned to Nancy. 'Got everything you need? Sorry there's no M-16.'

'I feel like something out of *Star Wars*,' she laughed, brandishing the FAMAS at him. The standard French infantry assault rifle, it was known to the troops as *le clairon*, the bugle, from its strikingly modernistic shape. 'But now I've shot off a couple of magazines, we'll get along fine.'

Bruno was also taking a FAMAS, and the guns were short enough to fit into the sports bag they'd use to conceal them when changing cars.

'We've only got the one size of flak vest,' the sergeant said apologetically, bringing them up from the bag at his feet. 'But they've got the Kevlar plates, they'll stop most rounds.'

Without hesitation, Nancy stripped off her shirt and jacket, down to her bra. The other men turned their heads away to give her privacy. Taking off his own gear, Bruno didn't notice until he began shrugging on the heavy vest and suddenly saw her eyes on him and taking her time before she pulled the vest over her head and her black bra. He caught his breath as his eyes lingered and he felt himself flush, knowing the sight would stay in his memory. And then her head poked out of the neck and she was grinning at him cheekily. He laughed and ducked his own head into his vest and began to adjust the straps. This was a remarkable woman.

'Roll up your right trouser leg, mademoiselle, if you please,' the sergeant said, and knelt to strap the black velcro scabbard around her ankle and shin. Bruno was already fitting his own when the sergeant handed her a blackened commando knife, serrated down one side. Bruno checked the blade against the hairs on the back of his forearm and nodded, thinking if it came down to that, they were in real trouble.

'One more thing,' the sergeant said, and pushed forward a short soldier with a Red Cross armband and a wide grin on his coal-black face.

'Field dressings, just in case,' he said. 'If either of you gets hit, I'm in the chopper and I'll be with you very fast. Count on it. And there's a morphine ampoule wrapped inside each dressing. There's a carbon pencil attached and remember to write M on the forehead if you have to use it.'

They climbed into Bruno's Land Rover, checked their equipment, and he told her to duck down as he drove past the small media encampment of satellite vans on the access road. He headed for Bergerac, seeing the helicopter dip over them in salute before wheeling and heading off toward Trémolat. Nancy began checking their radios. Standard French infantry kit, they were clipped to the flak vests and covered by the civilian jackets. Hers was the same red that Maya had been wearing on her visit to the school, the colour the jihadis would be expecting from monitoring the *Sud Ouest* news site. Bruno was certain now that they would be; every time he came on the radio Philippe gave a plug for his newspaper story.

'Comms are good,' she said. 'Let me check the cellphones, if we can hear anything over the rotor blades.' He felt her hand snake under his civilian jacket, feeling for the pouch on his belt. He caught his breath. She gave his thigh a friendly pat once she'd extracted the phone.

'There,' she said. 'That didn't hurt a bit, did it? First contact, Bruno, and don't tell me you weren't counting.'

Not sure what to say, he said nothing as she began punching the speed-dial buttons they had programmed into the phones.

'OK, they work, not great, but if all else fails they'll probably hear me scream for help.' She sat back, watching the road. 'Trémolat is over to the right, west of here, if I recall the map.'

'You do, and if this works out, you're my guest for dinner at the Vieux Logis at your convenience. It's my favourite restaurant.'

'Done, but tonight we'll be busy whether this works or not, and tomorrow I may be on a plane to Washington. So you're saying I'm welcome to come back.'

'Any time you want. I imagine you'll be back in France some day. And I'll always be in St Denis.'

'Isabelle said that was the trouble. She could never compete with St Denis.'

'I'm not inviting you to move here, I'm inviting you to dinner.'

'And I'm accepting with pleasure, but you have to pick the menu.'

'It will be a surprise, their *menu du marché*. It's about all I can afford.'

'Better still. I like surprises.' She paused. 'Talking of surprises, what do you plan to do if the sniper's first shot is a good one?'

'You mean if it hits me?'

'Of course.' She looked at him oddly.

'We stop at a friend of mine in Lalinde. He's a hunter, but he runs a clothes shop. We'll be there in a few minutes.' He gestured to his right. 'That's the turnoff we'll take to Trémolat.'

She mulled over his answer for a long moment, then said with delight, 'Clothes shop – you're going to borrow a mannequin.'

'Very good, but it's a bit more tricky than that, you'll see.'

In Lalinde, he parked opposite the small lake, darted from the car and was back within minutes carrying the top half of a mannequin. He put it down on the back seat.

'It's a she,' Nancy said. 'Won't they be able to tell the difference?'

'I've got a baseball cap to put on her, and a jacket. And they won't be seeing too well; we're coming from the west, from the setting sun.'

She began to sing what sounded like a country song about some dam in the American West and Bruno picked out the words Grand Coulee.

'Is that Bob Dylan?' he asked.

'A good try, but it's Woody Guthrie. Dylan did a cover version.'

'I like your voice,' he said. 'You can keep a tune.'

'Ah, a dangerous man, one who knows how women really like to be flattered.'

'If only I'd known it was so easy . . . We're coming into

Mouleydier, where Maya Halévy and her brother were almost killed in the war. They ran into a battle.'

'Sounds a bit like us, which reminds me, what do we do when the shooting starts? Do you have a plan?'

'Napoleon said no plan ever survives contact with the enemy,' Bruno said. 'But this is what I think. If it goes as we expect, they shoot and hit the mannequin, I spin the car to give some cover and we both roll out of the blind side with our weapons. By then I'm hoping you'll have called in the seventh cavalry. That's why there's a second bag, so we can each strap one round our shoulders and don't lose the weapons when we bale out.

'Once on the ground I go forward to shelter behind the front wheel and toss a smoke grenade, red to mark us for the chopper and to give us some cover. You go to the rear,' he went on. 'Then I throw a grenade to where I think the shooter was, you lay down some fire and then move. I'll try to move right, you move left. That will widen their angle and give us a chance of crossfire. But we have to take out their machine gun. And start counting. If the chopper takes more than ninety seconds, or if I go down, you need to start pulling back and finding cover. There are hedgerows and copses and a barn as you head away from the road.'

'Three-round bursts?' she asked.

'Three-round bursts, unless you get a clear target for single shots. We're not short of magazines and they'll be stunned to hear us with guns. That's our margin of surprise, that and the mannequin. Once they hear us shoot, they'll panic and rethink, they may start to run. I imagine they'll have their car somewhere near. If you see it, immobilize it.'

'And if it doesn't go according to plan?'

'We still follow our own plan as far as we can. Unless West Point taught you something different.'

'The West Point rule is always apply more firepower.' He could hear the tension in her voice, a slight rise in the register as this started to become real for her.

'That's why I'm more worried about RPGs and the Minimi than I am about the sniper,' he said. 'That's a lot of firepower, and it's why I'm carrying smoke grenades along with the frags. And we'll have an advantage if we move. The *Niqab* was hurt in a jumping accident. That means his back. He won't be sprinting. Big Mustaf has got a wrecked knee, I hit him pretty hard and I was surprised he could even walk. But he certainly won't be running. They'll only have one agile unit, the *Caïd*.'

'But we're both agile.'

'Right, they have the firepower, until the chopper turns up. We have surprise, smoke, grenades and movement. Whatever you do, don't stay in one place for more than a couple of bursts. And change your height of fire, don't always fire from a ditch. Stand behind a tree, get some higher ground. Force them to keep shifting their points of aim.'

'I was thinking what the sergeant said, that maybe they'd want to take Maya hostage.'

'It's possible, and it could mean they won't use the RPG. But don't count on it, don't count on anything.'

'One thing, Bruno, take this and read it when you want but only act on it if I'm out of commission, you understand?'

She handed him an envelope. He said OK and tucked it into an inside pocket, suddenly flooded with memories of doing it for other comrades in arms before going into action. He'd never had anyone to leave an envelope for. He supposed he had, these days, for Pamela, for the Mayor and in spite of everything for Isabelle. It had never crossed his mind to write a farewell note.

'It wasn't Napoleon who said no plan survives meeting the enemy,' Nancy said suddenly. 'It was a German, von Moltke. Napoleon's version was that first he engaged the enemy and then he'd see what to do.'

Bruno glanced at her, amused. 'Correction noted, but I think we'd better do it Napoleon's way.'

They had reached Bergerac and he drove straight to the centre, to Place Gambetta, and turned into the parking lot of the Hôtel de Bordeaux. The Rolls was there and Bruno parked in front of it to shield the exchange of cars, although there was no one in sight. He heard a door close and Yacov was there, Maya a small shadow following behind.

'Key is in the ignition,' Bruno said. 'Give us a moment to shift the equipment. You drive back the way I told you, the long way round through Sainte Alvère. When you get to Pamela's place there'll be some soldiers to take you on to the château. You have your mobile phone? And the Brigadier's numbers? And mine? Read them back to me.'

Yacov complied, a man accustomed to taking orders. But then chivalry intervened and he said, 'You can't take a woman on this job, take me instead.'

'It has to be a woman in the back of the car, obviously. And Nancy's a better shot than I am and she went through West Point. She comes with me, you don't.'

'He's right, Yacov,' said Maya, pushing him toward the Land Rover. 'You just do what you're told.'

'I won't forget this, Bruno,' Maya said, and reached up to embrace him. He gave her a smacking kiss on the lips and a hug to the waiflike frame and pushed her to the car.

'We're all loaded,' Nancy said, from the side of the Rolls. 'Your bag's on the front seat, mine is with me. Long guns and handguns both loaded. We are both carrying sidearms. All safeties are checked and on. Your mannequin has got her jacket and cap on and she's strapped in. I think I'll call her Maya.'

'And don't forget to call the Brigadier when you get close to St Denis,' Bruno told Yacov, closed the Land Rover door behind him and watched it drive away. When he turned back, Nancy was still standing by the side of the door.

'For my first time in a Rolls, I think a man ought to open the door for me and steward me inside,' she said, giving him that cheeky grin once more.

He opened the door, gave her his arm, and suddenly her face was against his.

'If all this goes wrong, I don't want your last kiss to come from an eighty-year-old woman,' she murmured, put a hand to the back of his neck and placed her lips softly, and then very firmly against his. For a brief moment, her tongue teased at his lips and her teeth gave the gentlest of nips to his lower lip.

She pulled back, pressed her cheek against his, and whispered into his ear, 'And if it's to be my last kiss, I'm glad it's you.' Then, trailing her hand across his neck and cheek, she sank into the back of the car and pulled the door shut behind her with a sound as discreet and as rich as it was final.

28

They drove in silence out of Bergerac, ignoring the pedestrians who stopped and pointed and some of them waved at the stately Rolls-Royce. Cars slowed and pulled aside to give the huge car room as they cruised around roundabouts and took the road that ran along the north bank of the river Dordogne.

'I was trying to work out what's wrong and suddenly I get it,' she said. 'This is a British car, right-hand drive, but they don't know that. The mannequin is in what the French think is the driver's seat. You're expecting the sniper to aim for that side.'

He nodded and raised his left hand in a vague salute. 'It gives us an edge, perhaps just a second, but that's all we'll need if you shoot like you did before.'

'What were you saluting?'

'A vineyard, Château de Tiregand. The château is on top of that slope and in a moment you'll see a stone pavilion against the skyline. It's given me a lot of pleasure over the years.'

'Sometimes I think you're slightly mad.' She spoke softly, almost to herself. 'Maybe we both are, doing this. I want you to know, if I get hit, don't come for me. Leave me, keep fighting, it will give me cover.'

Bruno didn't reply, running through the usual checklist, rules of engagement, objective, weapons, ammo, support. He kept swallowing, the tension making his saliva glands work. Some men became dry-mouthed before action, he'd always been the reverse.

He knew he was not in the least mad. There was a cold but deeply personal logic to this mission. These men had come to his town and tortured and killed Rafiq. For that, he had vowed to bring them to justice. Then they had attacked him, hurt and humiliated him in a college full of schoolchildren he knew, kids he had taught to have respect and trust in the police and in the law. For that, these men would face his own justice. And now they were back to kill again and he would stop them. It was his job, his town, his duty.

Bruno wondered what Nancy was going through. Her kiss had surprised him, unsettled him, triggering dreams and fantasies that lingered seductively in his mind, a distraction at a time when he needed to focus. Perhaps it had been a sign of her own nervousness. He didn't know if she'd ever seen action, and known the difference between shooting on a range and doing it when somebody was firing back.

'I know you went through West Point,' he said. 'But that Iraq tour you mentioned, was that with the military or with the FBI?'

'The military, tail-end of the war and then ten more months, I was running a communications platoon, a geek in uniform trying to keep the radios and computers running when dust got into everything and the troops sweated into their handsets. It didn't really get hairy when I was there and I saw more motherboards than action. Biggest priority was keeping the phone and emails open for the troops to stay in touch with home.'

'Any combat?'

'Just a bit, Baghdad airport at the very end, and then we were trying to fix shot-off aerials on some of our tanks when orders came through for a Thunder Run, did you hear about that?'

'Tanks columns racing though the city and out again, it sounded crazy to me.'

'It would have been, if they'd been organized or had any modern anti-tank weapons. It was certainly noisy but I don't think it was too dangerous. So, yes, technically I've been under fire, but for most of it I was on the inside of a Bradley, that's an armoured vehicle.'

'Well, you're in another one now, or very nearly. There must be a ton of metal in front of us.'

'I meant to ask, how does it drive?'

'Apart from the way I can't feel the road, can't feel the steering and think I'm riding on an air cushion, it's a pretty nice way to travel as long as you don't think of it as driving. If it's still on the road when we're done, you can drive her back.'

'It's a deal. This bridge we're crossing, that's Lalinde, so we turn off soon. I'll check the comms again.'

'Happy to know we have a comms expert on the strength.'

'I'm glad I'm here,' she said. 'I'm trained to do this.'

He heard her check the radios one by one, then her mobile phone. He took his own from his belt pouch and handed it back to her.

'All good, chopper in place, and the Brigadier wants you to know the *Caïd* was a *sous-off* in the Algerian army, left as a sergeant in a motorized infantry unit. That was sixteen years ago so they have his age as forty-six. That's it. The Algerians were vague about his postings and he suspects the guy deserted and went into GIA.'

She handed him back his phone and Bruno was struck by the symmetry of it all. The *Groupe Islamique Armée* were the ones who had killed Sami's family before the boy's eyes and triggered the whole chain of events that had led to this day, to this mission. It would end here, he told himself.

'OK, thanks, time to keep the secure channel open,' Bruno replied. 'Tell them we're turning off the main road now, estimated arrival at first likely ambush point about six, seven minutes.'

'Times like this I wish we had a nice discreet drone searching ahead. Do you want me to release your safety catches?'

'No thanks, leave them on. When we roll out of the car I want to make sure the weapons only fire when I want to.'

'In the States, before you go on stage or into something, we say "Break a leg," so break a leg, Bruno. What do you say in France?'

'We just say *merde*, whether in the theatre or in sports or in combat. So *merde* and break another leg.'

'But you're always saying *merde*. Don't you save it for something important?'

'Whenever we say it, it feels important.' The chatter was a sign that she was nervous. That was fine. So was he. If it helped, he was happy to chatter back. 'OK, tell the chopper we're into the valley and onto the flat land, if they're watching they may be able to see us coming.'

He settled the sports bag onto his lap and tightened the shoulder strap. He removed his seat belt and began settling lower into his seat, watching the road ahead through the narrow gap between the top of the steering wheel and the dashboard. It was like trying to drive through the slit of a postbox, but he wanted the only head they'd see to be the mannequin's.

'How's the sun?' he asked. His pulse was fast but steady and he was swallowing almost constantly now.

'Low and bright, a few scattered clouds, it should be shining into their eyes as you planned.'

'OK, here we go, turning point in sight, get ready . . . slowing for the bend and turning now.'

At first it seemed clear but then the windscreen to his left shattered, the mannequin's head exploded and he saw a bright flash from the left front. He yelled 'RPG' and braked as he turned the car toward it to put the engine between him and the explosion.

'Out now and call the chopper,' he called, opening his driver's-side door and rolling out, eyes closed against glare when the RPG hit and still rolling as he landed on a grass verge and then dived for a shallow ditch as the grenade hit the car somewhere in front. The Rolls was still moving but slower and he saw Nancy's door was open. He pulled the smoke grenade from his chest pocket, jerked the ignition cord and tossed it ahead of the car then ripped open the sports bag, pulled out his weapon and released the safety. Another RPG round hit the Rolls and it rocked as the explosion flared and the car stopped, lopsided and sagging now. It must have got the wheel.

He cast a quick glance behind and saw Nancy was out of the car and had moved with it, sheltered behind the rear wheels. A third RPG hit the Rolls and he saw her stagger and fall back, but she waved at him to signal she was still functional. She leopard-crawled into the slight cover of a roadside hedge.

He was belly-crawling along the ditch to get a field of fire when he heard the ripping sound of the Minimi opening up, long bursts, three seconds for the first one, four for the second. That was almost a full belt. They'd have to change. That gave him four seconds, maybe five.

He felt old skills come to life, awakening from a long sleep, and his vision narrowed to a single cone where he could see clearly and he felt time slowing so that he could think as well as fight. He popped his head up and saw two shapes bending together through drifting red smoke. That would be the guys on the Minimi, he thought, and gave them three aimed bursts. He pulled out a fragmentation grenade, released the pin, counted to three and still lying prone, rolled and threw. He followed it with another smoke grenade and another burst of automatic fire before rolling back into the ditch.

Bruno changed magazines and considered. The RPG had come from left front. The sniper round had almost certainly come from straight ahead, roughly where the Minimi had been. So the sniper was doubling as machine gunner, which put the RPG man on Nancy's side of the action. The Minimi's firepower was now the main threat.

He looked around, keeping his head low, and heard Nancy's weapon firing short, controlled bursts. There was an open field to his right, the hedge behind him where Nancy was, and about thirty metres ahead he saw the start of a stone wall. It was too far to reach and the Minimi would chew up the stone into lethal shards. Where in hell was that chopper?

Bruno squirmed backwards along the ditch as the Minimi opened up again, short bursts this time, searching the terrain through the red smoke, looking for the spot where he had been. He kept squirming back toward the stalled Rolls, which was now pumping out its own black smoke. The risk now was that the petrol tank would blow, but he saw no flames and all the smoke was coming from the front of the vehicle.

He might get a clear shot from beneath the car. The smoke was thick so he risked a quick crouching run and dive and saw the fire from the Minimi smashing into the stone wall to his right. He selected single-shot mode, threw another frag grenade over the top of the Rolls toward the gun, and then he had a narrow window of sight between the car and the road. It gave him a clear shot at the Minimi and he aimed and took it.

The man feeding the belt jerked, half-rose as if trying to stand and then fell against the gun. Bruno's grenade exploded uselessly, too far to the left. He fired again, trying for the man behind, but the bulk of the fallen man was shielding him. This time he took his time with the frag grenade, counted to three before he threw it and then rolled back into the familiar ditch, so shallow here it barely gave cover.

Nancy's weapon fired again, two short bursts and then another that went on and on, too long to be controlled fire. Had she been hit?

Bruno knew he would have to change position and they'd expect him to come from the right again so he began crawling left, hoping that Nancy had kept moving so they wouldn't bunch together. Using his elbows and knees to crawl, his weapon cradled in his arms, he suddenly saw his left hand bright with blood. It wasn't his. Nancy must have been hit. There was a trail of blood ahead, not much, but enough to follow. He couldn't see her.

And then came the sound of rotor blades and more automatic fire from a new direction as the men on board fired from the swooping helicopter.

Bruno was clear of the Rolls now and the chopper's blades were clearing the smoke that had sheltered him so well. He fired three more short bursts at the point where the Minimi had been and changed magazines. He peered ahead and slightly left, where he assumed the RPG man had taken position. Surely he'd have moved by now? Or put another grenade into the back of the car to explode the petrol tank and force Bruno out of cover?

And then he saw him, camouflage gear and a headscarf, coming from the brush and scrubland on the far side of the road and onto the road itself. Bruno knew that face well, remembered its bland look as the *Caïd* had walked toward him in the corridor of the *collège* readying his electric stick. The *Caïd* was firing from the hip but aiming high, going for the helicopter. It was a doomed attempt but it might buy time for the others to get away. Even before the thought was formed, Bruno's weapon was in his hands and firing. But it gave him just one round and then it jammed.

There was no time to clear it. Bruno opened his holster and pulled out the PAMAS, released the de-cocking lever and took double-handed aim from his position outstretched on the ground. The first double tap hit the man in the trunk and spun him round and before Bruno had time to shift to a head shot he saw the man jerk like a marionette, puffs of red mist and cloth stitching their way up his body as the helicopter guns cut him down.

Bruno turned, looking back to the Minimi. Two dark lumps lay side by side, one moving feebly. The gun was toppled onto its side, no belt in it. Another long burst from the helicopter and the movement stopped.

He got up, leaving the assault rifle but the PAMAS still in his hand, and scanned the ground to both sides as he walked along the ditch to the hedge where he'd last seen Nancy. He saw nothing from this side but pushed his way through, careless of the scratches, and looked low to left and right. He saw a small pool of blood, and then two splashes of blood in a row. He followed the trail and found her curled up behind the bole of a scrubby tree, a spreading pool of blood around her.

'It's me, Bruno, it's all clear,' he shouted and saw a pale face turn slowly toward him.

'My leg,' Nancy said. She had been trying to apply a tourniquet but her hands were too slick with her own blood. Bruno used his commando knife to rip open her slacks, cleaned her with a field dressing and saw two jagged entry wounds in her thigh and one just by her knee. Those weren't bullet marks. It must have been shrapnel from the RPG that got her. The thigh wound was pumping so he pressed on the field dressing, shouting 'Medic, Medic,' as he ripped off his belt with the other hand and tightened it around the top of her thigh.

The pumping slowed, but didn't stop. Bruno tried to remember the pressure point for the femoral artery, but wasn't sure, so he turned her onto her side, put his fist into her groin at the top of the thigh and leaned down with all his weight. The pumping stopped.

'You did well, Nancy, you were great. We got them all. The bad guys are all dead. Now stay with me, keep your eyes open, look at me, talk if you can. Just stay with me. You're going to be alright.'

'Hurts,' she said feebly. 'You heavy, hurts.'

'It's just to stop the bleeding, it won't be long, the medic's here, you can hear the chopper.'

He heard it flare and land but the rotors kept churning. He didn't dare shift position to signal them but kept his weight on that artery. He didn't know how much blood she'd lost but she was very pale and weak.

'Medic,' he roared again and suddenly there were two men there, the sergeant he recognized and the young soldier with the Red Cross armband taking a bottle from a bulky bag, inserting a tube, attaching a fat needle and sticking it into Nancy's arm, making her jerk.

'Plasma,' said the medic. 'Don't you dare fucking move,' he said to Bruno. 'Keep that pressure on.'

'Sarge,' he went on, 'hold this bottle above her and get someone else over here to tell the chopper we've an urgent medevac.'

He checked Nancy's pulse and lifted one of her eyelids to check the colour. He looked grim but focused. The lieutenant arrived running, panting as he tried to tell Bruno the terrorists were all accounted . . .

'Shut your mouth,' the medic snapped, not even looking at him. 'There's another medical bag in the chopper, bring it here now and get that chopper to land as close to me as he can. Then bring the stretcher.'

The lieutenant ran back even faster and Bruno heard the

engine revs mount to screaming pitch and then the wind came and the chopper seemed just a few metres away, rocking on its skids. The lieutenant put the extra medical bag beside Nancy and got busy with the folding stretcher. The bottle the sergeant was holding was almost empty. The medic attached a second tube to the one pumping the last drops of plasma into Nancy's arm and then the second bottle was there to take over.

'Stay in that position,' the medic said to Bruno. 'You're doing fine and so is she. Now we're going to roll her onto that stretcher and I want you to move with her and as soon as we have her on that chopper you get that pressure back on just as you had it, understand.'

'Yes, but when we move her . . .' he began.

'It's fine. We always relax the tourniquet, remember. We want to keep some circulation in that leg. That's what the second bottle is for. She might lose a drop but we'll get this done in three seconds, right Sarge?'

'That's right, son. When you're ready.' The stretcher was in place, the chopper side door open.

'On my count of three,' the medic said. 'One, two, and three, now.' He deftly rolled Nancy onto the stretcher and then he and the lieutenant picked it up and Bruno scrambled sideways with them, his fist still in place and the sergeant on Nancy's far side still holding his plasma bottle. As they slid the stretcher into the chopper, Bruno noticed the bottle was still almost full. Clumsily, he scrambled aboard using his knees and one hand as he struggled to keep his fist in place on the artery. The medic followed, took the plasma bottle and attached it to a hook by the chopper door.

'Thanks, Sarge,' the medic said as the engine screamed again and they began lifting off, leaving the sergeant and lieutenant behind, mouthing what looked like 'Don't worry' at Bruno as they scurried back, bending low to stay beneath the blades. The sergeant would know what to do, secure all weapons and ammo, clear the battlefield.

Back in place, his arm aching from the pressure but no more of Nancy's lifeblood pumping, Bruno could see that her eyes were open but most of what he could see were the whites. That was a bad sign, he remembered. He gestured with his head and the medic bent over, lifted her eyelids, checked her pulse and the plasma bottle and then gave Bruno the thumbs up. He bent down, put his mouth to Nancy's ear and shouted, 'You're gonna be fine. We got you sorted. Try to stay awake.'

He took a set of earphones from a row of them hanging on a hook and put them on Bruno's head, pulled out a mike from another set of phones and now Bruno could hear him clearly.

'We're going to St Denis medical centre and there's a doctor waiting. I'm going to put this other set of earphones on her and I want you to keep talking to her while I get an injection ready. OK? We've got to keep her awake.'

Bruno nodded and felt the medic adjust the mouthpiece so it was directly in front of Bruno's face. The medic fixed a set of phones on Nancy.

'It's me, Bruno, still here and you're going to be fine,' he said, and feeling too tired and drained to work out things to say he just babbled and watched the whites of her eyes. 'You got the jihadis, all three of them down.

'The bleeding has stopped and we're on our way to hospital in my home town. It's St Denis and you'll always remember that. You're doing well and it's going to be alright and we'll have that dinner together when you come back here to visit and we'll take a walk over that ambush site and relive it all. You'll be as beautiful as ever and if I'm very lucky you'll kiss me again . . .'

The medic edged around him, a syringe held point upwards in his hand. He squeezed gently and a little spray of liquid spurted from the needle. To Bruno's surprise, he didn't put it into Nancy's arm but into the tube from the plasma bottle.

'Go on, keep talking, she liked that bit about the kiss,' the medic said. 'Her eyes are coming back, look!'

And they were, half a circle of blue had come back into view below her fluttering eyelids and then the first black of the iris and she was looking at him and Bruno felt his heart swell with happiness.

'Say it again, mate, it's doing her good. Go on, keep telling her about that kiss all the way to St Denis.'

29

They landed in the open stretch of parkland behind the medical centre and as soon as the rotor blades jerked to a halt the paramedics rushed toward them wheeling a stretcher trolley. It already had a fresh plasma bottle attached. As they began to slide the stretcher from the floor of the chopper one of the attendants gently pressed Bruno's arm to lift it from his desperate grip on Nancy's thigh.

'It's alright now, we've got her,' he said, and suddenly she was gone. Bruno stayed on his knees, eyes closed, mouth dry from never ceasing to talk to her and his arm still locked in position, rigid as an iron bar.

'Come on, mate,' said the soldier who'd worked on Nancy throughout the flight. 'Time to go, you deserve a nice cold beer and there's people waiting. Your arm will be fine in a minute.'

Bruno clambered clumsily out, blinking in the sudden sunlight, and saw J-J, looking solemn, hands behind his back, Yveline at his side in full uniform, her hand up to her brow in a salute. Behind them were more people, Pamela and Florence and the Mayor at their head. No Fabiola, but of course she'd be in the clinic, working with all her skill to repair Nancy's mangled leg.

J-J came forward, looking apologetic but determined. 'Sorry, Bruno, but you know the rules. Your weapon, please.'

Bruno undid his holster and handed it over, knowing the regulations mandated an inquiry whenever a police officer had fired while on duty. It wasn't the first time.

'My FAMAS is back at the battle ground, outside Trémolat, and so are Nancy's weapons. There's an army lieutenant in charge there, cleaning up.'

'I understand. I'll need a statement from you before the end of the day,' J-J replied. 'It's just a formality, we know they fired first. The comms guys were monitoring the audio feed from the chopper.'

He slapped Bruno on the back and Yveline dropped her hand from her salute and squeezed his arm, making him wince. He nodded his head and smiled, wondering how much more of this there would be. Then came the flash of a camera, Philippe Delaron again, and for the first time Bruno was aware of how he looked and how he stank.

It was as if he'd just come from a slaughterhouse. It had dried on his hands but his sleeve and pants and the front of his tunic were sodden with Nancy's blood. It would probably be on his face as well, along with blowback from the weapons and the smoke particles. Well, let them learn that gunfights are squalid, messy places, he thought; they should know that human bodies like Nancy's are thin and vulnerable bags of skin that pour out blood when pierced.

And suddenly there was a tiny, elderly woman. Still full of fire and energy and careless of her expensive clothes she came forward and hugged him tightly, her face no higher than his chest.

'I'm sorry about your car, Maya,' he said. 'It's gone.'

'Bugger the silly old car. Pamela told me what you'd done, so thank you. It looks like St Denis has saved me all over again. How's the American girl? We saw her rushed into the clinic.'

'The medic said she'll be fine.'

And then Pamela was there, her lips held tightly together, whether in anger or to stop them from trembling, he couldn't tell, but her eyes were soft with compassion. She leaned forward to kiss him, keeping her body well back from the gore that covered his front.

'Ah, dear Bruno, it always has to be you. I only know what Yveline told me but that sounded dreadful enough,' she said. 'You'll never change, damn you.' But there was affection in her voice. She leaned forward to whisper into his ear. 'There's a message from Annette – the *Procureur* has assigned a *juge d'instruction*. They're going to bring charges against Deutz. I think you may have to arrest him, but you have to call her.'

Christ, he thought, that on top of everything else. Yacov was suddenly at his side, grabbing his hand to pump it firmly, and a woman's voice gave a shout of command and he heard a stamp of boots as a group of Gendarmes came to attention. Yveline got them lined up, holding back more people who were craning to see. They made a path for him to the Mayor's car and the Mayor was holding open the rear door. Newspapers were spread all across the rear seat to keep the blood off and he climbed in, leaned back and closed his eyes. Pamela got into the passenger seat and the Mayor started the big Citroën and drove slowly through the crowd.

'You can shower at my place, it's closest,' the Mayor said, his voice coming from far away. 'Pamela has a change of clothes

333

for you then the Brigadier wants you at the château. Apparently there has to be a press conference and we both have to be there. I'll stay in touch with the clinic to let you know of any change.'

Bruno pulled Nancy's envelope from the pocket where he'd stuffed it, opened the seal and read her note:

If you're reading this, please call my dad in Virginia, 703-463-1766, and tell him what happened. He speaks French. In my room at the château you'll find my annotated copy of Deutz's full report, the unsanitized version with the names and photos of the jihadists he worked with in the maximum security wing. I have now identified Deutz's case study number 7, Ali, as the Caïd, the guy who hit you with the cattle prod. Deutz's report claimed this Ali was now under control, which is why he was released. Please let my dad know, and the Brigadier. We have to discredit Deutz's work; it's dangerously wrong. I can prove he's been letting out the wrong people. And if we get through whatever has you reading this, I'd very much like to meet up again. My private email is my name, surname first, followed by the month and day of my birth, on gmail.com. You're a cop, a good one; you can find that out. So if I don't hear from you, I'll understand, and wish you a great life. Bisous, Nancy.

Merde, thought Bruno, what a piece of work that Deutz turned out to be. He didn't want to think about the personal part of the message, not yet. He was about to stuff the note back into his pocket, but this jacket would have to be thrown away. He pulled his wallet from his hip pocket, folded the letter and put it with the banknotes. He felt the car slow and begin the turn into the Mayor's driveway.

Pamela helped him strip off his clothes and handed him a small bag containing a razor, shaving cream, fresh toothbrush, toothpaste, shampoo and soap and a tube of the liniment she knew he used after a rugby match to rub into his bruises and aching muscles. She claimed to like the menthol smell of the stuff.

He leaned against the tiles as the hot water splashed over him and watched Nancy's blood diluting as it spilled down his belly and legs and swirled around the drain. He braced himself, used the shampoo and soap, scrubbed the dried blood from his encrusted fingernails and started to feel better. He turned on the cold water for a thirty-second blast and then climbed out and towelled himself dry, gentle with the bruises and abrasions in his skin. He combed his hair, shaved, and then brushed his teeth, gargling to get the dry cordite taste from his throat. Finally he rubbed the liniment into his shoulders and neck, into his thighs and the small of his back.

He opened the door and Pamela was standing there, reliable Pamela, with his clean uniform in hand, and he could smell coffee. He'd give a fortune for a cup of coffee. He turned down the Mayor's offer of a cognac. He didn't want to confront Deutz smelling of booze.

'Have you told the Mayor about Deutz and Fabiola?' he asked Pamela. She nodded and handed him a cup of coffee and a phone. 'You have to call Annette,' she said firmly.

'No,' he said. 'I can't discuss this with the *Proc*'s office until I've talked to the Brigadier. If the decision has been taken to bring formal charges, that's fine, but the Brigadier needs to know that we're about to put a bomb under his tribunal. You call Annette and tell her that and now I have to get to the château. Right after another cup of coffee.'

Back in the Mayor's car Bruno noticed that somebody had cleared away the fouled newspapers and then he spotted J-J's car parked discreetly down the street, pulling out to follow them.

Pamela turned from the front passenger seat, looked at him brightly and said, 'I've found a horse, a Selle Français, just like yours, only a mare. Only six years old, amazingly cheap, from a stables near Agen that's just gone bankrupt. I'm driving down tomorrow to see it, if you'd like to come.'

'I'd love to, if the Brigadier lets me go,' he said.

'I think you deserve a rest after what you've been through today,' the Mayor said. 'And if the terrorist threat is over, so is the Brigadier's authority over you. You're working for me again.'

Somebody must have warned the guardhouse at the château because they were waved straight through, but not before passing the media gauntlet of camera lenses and shouted questions. The Brigadier was waiting on the outer steps and came down to shake his hand. 'Well done and I'm very glad to see you in one piece,' he said. 'A pity you didn't leave any of the bastards alive for us to interrogate.'

'That wasn't our main priority at the time,' Bruno replied.

'Quite. I'm not criticizing. I think Rafiq can rest easy now. What's the latest from the hospital? The Americans are flying a hospital jet into Bergerac to take her back to their big military hospital at Ramstein in Germany and they want to know when Nancy can be helicoptered across.'

'Dr Stern is still working to keep her alive. We'll know as soon as she has anything to tell us.'

'Right, this press conference, the minister is very keen . . .' Bruno held up a hand.

'Wait, sir,' he said. 'You need to know that the *Procureur* has just signed off on charges of multiple rape against Deutz and I'm supposed to be in attendance for the formal arrest to take place here as soon as possible. I've informed the *Proc*'s office that I had to brief you first because of the tribunal. Now it's between you and him, sir.'

'Don't "Sir" me, Bruno, I know your old soldier's tricks. Did you know this was coming?'

'No, sir, not precisely. I knew that inquiries were under way but I just heard of this while on the way here.'

'*Putain de merde*, is this for real? Is he guilty?'

'I believe so. One of the women is Dr Stern, currently trying to save Nancy's life and I trust her implicitly. But as you'll understand, for a policeman like me it was a question of waiting for evidence.'

'Well, at least we've got a verdict from the tribunal. They're unanimous. Sami is not responsible for his actions and not fit to stand trial. They recommend he remain under medical supervision, but that's where they divide. Deutz wants him in a prison hospital, under his supervision. Weill and Chadoub think he should be an out-patient and that his parents should remain as his *tuteurs*.'

'That's not practical,' Bruno said. 'We stopped the three from Toulouse but eventually there'll be more killers coming. They can't afford to let Sami stay alive after all the publicity about his cooperating with us.'

The Brigadier nodded and looked at his watch.

'If I may make a suggestion,' Bruno said. The Brigadier looked at him quizzically.

'You could announce that Deutz has been suddenly taken ill and has been placed on medical leave, but that his work with the tribunal was complete and is much appreciated. Get that out tonight and let the announcement of the arrest come out tomorrow. But cut him loose while you can. He's facing five years, minimum, maybe twice that if all the other cases stand up.'

'Is that the best you can do?'

'Yes, sir, short of leaving the bastard alone in a locked room with a loaded revolver.'

'We're not in the nineteenth century now, Bruno.' The Brigadier tried to sound crisp but his heart wasn't in it. '*Merde*, I suppose there's no choice. I'd better call the minister and tell him why Deutz will be suddenly taken ill.'

'May I tell Sami's family that the threat from Toulouse is over? I think they have a right to know.'

'Go ahead, but don't tell them about the Tribunal decision. I still have to draft the report. And not a word about Deutz to anybody.'

The sergeant of the guard trotted up, came to attention and announced, 'The *Procureur de la République* is demanding access, sir.' He handed the Brigadier the *Procureur*'s laminated and outsized identity card, crossed with red and blue stripes.

'Sergeant, you'll have to gain me five minutes,' the Brigadier snapped. 'Go back and give the *Procureur* my compliments, say I'm tied up on a call to my minister and apologize profusely but under the security precautions in force tell him you have to double-check his identity. Then get on the phone and call his office, but whatever you do, get me those five minutes.'

He speed-dialled a number while Bruno saluted and headed briskly up the stairs, leaving Pamela and the Mayor looking baffled at the foot of the steps. The salute was for their benefit; they'd assume he was under orders. As soon as he rounded the first bend in the stairs, he slowed his pace, feeling the aches in his muscles.

As he came out onto the wide balcony, he was surprised to see that the sun had not yet sunk. It had been getting lower in the sky as he drove the Rolls-Royce to Trémolat only – what, he checked his watch – barely ninety minutes ago. Where had the time gone? Two minutes of battle, ten minutes before getting Nancy into the chopper, five minutes to St Denis, the greeting at the medical centre, his shower and change and the drive here.

'Bruno, Bruno,' came a familiar sing-song voice and Sami was coming towards him, Balzac squirming in his arms in the effort to reach his master. Sami looked behind Bruno and said inquisitively, 'Fabiola? Nancy?'

'Not today, Sami,' he said, embracing the youth, surprised by the strength he could feel in the skinny frame. The jogging and the food had done Sami good. His arm around Sami's shoulders, he walked across to shake hands with Momu and touch cheeks with Dillah and said, 'Good news. The threat from the Toulouse mosque is over. The three men who were hunting you are in custody.'

Technically, it was true, but he didn't want to add in front of Sami that they were dead.

'Does that mean we can go home? Dr Weill told us the

339

tribunal had completed its work.' Dillah gestured to the other end of the balcony where Dr Weill and Dr Chadoub were enjoying the last rays of the sun. They raised hands and smiled in greeting.

'I hope you'll be home very soon. That's good news about the tribunal. Did Dr Weill say what they had decided?'

'No, but he gave us a wink and a very big grin,' said Momu.

'And Dr Chadoub said she couldn't think of anything better for Sami than being with us,' added Dillah.

'That sounds promising. I truly hope it all works out. Excuse me a moment while I greet the doctors.' Bruno walked across to the two of them. 'Thank you most sincerely for your work here,' he said, shaking their hands.

'What was that about the threat being over?' asked Dr Chadoub. 'You mean the family can go home now?'

'That's not my decision, but you probably heard that we took these security precautions at the château for a reason. The immediate threat has now been removed.'

'The soldiers coming from the guardroom were clustered around a military radio and talking about what sounded like a battle,' Dr Chadoub went on. 'Was that what you meant?'

Bruno nodded.

'If you think that's the end of it you don't know these Salafi monsters,' she said. 'They'll send more killers.'

'That's a concern, certainly. Have you seen Dr Deutz?'

'After we heard about the battle, he went down to talk to the soldiers, pumping them for more details. Do you know what happened?'

He evaded the question. 'Are you staying here tonight?'

'I believe so. We're expected to sign the final report which is being drafted as we speak. We're unanimous, you'll be glad to hear, but there's still a question about Sami's future treatment.'

The door behind Dr Chadoub opened and Deutz appeared wearing a suit and tie. He must have been expecting the press conference. He bustled onto the balcony, words spilling out from him. 'You won't believe what's been happening, three terrorists shot dead just down the road. That pretty American Nancy was involved and was wounded and the local policeman Bruno was in the thick . . .'

'He's right here,' said Dr Weill, and then turned to the sound of commotion coming up the stairs from the other door at the far end of the balcony.

Deutz gaped at Bruno, and then came forward and grabbed his hand and began to pump it and murmur congratulations until Bruno wrenched his hand away. He didn't want to be touched by this man, so he turned to watch a confused knot of people tumbling through the door from the stairs.

The *Procureur* was shouting 'Outrageous' as a soldier hung half-heartedly onto his sleeve. The Brigadier was spluttering about national security while Annette, beside him, spotted Bruno and gave a cheerful wave. Yveline, still in uniform, brought up the rear. The Brigadier shook his head in despair and sat down at the nearest table. The soldier wisely ducked back to the door.

'Dr Deutz,' called the *Procureur*, striding across to confront him before glancing at Bruno. 'I'm glad to see you here, Chief of Police Courrèges. I'm sure you know your duty.' He darted a withering glance at the Brigadier.

Curious at these new arrivals, Sami crept up and stood

341

beside Bruno, Balzac still in his arms. Momu and Dillah had turned in their chairs to watch this sudden drama.

'Yes, I'm Deutz, what can I do for you?' He stood casually by the battlements, silhouetted against the setting sun, posed so that he was one of the few who did not have the sun in their eyes.

'Pascal Deutz, you are accused of multiple crimes of rape under Article 222.23 of the Penal Code,' the *Procureur* said, brandishing a warrant. 'You will be taken into *garde à vue* overnight in Sarlat and interrogated in custody there by the assigned *juge d'instruction* Bernard Ardouin, who will be your investigating magistrate.'

Deutz did not move from his place but glanced quickly at Annette and Yveline and then at Bruno and the Brigadier. He raised his eyebrows and then gave an elaborate shrug and put his hands in his trouser pockets. He looked to be the most relaxed man on the balcony.

'You are charged with the violent rape and actual bodily harm on or about February the fourth, two thousand and seven, of Doctor Fabiola Stern,' the *Procureur* began.

Sami tugged at Bruno's sleeve, looking confused and asked, 'Fabiola?'

'. . . and with the violent rape of Iphigène Vaugaudry on or about the tenth of May, two thousand and six,' the *Procureur* went on. 'And with the attempted rape of Monique Jouard on the second of March, two thousand and seven; each of these young women being *in statu pupilari* of you as an accredited member of the medical faculty of the university of Marseille and all the said offences having been committed in that city.'

'Fabiola?' Sami repeated. 'He did bad thing to Fabiola?'

'This is ridiculous,' Deutz declared calmly. 'I demand to consult a lawyer.'

'Yes, he did a very bad thing to Fabiola,' Bruno said distractedly to Sami, trying to pay attention to the drama before him.

The *Procureur* was stiff with anger and Deutz was looking at him with his usual arrogance mixed with contempt. He was leaning against the battlements, hands still in his pockets, the picture of a man who might be the victim of some foolish misunderstanding but wasn't in the least worried by it.

'What did he do to Fabiola? He hurt her?'

'Yes, he hurt her,' Bruno whispered, trying to shush Sami.

Suddenly he felt Sami thrust Balzac into his arms and before he could react, Sami had taken off like a sprinter, head down and arms pumping as he closed the ten or so metres between him and Deutz and launched himself at him. There was a sound like an axe striking flesh as Sami's head collided with Deutz's chin. Deutz reeled back, off balance and unable to save himself with his hands tangled in his pockets. The back of his hips caught on the lower level of the wide battlements and he began to topple backwards.

Bruno began running forward to hold them but he lost a vital half-second in putting Balzac down. Sami had the power of rage and his bare feet gripped the stone floor and powered on, his hands tight around Deutz's neck and his height and momentum pressing Deutz further back and further back. Deutz's legs slid out from under him and he was going over the edge.

Bruno launched a flailing dive, more a rugby tackle to try

and grab Sami's legs. But he was too late. His hand just brushed Sami's heel as the young man went over the battlements still clutching at Deutz. Bruno landed hard, slid forward, and his head cracked against the stone wall, protected a little by his képi. He groped a hand up, still groggy, and felt cloth and then a leg, sliding through his grip. And then he felt an ankle and gripped it hard and rolled to get his other hand onto the foot.

He heard a high scream and then a thud and then a scrambling of bodies and other men were beside him, one of them in uniform, helping hold the weight that seemed to be hauling his arms from their sockets.

'It's alright, we've got him,' came the *Procureur*'s voice.

Bruno scrambled to his feet and joined the *Procureur* and the soldier as they hauled Deutz back over the battlements. A long, keening cry came from just along the wall, where Momu was leaning out and staring down. His face ashen, Deutz crumpled in the arms of the two men who held him, trembling and panting as if he'd just run a race.

'Can we get a doctor here?' the *Procureur* cried.

Telling himself he had saved the wrong man, Bruno turned to the battlements and looked over at the sprawled and broken body in the courtyard nearly thirty metres below. Soldiers were running to the place where Sami lay, one of them the medic with his Red Cross armband. He kneeled down, careless of the blood spreading from Sami's head, and after a moment looked up and shook his head.

From behind him, Bruno heard a short bark from Balzac and then, for the first time, the tone turned into the full-hearted, deep and mournful bay of an adult dog. As he continued looking down and saw the soldiers drape a blanket over Sami's corpse, Bruno felt a cool wind on his face and the sky darkened. The sun had finally set.

Epilogue

It was a cold, grey November morning and the German sky seemed ready to rain when the small passenger jet with the US Air Force markings landed at the Ramstein airbase. The three congressmen filed off first with their escorting officer and Bruno brought up the rear. A minibus in Air Force blue waited on the tarmac as their baggage was unloaded and they all climbed aboard, Bruno squeezing in beside a large man wearing a stetson and a blue turquouse jewel at his collar instead of a tie. Bruno had learned he was a congressman from Arizona, who seemed to know Nancy and described Bruno to the others on board as 'the French cop who saved the life of Jeff Sutton's little girl.'

The call from the embassy in Paris had told him to board the plane at Bergerac, where it was making a special stop for him on its journey from a NATO conference at the French naval base at Toulon to Ramstein. Another US military aircraft would take him back to Bordeaux airport that evening, he had been told, along with some American sailors who were doing an exercise on maritime patrols with the French navy.

The minibus took them to the Landstuhl medical centre. There the congressmen each gave Bruno a crushing farewell handshake as they left with an Army colonel who commanded the three thousand personnel who ran the biggest military hospital in Europe. A young lieutenant with a clipboard came up to Bruno, who was wearing his full-dress police uniform as instructed, and asked, 'Chief of Police Courrèges?'

He led Bruno into a large concrete building, functional and rather depressing with its blocks of grey and slits for windows, and into a lobby with a bewildering array of signposts, most of them using acronyms. Bruno's command of English was adequate to help lost tourists and record details of mislaid passports but the jumble of speech coming from the tannoy and the brisk American voices left him lost. He followed closely behind the lieutenant as people around them, some in military uniform, some in green or blue medical clothes, stared at his French uniform. Only the receptionists seemed to wear white.

'This facility is one of the biggest organ donors in Europe,' the lieutenant said. 'And we average two to three births a day.' Bruno murmured a polite acknowledgement. They took the stairs up to a long corridor as the lieutenant explained they preferred to reserve the lifts for wheelchairs and stretchers. They entered a lobby area with potted plants and soft music. Bruno thought it was quite a contrast to the grim French military hospital where he'd been taken after Sarajevo. Suddenly they were out of the fluorescent lights and walking past windows into a corridor with doors on each side like an apartment building. A reception desk guarded the way but it was unoccupied. The lieutenant sighed, consulted his checklist, and started looking for numbers. He stopped at 174-A and knocked.

'Agent Sutton,' said the lieutenant, opened the door and showed Bruno inside. 'Your visitor, Ma'am,' he said, touching his cap, and left, closing the door behind him.

Nancy used a cane to rise from an easy chair by a large window that looked out onto a lawn and some trees. The light coming from it was behind her and bright enough that Bruno could hardly see her face. He advanced, saying something bland about how well she looked to conceal his nervousness, and kissed her on both cheeks.

'I don't think that will do, Bruno,' she said, and kissed him warmly on the lips. 'I have a memory of you talking endlessly about kissing me and me thinking why doesn't he just shut up and do it.'

'I didn't think the medic would have approved, given your condition.' He helped her back into her seat and pulled up a smaller straight-backed wooden chair to sit beside her. She smelled of toilet soap and shampoo, almost austere amid the scents of flowers in the room. Her hair had been recently done and she was wearing make-up, which she had never done at the château. It reminded him of the time he'd first seen her at the airport in Périgueux, when she'd looked coolly elegant and Parisian, and rather forbidding. She was wearing a dark blue silk dressing gown. She stretched out her legs, revealing ivory-coloured silk pyjamas and red velvet slippers.

'You look wonderful, like the queen of a literary salon receiving her admirers. How do you feel? How long before they let you out of here?'

'I'm well enough to get through dozens of layers of bureaucracy to get you here. How did you like the congressmen?'

'Very impressive handshakes, less self-important than our own politicians. They seemed to know my name.'

'Yes, I made sure of that, and of what you did. And thank

you for the flowers you sent.' She gestured around the room where every flat surface seemed to hold a vase, each with an impressive bouqet of roses, carnations, lilies and some exotic flowers he didn't recognise.

'I don't think I sent all those,' he said, embarrassed. His own modest offering now seemed very much less than adequate.

'Those roses are yours,' she said, pointing to a smaller vase with roses that were long past their best. 'I refuse to throw them away. The brigadier sent some, and Isabelle. Most of the others are from Maya and Yacov. They send a new batch every week. What's in that bag?'

He'd almost forgotten, putting it to one side as he'd drawn up the chair. He felt confused by her presence, not sure what to say, nor what he should ask about her wounds and her future. The drama that had drawn them together in St Denis and in the Rolls-Royce seemed a long time past.

'Foie gras, a fresh baguette, a bottle of *Chateau de Tirecul* Monbazillac that we ought to chill, and a bottle of my own *vin de noix* to build you up.' He forced some jollity into his voice. 'A glass each night as you go to bed and you'll sleep well. At Bergerac airport I thought they might not let me onto the aircraft with them. A congressman from Arizona told them not to be so foolish.'

'He's a friend of my dad, who sends you his regards and thanks. It was kind of you to call him. You beat his official notification by two days so he was here the day after my first operation.'

She gave a nervous smile and asked if he'd like some coffee or a soda. Like him, she seemed to be on edge, wondering how this reunion might go.

'I keep expecting one of the nurses to drop by,' she said, with a laugh that sounded forced. 'They're very curious about this dashing French visitor of mine.'

'How many operations did you have?' He deflected her compliment.

'Four, one to put some reinforcement grafts on my artery and the rest on my knee. But I was lucky to have you and the medic on the chopper and to have Fabiola work on me when we landed. The doctors here were impressed with what she'd done. The artery is fine and they've given me a new knee. I can stand and walk and it gets better every day. They say I'll soon be almost as good as new except that my skiing days are over. I'm doing physio and swimming every day and they promise to have me home with the family for Christmas. I'll even be able to dance.'

'And then?' He swallowed, thinking he sounded pathetic. He'd spent the flight composing far more eloquent speeches and now he could barely summon a single word.

'Three months convalescent leave and then back to the embassy in Paris. They want to capitalize on my new reputation with the French. Apparently the Brigadier is being unusually helpful. But tell me about St Denis. I heard about poor Sami. How are Momu and Dillah?'

'They're well, still grieving but they send ▉▉▉ you their best wishes. They know Sami thought of you as a friend. They miss him but I think they're resigned. They know that there could never have been a normal life with Sami. Momu is back at work, Dillah helps Rashida with the grandchildren. And Fabiola is blossoming now that Gilles has moved in with her while he works on his book. That solemnity she always had seems to have lifted.'

'That's good. When does Deutz go to trial?'

'Next month. He's had one hearing that confirmed he remains detained but they're having trouble finding a place secure enough to keep him alive. Word seems to have spread about him among the Muslims in prison. He knows it, too. I saw him at the hearing and he's lost weight, looks haunted and grey. He seemed to be years older.'

'Just as important, his fate seems to have helped discredit those damn techniques of his. My dad went ballistic when he learned Deutz had freed one of the guys who shot me up. What happens to Deutz now?'

'The Procureur is going for the maximum sentence, ten years.'

She nodded slowly and they fell silent, looking at each other. Suddenly each one started to say something simultaneously and then stopped. 'Go ahead,' she said.

'I was going to ask where you were spending your convalescent leave.' He paused and she raised her eyebrows.

'January and February, I'll go to my uncle's place in Florida and get some sun. It's a condo, right on the seafront at Longboat Key, one of the best beaches I know. It's just a few minutes from Sarasota airport. Have you ever been?'

He shook his head. Palm trees and beaches in mid-winter, he felt a touch of envy. 'What about March, before you start work at the embassy again?' he steeled himself to take the risk. 'You'd have a hero's welcome if you'd like to come to St Denis. I was wondering if I might see you again. Don't forget that I promised you a dinner.'

'I haven't forgotten and I'm going to take you up on it,' she said, and took his hand. 'In the meantime I'd like to try some of that foie gras.'

He let go of her hand to rummage in the bag, then looked around for a knife and plate. She pointed to a small cabinet that held everything he needed including glasses, a corkscrew and a bucket of ice. As he began opening the bottle of Monbazillac, she cleared her throat.

'You've never cooked for me yet, and Isabelle said that's a treat not to miss,' she said. 'I was wondering if you'd like to spend some time with me in Florida. My uncle has a very sophisticated kitchen.'

He handed her a glass, kissed her lightly on the lips and said, 'That sounds wonderful and I'd love to cook for you. But the kitchen is not the attraction.'

'So you're coming for the palm trees and the beach?'

'No,' he said. And he kissed her again.

Acknowledgements

This is a work of fiction and all living characters are invented, although as always their inspiration owes a great deal to my genial neighbours and friends in the enchanting valley of the river Vézère. There are, however, references to a number of historical characters involved in the Resistance and in saving Jewish children from the Holocaust. I have tried to stick with the known facts of their work, knowing that no words of mine could hope to do justice to their nobility and their courage.

Although the tale of David and Maya Halévy is invented, their experiences were not uncommon for those Jewish children in France who survived the Second World War. The round-up of July 1942 at the Vélodrome d'Hiver did take place and the heroic efforts of the Jewish Scouts under Robert Gamzon to save the children are exactly as related here. The Protestant communities of southern France played a noble role and the old Huguenot village of Le Chambon-sur-Lignon found refuge for more than 3,000 Jewish children. The woman I call Tante Simone existed; the name Simone Mairesse is inscribed among the names of the righteous. The town and Simone and many other heroic figures were finally given the honour they deserved in their homeland by President Jacques Chirac at a ceremony at the Panthéon in Paris in January 2007.

The two battles of Mouleydier in June 1944 took place much as I describe them, although there are confused and contradictory accounts in the various memoirs of those who took part. These disputes reflect the bitter political antagonisms between the rival Francs Tireurs et Partisans, mainly Communists, and the more conservative and Gaullist Armée Secrète. I relied on the memoirs of René Coustellier, leader of the Resistance Group Soleil; on Guy Penaud's *Histoire de la Résistance en Périgord*; Pierre Louty's *Histoires Tragiques du Maquis*; and on Christian Bourrier's *La Résistance en Pays lindois*. As so often, I am grateful to my friend Jean-Jacques Gillot, a distinguished local historian, for his invaluable encyclopedia, *Résistants du Périgord*. André Roulland's *La Vie en Périgord sous l'Occupation, 1940–44* was of great help in reconstructing the lives of David and Maya on the farm. I would also like to thank several friends in the Périgord, including Jean-Pierre Picot, Colette and Joseph da Cunha and the Bounichou family of Lalinde for sharing with me their recollections of those heroic but tragic days.

For the story of Sami, I read widely in the available journalists' accounts of modern Afghanistan, but I have not visited that harsh, magnificent land for over twenty years. Abdul Salam Zaeef's memoir, *My Life With the Taliban*, and the more recent *Facing the Taliban*, the memoir of Anoja Wijeyesekera, a Sri Lankan woman who worked for the United Nations, were informative. My account of the horrors of the Algerian civil war is based on a number of sources, including Derradji Abder-Rahmane's *Concise History of Political Violence in Algeria*; Hugh Roberts's *The Battlefield: Algeria 1988–2002*; and the Amnesty International report *Algeria: A human rights crisis*; Mohammed Samraoui's *Chronique des Années de Sang* and Habib Souaïdia's

La Sale Guerre, an extraordinary memoir by a member of the Algerian special forces.

The Toulouse mosque, its Imams and its security services are pure inventions for literary purposes, and so is the report on Islam and jihadist recruitment in French prisons. But, having visited mosques in Paris, Toulouse and elsewhere in Europe and the Middle East, and having published several articles on Islam in Europe (see, for example, 'Europe's Mosque Hysteria', *Wilson Quarterly*, Washington DC, Spring 2006), I know something of the terrain. I am grateful to Professor Tariq Ramadan of St Antony's College, Oxford, and to the French scholar of Islam Professor Olivier Roy, for sharing with me their insights into the challenges and prospects of Islam in Europe.

My friend Linda Stern, a truly gifted psychologist in Washington DC, helped me to understand something of the challenges and features of the range of difficulties we call autism. I am most grateful for her help, but any errors in the description of Sami and his behaviour are entirely my own.

The château to which Sami is taken is an invention, drawn in part from the château de Campagne, now splendidly restored as an archaeological research centre, and partly from the château de la Roque des Péagers near Meyrals. There are more than a thousand châteaux and historic manor houses in the Dordogne and Vézère valleys, so we fortunate local novelists have a wondrous range of locations from which to choose.

As always, I am most grateful to Jane and Caroline Wood in Britain, to Jonathan Segal in New York and to Anna von Planta in Zurich for their irreplaceable editing skills. My family has been part of the Bruno project from the beginning and are always the first to read and comment on my drafts. My wife

Julia, who is co-author of the Bruno cookbook, also checks the recipes; our elder daughter Kate runs the brunochiefofpolice. com website; and our younger daughter Fanny is the continuity expert, keeping track of meals, characters, events and places as Bruno's life and biography grow ever more complex with each new book. And Benson, our basset hound, thoughtfully ensures that I never spend too long at the writing desk, but get out often to enjoy the magical Périgord landscape that continues to inspire me to spin the tales of Bruno and the fictional town of St Denis.